W9-CCT-919

THE
CHOSEN

"*The Chosen* is a major addition to contemporary American fiction."

—*Washington Sunday Star*

"A rare reading experience. . . . Arresting, original. . . . There are chapters unlike anything else I have read."

—John Barkham

"It is the kind of work that . . . pulls deeply and fulfills your strongest expectations. It could be the best thing you'll read this year—or a great many more to come."

—*Dallas Times-Herald*

"*The Chosen* is a compelling, absorbing book. It offers deep, sympathetic insight into the variety and profundity of Jewish tradition and heritage. It's interesting as social commentary and as, simply, story. It's a joy to read for its splendid, singing prose style as much as for its message."

—*Minneapolis Tribune*

"It is a simple, almost meager story about Jewish people who are far from typical—yet the warmth and pathos of the dealings between fathers and sons, the understated odyssey from boyhood to manhood, give the book a range that makes it worth anybody's reading."

—*Christian Science Monitor*

TO

ADENA

When a trout rising to a fly gets hooked on a line and finds himself unable to swim about freely, he begins with a fight which results in struggles and splashes and sometimes an escape. Often, of course, the situation is too tough for him.

In the same way the human being struggles with his environment and with the hooks that catch him. Sometimes he masters his difficulties; sometimes they are too much for him. His struggles are all that the world sees and it naturally misunderstands them. It is hard for a free fish to understand what is happening to a hooked one.

—KARL A. MENNINGER

True happiness
Consists not in the multitude of friends,
But in the worth and choice.

—BEN JONSON

To Dr. Israel Charny, Mrs. Jonas Greenfield, Rabbi Raphael Posner, and Dr. Aaron Rosen, all of whom helped with the research, I offer my gratitude.

C. P.

THE
CHOSEN

Chaim Potok

FAWCETT CREST • NEW YORK

The characters and events in this novel are creations of the author's imagination. What likeness they may bear to persons or events, living or dead, present or past, is the likeness of coincidence.

A Fawcett Crest Book

Published by Ballantine Books

Copyright © 1967 by Chaim Potok

ISBN 0-449-20334-4

This edition published by arrangement with
Simon & Schuster, Inc.

Selection of the Literary Guild, April 1967

Manufactured in the United States of America

First Fawcett Crest Edition: June 1968
First Ballantine Books Edition: December 1982

BOOK ONE

I was a son to my father . . .
And he taught me and said to me,
"Let your heart hold fast my words. . . ."
                                                    —PROVERBS

CHAPTER ONE
✥✥✥✥✥✥✥✥✥✥✥✥✥✥✥

FOR THE FIRST FIFTEEN YEARS of our lives, Danny and I lived within five blocks of each other and neither of us knew of the other's existence.

Danny's block was heavily populated by the followers of his father, Russian Hasidic Jews in somber garb, whose habits and frames of reference were born on the soil of the land they had abandoned. They drank tea from samovars, sipping it slowly through cubes of sugar held between their teeth; they ate the foods of their homeland, talked loudly, occasionally in Russian, most often in a Russian Yiddish, and were fierce in their loyalty to Danny's father.

A block away lived another Hasidic sect, Jews from southern Poland, who walked the Brooklyn streets like specters, with their black hats, long black coats, black beards, and earlocks. These Jews had their own rabbi, their own dynastic ruler, who could trace his family's position of rabbinic leadership back to the time of the Ba'al Shem Tov, the eighteenth-century founder of Hasidism, whom they all regarded as a God-invested personality.

About three or four such Hasidic sects populated the area in which Danny and I grew up, each with its own rabbi, its own little synagogue, its own customs, it own fierce loyalties. On a Shabbat or festival morning, the members of each sect could be seen walking to their respective synagogues, dressed in their particular garb, eager to pray with their particular rabbi and forget the tumult of the week and the hungry grabbing for money which they needed to feed their large families during the seemingly endless Depression.

The sidewalks of Williamsburg were cracked squares of cement, the streets paved with asphalt that softened in the stifling summers and broke apart into potholes in the bitter winters. Many of the houses were brownstones, set tightly together, none taller than three or four stories. In these houses lived Jews, Irish, Germans, and some Spanish Civil War refugee families that had fled the new Franco regime before the onset of the Second World War. Most of the stores were run by gentiles, but some were owned by Orthodox Jews, members of the Hasidic sects in the area. They could be seen behind their counters, wearing black skullcaps, full beards, and long earlocks, eking out their meager livelihoods and dreaming of Shabbat and festivals when they could close their stores and turn their attention to their prayers, their rabbi, their God.

Every Orthodox Jew sent his male children to a yeshiva, a Jewish parochial school, where they studied from eight or nine in the morning to four or five in the evening. On Fridays the students were let out at about one o'clock to prepare for the Shabbat. Jewish education was compulsory for the Orthodox, and because this was America and not Europe, English education was compulsory as well—so each student carried a double burden: Hebrew studies in the mornings and English studies in the afternoons. The test of intellectual excellence, however, had been reduced by tradition and unvoiced unanimity to a single area of study: Talmud. Virtuosity in Talmud was the achievement most sought after by every student of a yeshiva, for it was the automatic guarantee of a reputation for brilliance.

Danny attended the small yeshiva established by his father. Outside of the Williamsburg area, in Crown Heights, I attended the yeshiva in which my father taught. This latter yeshiva was somewhat looked down upon by the students of other Jewish parochial schools of Brooklyn: it offered more English subjects than the required minimum, and it taught its Jewish subjects in Hebrew rather than Yiddish. Most of the students were children of immigrant Jews who preferred to regard themselves as having been emancipated from the fenced-off ghetto mentality typical of the other Jewish parochial schools in Brooklyn.

Danny and I probably would never have met—or we would have met under altogether different circumstances—had it not been for America's entry into the Second World War and the desire this bred on the part of some English teachers in the Jewish parochial schools to show the gentile world that yeshiva students were as physically fit, despite their long hours of study, as any other American student. They went about proving this by organizing the Jewish parochial schools in and around our area into competitive leagues, and once every two weeks the schools would compete against one another in a variety of sports. I became a member of my school's varsity softball team.

On a Sunday afternoon in early June, the fifteen members of my team met with our gym instructor in the play yard of our school. It was a warm day, and the sun was bright on the asphalt floor of the yard. The gym instructor was a short, chunky man in his early thirties who taught in the mornings in a nearby public high school and supplemented his income by teaching in our yeshiva during the afternoons. He wore a white polo shirt, white pants, and white sweater, and from the awkward way the little black skullcap sat perched on his round, balding head, it was clearly apparent that he was not accustomed to wearing it with any sort of regularity. When he talked he frequently thumped his right fist into his left palm to emphasize a point. He walked on the balls of his feet, almost in imitation of a boxer's ring stance, and he was fanatically addicted to professional baseball. He had nursed our softball team along for two years, and by a mixture of patience, luck, shrewd manipulations during some tight ball games, and hard, fist-thumping harangues calculated to shove us into a patriotic awareness of the importance of athletics and physical fitness for the war effort, he was able to mold our original team of fifteen awkward fumblers into the top team of our league. His name was Mr. Galanter, and all of us wondered why he was not off somewhere fighting in the war.

During my two years with the team, I had become quite adept at second base and had also developed a swift underhand pitch that would tempt a batter into a swing but would drop into a curve at the last moment and slide just below the flaying bat for a strike. Mr. Galanter always began a ball game by putting me at second base and would use me as a pitcher only in very tight moments, because, as he put it once, "My baseball philosophy is grounded on the defensive solidarity of the infield."

That afternoon we were scheduled to play the winning team of another neighborhood league, a team with a reputation for wild, offensive slugging and poor fielding. Mr. Galanter said he was counting upon our infield to act as a solid defensive front. Throughout the warm-up period, with only our team in the yard, he kept thumping his right fist into his left palm and shouting at us to be a solid defensive front.

"No holes," he shouted from near home plate. "No holes, you hear? Goldberg, what kind of solid defensive front is that? Close in. A battleship could get between you and Malter. That's it. Schwartz, what are you doing, looking for paratroops? This is a ball game. The enemy's on the ground. That throw was wide, Goldberg. Throw it like a sharpshooter. Give him the ball again. Throw it. Good. Like a sharpshooter. Very good. Keep the infield solid. No defensive holes in this war."

We batted and threw the ball around, and it was warm and sunny, and there was the smooth, happy feeling of the summer soon to come, and the tight excitement of the ball game. We wanted very much to win, both for ourselves and, more especially, for Mr. Galanter, for we had all come to like his fist-thumping sincerity. To the rabbis who taught in the Jewish parochial schools, baseball was an evil waste of time, a spawn of the potentially assimilationist English portion of the yeshiva day. But to the students of most of the parochial schools, an inter-league baseball victory had come to take on only a shade less significance than a top grade in Talmud, for it was an unquestioned mark of one's Americanism, and to be counted a loyal American had become increasingly important to us during these last years of the war.

So Mr. Galanter stood near home plate, shouting instructions and words of encouragement, and we batted and tossed the ball around. I walked off the field for a moment to set up my eyeglasses for the game. I wore shell-rimmed glasses, and before every game I would bend the earpieces in so the glasses would stay tight on my head and not slip down the bridge of my nose when I began to sweat. I always waited until just before a game to bend down the earpieces, because, bent, they would cut into the skin over my ears, and I did not want to feel the pain a moment longer than I had to. The tops of my ears would be sore for days after every game, but better that, I thought, than the need to keep pushing my glasses up the bridge of my nose or the possibility of having them fall off suddenly during an important play.

Davey Cantor, one of the boys who acted as a replacement if a first-stringer had to leave the game, was standing near the wire screen behind home plate. He was a short boy, with a round face, dark hair, owlish glasses, and a very Semitic nose. He watched me fix my glasses.

"You're looking good out there, Reuven," he told me.

"Thanks," I said.

"Everyone is looking real good."

"It'll be a good game."

He stared at me through his glasses. "You think so?" he asked.

"Sure, why not?"

"You ever see them play, Reuven?"

"No."

"They're murderers."

"Sure," I said.

"No, really. They're wild."

"You saw them play?"

"Twice. They're murderers."

"Everyone plays to win, Davey."

"They don't only play to win. They play like it's the first of the Ten Commandments."

I laughed. "That yeshiva?" I said. "Oh, come on, Davey."

"It's the truth."

"Sure," I said.

"Reb Saunders ordered them never to lose because it would shame their yeshiva or something. I don't know. You'll see."

"Hey, Malter!" Mr. Galanter shouted. "What are you doing, sitting this one out?"

"You'll see," Davey Cantor said.

"Sure." I grinned at him. "A holy war."

He looked at me.

"Are you playing?" I asked him.

"Mr. Galanter said I might take second base if you have to pitch."

"Well, good luck."

"Hey, Malter!" Mr. Galanter shouted. "There's a war on, remember?"

"Yes, sir!" I said, and ran back out to my position at second base.

We threw the ball around a few more minutes, and then I went up to home plate for some batting practice. I hit a long one out to left field, and then a fast one to the shortstop, who fielded it neatly and whipped it to first. I had the bat ready for another swing when someone said, "Here they are," and I rested the bat on my shoulder and saw the team we were going to play turn up our block and come into the yard. I saw Davey Cantor kick nervously at the wire screen behind home plate, then put his hands into the pockets of his dungarees. His eyes were wide and gloomy behind his owlish glasses.

I watched them come into the yard.

There were fifteen of them, and they were dressed alike in white shirts, dark pants, white sweaters, and small black skullcaps. In the fashion of the very Orthodox, their hair was closely cropped, except for the area near their ears from which mushroomed the untouched hair that tumbled down into the long side curls. Some of them had the beginnings of beards, straggly tufts of hair that stood in isolated clumps on their chins, jawbones, and upper lips. They all wore the traditional undergarment beneath their shirts, and the tzitzit, the long fringes appended to the four corners of the garment, came out above their belts and swung against their pants as they walked. These were the very Orthodox, and they obeyed literally the Biblical commandment *And ye shall look upon it*, which pertains to the fringes.

In contrast, our team had no particular uniform, and each of us wore whatever he wished: dungarees, shorts, pants, polo shirts, sweat shirts, even undershirts. Some of us wore the garment, others did not. None of us wore the fringes outside his trousers. The only element of uniform that we had in common was the small, black skullcap which we, too, wore.

They came up to the first-base side of the wire screen behind home plate and stood there in a silent black-and-white mass, holding bats and balls and gloves in their hands. I looked at them. They did not seem to me to present any picture of ferocity. I saw Davey Cantor kick again at the wire screen, then walk away from them to the third-base line, his hands moving nervously against his dungarees.

Mr. Galanter smiled and started toward them, moving quickly on the balls of his feet, his skullcap perched precariously on the top of his balding head.

A man disentangled himself from the black-and-white mass of players and took a step forward. He looked to be in his late twenties and wore a black suit, black shoes, and a black hat. He had a black beard, and he carried a book under one arm. He was obviously a rabbi, and I marveled that the yeshiva had placed a rabbi instead of an athletic coach over its team.

Mr. Galanter came up to him and offered his hand.

"We are ready to play," the rabbi said in Yiddish, shaking Mr. Galanter's hand with obvious uninterest.

"Fine," Mr. Galanter said in English, smiling.

The rabbi looked out at the field. "You played already?" he asked.

"How's that?" Mr. Galanter said.

"You had practice?"

"Well, sure—"

"We want to practice."

"How's that?" Mr. Galanter said again, looking surprised.

"You practiced, now we practice."

"You didn't practice in your own yard?"

"We practiced."

"Well, then—"

"But we have never played in your yard before. We want a few minutes."

"Well, now," Mr. Galanter said, "there isn't much time. The rules are each team practices in its own yard."

"We want five minutes," the rabbi insisted.

"Well—" Mr. Galanter said. He was no longer smiling. He always liked to go right into a game when we played in our own yard. It kept us from cooling off, he said.

"Five minutes," the rabbi said. "Tell your people to leave the field."

"How's that?" Mr. Galanter said.

"We cannot practice with your people on the field. Tell them to leave the field."

"Well, now," Mr. Galanter said, then stopped. He thought

for a long moment. The black-and-white mass of players behind the rabbi stood very still, waiting. I saw Davey Cantor
kick at the asphalt floor of the yard. "Well, all right. Five
minutes. Just five minutes, now."

"Tell your people to leave the field," the rabbi said.

Mr. Galanter stared gloomily out at the field, looking a little deflated. "Everybody off!" he shouted, not very loudly.
"They want a five-minute warm-up. Hustle, hustle. Keep
those arms going. Keep it hot. Toss some balls around behind
home. Let's go!"

The players scrambled off the field.

The black-and-white mass near the wire screen remained
intact. The young rabbi turned and faced his team.

He talked in Yiddish. "We have the field for five minutes,"
he said. "Remember why and for whom we play."

Then he stepped aside, and the black-and-white mass dissolved into fifteen individual players who came quickly onto
the field. One of them, a tall boy with sand-colored hair and
long arms and legs that seemed all bones and angles, stood at
home plate and commenced hitting balls out to the players.
He hit a few easy grounders and pop-ups, and the fielders
shouted encouragement to one another in Yiddish. They handled themselves awkwardly, dropping easy grounders, throwing wild, fumbling fly balls. I looked over at the young rabbi.
He had sat down on the bench near the wire screen and was
reading his book.

Behind the wire screen was a wide area, and Mr. Galanter
kept us busy there throwing balls around.

"Keep those balls going!" he fist-thumped at us. "No one
sits out this fire fight! Never underestimate the enemy!"

But there was a broad smile on his face. Now that he was
actually seeing the other team, he seemed not at all concerned about the outcome of the game. In the interim between throwing a ball and having it thrown back to me, I told
myself that I liked Mr. Galanter, and I wondered about his
constant use of war expressions and why he wasn't in the
army.

Davey Cantor came past me, chasing a ball that had gone
between his legs.

"Some murderers," I grinned at him.

"You'll see," he said as he bent to retrieve the ball.

"Sure," I said.

"Especially the one batting. You'll see."

The ball was coming back to me, and I caught it neatly and flipped it back.

"Who's the one batting?" I asked.

"Danny Saunders."

"Pardon my ignorance, but who is Danny Saunders?"

"Reb Saunders' son," Davey Cantor said, blinking his eyes.

"I'm impressed."

"You'll see," Davey Cantor said, and ran off with his ball.

My father, who had no love at all for Hasidic communities and their rabbinic overlords, had told me about Rabbi Isaac Saunders and the zealousness with which he ruled his people and settled questions of Jewish law.

I saw Mr. Galanter look at his wristwatch, then stare out at the team on the field. The five minutes were apparently over, but the players were making no move to abandon the field. Danny Saunders was now at first base, and I noticed that his long arms and legs were being used to good advantage, for by stretching and jumping he was able to catch most of the wild throws that came his way.

Mr. Galanter went over to the young rabbi who was still sitting on the bench and reading.

"It's five minutes," he said.

The rabbi looked up from his book. "Ah?" he said.

"The five minutes are up," Mr. Galanter said.

The rabbi stared out at the field. "Enough!" he shouted in Yiddish. "It's time to play!" Then he looked down at the book and resumed his reading.

The players threw the ball around for another minute or two, and then slowly came off the field. Danny Saunders walked past me, still wearing his first baseman's glove. He was a good deal taller than I, and in contrast to my somewhat ordinary but decently proportioned features and dark hair, his face seemed to have been cut from stone. His chin, jaw and cheekbones were made up of jutting hard lines, his nose was straight and pointed, his lips full, rising to a steep angle from the center point beneath his nose and then slanting off to form a too-wide mouth. His eyes were deep blue, and the sparse tufts of hair on his chin, jawbones, and upper lip, the close-cropped hair on his head, and the flow of side curls along his ears were the color of sand. He moved in a loose-jointed, disheveled sort of way, all arms and legs, talking in Yiddish to one of his teammates and ignoring me completely as he passed by. I told myself that I did not like his Hasidic-bred sense of superiority and that it would be a great pleasure to defeat him and his team in this afternoon's game.

The umpire, a gym instructor from a parochial school two blocks away, called the teams together to determine who would bat first. I saw him throw a bat into the air. It was caught and almost dropped by a member of the other team.

During the brief hand-over-hand choosing, Davey Cantor came over and stood next to me.

"What do you think?" he asked.

"They're a snooty bunch," I told him.

"What do you think about their playing?"

"They're lousy."

"They're murderers."

"Oh, come on, Davey."

"You'll see," Davey Cantor said, looking at me gloomily.

"I just did see."

"You didn't see anything."

"Sure," I said. "Elijah the prophet comes in to pitch for them in tight spots."

"I'm not being funny," he said, looking hurt.

"Some murderers," I told him, and laughed.

The teams began to disperse. We had lost the choosing, and they had decided to bat first. We scampered onto the field. I took up my position at second base. I saw the young rabbi sitting on the bench near the wire fence and reading. We threw a ball around for a minute. Mr. Galanter stood alongside third base, shouting his words of encouragement at us. It was warm, and I was sweating a little and feeling very good. Then the umpire, who had taken up his position behind the pitcher, called for the ball and someone tossed it to him. He handed it to the pitcher and shouted, "Here we go! Play ball!" We settled into our positions.

Mr. Galanter shouted, "Goldberg, move in!" and Sidney Goldberg, our shortstop, took two steps forward and moved a little closer to third base. "Okay fine," Mr. Galanter said. "Keep that infield solid!"

A short, thin boy came up to the plate and stood there

with his feet together, holding the bat awkwardly over his head. He wore steel-rimmed glasses that gave his face a pinched, old man's look. He swung wildly at the first pitch, and the force of the swing spun him completely around. His earlocks lifted off the sides of his head and followed him around in an almost horizontal circle. Then he steadied himself and resumed his position near the plate, short, thin, his feet together, holding his bat over his head in an awkward grip.

The umpire called the strike in a loud, clear voice, and I saw Sidney Goldberg look over at me and grin broadly.

"If he studies Talmud like that, he's dead," Sidney Goldberg said.

I grinned back at him.

"Keep that infield solid!" Mr. Galanter shouted from third base. "Malter, a little to your left! Good!"

The next pitch was too high, and the boy chopped at it, lost his bat and fell forward on his hands. Sidney Goldberg and I looked at each other again. Sidney was in my class. We were similar in build, thin and lithe, with somewhat spindly arms and legs. He was not a very good student, but he was an excellent shortstop. We lived on the same block and were good but not close friends. He was dressed in an undershirt and dungarees and was not wearing the four-cornered garment. I had on a light-blue shirt and dark-blue work pants, and I wore the four-cornered garment under the shirt.

The short, thin boy was back at the plate, standing with his feet together and holding the bat in his awkward grip. He let the next pitch go by, and the umpire called it a strike. I saw the young rabbi look up a moment from his book, then resume reading.

"Two more just like that!" I shouted encouragingly to the pitcher. "Two more, Schwartzie!" And I thought to myself, Some murderers.

I saw Danny Saunders go over to the boy who had just struck out and talk to him. The boy looked down and seemed to shrivel with hurt. He hung his head and walked away behind the wire screen. Another short, thin boy took his place at the plate. I looked around for Davey Cantor but could not see him.

The boy at bat swung wildly at the first two pitches and

missed them both. He swung again at the third pitch, and I heard the loud *thwack* of the bat as it connected with the ball, and saw the ball move in a swift, straight line toward Sidney Goldberg, who caught it, bobbled it for a moment, and finally got it into his glove. He tossed the ball to me, and we threw it around. I saw him take off his glove and shake his left hand.

"That hurt," he said, grinning at me.

"Good catch," I told him.

"That hurt like hell," he said, and put his glove back on his hand.

The batter who stood now at the plate was broad-shouldered and built like a bear. He swung at the first pitch, missed, then swung again at the second pitch and sent the ball in a straight line over the head of the third baseman into left field. I scrambled to second, stood on the base and shouted for the ball. I saw the left fielder pick it up on the second bounce and relay it to me. It was coming in a little high, and I had my glove raised for it. I felt more than saw the batter charging toward second, and as I was getting my glove on the ball he smashed into me like a truck. The ball went over my head, and I fell forward heavily onto the asphalt floor of the yard, and he passed me, going toward third, his fringes flying out behind him, holding his skullcap to his head with his right hand so it would not fall off. Abe Goodstein, our first baseman, retrieved the ball and whipped it home, and the batter stood at third, a wide grin on his face.

The yeshiva team exploded into wild cheers and shouted loud words of congratulations in Yiddish to the batter.

Sidney Goldberg helped me get to my feet.

"That momzer!" he said. "You weren't in his way!"

"Wow!" I said, taking a few deep breaths. I had scraped the palm of my right hand.

"What a momzer!" Sidney Goldberg said.

I saw Mr. Galanter come storming onto the field to talk to the umpire. "What kind of play was that?" he asked heatedly. "How are you going to rule that?"

"Safe at third," the umpire said. "Your boy was in the way."

Mr. Galanter's mouth fell open. "How's that again?"

"Safe at third," the umpire repeated.

Mr. Galanter looked ready to argue, thought better of it, then stared over at me. "Are you all right, Malter?"

"I'm okay," I said, taking another deep breath.

Mr. Galanter walked angrily off the field.

"Play ball!" the umpire shouted.

The yeshiva team quieted down. I saw that the young rabbi was now looking up from his book and smiling faintly.

A tall, thin player came up to the plate, set his feet in correct position, swung his bat a few times, then crouched into a waiting stance. I saw it was Danny Saunders. I opened and closed my right hand, which was still sore from the fall.

"Move back! Move back!" Mr. Galanter was shouting from alongside third base, and I took two steps back.

I crouched, waiting.

The first pitch was wild, and the yeshiva team burst into loud laughter. The young rabbi was sitting on the bench, watching Danny Saunders intently.

"Take it easy, Schwartzie!" I shouted encouragingly to the pitcher. "There's only one more to go!"

The next pitch was about a foot over Danny Saunders' head, and the yeshiva team howled with laughter. Sidney Goldberg and I looked at each other. I saw Mr. Galanter standing very still alongside third, staring at the pitcher. The rabbi was still watching Danny Saunders.

The next pitch left Schwartzie's hand in a long, slow line, and before it was halfway to the plate I knew Danny Saunders would try for it. I knew it from the way his left foot came forward and the bat snapped back and his long, thin body began its swift pivot. I tensed, waiting for the sound of the bat against the ball, and when it came it sounded like a gunshot. For a wild fraction of a second I lost sight of the ball. Then I saw Schwartzie dive to the ground, and there was the ball coming through the air where his head had been and I tried for it but it was moving too fast, and I barely had my glove raised before it was in center field. It was caught on a bounce and thrown to Sidney Goldberg, but by that time Danny Saunders was standing solidly on my base and the yeshiva team was screaming with joy.

Mr. Galanter called for time and walked over to talk to Schwartzie. Sidney Goldberg nodded to me, and the two of us went over to them.

"That ball could've killed me!" Schwartzie was saying. He was of medium size, with a long face and a bad case of acne. He wiped sweat from his face. "My God, did you see that ball?"

"I saw it," Mr. Galanter said grimly.

"That was too fast to stop, Mr. Galanter," I said in Schwartzie's defense.

"I heard about that Danny Saunders," Sidney Goldberg said. "He always hits to the pitcher."

"You could've told me," Schwartzie lamented. "I could've been ready."

"I only *heard* about it," Sidney Goldberg said. "You always believe everything you hear?"

"God, that ball could've killed me!" Schwartzie said again.

"You want to go on pitching?" Mr. Galanter said. A thin sheen of sweat covered his forehead, and he looked very grim.

"Sure, Mr. Galanter," Schwartzie said. "I'm okay."

"You're sure?"

"Sure I'm sure."

"No heroes in this war, now," Mr. Galanter said "I want live soldiers, not dead heroes."

"I'm no hero," Schwartzie muttered lamely. "I can still get it over, Mr. Galanter. God, it's only the first inning."

"Okay, soldier," Mr. Galanter said, not very enthusiastically. "Just keep our side of this war fighting."

"I'm trying my best, Mr. Galanter," Schwartzie said.

Mr. Galanter nodded, still looking grim, and started off the field. I saw him take a handkerchief out of his pocket and wipe his forehead.

"Jesus Christ!" Schwartzie said, now that Mr. Galanter was gone. "That bastard aimed right for my head!"

"Oh, come on, Schwartzie," I said. "What is he, Babe Ruth?"

"You heard what Sidney said."

"Stop giving it to them on a silver platter and they won't hit it like that."

"Who's giving it to them on a silver platter?" Schwartzie lamented. "That was a great pitch."

"Sure," I said.

The umpire came over to us. "You boys planning to chat

here all afternoon?" he asked. He was a squat man in his late forties, and he looked impatient.

"No, sir," I said very politely, and Sidney and I ran back to our places.

Danny Saunders was standing on my base. His white shirt was pasted to his arms and back with sweat.

"That was a nice shot," I offered.

He looked at me curiously and said nothing.

"You always hit it like that to the pitcher?" I asked.

He smiled faintly. "You're Reuven Malter," he said in perfect English. He had a low, nasal voice.

"That's right," I said, wondering where he had heard my name.

"Your father is David Malter, the one who writes articles on the Talmud?"

"Yes."

"I told my team we're going to kill you apikorsim this afternoon." He said it flatly, without a trace of expression in his voice.

I stared at him and hoped the sudden tight coldness I felt wasn't showing on my face. "Sure," I said. "Rub your tzitzit for good luck."

I walked away from him and took up my position near the base. I looked toward the wire screen and saw Davey Cantor standing there, staring out at the field, his hands in his pockets. I crouched down quickly, because Schwartzie was going into his pitch.

The batter swung wildly at the first two pitches and missed each time. The next one was low, and he let it go by, then hit a grounder to the first baseman, who dropped it, flailed about for it wildly, and recovered it in time to see Danny Saunders cross the plate. The first baseman stood there for a moment, drenched in shame, then tossed the ball to Schwartzie. I saw Mr. Galanter standing near third base, wiping his forehead. The yeshiva team had gone wild again, and they were all trying to get to Danny Saunders and shake his hand. I saw the rabbi smile broadly, then look down at his book and resume reading.

Sidney Goldberg came over to me. "What did Saunders tell you?" he asked.

"He said they were going to kill us apikorsim this afternoon."

He stared at me. "Those are nice people, those yeshiva people," he said, and walked slowly back to his position.

The next batter hit a long fly ball to right field. It was caught on the run.

"Hooray for us," Sidney Goldberg said grimly as we headed off the field. "Any longer and they'd be asking us to join them for the Mincha Service."

"Not us," I said. "We're not holy enough."

"Where did they learn to hit like that?"

"Who knows?" I said.

We were standing near the wire screen, forming a tight circle around Mr. Galanter.

"Only two runs," Mr. Galanter said, smashing his right fist into his left hand. "And they hit us with all they had. Now we give them *our* heavy artillery. Now *we* barrage *them!*" I saw that he looked relieved but that he was still sweating. His skullcap seemed pasted to his head with sweat. "Okay!" he said. "Fire away!"

The circle broke up, and Sidney Goldberg walked to the plate, carrying a bat. I saw the rabbi was still sitting on the bench, reading. I started to walk around behind him to see what book it was, when Davey Cantor came over, his hands in his pockets, his eyes still gloomy.

"Well?" he asked.

"Well what?" I said.

"I told you they could hit."

"So you told me. So what?" I was in no mood for his feelings of doom, and I let my voice show it.

He sensed my annoyance. "I wasn't bragging or anything," he said, looking hurt. "I just wanted to know what you thought."

"They can hit," I said.

"They're murderers," he said.

I watched Sidney Goldberg let a strike go by and said nothing.

"How's your hand?" Davey Cantor asked.

"I scraped it."

"He ran into you real hard."

"Who is he?"

"Dov Shlomowitz," Davey Cantor said. "Like his name, that's what he is," he added in Hebrew. "Dov" is the Hebrew word for bear.

"Was I blocking him?"

Davey Cantor shrugged. "You were and you weren't. The ump could've called it either way."

"He felt like a truck," I said, watching Sidney Goldberg step back from a close pitch.

"You should see his father. He's one of Reb Saunders' shamashim. Some bodyguard he makes."

"Reb Saunders has bodyguards?"

"Sure he has bodyguards," Davey Cantor said. "They protect him from his own popularity. Where've you been living all these years?"

"I don't have anything to do with them."

"You're not missing a thing, Reuven."

"How do you know so much about Reb Saunders?"

"My father gives him contributions."

"Well, good for your father," I said.

"He doesn't pray there or anything. He just gives him contributions."

"You're on the wrong team."

"No, I'm not, Reuven. Don't be like that." He was looking very hurt. "My father isn't a Hasid or anything. He just gives them some money a couple times a year."

"I was only kidding, Davey." I grinned at him. "Don't be so serious about everything."

I saw his face break into a happy smile, and just then Sidney Goldberg hit a fast, low grounder and raced off to first. The ball went right through the legs of the shortstop and into center field.

"Hold it at first!" Mr. Galanter screamed at him, and Sidney stopped at first and stood on the base.

The ball had been tossed quickly to second base. The second baseman looked over toward first, then threw the ball to the pitcher. The rabbi glanced up from the book for a moment, then went back to his reading.

"Malter, coach him at first!" Mr. Galanter shouted, and I ran up the base line.

"They can hit, but they can't field," Sidney Goldberg said, grinning at me as I came to a stop alongside the base.

"Davey Cantor says they're murderers," I said.

"Old gloom-and-doom Davey," Sidney Goldberg said, grinning.

Danny Saunders was standing away from the base, making a point of ignoring us both.

The next batter hit a high fly to the second baseman, who caught it, dropped it, retrieved it, and made a wild attempt at tagging Sidney Goldberg as he raced past him to second.

"Safe all around!" the umpire called, and our team burst out with shouts of joy. Mr. Galanter was smiling. The rabbi continued reading, and I saw that he was now slowly moving the upper part of his body back and forth.

"Keep your eyes open, Sidney!" I shouted from alongside first base. I saw Danny Saunders look at me, then look away. Some murderers, I thought. Shleppers is more like it.

"If it's on the ground run like hell," I said to the batter who had just come onto first base, and he nodded at me. He was our third baseman, and he was about my size.

"If they keep fielding like that we'll be here till tomorrow," he said, and I grinned at him.

I saw Mr. Galanter talking to the next batter, who was nodding his head vigorously. He stepped to the plate, hit a hard grounder to the pitcher, who fumbled it for a moment then threw it to first. I saw Danny Saunders stretch for it and stop it.

"Out!" the umpire called. "Safe on second and third!"

As I ran up to the plate to bat, I almost laughed aloud at the pitcher's stupidity. He had thrown it to first rather than third, and now we had Sidney Goldberg on third, and a man on second. I hit a grounder to the shortstop and instead of throwing it to second he threw it to first, wildly, and again Danny Saunders stretched and stopped the ball. But I beat the throw and heard the umpire call out, "Safe all around! One in!" And everyone on our team was patting Sidney Goldberg on the back. Mr. Galanter smiled broadly.

"Hello again," I said to Danny Saunders, who was standing near me, guarding his base. "Been rubbing your tzitzit lately?"

He looked at me, then looked slowly away, his face expressionless.

Schwartzie was at the plate, swinging his bat.

"Keep your eyes open!" I shouted to the runner on third. He looked too eager to head for home. "It's only one out!"

He waved a hand at me.

Schwartzie took two balls and a strike, then I saw him begin to pivot on the fourth pitch. The runner on third started for home. He was almost halfway down the base line when the bat sent the ball in a hard line drive straight to the third baseman, the short, thin boy with the spectacles and the old man's face, who had stood hugging the base and who now caught the ball more with his stomach than with his glove, managed somehow to hold on to it, and stood there, looking bewildered and astonished.

I returned to first and saw our player who had been on third and who was now halfway to home plate turn sharply and start a panicky race back.

"Step on the base!" Danny Saunders screamed in Yiddish across the field, and more out of obedience than awareness the third baseman put a foot on the base.

The yeshiva team howled its happiness and raced off the field. Danny Saunders looked at me, started to say something stopped, then walked quickly away.

I saw Mr. Galanter going back up the third-base line, his face grim. The rabbi was looking up from his book and smiling.

I took up my position near second base, and Sidney Goldberg came over to me.

"Why'd he have to take off like that?" he asked.

I glared over at our third baseman, who was standing near Mr. Galanter and looking very dejected.

"He was in a hurry to win the war," I said bitterly.

"What a jerk," Sidney Goldberg said.

"Goldberg, get over to your place!" Mr. Galanter called out. There was an angry edge to his voice. "Let's keep that infield solid!"

Sidney Goldberg went quickly to his position. I stood still and waited.

It was hot, and I was sweating beneath my clothes. I felt the earpieces of my glasses cutting into the skin over my ears, and I took the glasses off for a moment and ran a finger over the pinched ridges of skin, then put them back on quickly because Schwartzie was going into a windup. I crouched down, waiting, remembering Danny Saunders' promise to his team that they would kill us apikorsim. The word had meant, originally, a Jew educated in Judaism who denied basic tenets of his faith, like the existence of God, the revelation, the resurrection of the dead. To people like Reb Saunders, it also meant any educated Jew who might be reading, say, Darwin, and who was not wearing side curls and fringes outside his trousers. I was an apikoros to Danny Saunders, despite my belief in God and Torah, because I did not have side curls and was attending a parochial school where too many English subjects were offered and where Jewish subjects were taught in Hebrew instead of Yiddish, both unheard-of sins, the former because it took time away from the study of Torah, the latter because Hebrew was the Holy Tongue and to use it in ordinary classroom discourse was a desecration of God's Name. I had never really had any personal contact with this kind of Jew before. My father had told me he didn't mind their beliefs. What annoyed him was their fanatic sense of righteousness, their absolute certainty that they and they alone had God's ear, and every other Jew was wrong, totally wrong, a sinner, a hypocrite, an apikoros, and doomed, therefore, to burn in hell. I found myself wondering again how they had learned to hit a ball like that if time for the study of Torah was so precious to them and why they had sent a rabbi along to waste his time sitting on a bench during a ball game.

Standing on the field and watching the boy at the plate swing at a high ball and miss, I felt myself suddenly very angry, and it was at that point that for me the game stopped being merely a game and became a war. The fun and excitement was out of it now. Somehow the yeshiva team had translated this afternoon's baseball game into a conflict between what they regarded as their righteousness and our sinfulness. I found myself growing more and more angry, and I felt the anger begin to focus itself upon Danny Saunders, and suddenly it was not at all difficult for me to hate him.

Schwartzie let five of their men come up to the plate that half inning and let one of those five score. Sometime during that half inning, one of the members of the yeshiva team had shouted at us in Yiddish, "Burn in hell, you apikorsim!" and by the time that half inning was over and we were standing around Mr. Galanter near the wire screen, all of us knew that this was not just another ball game.

Mr. Galanter was sweating heavily, and his face was grim. All he said was, "We fight it careful from now on. No more mistakes." He said it very quietly, and we were all quiet, too, as the batter stepped up to the plate.

We proceeded to play a slow, careful game, bunting whenever we had to, sacrificing to move runners forward, obeying Mr. Galanter's instructions. I noticed that no matter where the runners were on the bases, the yeshiva team always threw to Danny Saunders, and I realized that they did this because he was the only infielder who could be relied upon to stop their wild throws. Sometime during the inning, I walked over behind the rabbi and looked over his shoulder at the book he was reading. I saw the words were Yiddish. I walked back to the wire screen. Davey Cantor came over and stood next to me, but he remained silent.

We scored only one run that inning, and we walked onto the field for the first half of the third inning with a sense of doom.

Dov Shlomowitz came up to the plate. He stood there like a bear, the bat looking like a matchstick in his beefy hands. Schwartzie pitched, and he sliced one neatly over the head of the third baseman for a single. The yeshiva team howled, and again one of them called out to us in Yiddish, "Burn, you apikorsim!" and Sidney Goldberg and I looked at each other without saying a word.

Mr. Galanter was standing alongside third base, wiping his forehead. The rabbi was sitting quietly, reading his book.

I took off my glasses and rubbed the tops of my ears. I felt a sudden momentary sense of unreality, as if the play yard, with its black asphalt floor and its white base lines, were my entire world now, as if all the previous years of my life had led me somehow to this one ball game, and all the future years of my life would depend upon its outcome. I stood there for a moment, holding the glasses in my hand and feeling frightened. Then I took a deep breath, and the feeling passed. It's only a ball game, I told myself. What's a ball game?

Mr. Galanter was shouting at us to move back. I was standing a few feet to the left of second, and I took two steps

back. I saw Danny Saunders walk up to the plate, swinging a
bat. The yeshiva team was shouting at him in Yiddish to kill
us apikorsim.

Schwartzie turned around to check the field. He looked
nervous and was taking his time. Sidney Goldberg was standing up straight, waiting. We looked at each other, then
looked away. Mr. Galanter stood very still alongside third
base, looking at Schwartzie.

The first pitch was low, and Danny Saunders ignored it.
The second one started to come in shoulder-high, and before
it was two thirds of the way to the plate, I was already standing on second base. My glove was going up as the bat
cracked against the ball, and I saw the ball move in a straight
line directly over Schwartzie's head, high over his head, moving so fast he hadn't even had time to regain his balance
from the pitch before it went past him. I saw Dov Shlomowitz heading toward me and Danny Saunders racing to first
and I heard the yeshiva team shouting and Sidney Goldberg
screaming, and I jumped, pushing myself upward off the
ground with all the strength I had in my legs and stretching
my glove hand till I thought it would pull out of my shoulder. The ball hit the pocket of my glove with an impact that
numbed my hand and went through me like an electric
shock, and I felt the force pull me backward and throw me
off balance, and I came down hard on my left hip and elbow.
I saw Dov Shlomowitz whirl and start back to first, and I
pushed myself up into a sitting position and threw the ball
awkwardly to Sidney Goldberg, who caught it and whipped it
to first. I heard the umpire scream "Out!" and Sidney Goldberg ran over to help me to my feet, a look of disbelief and
ecstatic joy on his face. Mr. Galanter shouted "Time!" and
came racing onto the field. Schwartzie was standing in his
pitcher's position with his mouth open. Danny Saunders
stood on the base line a few feet from first, where he had
stopped after I had caught the ball, staring out at me, his face
frozen to stone. The rabbi was staring at me, too, and the
yeshiva team was deathly silent.

"That was a great catch, Reuven!" Sidney Goldberg said,
thumping my back. "That was sensational!"

I saw the rest of our team had suddenly come back to life
and was throwing the ball around and talking up the game.

Mr. Galanter came over. "You all right, Malter?" he asked. "Let me see that elbow."

I showed him the elbow. I had scraped it, but the skin had not been broken.

"That was a good play," Mr. Galanter said, beaming at me. I saw his face was still covered with sweat, but he was smiling broadly now.

"Thanks, Mr. Galanter."

"How's the hand?"

"It hurts a little."

"Let me see it."

I took off the glove, and Mr. Galanter poked and bent the wrist and fingers of the hand.

"Does that hurt?" he asked.

"No," I lied.

"You want to go on playing?"

"Sure, Mr. Galanter."

"Okay," he said, smiling at me and patting my back. "We'll put you in for a Purple Heart on that one, Malter."

I grinned at him.

"Okay," Mr. Galanter said. "Let's keep this infield solid!"

He walked away, smiling.

"I can't get over that catch," Sidney Goldberg said.

"You threw it real good to first," I told him.

"Yeah," he said. "While you were sitting on your tail."

We grinned at each other, and went to our positions.

Two more of the yeshiva team got to bat that inning. The first one hit a single, and the second one sent a high fly to short, which Sidney Goldberg caught without having to move a step. We scored two runs that inning and one run the next, and by the top half of the fifth inning we were leading five to three. Four of their men had stood up to bat during the top half of the fourth inning, and they had got only a single on an error to first. When we took to the field in the top half of the fifth inning, Mr. Galanter was walking back and forth alongside third on the balls of his feet, sweating, smiling, grinning, wiping his head nervously; the rabbi was no longer reading; the yeshiva team was silent as death. Davey Cantor was playing second, and I stood in the pitcher's position. Schwartzie had pleaded exhaustion, and since this was the final inning—our parochial school schedules only permitted

us time for five-inning games—and the yeshiva team's last
chance at bat, Mr. Galanter was taking no chances and told
me to pitch. Davey Cantor was a poor fielder, but Mr. Galanter was counting on my pitching to finish off the game. My
left hand was still sore from the catch, and the wrist hurt
whenever I caught a ball, but the right hand was fine, and the
pitches went in fast and dropped into the curve just when I
wanted them to. Dov Schlomowitz stood at the plate, swung
three times at what looked to him to be perfect pitches, and
hit nothing but air. He stood there looking bewildered after
the third swing, then slowly walked away. We threw the ball
around the infield, and Danny Saunders came up to the plate.

The members of the yeshiva team stood near the wire
fence, watching Danny Saunders. They were very quiet. The
rabbi was sitting on the bench, his book closed. Mr. Galanter
was shouting at everyone to move back. Danny Saunders
swung his bat a few times, then fixed himself into position
and looked out at me.

Here's a present from an apikoros, I thought, and let go the
ball. It went in fast and straight, and I saw Danny Saunders'
left foot move out and his bat go up and his body begin to
pivot. He swung just as the ball slid into its curve, and the
bat cut savagely through empty air, twisting him around and
sending him off balance. His black skullcap fell off his head,
and he regained his balance and bent quickly to retrieve it.
He stood there for a moment, very still, staring out at me.
Then he resumed his position at the plate. The ball came
back to me from the catcher, and my wrist hurt as I caught
it.

The yeshiva team was very quiet, and the rabbi had begun
to chew his lip.

I lost control of the next pitch, and it was wide. On the
third pitch, I went into a long, elaborate windup and sent him
a slow, curving blooper, the kind a batter always wants to hit
and always misses. He ignored it completely and the umpire
called it a ball.

I felt my left wrist begin to throb as I caught the throw
from the catcher. I was hot and sweaty, and the earpieces of
my glasses were cutting deeply into the flesh above my ears
as a result of the head movements that went with my
pitching.

Danny Saunders stood very still at the plate, waiting.

Okay, I thought, hating him bitterly. Here's another present.

The ball went to the plate fast and straight, and dropped just below his swing. He checked himself with difficulty so as not to spin around, but he went off his balance again and took two or three staggering steps forward before he was able to stand up straight.

The catcher threw the ball back, and I winced at the pain in my wrist. I took the ball out of the glove, held it in my right hand, and turned around for a moment to look out at the field and let the pain in my wrist subside. When I turned back I saw that Danny Saunders hadn't moved. He was holding his bat in his left hand, standing very still and staring at me. His eyes were dark, and his lips were parted in a crazy, idiot grin. I heard the umpire yell "Play ball!" but Danny Saunders stood there, staring at me and grinning. I turned and looked out at the field again, and when I turned back he was still standing there, staring at me and grinning. I could see his teeth between his parted lips. I took a deep breath and felt myself wet with sweat. I wiped my right hand on my pants and saw Danny Saunders step slowly to the plate and set his legs in position. He was no longer grinning. He stood looking at me over his left shoulder, waiting.

I wanted to finish it quickly because of the pain in my wrist, and I sent in another fast ball. I watched it head straight for the plate. I saw him go into a sudden crouch, and in the fraction of a second before he hit the ball I realized that he had anticipated the curve and was deliberately swinging low. I was still a little off balance from the pitch, but I managed to bring my glove hand up in front of my face just as he hit the ball. I saw it coming at me, and there was nothing I could do. It hit the finger section of my glove, deflected off, smashed into the upper rim of the left lens of my glasses, glanced off my forehead, and knocked me down. I scrambled around for it wildly, but by the time I got my hand on it Danny Saunders was standing safely on first.

I heard Mr. Galanter call time, and everyone on the field came racing over to me. My glasses lay shattered on the asphalt floor, and I felt a sharp pain in my left eye when I blinked. My wrist throbbed, and I could feel the bump com-

ing up on my forehead. I looked over at first, but without my
glasses Danny Saunders was only a blur. I imagined I could
still see him grinning.

I saw Mr. Galanter put his face next to mine. It was
sweaty and full of concern. I wondered what all the fuss was
about. I had only lost a pair of glasses, and we had at least
two more good pitchers on the team.

"Are you all right, boy?" Mr. Galanter was saying. He
looked at my face and forehead. "Somebody wet a handkerchief with cold water!" he shouted. I wondered why he was
shouting. His voice hurt my head and rang in my ears. I saw
Davey Cantor run off, looking frightened. I heard Sidney
Goldberg say something, but I couldn't make out his words.
Mr. Galanter put his arm around my shoulders and walked
me off the field. He sat me down on the bench next to the
rabbi. Without my glasses everything more than about ten
feet away from me was blurred. I blinked and wondered
about the pain in my left eye. I heard voices and shouts, and
then Mr. Galanter was putting a wet handkerchief on my
head.

"You feel dizzy, boy?" he said.

I shook my head.

"You're sure now?"

"I'm all right," I said, and wondered why my voice
sounded husky and why talking hurt my head.

"You sit quiet now," Mr. Galanter said. "You begin to feel
dizzy, you let me know right away."

"Yes, sir," I said.

He went away. I sat on the bench next to the rabbi, who
looked at me once, then looked away. I heard shouts in Yiddish. The pain in my left eye was so intense I could feel it in
the base of my spine. I sat on the bench a long time, long
enough to see us lose the game by a score of eight to seven,
long enough to hear the yeshiva team shout with joy, long
enough to begin to cry at the pain in my left eye, long
enough for Mr. Galanter to come over to me at the end of
the game, take one look at my face and go running out of the
yard to call a cab.

CHAPTER TWO
✠✠✠✠✠✠✠✠✠✠✠✠✠✠✠

WE RODE to the Brooklyn Memorial Hospital, which was a few blocks away, and Mr. Galanter paid the cab fare. He helped me out, put his arm around my shoulders, and walked me into the emergency ward.

"Keep that handkerchief over the eye," he said. "And try not to blink." He was very nervous, and his face was covered with sweat. He had taken off his skullcap, and I could see him sweating beneath the hairs on his balding head.

"Yes, sir," I said. I was frightened and was beginning to feel dizzy and nauseated. The pain in my left eye was fierce. I could feel it all along the left side of my body and in my groin.

The nurse at the desk wanted to know what was wrong.

"He was hit in the eye by a baseball," Mr. Galanter said.

She asked us to sit down and pressed a button on her desk. We sat down next to a middle-aged man with a blood-soaked bandage around a finger on his right hand. He sat there in obvious pain, resting his finger on his lap and nervously smoking a cigarette despite the sign on the wall that said NO SMOKING.

He looked at us. "Ball game?" he asked.

Mr. Galanter nodded. I kept my head straight, because it didn't hurt so much when I didn't move it.

The man held up his finger. "Car door," he said. "My kid slammed it on me." He grimaced and put his hand back on his lap.

A nurse came out of a door at the far end of the room and nodded to the man. He stood up. "Take care," he said, and went out.

"How're you doing?" Mr. Galanter asked me.

"My eye hurts," I told him.

"How's the head?"

"I feel dizzy."

"Are you nauseous?"

"A little."

"You'll be okay," Mr. Galanter said, trying to sound encouraging. "You get a Purple Heart for today's work, trooper." But his voice was tense, and he looked frightened.

"I'm sorry about all this, Mr. Galanter," I said.

"What are you sorry about, boy?" he said. "You played a great game."

"I'm sorry to be putting you to so much trouble."

"What trouble? Don't be silly. I'm glad to help one of my troopers."

"I'm also sorry we lost."

"So we lost. So what? There's next year, isn't there?"

"Yes, sir."

"Don't talk so much. Just take it easy."

"They're a tough team," I said.

"That Saunders boy," Mr. Galanter said, "the one who hit you. You know anything about him?"

"No, sir."

"I never saw a boy hit a ball like that."

"Mr. Galanter?"

"Yes?"

"My eye really hurts."

"We'll be going in in a minute, boy. Hold on. Would your father be home now?"

"Yes, sir."

"What's your phone number?"

I gave it to him.

A nurse came out the door and nodded to us. Mr. Galanter helped me get to my feet. We walked through a corridor and followed the nurse into an examination room. It had white walls, a white chair, a white, glass-enclosed cabinet, and a tall metal table with a white sheet over the mattress. Mr. Galanter helped me onto the table, and I lay there and stared up at the white ceiling out of my right eye.

"The doctor will be here in a moment," the nurse said, and went out.

"Feel any better?" Mr. Galanter asked me.

"No," I said.

A young doctor came in. He had on a white gown and was wearing a stethoscope around his neck. He looked at us and smiled pleasantly.

"Stopped a ball with your eye, I hear," he said, smiling at me. "Let's have a look at it."

I took off the wet handkerchief, opened my left eye, and gasped with the pain. He looked down at the eye, went to the cabinet, came back, and looked at the eye again through an instrument with a light attached to it. He straightened up and looked at Mr. Galanter.

"Was he wearing glasses?" he asked.

"Yes."

The doctor put the instrument over the eye again. "Can you see the light?" he asked me.

"It's a little blurred," I told him.

"I think I'll go call your father," Mr. Galanter said.

The doctor looked at him. "You're not the boy's father?"

"I'm his gym teacher."

"You had better call his father, then. We'll probably be moving him upstairs."

"You're going to keep him here?"

"For a little while," the doctor said pleasantly. "Just as a precaution."

"Oh," Mr. Galanter said.

"Could you ask my father to bring my other pair of glasses?" I said.

"You won't be able to wear glasses for a while, son," the doctor told me. "We'll have to put a bandage over that eye."

"I'll be right back," Mr. Galanter said, and went out.

"How does your head feel?" the doctor asked me.

"It hurts."

"Does that hurt?" he asked, moving my head from side to side.

I felt myself break out into a cold sweat. "Yes, sir," I said.

"Do you feel nauseous at all?"

"A little," I said, "My left wrist hurts, too."

"Let's take a look at it. Does that hurt?"

"Yes, sir."

"Well, you really put in a full day. Who won?"

"They did."

"Too bad. Now look, you lie as quiet as you can and try not to blink your eyes. I'll be right back."

He went quickly out.

I lay very still on the table. Except for the time I had had my tonsils out I had never been overnight in a hospital. I was frightened, and I wondered what was causing the pain in my eye. Some of the glass from the lens must have scratched it, I thought. I wondered why I hadn't anticipated Danny Saunders' going for the curve, and, thinking of Danny Saunders, I found myself hating him again and all the other side-curled fringe wearers on his yeshiva team. I thought of my father receiving the phone call from Mr. Galanter and rushing over to the hospital, and I had to hold myself back from crying. He was probably sitting at his desk, writing. The call would frighten him terribly. I found I could not keep back my tears, and I blinked a few times and winced with the pain.

The young doctor returned, and this time he had another doctor with him. The second doctor looked a little older and had blond hair. He came over to me without a word and looked at my eye with the instrument.

I thought I saw him go tense. "Is Snydman around?" he said, looking throught the instrument.

"I passed him a few minutes ago," the first doctor said.

"He had better have a look at it," the second doctor said. He straightened slowly.

"You lie still now, son," the first doctor said. "A nurse will be in in a minute."

They went out. A nurse came in and smiled at me. "This won't hurt a bit," she said, and put some drops into my left eye. "Now keep it closed and put this bit of cotton over it. That's a good boy." She went out.

Mr. Galanter came back. "He's on his way over," he said.

"How did he sound?"

"I don't know. He said he'd be right over."

"It's not good for him to be worried. He's not too well."

"You'll be okay, boy. This is a fine hospital. How's the eye?"

"It feels better. They put some drops in it."

"Good. Good. I told you this is a fine hospital. Had my appendix out here."

Three men came into the room, the two doctors and a

short, middle-aged man with a round face and a graying mustache. He had dark hair and was not wearing a gown.

"This is Dr. Snydman, son," the first doctor said to me. "He wants to have a look at your eye."

Dr. Snydman came over to me and smiled. "I hear you had quite a ball game there, young man. Let's have a look." He had a warm smile, and I liked him immediately. He took the cotton off the eye and looked through the instrument. He looked at the eye a long time. Then he straightened slowly and turned to Mr. Galanter.

"Are you the boy's father?"

"I called his father," Mr. Galanter said. "He's coming over right away."

"We'll need his signature," Dr. Snydman said. He turned to the other two doctors. "I don't think so," he said. "I think it's right on the edge. I'll have to have a better look at it upstairs." He turned to me and smiled warmly.

"An eye is not a thing to stop a ball with, young man."

"He hit it real fast," I said.

"I'm sure he did. We're going to have you brought upstairs so we can have a better look at it."

The three doctors went out.

"What's upstairs?" I asked Mr. Galanter.

"The eye ward, I guess. They have all the big instruments up there."

"What do they want to look at it up there for?"

"I don't know, boy. They didn't tell me anything."

Two hospital orderlies came into the room, wheeling a stretcher table. When they lifted me off the examination table, the pain rammed through my head and sent flashes of black, red and white colors into my eyes. I cried out.

"Sorry, kid," one of the orderlies said sympathetically. They put me down carefully on the stretcher table and wheeled me out of the room and along the corridor. Mr. Galanter followed.

"Here's the elevator," the other orderly said. They were both young and looked almost alike in their white jackets, white trousers, and white shoes.

The elevator took a long time going up. I lay on the stretcher table, staring up out of my right eye at the fluorescent light on the ceiling. It looked blurred, and I saw it change color, going from white to red to black, then back to white.

"I never saw a light like that," I said.

"Which light is that?" one of the orderlies asked.

"The fluorescent. How do they get it to change colors like that?"

The orderlies looked at each other.

"Just take it easy, kid," one of them said. "Just relax."

"I never saw a light change colors like that," I said.

"Jesus," Mr. Galanter said under his breath.

He was standing alongside the stretcher table with his back to the rear of the elevator. I tried turning my head to look at him, but the pain was too much and I lay still. I had never heard him use that word before, and I wondered what had made him use it now. I lay there, staring up at the light and wondering why Mr. Galanter had used that word, when I saw one of the orderlies glance down at me with a reassuring grin. I remembered Danny Saunders standing in front of the plate and staring at me with that idiot grin on his lips. I closed my right eye and lay still, listening to the noise of the elevator. This is a slow elevator, I thought. But how do they get the light to change colors like that? Then the light was bad all over and everyone crowded around me. Someone was wiping my forehead, and the light was suddenly gone.

I opened my right eye. A nurse in a white uniform said, "Well, now, how are we doing, young man?" and for a long moment I stared up at her and didn't know what was happening. Then I remembered everything—and I couldn't say a word.

I saw the nurse standing over my bed and smiling down at me. She was heavily built and had a round, fleshy face and short, dark hair.

"Well, now, let's see," she said. "Move your head a little, just a little, and tell me how it feels."

I moved my head from side to side on the pillow.

"It feels fine," I said.

"That's good. Are you at all hungry?"

"Yes, ma'am."

"That's very good." She smiled. "You won't need this now."

She pushed aside the curtain that enclosed the bed. I blinked in the sudden sunlight.

"Isn't that better?"

"Yes ma'am. Thank you. Is my father here?"

"He'll be in shortly. You lie still now and rest. They'll be bringing supper in soon. You're going to be just fine."

She went away.

I lay still for a moment, looking at the sunlight. It was coming in through tall windows in the wall opposite my bed. I could see the windows only through my right eye, and they looked blurred. I moved my head slowly to the left, not taking it off the pillow and moving it carefully so as not to disturb the thick bandage that covered my left eye. There was no pain at all in my head, and I wondered how they had got the pain to leave so quickly. That's pretty good, I thought, remembering what Mr. Galanter had said about this hospital. For a moment I wondered where he was and where my father was; then I forgot them both as I watched the man who was in the bed to my left.

He looked to be in his middle thirties, and he had broad shoulders and a lean face with a square jaw and a dark stubble. His hair was black, combed flat on top of his head and parted in the middle. There were dark curls of hair on the backs of his long hands, and he wore a black patch over his right eye. His nose was flat, and a half-inch scar beneath his lower lip stood out white beneath the dark stubble. He was sitting up in the bed, playing a game of cards with himself and smiling broadly. Some cards were arranged in rows on the blanket, and he was drawing other cards from the deck he held in his hands and adding them to the rows.

He saw me looking at him.

"Hello, there," he said, smiling. "How's the old punching bag?"

I didn't understand what he meant.

"The old noggin. The head."

"Oh. It feels good."

"Lucky boy. A clop in the head is a rough business. I went four once and got clopped in the head, and it took me a month to get off my back. Lucky boy." He held a card in his hands and looked down at the rows of cards on the blanket. "Ah, so I cheat a little. So what?" He tucked the card into a row. "I hit the canvas so hard I rattled my toenails. That was some clop." He drew another card and inspected it. "Caught me with that right and clopped me real good. A whole month on my back." He was looking at the rows of cards on the blanket. "Here we go," he smiled broadly, and added the card to one of the rows.

I couldn't understand most of what he was talking about, but I didn't want to be disrespectful and turn away, so I kept my head turned toward him. I looked at the black patch on his right eye. It covered the eye as well as the upper part of his cheekbone, and it was held in place by a black band that went diagonally under his right ear, around his head and across his forehead. After a few minutes of looking at him, I realized he had completely forgotten about me, and I turned my head slowly away from him and to the right.

I saw a boy of about ten or eleven. He was lying in the bed with his head on the pillow, his palms flat under his head and his elbows jutting upward. He had light blond hair and a fine face, a beautiful face. He lay there with his eyes open, staring up at the ceiling and not noticing me looking at him. Once or twice I saw his eyes blink. I turned my head away.

The people beyond the beds immediately to my right and left were blurs, and I could not make them out. Nor could I make out much of the rest of the room, except to see that it had two long rows of beds and a wide middle aisle, and that it was clearly a hospital ward. I touched the bump on my forehead. It had receded considerably but was still very sore. I looked at the sun coming through the windows. All up and down the ward people were talking to each other, but I was not interested in what they were saying. I was looking at the sun. It seemed strange to me now that it should be so bright. The ball game had ended shortly before six o'clock. Then there had been the ride in the cab, the time in the waiting and examination rooms, and the ride up in the elevator. I couldn't remember what had happened afterwards, but it couldn't all have happened so fast that it was now still Sunday afternoon. I thought of asking the man to my left what day it was, but he seemed absorbed in his card game. The boy to my right hadn't moved at all. He lay quietly staring up at the ceiling, and I didn't want to disturb him.

I moved my wrist slowly. It still hurt. That Danny Saunders was a smart one, and I hated him. I wondered what he was thinking now. Probably gloating and bragging about the ball game to his friends. That miserable Hasid!

An orderly came slowly up the aisle, pushing a metal table piled high with food trays. There was a stir in the ward as people sat up in their beds. I watched him hand out the trays and heard the clinking of silverware. The man on my left scooped up the cards and put them on the table between our beds.

"Chop-chop," he said, smiling at me. "Time for the old feed bag. They don't make it like in training camp, though. Nothing like eating in training camp. Work up a sweat, eat real careful on account of watching the weight, but eat real good. What's the menu, Doc?"

The orderly grinned at him. "Be right with you, Killer." He was still three beds away.

The boy in the bed to my right moved his head slightly and put his hands down on top of his blanket. He blinked his eyes and lay still, staring up at the ceiling.

The orderly stopped at the foot of his bed and took a tray from the table.

"How you doing, Billy?"

The boy's eyes sought out the direction from which the orderly's voice had come.

"Fine," he said softly, very softly, and began to sit up.

The orderly came around to the side of the bed with a tray of food, but the boy kept staring in the direction from which the orderly's voice had come. I looked at the boy and saw that he was blind.

"It's chicken, Billy," the orderly said. "Peas and carrots, potatoes, real hot vegetable soup, and applesauce."

"Chicken!" the man to my left said. "Who can do a ten-rounder on chicken?"

"You doing a ten-rounder tonight, Killer?" the orderly asked pleasantly.

"Chicken!" the man to my left said again, but he was smiling broadly.

"You all set, Billy?" the orderly asked.

"I'm fine," the boy said. He fumbled about for the silverware, found the knife and fork, and commenced eating.

I saw the nurse come up the aisle and stop at my bed.
"Hello, young man. Are we still hungry?"

"Yes, ma'am."

"That's good. Your father said to tell you this is a kosher
hospital, and you are to eat everything."

"Yes, ma'am. Thank you."

"How does your head feel?"

"It feels fine, ma'am."

"No pain?"

"No."

"That's very good. We won't ask you to sit up, though.
Not just yet. We'll raise the bed up a bit and you can lean
back against the pillow."

I saw her bend down. From the motions of her shoulders I could see she was turning something set into the foot
of the bed. I felt the bed begin to rise.

"Is that comfortable?" she asked me.

"Yes, ma'am. Thank you very much."

She went to the night table between my bed and the bed to
my right and opened a drawer. "Your father asked that we
give you this." She was holding a small, black skullcap in her
hand.

"Thank you, ma'am."

I took the skullcap and put it on.

"Enjoy your meal," she said, smiling.

"Thank you very much," I said. I had been concerned
about eating. I wondered when my father had been to the
hospital and why he wasn't here now.

"Mrs. Carpenter," the man to my left said, "how come
chicken again?"

The nurse looked at him sternly. "Mr. Savo, please behave
yourself."

"Yes, *ma'am*," the man said, feigning fright.

"Mr. Savo, you are a poor example to your young neigh-
bors."

She turned quickly and went away.

"Tough as a ring post," Mr. Savo said, grinning at me.
"But a great heart."

The orderly put the food tray on his bed, and he began
eating ravenously. While chewing on a bone, he looked at me
and winked his good eye. "Good food. Not enough zip, but

that's the kosher bit for you. Love to kid them along. Keeps them on their toes like a good fighter."

"Mr. Savo, sir?"

"Yeah, kid?"

"What day is today?"

He took the chicken bone out of his mouth. "It's Monday."

"Monday, June fifth?"

"That's right, kid."

"I slept a long time," I said quietly.

"You were out like a light, boy. Had us all in a sweat." He put the chicken bone back in his mouth. "Some clop that must've been," he said, chewing on the bone.

I decided it would be polite to introduce myself. "My name is Reuven Malter."

His lips smiled at me from around the chicken bone in his mouth. "Good to meet you, Reu— Reu— how's that again?"

"Reuven—Robert Malter."

"Good to meet you, Bobby boy." He took the chicken bone from his mouth, inspected it, then dropped it onto the tray. "You always eat with a hat on?"

"Yes, sir."

"What's that, part of your religion or something?"

"Yes, sir."

"Always like kids that hold to their religion. Important thing, religion. Wouldn't mind some of it in the ring. Tough place, the ring. Tony Savo's my name."

"Are you a professional prizefighter?"

"That's right, Bobby boy. I'm a prelim man. Could've been on top if that guy hadn't clopped me with that right the way he did. Flattened me for a month. Manager lost faith. Lousy manager. Tough racket, the ring. Good food, eh?"

"Yes, sir."

"Not like in training camp, though. Nothing like eating in training camp."

"Are you feeling better now?" I heard the blind boy ask me, and I turned to look at him. He had finished eating and was sitting looking in my direction. His eyes were wide open and a pale blue.

"I'm a lot better," I told him. "My head doesn't hurt."

"We were all very worried about you."

I didn't know what to say to that. I thought I would just nod and smile, but I knew he wouldn't see it. I didn't know what to say or do, so I kept silent.

"My name's Billy," the blind boy said.

"How are you, Billy? I'm Robert Malter."

"Hello, Robert. Did you hurt your eye very badly?"

"Pretty badly."

"You want to be careful about your eyes, Robert."

I didn't know what to say to that, either.

"Robert's a grown-up name, isn't it? How old are you?"

"Fifteen."

"That's grown up."

"Call me Bobby," I said to him. "I'm not really that grown up."

"Bobby is a nice name. All right. I'll call you Bobby."

I kept looking at him. He had such a beautiful face, a gentle face. His hands lay limply on the blanket, and his eyes stared at me vacantly.

"What kind of hair do you have, Bobby? Can you tell me what you look like?"

"Sure. I have black hair and brown eyes, and a face like a million others you've seen—you've heard about. I'm about five foot six, and I've got a bump on my head and a bandaged left eye."

He laughed with sudden delight. "You're a nice person," he said warmly. "You're nice like Mr. Savo."

Mr. Savo looked over at us. He had finished eating and was holding the deck of cards in his hands. "That's what I kept telling my manager. I'm a nice guy, I kept telling him. Is it my fault I got clopped? But he lost faith. Lousy manager."

Billy stared in the direction of his voice. "You'll be all right again, Mr. Savo," he said earnestly. "You'll be right back up there on top again."

"Sure, Billy," Tony Savo said, looking at him. "Old Tony'll make it up there again."

"Then I'll come to your training camp and watch you practice and we'll have that three-rounder you promised me."

"Sure, Billy."

"Mr. Savo promised me a three-rounder after my operation," Billy explained to me eagerly, still staring in the direction of Tony Savo's voice.

"That's great," I said.

"It's a new kind of operation," Billy said, turning his face in my direction. "My father explained it to me. They found out how to do it in the war. It'll be wonderful doing a three-rounder with you, Mr. Savo."

"Sure, Billy. Sure." He was sitting up in his bed, looking at the boy and ignoring the deck of cards he held in his hands.

"It'll be wonderful to be able to see again," Billy said to me. "I had an accident in the car once. My father was driving. It was a long time ago. It wasn't my father's fault, though."

Mr. Savo looked down at the deck of cards, then put it back on top of the night table.

I saw the orderly coming back up the aisle to collect the food trays. "Did you enjoy the meal?" he asked Billy.

Billy turned his head in the direction of his voice. "It was a fine meal."

"How about you, Killer?"

"Chicken!" Tony Savo said. "What can be good about chicken?" His voice was flat though now, and all the excitement was out of it.

"How come you left the bones this time?" the orderly asked, grinning.

"Who can do a ten-rounder on chicken?" Tony Savo said. But he didn't seem to have his heart anymore in what he was saying. I saw him lie back on his pillow and stare up at the ceiling out of his left eye. Then he closed the eye and put his long hairy hands across his chest.

"We'll lower this for you," the orderly said to me after he took my tray. He bent down at the foot of the bed, and I felt the head of the bed go flat.

Billy lay back on his pillow. I turned my head and saw him lying there, his eyes open and staring up, his palms under his head, his elbows jutting outward. Then I looked beyond his bed and saw a man hurrying up the aisle, and when he came into focus I saw it was my father.

I almost cried out, but I held back and waited for him to come up to my bed. I saw he was carrying a package wrapped in newspapers. He had on his dark gray, striped, double-breasted suit and his gray hat. He looked thin and worn, and his face was pale. His eyes seemed red behind his steel-rimmed spectacles, as though he hadn't slept in a long time. He came quickly around to the left side of the bed and looked down at me and tried to smile. But the smile didn't come through at all.

"The hospital telephoned me a little while ago," he said, sounding a little out of breath. "They told me you were awake."

I started to sit up in the bed.

"No," he said. "Lie still. They told me you were not to sit up yet."

I lay back and looked up at him. He sat down on the edge of the bed and put the package down next to him. He took off his hat and put it on top of the package. His sparse gray hair lay uncombed on his head. That was unusual for my father. I never remembered him leaving the house without first carefully combing his hair.

"You slept almost a full day," he said, trying another smile. He had a soft voice, but it was a little husky now. "How are you feeling, Reuven?"

"I feel fine now," I said.

"They told me you had a slight concussion. Your head does not hurt?"

"No."

"Mr. Galanter called a few times today. He wanted to know how you were. I told him you were sleeping."

"He's a wonderful man, Mr. Galanter."

"They told me you might sleep for a few days. They were surprised you woke so soon."

"The ball hit me very hard."

"Yes," he said. "I heard all about the ball game."

He seemed very tense, and I wondered why he was still worried.

"The nurse didn't say anything to me about my eye," I said. "Is it all right?"

He looked at me queerly.

"Of course it is all right. Why should it not be all right? Dr. Snydman operated on it, and he is a very big man."

"He operated on my eye?" It had never occurred to me that I had been through an operation. "What was wrong? Why did he have to operate?"

My father caught the fear in my voice.

"You will be all right now," he calmed me. "There was a piece of glass in your eye and he had to get it out. Now you will be all right."

"There was glass in my eye?"

My father nodded slowly. "It was on the edge of the pupil."

"And they took it out?"

"Dr. Snydman took it out. They said he performed a miracle." But somehow my father did not look as though a miracle had been performed. He sat there, tense and upset.

"Is the eye all right now?" I asked him.

"Of course it is all right. Why should it not be all right?"

"It's not all right," I said. "I want you to tell me."

"There is nothing to tell you. They told me it was all right."

"Abba, please tell me what's the matter."

He looked at me, and I heard him sigh. Then he began to cough, a deep, rasping cough that shook his frail body terribly. He took a handkerchief from his pocket and held it to his lips and coughed a long time. I lay tense in the bed, watching him. The coughing stopped. I heard him sigh again, and then he smiled at me. It was his old smile, the warm smile that turned up the corners of his thin lips and lighted his face.

"Reuven, Reuven," he said, smiling and shaking his head, "I have never been good at hiding things from you, have I?"

I was quiet.

"I always wanted a bright boy for a son. And you are bright. I will tell you what they told me about the eye. The eye is all right. It is fine. In a few days they will remove the bandages and you will come home."

"In only a few days?"

"Yes."

"So why are you so worried? That's wonderful!"

"Reuven, the eye has to heal."

I saw a man walk up the aisle and come alongside Billy's bed. He looked to be in his middle thirties. He had light blond hair, and from his face I could tell immediately that he was Billy's father. I saw him sit down on the edge of the bed, and I saw Billy turn his face toward him and sit up. The father kissed the boy gently on the forehead. They talked quietly.

I looked at my father. "Of course the eye has to heal," I said.

"It has a tiny cut on the edge of the pupil, and the cut has to heal."

I stared at him. "The scar tissue," I said slowly. "The scar tissue can grow over the pupil." And I felt myself go sick with fear.

My father blinked, and his eyes were moist behind the steel-rimmed spectacles.

"Dr. Snydman informed me he had a case like yours last year, and the eye healed. He is optimistic everything will be all right."

"But he's not sure."

"No," my father said. "He is not sure."

I looked at Billy and saw him and his father talking together quietly and seriously. The father was caressing the boy's cheek. I looked away and turned my head to the left. Mr. Savo seemed to be asleep.

"Reb Saunders called me twice today and once last night," I heard my father say softly.

"Reb Saunders?"

"Yes. He wanted to know how you were. He told me his son is very sorry over what happened."

"I'll bet," I said bitterly.

My father stared at me for a moment, then leaned forward a little on the bed. He began to say something, but his words broke into a rasping cough. He put the handkerchief in front of his mouth and coughed into it. He coughed a long time, and I lay still and watched him. When he stopped, he took off his spectacles and wiped his eyes. He put the spectacles back on and took a deep breath.

"I caught a cold," he apologized. "There was a draft in the classroom yesterday. I told the janitor, but he told me he could not find anything wrong. So I caught a cold. In June yet. Only your father catches colds in June."

"You're not taking care of yourself, abba."

"I am worried about my baseball player." He smiled at me. "I worry all the time you will get hit by a taxi or a trolley car, and you go and get hit by a baseball."

"I hate that Danny Saunders for this. He's making you sick."

"Danny Saunders is making me sick? How is he making me sick?"

"He deliberately aimed at me, abba. He hit me deliberately. Now you're getting sick worrying about me."

My father looked at me in amazement. "He hit you deliberately?"

"You should see how he hits. He almost killed Schwartzie. He said his team would kill us apikorsim."

"Apikorsim?"

"They turned the game into a war."

"I do not understand. On the telephone Reb Saunders said his son was sorry."

"Sorry! I'll bet he's sorry! He's sorry he didn't kill me altogether!"

My father gazed at me intently, his eyes narrowing. I saw the look of amazement slowly leave his face.

"I do not like you to talk that way," he said sternly.

"It's true, abba."

"Did you ask him if it was deliberate?"

"No."

"How can you say something like that if you are not sure? That is a terrible thing to say." He was controlling his anger with difficulty.

"It seemed to be deliberate."

"Things are always what they seem to be, Reuven? Since when?"

I was silent.

"I do not want to hear you say that again about Reb Saunders' son."

"Yes, abba."

"Now, I brought you this." He undid the newspapers around the package, and I saw it was our portable radio. "Just because you are in the hospital does not mean you should shut yourself off from the world. It is expected Rome will fall any day now. And there are rumors the invasion of Europe will be very soon. You should not forget there is a world outside."

"I'll have to do my schoolwork, abba. I'll have to keep up with my classes."

"No schoolwork, no books, and no newspapers. They told me you are not allowed to read."

"I can't read at all?"

"No reading. So I brought you the radio. Very important things are happening, Reuven, and a radio is a blessing."

He put the radio on the night table. A radio brought the world together, he said very often. Anything that brought the world together he called a blessing.

"Now, your schoolwork," he said. "I talked with your teachers. If you cannot prepare in time for your examinations, they will give them to you privately at the end of June or in September. So you do not have to worry."

"If I'm out of the hospital in a few days, I'll be able to read soon."

"We will see. We have to find out first about the scar tissue."

I felt myself frightened again. "Will it take long to find out?"

"A week or two."

"I can't read for two weeks?"

"We will ask Doctor Snydman when you leave the hospital. But no reading now."

"Yes, abba."

"Now I have to go," my father said. He put his hat on, folded the newspaper and put it under his arm. He coughed again, briefly this time, and stood up. "I have to prepare examinations, and I must finish an article. The journal gave me a deadline." He looked down at me and smiled, a little nervously, I thought. He seemed so pale and thin.

"Please take care of yourself, abba. Don't get sick."

"I will take care of myself. You will rest. And listen to the radio."

"Yes, abba."

He looked at me, and I saw him blink his eyes behind his steel-rimmed spectacles. "You are not a baby anymore. I hope—" He broke off. I thought I saw his eyes begin to mist and his lips tremble for a moment.

Billy's father said something to the boy, and the boy laughed loudly. I saw my father glance at them briefly, then look back at me. Then I saw him turn his head and look at them again. He looked at them a long time. Then he turned back to me. I saw from his face that he knew Billy was blind.

"I brought you your tefillin and prayer book," he said very quietly. His voice was husky, and it trembled. "If they tell you it is all right, you should pray with your tefillin. But only if they tell you it is all right and will not be harmful to your head or your eye." He stopped for a moment to clear his throat. "It is a bad cold, but I will be all right. If you cannot pray with your tefillin, pray anyway. Now I have to go." He bent and kissed me on the forehead. As he came close to me, I saw his eyes were red and misty. "My baseball player," he said, trying to smile. "Take care of yourself and rest. I will be back to see you tomorrow." He turned and walked quickly away up the aisle, small and thin, but walking with a straight, strong step the way he always walked no matter how he felt. Then he was out of focus and I could no longer see him.

I lay on the pillow and closed my right eye. I found myself crying after a while, and I thought that might be bad for my eye, and I forced myself to stop. I lay still and thought about my eyes. I had always taken them for granted, the way I took for granted all the rest of my body and also my mind. My father had told me many times that health was a gift, but I never really paid much attention to the fact that I was rarely sick or almost never had to go to a doctor. I thought of Billy and Tony Savo. I tried to imagine what my life might be like if I had only one good eye, but I couldn't. I had just never thought of my eyes before. I had never thought what it might be like to be blind. I felt the wild terror again, and I tried to control it. I lay there a long time, thinking about my eyes.

I heard a stir in the ward, opened my right eye, and saw that Billy's father had gone. Billy was lying on his pillow with his palms under his head and his elbows jutting outward. His eyes were open and staring at the ceiling. I saw nurses alongside some of the beds, and I realized that everyone was preparing for sleep. I turned my head to look at Mr. Savo. He seemed to be asleep. My head was beginning to hurt a little, and my left wrist still felt sore. I lay very still. I saw the nurse come up to my bed and look down at me with a bright smile.

"Well, now," she said. "How are we feeling, young man?"

"My head hurts a little," I told her.

"That's to be expected." She smiled at me. "We'll give you this pill now so you'll have a fine night's sleep."

She went to the night table and filled a glass with water from a pitcher that stood on a little tray. She helped me raise my head, and I put the pill in my mouth and swallowed it down with some of the water.

"Thank you," I said, lying back on the pillow.

"You're very welcome, young man. It's nice to meet polite young people. Goodnight, now."

"Goodnight, ma'am. Thank you."

She went away up the aisle.

I turned my head and looked at Billy. He lay very still with his eyes open. I watched him for a moment, then closed my eye. I wondered what it was like to be blind, completely blind. I couldn't imagine it, but I thought it must be something like the way I was feeling now with my eyes closed. But it's not the same, I told myself. I know if I open my right eye I'll see. When you're blind it makes no difference whether you open your eyes or not. I couldn't imagine what it was like to know that no matter whether my eyes were opened or closed it made no difference, everything was still dark.

CHAPTER THREE
▶▶▶▶▶▶▶▶▶▶▶▶▶▶▶▶▶▶▶▶◀

ASLEEP, I HEARD A SHOUT and a noise that sounded like a cheer, and I woke immediately. There was a lot of movement in the ward, and loud voices. I wondered what was happening, there was so much noise and shouting going on and a radio was blaring. I began to sit up, then remembered that I was not yet permitted to sit and put my head back on the pillow. It was light outside, but I could not see the sun. I wondered what the noise was all about, and then I saw Mrs. Carpenter walking sternly up the aisle. She was telling people to stop all the shouting and to remember that this was a hospital and not Madison Square Garden. I looked over at Billy. He was sitting straight up in his bed, and I could tell he was trying to make out what was going on. His face looked puzzled and a little frightened. I turned to look at Mr. Savo, and I saw he was not in his bed.

The noise quieted a little, but the radio was still blaring. I couldn't make it out too clearly because every now and then someone would interrupt with a shout or a cheer. The announcer was talking about places called Caen and Carentan. He said something about a British airborne division seizing bridgeheads and two American airborne divisions stopping enemy troops from moving into the Cotentin Peninsula. I didn't recognize any of the names, and I wondered why everyone was so excited. There was war news all the time, but no one got this excited unless something very special was happening. I thought I could see Mr. Savo sitting on one of the beds. Mrs. Carpenter went over to him, and from the way she walked I thought she was angry. I saw Mr. Savo get to his feet and come back up the aisle. The announcer was saying something about the Isle of Wight and the Normandy coast and Royal Air Force bombers attacking enemy coast-defense guns

55

and United States Air Force bombers attacking shore defenses. I suddenly realized what was happening and felt my heart begin to beat quickly.

I saw Mr. Savo come up to my bed. He was angry, and his long, thin face with the black eyepatch made him look like a pirate.

" 'Go back to your bed, Mr. Savo,' " he mimicked. " 'Go back to your bed this instant.' You'd think I was dying. This is no time to be in bed."

"Is it the invasion of Europe, Mr. Savo?" I asked him eagerly. I was feeling excited and a little tense, and I wished the people who were cheering would be quiet.

He looked down at me. "It's D day, Bobby boy. We're clopping them good. And Tony Savo has to go back to his bed." Then he spotted the portable radio my father had brought me the night before. "Hey, Bobby boy, is that your radio?"

"That's right," I said excitedly. "I forgot all about it."

"Lucky, lucky us." He was smiling broadly and no longer looked like a pirate. "We'll put it on the table between our beds and give it a listen, eh?"

"I think Billy will want to hear it too, Mr. Savo." I looked over at Billy.

Billy turned and stared in the direction of my voice. "Do you have a radio here, Bobby?" He seemed very excited.

"It's right here, Billy. Right between our beds."

"My uncle is a pilot. He flies big planes that drop bombs. Can you turn it on?"

"Sure, kid." Mr. Savo turned on the radio, found the station with the same announcer who was coming over the other radio, then got into his bed and lay back on his pillow. The three of us lay in our beds and listened to the news of the invasion.

Mrs. Carpenter came up the aisle. She was still a little angry over all the noise in the ward, but I could see she was also excited. She asked me how I was feeling.

"I'm feeling fine, ma'am."

"That's very good. Is that your radio?"

"Yes, ma'am. My father brought it to me."

"How nice. You may sit up a little if you wish."

"Thank you." I was happy to hear that. "May I pray with my tefillin?"

"Your phylacteries?"

"Yes, ma'am."

"I don't see why not. You'll be careful of the bump on your head, now."

"Yes, ma'am. Thank you."

She looked sternly at Mr. Savo. "I see you're behaving yourself, Mr. Savo."

Mr. Savo looked at her out of his left eye and grunted. "You'd think I was dying."

"You are to remain in bed, Mr. Savo."

Mr. Savo grunted again.

She went back up the aisle.

"Tough as a ring post," Mr. Savo said, grinning. "Turn it up a bit, Bobby boy. Can't hear it too good."

I leaned over and turned up the volume of the radio. It felt good to be able to move again.

I got the tefillin and prayer book out of the drawer of the night table and began to put on the tefillin. The head strap rubbed against the bump, and I winced. It was still sore. I finished adjusting the hand strap and opened the prayer book. I saw Mr. Savo looking at me. Then I remembered that I wasn't allowed to read, so I closed the prayer book. I prayed whatever I remembered by heart, trying not to listen to the announcer. I prayed for the safety of all the soldiers fighting on the beaches. When I finished praying, I took off the tefillin and put them and the prayer book back in the drawer.

"You're a real religious kid, there, Bobby boy," Mr. Savo said to me.

I didn't know what to say to that, so I looked at him and nodded and didn't say anything.

"You going to be a priest or something?"

"I might," I said. "My father wants me to be a mathematician, though."

"You good at math?"

"Yes. I get all A's in math."

"But you want to be a priest, eh? A—rabbi, you call it."

"Sometimes I think I want to be a rabbi. I'm not sure."

"It's a good thing to be, Bobby boy. Cockeyed world needs people like that. I could've been a priest. Had a chance once.

Made a wrong choice. Wound up clopping people instead. Lousy choice. Hey, listen to that!"

The correspondent was saying excitedly that some German torpedo boats had attacked a Norwegian destroyer and that it looked like it was sinking. There were sailors jumping overboard and lifeboats being lowered.

"They got clopped," Mr. Savo said, looking grim. "Poor bas—poor guys."

The correspondent sounded very excited as he described the Norwegian destroyer sinking.

The rest of that morning I did nothing but listen to the radio and talk about the war with Mr. Savo and Billy. I explained to Billy as best I could some of the things that were going on, and he kept telling me his uncle was the pilot of a big plane that dropped bombs. He asked me if I thought he was dropping them now to help with the invasion. I told him I was sure he was.

Shortly after lunch, a boy came in from the other ward bouncing a ball. I saw he was about six years old, had a thin pale face and dark uncombed hair which he kept brushing away from his eyes with his left hand while he walked along bouncing the ball with his right. He wore light brown pajamas and a dark brown robe.

"Poor kid," said Mr. Savo. "Been in the ward across the hall most of his life. Stomach's got no juices or something." He watched him come up the aisle. "Crazy world. Cockeyed."

The boy stood at the foot of Mr. Savo's bed, looking very small and pale. "Hey, Mr. Tony. You want to catch with Mickey?"

Mr. Savo told him this was no day to toss a ball around, there was an invasion going on. Mickey didn't know what an invasion was, and began to cry. "You promised, Mr. Tony. You said you would catch with little Mickey."

Mr. Savo looked uncomfortable. "Okay, kid. Don't start bawling again. Just two catches. Okay?"

"Sure, Mr. Tony," Mickey said, his face glowing. He threw the ball to Mr. Savo, who had to stretch his right hand high over his head to catch it. He tossed it back lightly to the boy, who dropped it and went scrambling for it under the bed.

I saw Mrs. Carpenter come rushing up the aisle, looking furious.

"Mr. Savo, you are simply impossible!" she almost shouted.

Mr. Savo sat in his bed, breathing very hard and not saying anything.

"You are going to make yourself seriously ill unless you stop this nonsense and rest!"

"Yes, ma'am," Mr. Savo said. His face was pale. He lay back on his pillow and closed his left eye.

Mrs. Carpenter turned to the boy, who had found his ball and was looking expectantly at Mr. Savo.

"Mickey, there will be no more catching with Mr. Savo."

"Aw, Mrs. Carpenter—"

"Mickey!"

"Yes'm," Mickey said, suddenly docile. "Thanks for the catch, Mr. Tony."

Mr. Savo lay on his pillow and didn't say anything. Mickey went back up the aisle, bouncing his ball.

Mrs. Carpenter looked down at Mr. Savo. "Are you feeling all right?" she asked, sounding concerned.

"I'm a little pooped," Mr. Savo said, not opening his eye.

"You should know better than to do something like that."

"Sorry, ma'am."

Mrs. Carpenter went away.

"Tough as a ring post," Mr. Savo said. "But a big heart." He lay still with his eye closed, and after a while I saw he was asleep.

The announcer was talking about the supply problems involved in a large-scale invasion, when I saw Mr. Galanter coming up the aisle. I turned the radio down a little. Mr. Galanter came up to my bed. He was carrying a copy of the *New York Times* under his arm, and his face was flushed and excited.

"Came up to say hello, soldier. I'm between schools, so I've only got a few minutes. Couldn't've seen you otherwise today. How are we doing?"

"I'm a lot better, Mr. Galanter." I was happy and proud that he had come to see me. "My head doesn't hurt at all, and the wrist is a lot less sore."

"That's good news, trooper. Great news. This is some day,

isn't it? One of the greatest days in history. Fantastic under-taking."

"Yes, sir. I've been listening to it on the radio."

"We can't begin to imagine what's going on, trooper. That's the incredible part. Probably have to land more than a hundred fifty thousand troops today and tomorrow, and thousands and thousands of tanks, artillery pieces, jeeps, bulldozers, everything, and all on those beaches. It staggers the mind!"

"I told little Billy here that they were using the big bombing planes an awful lot. His uncle is a bomber pilot. He's probably flying his plane right now."

Mr. Galanter looked at Billy, who had turned his head in our direction, and I saw Mr. Galanter notice immediately that he was blind.

"How are you, young feller?" Mr. Galanter said, his voice sounding suddenly a lot less excited.

"My uncle flies a big plane that drops bombs," Billy said. "Are you a flier?"

I saw Mr. Galanter's face go tight.

"Mr. Galanter is my gym teacher in high school," I told Billy.

"My uncle's been a pilot for a long time now. My father says they have to fly an awful lot before they can come home. Were you wounded or something, Mr. Galanter, sir, that you're home now?"

I saw Mr. Galanter stare at the boy. His mouth was open, and he ran his tongue over his lips. He looked uncomfortable.

"Couldn't make it as a soldier," he said, looking at Billy. "I've got a bad—" He stopped. "Tried to make it but couldn't."

"I'm sorry to hear that, sir."

"Yeah," Mr. Galanter said.

I was feeling embarrassed. Mr. Galanter's excitement had disappeared, and now he stood there, staring at Billy and looking deflated. I felt sorry for him, and I regretted having mentioned Billy's uncle.

"I wish your uncle all the luck in the world," Mr. Galanter said quietly to Billy.

"Thank you, sir," Billy said.

Mr. Galanter turned to me. "They did quite a job getting that piece of glass out of your eye, trooper." He was trying to sound cheerful, but he wasn't succeeding too well. "How soon will you be out?"

"My father said in a few days."

"Well, that's great. You're a lucky boy. It could've been a lot worse."

"Yes, sir."

I wondered if he knew about the scar tissue and didn't want to talk to me about it. I decided not to mention it; he was looking a little sad and uneasy, and I didn't want to make him any more uncomfortable than he already was.

"Well, I got to go teach a class, trooper. Take care of yourself and get out of here soon."

"Yes, sir. Thank you for everything and for coming to see me."

"Anything for one of my troopers," he said.

I watched him walk away slowly up the aisle.

"It's too bad he couldn't be a soldier," Billy said. "My father isn't a soldier, but that's because my mother was killed in the accident and there's no one else to take care of me and my little sister."

I looked at him and didn't say anything.

"I think I'll sleep a little now," Billy said. "Would you turn off the radio?"

"Sure, Billy."

I saw him put his palms under his head on the pillow and lie there, staring vacantly up at the ceiling.

I lay back and after a few minutes of thinking about Mr. Galanter I fell asleep. I dreamed about my left eye and felt very frightened. I thought I could see sunlight through the closed lid of my right eye, and I dreamed about waking up in the hospital yesterday afternoon and the nurse moving the curtain away. Now something was blocking the sunlight. Then the sunlight was back again, and I could see it in my sleep through the lid of my right eye. Then it was gone again, and I felt myself getting a little angry at whoever was playing with the sunlight. I opened my eye and saw someone standing alongside my bed. Whoever it was stood silhouetted against the sunlight, and for a moment I couldn't make out the face. Then I sat up quickly.

"Hello," Danny Saunders said softly. "I'm sorry if I woke you. The nurse told me it was all right to wait here."

I looked at him in amazement. He was the last person in the world I had expected to visit me in the hospital.

"Before you tell me how much you hate me," he said quietly, "let me tell you that I'm sorry about what happened."

I stared at him and didn't know what to say. He was wearing a dark suit, a white shirt open at the collar, and a dark skullcap. I could see the earlocks hanging down alongside his sculptured face and the fringes outside the trousers below the jacket.

"I don't hate you," I managed to say, because I thought it was time for me to say something even if what I said was a lie.

He smiled sadly. "Can I sit down? I've been standing here about fifteen minutes waiting for you to wake up."

I sort of nodded or did something with my head, and he took it as a sign of approval and sat down on the edge of the bed to my right. The sun streamed in from the windows behind him, and shadows lay over his face and accentuated the lines of his cheeks and jaw. I thought he looked a little like the pictures I had seen of Abraham Lincoln before he grew the beard—except for the small tufts of sand-colored hair on his chin and cheeks, the close-cropped hair on his head, and the side curls. He seemed ill at ease, and his eyes blinked nervously.

"What do they say about the scar tissue?" he asked.

I was astonished all over again. "How did you find out about that?"

"I called your father last night. He told me."

"They don't know anything about it yet. I might be blind in that eye."

He nodded slowly and was silent.

"How does it feel to know you've made someone blind in one eye?" I asked him. I had recovered from my surprise at his presence and was feeling the anger beginning to come back.

He looked at me, his sculptured face expressionless. "What do you want me to say?" His voice wasn't angry, it was sad. "You want me to say I'm miserable? Okay, I'm miserable."

"That's all? Only miserable? How do you sleep nights?"

He looked down at his hands. "I didn't come here to fight with you," he said softly. "If you want to do nothing but fight, I'm going to go home."

"For my part," I told him, "you can go to hell, and take your whole snooty bunch of Hasidim along with you!"

He looked at me and sat still. He didn't seem angry, just sad. His silence made me all the angrier, and finally I said, "What the hell are you sitting there for? I thought you said you were going home!"

"I came to talk to you," he said quietly.

"Well, I don't want to listen," I told him. "Why don't you go home? Go home and be sorry over my eye!"

He stood up slowly. I could barely see his face because of the sunlight behind him. His shoulders seemed bowed.

"I *am* sorry," he said quietly.

"I'll just bet you are," I told him.

He started to say something, stopped, then turned and walked slowly away up the aisle. I lay back on the pillow, trembling a little and frightened over my own anger and hate.

"He a friend of yours?" I heard Mr. Savo ask me.

I turned to him. He was lying with his head on his pillow.

"No," I said.

"He give you a rough time or something? You don't sound so good, Bobby boy."

"He's the one who hit me in the eye with the ball."

Mr. Savo's face brightened. "No kidding? The clopper himself. Well, well!"

"I think I'll get some more sleep," I said. I was feeling depressed.

"He one of these real religious Jews?" Mr. Savo asked.

"Yes."

"I've seen them around. My manager had an uncle like that. Real religious guy. Fanatic. Never had anything to do with my manager, though. Small loss. Some lousy manager."

I didn't feel like having a conversation just then, so I remained silent. I was feeling a little regretful that I had been so angry with Danny Saunders.

I saw Mr. Savo sit up and take the deck of cards from his night table. He began to set up his rows on the blanket. I no-

ticed Billy was asleep. I lay back in my bed and closed my
eyes. But I couldn't sleep.

My father came in a few minutes after supper, looking
pale and worn. When I told him about my conversation with
Danny Saunders, his eyes became angry behind the glasses.

"You did a foolish thing, Reuven," he told me sternly.
"You remember what the Talmud says. If a person comes to
apologize for having hurt you, you must listen and forgive
him."

"I couldn't help it, abba."

"You hate him so much you could say those things to
him?"

"I'm sorry," I said, feeling miserable.

He looked at me and I saw his eyes were suddenly sad. "I
did not intend to scold you," he said.

"You weren't scolding," I defended him.

"What I tried to tell you, Reuven, is that when a person
comes to talk to you, you should be patient and listen. Especially if he has hurt you in any way. Now, we will not talk
anymore tonight about Reb Saunders' son. This is an important day in the history of the world. It is the beginning of the
end for Hitler and his madmen. Did you hear the announcer
on the boat describing the invasion?"

We talked for a while about the invasion. Finally, my father left, and I lay back in my bed, feeling depressed and
angry with myself over what I had said to Danny Saunders.

Billy's father had come to see him again, and they were
talking quietly. He glanced at me and smiled warmly. He was
a fine-looking person, and I noticed he had a long white scar
on his forehead running parallel to the line of his light blond
hair.

"Billy tells me you've been very nice to him," he said to
me.

I sort of nodded my head on the pillow and tried to smile
back.

"I appreciate that very much," he said. "Billy wonders if
you would call us when he gets out of the hospital."

"Sure," I said.

"We're in the phone book. Roger Merrit. Billy says that

after his operation, when he can see again, he would like to see what you look like."

"Sure, I'll give you a call," I said.

"Did you hear that, Billy?"

"Yes," Billy said happily. "Didn't I tell you he was nice, Daddy?"

The man smiled at me, then turned back to Billy. They went on talking quietly.

I lay in the bed and thought about all the things that had happened during the day, and felt sad and depressed.

The next morning, Mrs. Carpenter told me I could get out of bed and walk around a bit. After breakfast, I went out into the hall for a while. I looked out a window and saw people outside on the street. I stood there, staring out the window a long time. Then I went back to my bed and lay down.

I saw Mr. Savo sitting up in his bed, playing cards and grinning.

"How's it feel to be on your feet, Bobby boy?" he asked me.

"It feels wonderful. I'm a little tired, though."

"Take it real slow, kid. Takes a while to get the old strength back."

One of the patients near the radio at the other end of the ward let out a shout. I leaned over and turned on my radio. The announcer was talking about a breakthrough on one of the beaches.

"That's clopping them!" Mr. Savo said, grinning broadly.

I wondered what that beach must look like now, and I could see it filled with broken vehicles and dead soldiers.

I spent the morning listening to the radio. When Mrs. Carpenter came over, I asked her how long I would be in the hospital, and she smiled and said Dr. Snydman would have to decide that. "Dr. Snydman will see you Friday morning," she added.

I was beginning to feel a lot less excited over the war news and a lot more annoyed that I couldn't read. In the afternoon, I listened to some of the soap operas—*Life Can Be Beautiful, Stella Dallas, Mary Noble, Ma Perkins*—and what I heard depressed me even more. I decided to turn off the radio and get some sleep.

"Do you want to hear any more of this?" I asked Billy.

He didn't answer, and I saw he was sleeping.

"Turn it off, kid," Mr. Savo said. "How much of that junk can a guy take?"

I turned off the radio and lay back on my pillow.

"Never knew people could get clopped so hard the way they clop them on those soap operas," Mr. Savo said. "Well, well, look who's here."

"Who?" I sat up.

"Your real religious clopper."

I saw it was Danny Saunders. He came up the aisle and stood alongside my bed, wearing the same clothes he had the day before.

"Are you going to get angry at me again?" he asked hesitantly.

"No," I said.

"Can I sit down?"

"Yes."

"Thanks," he said, and sat down on the edge of the bed to my right. I saw Mr. Savo stare at him for a moment, then go back to his cards.

"You were pretty rotten yesterday, you know," Danny Saunders said.

"I'm sorry about that." I was surprised at how happy I was to see him.

"I didn't so much mind you being angry," he said. "What I thought was rotten was the way you wouldn't let me talk."

"That was rotten, all right. I'm really sorry."

"I came up to talk to you now. Do you want to listen?"

"Sure," I said.

"I've been thinking about that ball game. I haven't stopped thinking about it since you got hit."

"I've been thinking about it, too," I said.

"Whenever I do or see something I don't understand, I like to think about it until I understand it." He talked very rapidly, and I could see he was tense. "I've thought about it a lot, but I still don't understand it. I want to talk to you about it. Okay?"

"Sure," I said.

"Do you know what I don't understand about that ball game? I don't understand why I wanted to kill you."

I stared at him.

"It's really bothering me."

"Well, I should hope so," I said.

"Don't be so cute, Malter. I'm not being melodramatic. I really wanted to kill you."

"Well, it was a pretty hot ball game," I said. "I didn't exactly love you myself there for a while."

"I don't think you even know what I'm talking about," he said.

"Now, wait a minute—"

"No, listen. Just listen to what I'm saying, will you? Do you remember that second curve you threw me?"

"Sure."

"Do you remember I stood in front of the plate afterwards and looked at you?"

"Sure." I remembered the idiot grin vividly.

"Well, that's when I wanted to walk over to you and open your head with my bat."

I didn't know what to say.

"I don't know why I didn't. I wanted to."

"That was some ball game," I said, a little awed by what he was telling me.

"It had nothing to do with the ball game," he said. "At least I don't think it did. You weren't the first tough team we played. And we've lost before, too. But you really had me going, Malter. I can't figure it out. Anyway, I feel better telling you about it."

"Please stop calling me Malter," I said.

He looked at me. Then he smiled faintly. "What do you want me to call you?"

"If you're going to call me anything, call me Reuven," I said. "Malter sounds as if you're a schoolteacher or something."

"Okay," he said, smiling again. "Then you call me Danny."

"Fine," I said.

"It was the wildest feeling," he said. "I've never felt that way before."

I looked at him, and suddenly I had the feeling that everything around me was out of focus. There was Danny Saunders, sitting on my bed in the hospital dressed in his Hasidic-style clothes and talking about wanting to kill me because I

had pitched him some curve balls. He was dressed like a
Hasid, but he didn't sound like one. Also, yesterday I had
hated him; now we were calling each other by our first
names. I sat and listened to him talk. I was fascinated just
listening to the way perfect English came out of a person in
the clothes of a Hasid. I had always thought their English
was tinged with a Yiddish accent. As a matter of fact, the
few times I had ever talked with a Hasid, he had spoken only
Yiddish. And here was Danny Saunders talking English, and
what he was saying and the way he was saying it just didn't
seem to fit in with the way he was dressed, with the side curls
on his face and the fringes hanging down below his dark
jacket.

"You're a pretty rough fielder and pitcher," he said, smiling at me a little.

"You're pretty rough yourself," I told him. "Where did
you learn to hit a ball like that?"

"I practiced," he said. "You don't know how many hours I
spent learning how to field and hit a baseball."

"Where do you get the time? I thought you people always
studied Talmud."

He grinned at me. "I have an agreement with my father. I
study my quota of Talmud every day, and he doesn't care
what I do the rest of the time."

"What's your quota of Talmud?"

"Two blatt."

"Two blatt?" I stared at him. That was four pages of Talmud a day. If I did one page a day, I was delighted. "Don't
you have any English work at all?"

"Of course I do. But not too much. We don't have too
much English work at our yeshiva."

"Everybody has to do two blatt of Talmud a day *and* his
English?"

"Not everybody. Only me. My father wants it that way."

"How do you do it? That's a fantastic amount of work."

"I'm lucky." He grinned at me. "I'll show you how. What
Talmud are you studying now?"

"*Kiddushin,*" I said.

"What page are you on?"

I told him.

"I studied that two years ago. Is this what it reads like?"

He recited about a third of the page word for word, including the commentaries and the Maimonidean legal decisions of the Talmudic disputations. He did it coldly, mechanically, and, listening to him, I had the feeling I was watching some sort of human machine at work.

I sat there and gaped at him. "Say, that's pretty good," I managed to say, finally.

"I have a photographic mind. My father says it's a gift from God. I look at a page of Talmud, and I remember it by heart. I understand it, too. After a while, it gets a little boring, though. They repeat themselves a lot. I can do it with *Ivanhoe,* too. Have you read *Ivanhoe?*"

"Sure."

"Do you want to hear it with *Ivanhoe?*"

"You're showing off now," I said.

He grinned. "I'm trying to make a good impression."

"I'm impressed," I said. "I have to sweat to memorize a page of Talmud. Are you going to be a rabbi?"

"Sure. I'm going to take my father's place."

"I may become a rabbi. Not a Hasidic-type, though."

He looked at me, an expression of surprise on his face. "What do you want to become a rabbi for?"

"Why not?"

"There are so many other things you could be."

"That's a funny way for you to talk. *You're* going to become a rabbi."

"I have no choice. It's an inherited position."

"You mean you wouldn't become a rabbi if you had a choice?"

"I don't think so."

"What would you be?"

"I don't know. Probably a psychologist."

"A psychologist?"

He nodded.

"I'm not even sure I know what it's about."

"It helps you understand what a person is really like inside. I've read some books on it."

"Is that like Freud and psychoanalysis and things like that?"

"Yes," he said.

I didn't know much at all about psychoanalysis, but Danny

Saunders, in his Hasidic clothes, seemed to me to be about the last person in the world who would qualify as an analyst. I always pictured analysts as sophisticated people with short pointed beards, monocles, and German accents.

"What would you be if you didn't become a rabbi?" Danny Saunders asked.

"A mathematician," I said. "That's what my father wants me to be."

"And teach in a university somewhere?"

"Yes."

"That's a very nice thing to be," he said. His blue eyes looked dreamy for a moment. "I'd like that."

"I'm not sure I want to do that, though."

"Why not?"

"I sort of feel I could be more useful to people as a rabbi. To our own people, I mean. You know, not everyone is religious, like you or me. I could teach them, and help them when they're in trouble. I think I would get a lot of pleasure out of that."

"I don't think I would. Anyway, I'm going to be a rabbi. Say, where did *you* learn to pitch like that?"

"I practiced, too." I grinned at him.

"But you don't have to do two blatt of Talmud a day."

"Thank God!"

"You certainly have a mean way of pitching."

"How about your hitting? Do you always hit like that, straight to the pitcher?"

"Yes."

"How'd you ever learn to do *that?*"

"I can't hit any other way. It's got something to do with my eyesight, and with the way I hold the bat. I don't know."

"That's a pretty murderous way to hit a ball. You almost killed me."

"You were supposed to duck," he said.

"I had no chance to duck."

"Yes you did."

"There wasn't enough time. You hit it so fast."

"There was time for you to bring up your glove."

I considered that for a moment.

"You didn't want to duck."

"That's right," I said, after a while.

"You didn't want to have to duck any ball that I hit. You had to try and stop it."

"That's right." I remembered that fraction of a second when I had brought my glove up in front of my face. I could have jumped aside and avoided the ball completely. I hadn't thought to do that, though. I hadn't wanted Danny Saunders to make me look like Schwartzie.

"Well, you stopped it," Danny Saunders said.

I grinned at him.

"No hard feelings anymore?" he asked me.

"No hard feelings," I said. "I just hope the eye heals all right."

"I hope so, too," he said fervently. "Believe me."

"Say, who was that rabbi on the bench? Is he a coach or something?"

Danny Saunders laughed. "He's one of the teachers in the yeshiva. My father sends him along to make sure we don't mix too much with the apikorsim."

"That apikorism thing got me angry at you. What did you have to tell your team a thing like that for?"

"I'm sorry about that. It's the only way we could have a team. I sort of convinced my father you were the best team around and that we had a duty to beat you apikorsim at what you were best at. Something like that."

"You really had to tell your father that?"

"Yes."

"What would have happened if you'd lost?"

"I don't like to think about that. You don't know my father."

"So you practically *had* to beat us."

He looked at me for a moment, and I saw he was thinking of something. His eyes had a kind of cold, glassy look. "That's right," he said, finally. He seemed to be seeing something he had been searching for a long time. "That's right," he said again.

"What was he reading all the time?"

"Who?"

"The rabbi."

"I don't know. Probably a book on Jewish law or something."

"I thought it might have been something your father wrote."

"My father doesn't write," Danny said. "He reads a lot, but he never writes. He says that words distort what a person really feels in his heart. He doesn't like to talk too much, either. Oh, he talks plenty when we're studying Talmud together. But otherwise he doesn't say much. He told me once he wishes everyone could talk in silence."

"Talk in silence?"

"I don't understand it, either," Danny said, shrugging. "But that's what he said."

"Your father must be quite a man."

He looked at me. "Yes," he said, with the same cold, glassy stare in his eyes. I saw him begin to play absent-mindedly with one of his earlocks. We were quiet for a long time. He seemed absorbed in something. Finally, he stood up. "It's late. I had better go."

"Thanks for coming to see me."

"I'll see you tomorrow again."

"Sure."

He still seemed to be absorbed in something. I watched him walk slowly up the aisle and out of the ward.

CHAPTER FOUR
✦✦✦✦✦✦✦✦✦✦✦✦✦✦✦✦✦

MY FATHER CAME IN a few minutes later, looking worse than he had the day before. His cheeks were sunken, his eyes were red, and his face was ashen. He coughed a great deal and kept telling me it was his cold. He sat down on the bed and told me he had talked to Dr. Snydman on the phone. "He will look at your eye Friday morning, and you will probably be able to come home Friday afternoon. I will come to pick you up when I am through teaching."

"That's wonderful!" I said.

"You will not be able to read for about ten days. He told me he will know by then about the scar tissue."

"I'll be happy to be out of this hospital," I said. "I walked around a little today and saw the people on the street outside."

My father looked at me and didn't say anything.

"I wish I was outside now," I said. "I envy them being able to walk around like that. They don't know how lucky they are."

"No one knows he is fortunate until he becomes unfortunate," my father said quietly. "That is the way the world is."

"It'll be good to be home again. At least I won't have to spend a Shabbat here."

"We'll have a nice Shabbat together," my father said. "A quiet Shabbat where we can talk and not be disturbed. We will sit and drink tea and talk." He coughed a little and put the handkerchief to his mouth. He took off his spectacles and wiped his eyes. Then he put them back on and sat on the bed, looking at me. He seemed so tired and pale, as if all his strength had been drained from him.

"I didn't tell you yet, abba. Danny Saunders came to see me today."

My father did not seem surprised. "Ah," he said. "And?"

"He's a very nice person. I like him."

"So? All of a sudden you like him." He was smiling. "What did he say?"

I told him everything I could remember of my conversation with Danny Saunders. Once, as I talked, he began to cough, and I stopped and watched helplessly as his thin frame bent and shook. Then he wiped his lips and eyes, and told me to continue. He listened intently. When I told him that Danny Saunders had wanted to kill me, his eyes went wide, but he didn't interrupt. When I told him about Danny Saunders' photographic mind, he nodded as if he had known about that all along. When I described as best I could what we had said about our careers, he smiled indulgently. And when I explained why Danny Saunders had told his team that they would kill us apikorsim, he stared at me and I could see the same look of absorption come into his eyes that I had seen earlier in the eyes of Danny Saunders. Then my father nodded. "People are not always what they seem to be," he said softly. "That is the way the world is, Reuven."

"He's going to come visit me again tomorrow, abba."

"Ah," my father murmured. He was silent for a moment. Then he said quietly, "Reuven, listen to me. The Talmud says that a person should do two things for himself. One is to acquire a teacher. Do you remember the other?"

"Choose a friend," I said.

"Yes. You know what a friend is, Reuven? A Greek philosopher said that two people who are true friends are like two bodies with one soul."

I nodded.

"Reuven, if you can, make Danny Saunders your friend."

"I like him a lot, abba."

"No. Listen to me. I am not talking only about liking him. I am telling you to make him your friend and to let him make you his friend. I think—" He stopped and broke into another cough. He coughed a long time. Then he sat quietly on the bed, his hand on his chest, breathing hard. "Make him your friend," he said again, and cleared his throat noisily.

"Even though he's a Hasid?" I asked, smiling.

"Make him your friend," my father repeated. "We will see."

"The way he acts and talks doesn't seem to fit what he

wears and the way he looks," I said. "It's like two different people."

My father nodded slowly but was silent. He looked over at Billy, who was still asleep.

"How is your little neighbor?" he asked me.

"He's very nice. There's a new kind of operation they'll be doing on his eyes. He was in an auto accident, and his mother was killed."

My father looked at Billy and shook his head. He sighed and stood up, then bent and kissed me on the forehead.

"I will be back to see you tomorrow. Is there anything you need?"

"No, abba."

"Are you able to use your tefillin?"

"Yes. I can't read though. I pray by heart."

He smiled at he. "I did not think of that. My baseball player. I will see you again tomorrow, Reuven."

"Yes, abba."

I watched him walk quickly up the aisle.

"That your father, kid?" I heard Mr. Savo ask me.

I turned to him and nodded. He was still playing his game of cards.

"Nice-looking man. Very dignified. What's he do?"

"He teaches."

"Yeah? Well, that's real nice, kid. My old man worked a pushcart. Down near Norfolk Street, it was. Worked like a dog. You're a lucky kid. What's he teach?"

"Talmud," I said. "Jewish law."

"No kidding? He in a Jewish school?"

"Yes," I said. "A high school."

Mr. Savo frowned at a card he had just pulled from the deck. "Damn," he muttered. "No luck nowhere. Story of my life." He tucked the card into a row on the blanket. "You looked kind of chummy there with your clopper, boy. You making friends with him?"

"He's a nice person," I said.

"Yeah? Well, you watch guys like that, kid. You watch them real good, you hear? Anyone clops you, he's got a thing going. Old Tony knows. You watch them."

"It was really an accident," I said.

"Yeah?"

"I could have ducked the ball."

Mr. Savo looked at me. His face was dark with the growth of beard, and his left eye seemed a little swollen and bloodshot. The black patch that covered his right eye looked like a huge skin mole. "Anyone out to clop you doesn't want you to duck, kid. I know."

"It wasn't really like that, Mr. Savo."

"Sure, kid. Sure. Old Tony doesn't like fanatics, that's all."

"I don't think he's a fanatic."

"No? What's he go around in those clothes for?"

"They all wear those clothes. It's part of their religion."

"Sure, kid. But listen. You're a good kid. So I'm telling you, watch out for those fanatics. They're the worse cloppers around." He looked at a card in his hands, then threw it down. "Lousy game. No luck." He scooped up the cards, patted them into a deck, and put them on the night table. He lay back on his pillow. "Long day," he said, talking almost to himself. "Like waiting for a big fight." He closed his left eye.

I woke during the night and lay still a long time, trying to remember where I was. I saw the dim blue night light at the other end of the ward, and took a deep breath. I heard a movement next to me and turned my head. The curtain had been drawn around Mr. Savo's bed, and I could hear people moving around. I sat up. A nurse came over to me from somewhere. "You go right back to sleep, young man," she ordered. "Do you hear?" She seemed angry and tense. I lay back on my bed. In a little while, I was asleep.

When I woke in the morning, the curtain was still drawn around Mr. Savo's bed. I stared at it. It was light brown, and it enclosed the area of the bed completely so that not even the metal legs of the bed could be seen. I remembered Monday afternoon when I had awakened with the curtain around my bed and Mrs. Carpenter bending over me, and I wondered what had happened to Mr. Savo. I saw Mrs. Carpenter coming quickly up the aisle, carrying a metal tray in her hands. There were instruments and bandages on the tray. I sat up and asked her what was wrong with Mr. Savo. She looked at me sternly, her round, fleshy face grim. "Mr. Savo will be all right, young man. Now you just go about your own business and let Mr. Savo be." She disappeared behind the curtain. I heard a soft moan. At the other end of the ward, the radio had been turned on and the announcer was talking about the war. I didn't want to turn my radio on for fear of disturbing Mr. Savo. I heard another moan, and then I couldn't stand it anymore. I got out of my bed and went to the bathroom. Then I walked around in the hall outside the ward and stared at the people on the street. When I came back, the curtain was still drawn around Mr. Savo's bed, and Billy was awake.

I sat down on my bed and saw him turn his head in my direction.

"Is that you, Bobby?" he asked me.

"Sure," I said.

"Is something wrong with Mr. Savo?"

I wondered how he knew about that.

"I think so," I told him. "They've got the curtain around his bed, and Mrs. Carpenter is in there with him."

"No," Billy said. "She just went away. I was calling him, and she told me not to disturb him. Is it something very bad?"

"I don't know. I think we ought to talk a little quieter, Billy. So we don't bother him."

"That's right," Billy said, lowering his voice.

"Also, I think we'll stop listening to the radio today. We don't want to wake him if he's sleeping."

Billy nodded fervently.

I got my tefillin from the night table and sat on my bed and prayed for a long time. Mostly, I prayed for Mr. Savo.

I was eating breakfast when I saw Dr. Snydman hurrying up the aisle with Mrs. Carpenter. He didn't even notice me as he passed my bed. He was wearing a dark suit, and he wasn't smiling. He went behind the curtain around Mr. Savo's bed, and Mrs. Carpenter followed. I heard them talking softly, and I heard Mr. Savo moan a few times. They were there quite a while. Then they came out and went back up the aisle.

I was really frightened now about Mr. Savo. I found I missed him and the way he talked and played cards. After breakfast, I lay in my bed and began to think about my left eye. I remembered tomorrow was Friday and that in the morning Dr. Snydman was supposed to examine it. I felt cold with fright. That whole morning and afternoon I lay in the bed and thought about my eye and became more and more frightened.

All that day the curtain remained around Mr. Savo's bed. Every few minutes, a nurse would go behind the curtain, stay there for a while, then come out and walk back up the aisle. In the afternoon, the radio at the other end of the ward was turned off. I tried to fall asleep, but couldn't. I kept watching nurses go in and out of the curtain around Mr. Savo's bed. By suppertime I was feeling so frightened and miserable that I could hardly eat. I nibbled at the food and sent the tray back almost untouched.

Then I saw Danny come up the aisle and stop at my bed. He was wearing the dark suit, the dark skullcap, the white shirt open at the collar, and the fringes showing below his jacket. My face must have mirrored my happiness at seeing him because he broke into a warm smile and said, "You look like I'm the Messiah. I must have made some impression yesterday."

I grinned at him. "It's just good to see you," I told him. "How are you?"

"How are *you?* You're the one in the hospital."

"I'm fed up being cooped up like this. I want to get out and go home. Say, it's really good to see you, you sonofagun!"

He laughed. "I *must* be the Messiah. No mere Hasid would get a greeting like that from an apikoros."

He stood at the foot of the bed, his hands in his trouser pockets, his face relaxed. "When do you go home?" he asked.

I told him. Then I remembered Mr. Savo lying in his bed behind the curtain. "Listen," I said, motioning with my head at the curtain. "Let's talk outside in the hall. I don't want to disturb him."

I got out of bed, put on my bathrobe, and we walked together out of the ward. We sat down on a bench in the hallway next to a window. The hallway was long and wide. Nurses, doctors, patients, orderlies, and visitors went in and out of the wards. It was still light outside. Danny put his hands in his pockets and stared out the window. "I was born in this hospital," he said quietly. "The day before yesterday was the first time I'd been in it since I was born."

"I was born here, too," I said. "It never occurred to me."

"I thought of it yesterday in the elevator coming up."

"I was back here to have my tonsils out, though. Didn't you ever have your tonsils out?"

"No. They never bothered me." He sat there with his hands in his pockets, staring out the window. "Look at that. Look at all those people. They look like ants. Sometimes I get the feeling that's all we are—ants. Do you ever feel that way?"

His voice was quiet, and there was an edge of sadness to it.

"Sometimes," I said.

"I told it to my father once."

"What did he say?"

"He didn't say anything. I told you, he never talks to me except when we study. But a few days later, while we were studying, he said that man was created by God, and Jews had a mission in life."

"What mission is that?"

"To obey God."

"Don't you believe that?"

He looked slowly away from the window. I saw his deep blue eyes stare at me, then blink a few times. "Sure I believe it," he said quietly. His shoulders were bowed. "Sometimes I'm not sure I know what God wants, though."

"That's a funny thing for you to say."

"Isn't it?" he said. He looked at me but didn't seem to be seeing me at all. "I've never said that to anyone before." He seemed to be in a strange, brooding mood. I was beginning to feel uneasy. "I read a lot," he said. "I read about seven or eight books a week outside of my schoolwork. Have you ever read Darwin or Huxley?"

"I've read a little of Darwin," I said.

"I read in the library so my father won't know. He's very strict about what I read."

"You read books about evolution and things like that?"

"I read anything good that I can get my hands on. I'm reading Hemingway now. You've heard of Hemingway."

"Sure."

"Have you read any of his works?"

"I read some of his short stories."

"I finished *A Farewell to Arms* last week. He's a great writer. It's about the First World War. There's this American in the Italian Army. He marries an English nurse. Only he doesn't really marry her. They live together, and she becomes pregnant, and he deserts. They run away to Switzerland, and she dies in childbirth."

"I didn't read it."

"He's a great writer. But you wonder about a lot of things when you read him. He's got a passage in the book about ants on a burning log. The hero, this American, is watching the ants, and instead of taking the log out of the fire and saving the ants, he throws water into the fire. The water turns into steam and that roasts some of the ants, and the others just burn to death on the log or fall off into the fire. It's a great passage. It shows how cruel people can be."

All the time he talked he kept staring out the window. I almost had the feeling he wasn't talking so much to me as to himself.

"I just get so tired of studying only Talmud all the time. I know the stuff cold, and it gets a little boring after a while. So I read whatever I can get my hands on. But I only read what the librarian says is worthwhile. I met a man there, and he keeps suggesting books for me to read. That librarian is funny. She's a nice person, but she keeps staring at me all the time. She's probably wondering what a person like me is doing reading all those books."

"I'm wondering a little myself," I said.

"I told you. I get bored studying just Talmud. And the English work in school isn't too exciting. I think the English teachers are afraid of my father. They're afraid they'll lose their jobs if they say something too exciting or challenging. I don't know. But it's exciting being able to read all those books." He began to play with the earlock on the right side of his face. He rubbed it gently with his right hand, twirled it around his forefinger, released it, then twirled it around the finger again. "I've never told this to anyone before," he said. "All the time I kept wondering who I would tell it to one day." He was staring down at the floor. Then he looked at me and smiled. It was a sad smile, but it seemed to break the mood he was in. "If you'd've ducked that ball I would still be wondering," he said, and put his hand back into his pockets.

I didn't say anything. I was still a little overwhelmed by

what he had told me. I couldn't get over the fact that this was Danny Saunders, the son of Reb Saunders, the tzaddik.

"Can I be honest with you?" I asked him.

"Sure," he said.

"I'm all mixed up about you. I'm not trying to be funny or anything. I really am mixed up about you. You look like a Hasid, but you don't sound like one. You don't sound like what my father says Hasidim are supposed to sound like. You sound almost as if you don't believe in God."

He looked at me but didn't respond.

"Are you really going to become a rabbi and take your father's place?"

"Yes," he said quietly.

"How can you do that if you don't believe in God?"

"I believe in God. I never said I didn't believe in God."

"You don't sound like a Hasid, though," I told him.

"What do I sound like?"

"Like a—an apikoros."

He smiled but said nothing. It was a sad smile, and his blue eyes seemed sad, too. He looked back out the window, and we sat in silence a long time. It was a warm silence, though, not in the least bit awkward. Finally, he said very quietly, "I have to take my father's place. I have no choice. It's an inherited position. I'll work it out—somehow. It won't be that bad, being a rabbi. Once I'm a rabbi my people won't care what I read. I'll be sort of like God to them. They won't ask any questions."

"Are you going to like being a rabbi?"

"No," he said.

"How can you spend your life doing what you don't like?"

"I have no choice," he said again. "It's like a dynasty. If the son doesn't take the father's place, the dynasty falls apart. The people expect me to become their rabbi. My family has been their rabbi for six generations now. I can't just walk out on them. I'm—I'm a little trapped. I'll work it out, though—somehow." But he didn't sound as if he thought he would be able to work it out. He sounded very sad.

We sat quietly a while longer, looking out the window at the people below. There were only a few minutes of sunlight left, and I found myself wondering why my father hadn't yet come to see me. Danny turned away from the window and began to play with his earlock again, caressing it and twirling it around his index finger. Then he shook his head and put his hands in his pockets. He sat back on the bench and looked at me. "It's funny," he said. "It's really funny. I have to be a rabbi and don't want to be one. You don't have to be a rabbi and do want to be one. It's a crazy world."

I didn't say anything. I had a sudden vivid picture of Mr. Savo sitting in his bed, saying, "Crazy world. Cockeyed." I wondered how he was feeling and if the curtain was still around his bed.

"What kind of mathematics are you interested in?" Danny asked.

"I'm really interested in logic. Mathematical logic."

He looked puzzled.

"Some people call it symbolic logic," I said.

"I never even heard of it," he confessed.

"It's really very new. A lot of it began with Russell and Whitehead and a book they wrote called *Principia Mathematica*."

"Bertrand Russell?"

"That's right."

"I didn't know he was a mathematician."

"Oh, sure. He's a great mathematician. And a logician, too."

"I'm very bad at mathematics. What's it all about? Mathematical logic, I mean."

"Well, they try to deduce all of mathematics from simple logical principles and show that mathematics is really based on logic. It's pretty complicated stuff. But I enjoy it."

"You have a course in *that* in your high school?"

"No. You're not the only person who reads a lot."

For a moment he looked at me in astonishment. Then he laughed.

"I don't read seven or eight books a week, though, like you," I said. "Only about three or four."

He laughed again. Then he got to his feet and stood facing me. His eyes were bright and alive with excitement.

"I never even heard of symbolic logic," he said. "It sounds fascinating. And you want to be a rabbi? How do they do it? I mean, how can you deduce arithmetic from logic? I don't see—" He stopped and looked at me. "What's the matter?" he asked.

"There's my father," I said, and got quickly to my feet.

My father had come out of the elevator at the other end of the hall and was walking toward the eye ward. I thought I would have to call out to attract his attention, but a few steps short of the entrance to the ward he saw us. If he felt any surprise at seeing me with Danny I didn't notice it. His face did not change expression. But as he came over to us, I saw Danny's face change radically. It went from curiosity to be-wildered astonishment. He looked for a moment as though he wanted to run away. I could see he was nervous and agitated, but I didn't have time to think about it, because my father was standing there, looking at the two of us. He was wearing his dark gray, double-breasted suit and his gray hat. He was a good deal shorter than Danny and a little shorter than I, and his face still looked pale and worn. He seemed out of breath, and he was carrying a handkerchief in his right hand.

"I am late," he said. "I was afraid they would not let me in." His voice was hoarse and raspy. "There was a faculty meeting. How are you, Reuven?"

"I'm fine, abba."

"Should you be out here in the hall now?"

"It's all right, abba. The man next to me became sick sud-denly, and we didn't want to disturb him. Abba, I want you to meet Danny Saunders."

I could see a faint smile begin to play around the corners of my father's lips. He nodded at Danny.

"This is my father, Danny."

Danny didn't say anything. He just stood there, staring at my father. I saw my father watching him from behind his steel-rimmed spectacles, the smile still playing around the corners of his lips.

"I didn't—" Danny began, then stopped.

There was a long moment of silence, during which Danny and my father stood looking at each other and I stared at the two of them and nothing was said.

It was my father who finally broke the silence. He did it gently and with quiet warmth. He said, "I see you play ball as well as you read books, Danny. I hope you are not as vi-olent with a book as you are with a baseball."

Now it was my turn to be astonished. "You know Danny?"

"In a way," my father said, smiling broadly.

"I—I had no idea," Danny stammered.

"And how could you have?" my father asked. "I never told you my name."

"You knew me all the time?"

"Only after the second week. I asked the librarian. You applied for membership once, but did not take out a card."

"I was afraid to."

"I understood as much," my father said.

I suddenly realized it was my father who all along had been suggesting books for Danny to read. My father was the man Danny had been meeting in the library!

"But you never told me!" I said loudly.

My father looked at me. "What did I never tell you?"

"You never told me you met Danny in the library! You never told me you were giving him books to read!"

My father looked from me to Danny, then back to me. "Ah," he said, smiling. "I see you know about Danny and the library."

"I told him," Danny said. He had begun to relax a bit, and the look of surprise was gone from his face now.

"And why should I tell you?" my father asked. "A boy asks me for books to read. What is there to tell?"

"But all this week, even after the accident, you never said a word!"

"I did not think it was for me to tell," my father said quietly. "A boy comes into the library, climbs to the third floor, the room with old journals, looks carefully around, finds a table behind a bookcase where almost no one can see him, and sits down to read. Some days I am there, and he comes over to me, apologizes for interrupting me in my work and asks me if I can recommend a book for him to read. He does not know me, and I do not know him. I ask him if he is interested in literature or science, and he tells me he is interested in anything that is worthwhile. I suggest a book, and two hours later he returns, thanks me, and tells me he has finished reading it, is there anything else I can recommend. I am a little astonished, and we sit for a while and discuss the book, and I see he has not only read it and understood it, but has memorized it. So I give him another book to read, one that is a little bit more difficult, and the same thing occurs. He finishes it completely, returns to me, and we sit and discuss it. Once I ask him his name, but I see he becomes very nervous, and I go to another topic quickly. Then I ask the librarian, and I understand everything because I have already heard of Reb Saunders' son from other people. He is very interested in psychology, he tells me. So I recommend more books. It is now almost two months that I have been making such recommendations. Isn't that so, Danny? Do you really think, Reuven, I should have told you? It was for Danny to tell if he wished, not for me."

My father coughed a little and wiped his lips with the handkerchief. The three of us stood there for a moment, not saying anything. Danny had his hands in his pockets and was looking down at the floor. I was still trying to get over my surprise.

"I'm very grateful to you, Mr. Malter," Danny said. "For everything."

"There is nothing to be grateful for, Danny," my father told him. "You asked me for books and I made recommendations. Soon you will be able to read on your own and not need anyone to make recommendations. If you continue to come to the library I will show you how to use a bibliography."

"I'll come," Danny said. "Of course I'll come."

"I am happy to hear that," my father told him, smiling.

"I—I think I'd better go now. It's very late. I hope the examination goes all right tomorrow, Reuven."

I nodded.

"I'll come over to your house Saturday afternoon. Where do you live?"

I told him.

"Maybe we can go out for a walk," he suggested.

"I'd like that," I said eagerly.

"I'll see you, then, on Saturday. Goodbye, Mr. Malter."

"Goodbye, Danny."

He went slowly up the hall. We watched him stop at the elevator and wait. Then the elevator came, and he was gone.

My father coughed into his handkerchief. "I am very tired," he said. "I had to rush to get here. Faculty meetings always take too long. When you are a professor in a university, you must persuade your colleagues not to have long faculty meetings. I must sit down."

We sat down on the bench near the window. It was almost dark outside, and I could barely make out the people on the sidewalk below.

"So," my father said, "how are you feeling?"

"I'm all right, abba. I'm a little bored."

"Tomorrow you will come home. Dr. Snydman will examine you at ten o'clock, and I will come to pick you up at one. If he could examine you earlier, I would pick you up earlier. But he has an operation in the early morning, and I must teach a class at eleven. So I will be here at one."

"Abba, I just can't get over that you've known Danny for so long. I can't get over him being the son of Reb Saunders."

"Danny cannot get over it, either," my father said quietly.

"I don't—"

My father shook his head and waved my unasked question away with his hand. He coughed again and took a deep breath. We sat for a while in silence. Billy's father came out of the ward. He walked slowly and heavily. I saw him go into the elevator.

My father took another deep breath and got to his feet.

"Reuven, I must go home and go to bed. I am very tired. I was up almost all last night finishing the article, and now rushing here to see you after the faculty meeting. . . . Too much. Too much. Come with me to the elevator."

We walked up the hall and stood in front of the double doors of the elevator.

"We will talk over the Shabbat table," my father said. He had almost no voice left. "It has been some day for you."

"Yes, abba."

The elevator came, and the doors opened. There were people inside. My father went in, turned, and faced me. "My two baseball players," he said, and smiled. The doors closed on his smile.

I went back up the hall to the eye ward. I was feeling very tired, and I kept seeing and hearing Danny and my father talking about what had been going on between them in the library. When I got to my bed, I saw that not only was the curtain still around Mr. Savo's bed, there was now a curtain around Billy's bed, too.

I went up to the glass-enclosed section under the blue light where two nurses were sitting and asked what had happened to Billy.

"He's asleep," one of the nurses said.

"Is he all right?"

"Of course. He is getting a good night's sleep."

"You should be in bed now, young man," the other nurse said.

I went back up the aisle and got into my bed.

The ward was quiet. After a while I fell asleep.

The windows were bright with sunlight. I lay in the bed a while, staring at the windows. Then I remembered it was Friday, and I sat up quickly. I heard someone say, "Good to see you again, Bobby boy. How've you been?" and I turned, and there was Mr. Savo, lying on his pillow, the curtain no longer drawn around his bed. His long, stubbled face looked pale, and he wore a thick bandage over his right eye in place of the black patch. But he was grinning at me broadly, and I saw him wink his left eye.

"Had a bad night, kid. Comes from playing ball. Never could see anything in chasing a ball around."

'It's wonderful to see you again, Mr. Savo!"

"Yeah, kid. Been quite a trip. Gave the Doc a real scare."

"You had Billy and me worried, too, Mr. Savo." I turned to look at Billy. I saw the curtain had been pulled back from his bed. Billy was gone.

"Took him out about two hours ago, kid. Big day for him. Good little kid. Lots of guts. Got to give him that three-rounder one day."

I stared at Billy's empty bed.

"I got to take it real easy, kid. Can't do too much talking. Have the old ring post down on my back."

He closed his eye and lay still.

When I prayed that morning it was all for Billy, every word. I kept seeing his face and vacant eyes. I didn't eat much breakfast. Soon it was ten o'clock, and Mrs. Carpenter came to get me. Mr. Savo lay very still in his bed, his eye closed.

The examination room was down the hall, a few doors away from the elevator. Its walls and ceiling were white, its floor was covered with squares of light and dark brown tile. There was a black leather chair over against one of the walls and instrument cabinets everywhere. A white examination table stood to the left of the chair. Attached to the floor at the right of the chair was a large, stubby-looking metal rod with a horizontal metal arm. Some kind of optical instrument formed part of the end of this metal arm.

Dr. Snydman was in the room, waiting for me. He looked tired. He smiled but didn't say anything. Mrs. Carpenter motioned me onto the examination table. Dr. Snydman came over and began to take the bandage off. I looked up at him out of my right eye. His hands worked very fast, and I could see the hairs on his fingers.

"Now, son, listen to me," Dr. Snydman said. "Your eye has been closed inside the bandage all the time. When the last bandage comes off, you may open it. We'll dim the light in here, so it won't hurt you."

I was nervous, and I could feel myself sweating. "Yes, sir," I said.

Mrs. Carpenter turned off some of the lights, and I felt the bandage come off the eye. I felt it before I knew it, because suddenly the eye was cold from the air.

"Now, open your eye slowly until you become accustomed to the light," Dr. Snydman said.

I did as he told me, and in a little while I was able to keep it open without difficulty. I could see now through both my eyes.

"We can have the lights now, nurse," Dr. Snydman said.

I blinked as the new lights came on.

"Now we'll have a look," Dr. Snydman said, and bent down and peered at the eye through an instrument. After a while, he told me to close the eye, and he pressed down on the lid with one of his fingers.

"Does that hurt?" he asked.

"No, sir."

"Let's have you on that chair now," he said.

I sat on the chair, and he looked at the eye through the instrument attached to the metal rod. Finally, he straightened, swung the instrument back, and gave me a tired smile.

"Nurse, this young man can go home. I want to see him in my office in ten days."

"Yes, Doctor," Mrs. Carpenter said.

Dr. Snydman looked at me. "Your father tells me you know about the scar tissue."

"Yes, sir."

"Well, I think you're going to be all right. I'm not absolutely certain, you understand, so I want to see you again in my office. But I think you'll be fine."

I was so happy I felt myself begin to cry.

"You're a very lucky young man. Go home, and for heaven's sake keep your head away from baseballs."

"Yes, sir. Thank you *very* much."

"You're quite welcome."

Outside in the hall, Mrs. Carpenter said, "We'll call your father right away. Isn't that wonderful news?"

"Yes, ma'am."

"You're lucky, you know. Dr. Snydman is a great surgeon."

"I'm very grateful to him," I said. "Ma'am?"

"Yes?"

"Is Billy's operation over yet?"

Mrs. Carpenter looked at me. "Why, yes, of course. It was Dr. Snydman who operated."

"Is he all right?"

"We hope for the best, young man. We always hope for the best. Come. We must call your father and get you ready to leave."

Mr. Savo was waiting for me. "How'd it go, boy?" he asked.

"Dr. Snydman says he thinks I'll be fine. I'm going home."

Mr. Savo grinned. "That's the way to do it, boy! Can't make a career out of lying around in hospitals."

"Are you going home soon, Mr. Savo?"

"Sure, kid. Maybe in a couple of days or so. If I don't go catching any more balls from little Mickey."

"Dr. Snydman operated on Billy," I said.

"Figured as much. Good man, the Doc. Got a big heart."

"I hope Billy's all right."

"He'll be okay, kid. Important thing is you're getting out."

An orderly came over with my clothes, and I began to dress. I was very nervous, and my knees felt weak. After a while, I stood there, wearing the same clothes I had worn on Sunday for the ball game. It's been some week, I thought.

I sat on my bed, talking with Mr. Savo, and couldn't eat any of my lunch. I was nervous and impatient for my father to come. Mr. Savo told me to relax, I was spoiling his lunch. I sat there and waited. Finally, I saw my father coming quickly up the aisle, and I jumped to my feet. His face was beaming, and his eyes were misty. He kissed me on the forehead.

"So," he said. "The baseball player is ready to come home."

"Did you hear what Dr. Snydman said, abba?"

"The nurse told me on the telephone. Thank God!"

"Can we go home now, abba?"

"Of course. We will go home and have a wonderful Shabbat. I will take your things from the table."

I looked at Mr. Savo, who was sitting up on his bed, grinning at us. "It was wonderful meeting you, Mr. Savo."

"Likewise, kid. Keep the old beanbag away from those baseballs."

"I hope your eye gets better soon."

"The eye's out, kid. They had to take it out. It was some clop. Didn't want the little blind kid to know, so kept it quiet."

"I'm awfully sorry to hear that, Mr. Savo."

"Sure, kid. Sure. That's the breaks. Should've been a priest. Lousy racket, boxing. Glad to be out of it. Would've been in the war if that guy hadn't clopped me in the head like that years back. Busted up something inside. That's the breaks."

"Goodbye, Mr. Savo."

"Goodbye, kid. Good luck."

I went out of the ward with my father, and out of the hospital.

BOOK TWO

++++++++++++++++++

*Silence is good everywhere, except
in connection with Torah.*
                              —The Zohar

CHAPTER FIVE

WE TOOK A CAB and on the way home my father handed me my other pair of glasses with a warning not to read until Dr. Snydman told me I could, and I put them on. The world jumped into focus and everything looked suddenly bright and fresh and clean, as it does on an early morning with the sun on the trees, and there was newness everywhere, a feeling that I had been away a long time in a dark place and was now returning home to sunlight.

We lived on the first floor of a three-story brownstone house that stood on a quiet street just off busy Lee Avenue. The brownstone row houses lined both sides of the street, and long, wide, stone stairways led from the sidewalks to the frosted-glass double doors of the entrances. Tall sycamores stood in front of the houses and their leaves threw cool shadows onto the paved ground. There was a gentle breeze and I could hear the leaves moving over my head.

In front of each house was a tiny lawn planted with either morning glories or a hydrangea bush. The hydrangea bush—or snowball bush, as we called it—on our lawn glowed in the sunlight, and I stared at it. I had never really paid any attention to it before. Now it seemed suddenly luminous and alive.

We climbed up the wide stone staircase and came through the vestibule into the long hallway where it was dark and cool, and narrow like the corridor of a railroad car. The door to our apartment was at the end of the hallway, below and to the right of the staircase that led to the two stories above us. My father put his key into the lock, and we stepped inside.

I could smell the chicken soup immediately, and I had only taken two or three steps when Manya, our Russian housekeeper, came running out of the kitchen in her long apron, her man-sized shoes, and with strands of dark hair falling across her forehead from the braided bun on the top of her head, scooped me into her huge arms as though I were a leaf, and smothered me with a hug that pushed the air from my lungs and left me breathless. She planted a wet kiss on my forehead, then held me at arm's length and began to babble in Ukrainian. I couldn't understand what she was saying, but I could see her eyes were moist and she was biting her lips to keep from crying. She released me, and I stood there, smiling and catching my breath, while my father talked to her.

"Are you hungry, Reuven?" my father asked me.

"I'm starved," I said.

"There is lunch on the table. We will eat together. Then you can lie on the porch and rest while I finish typing my article."

Lunch turned out to be a massive affair, with a thick soup, fresh rye bread, onion rolls, bagels, cream cheese, scrambled eggs, smoked salmon, and chocolate pudding. My father and I ate without talking, while Manya hovered over us like a protective bear, and afterwards my father went into his study and I walked slowly through the apartment. I had lived in it all my life, but I never really saw it until I went through it that Friday afternoon.

I came out of the kitchen and stood for a moment staring down at the strip of gray carpet that ran the length of the hall. I turned left and walked slowly along the hall, past the bathroom and the dumbwaiter to my left, past the telephone stand and the pictures of Herzl, Bialik, and Chaim Weizmann that hung from the wall on my right, and into my bedroom. It was a long, somewhat narrow room, with a bed against its right wall, a bookcase along its left wall, two closets near the door, and a desk and chair set a bit away from the wall facing the door. To the left of the desk, along the bookcase wall, was a window that looked out onto the alleyway and back yard beyond. The room had been cleaned, the bed carefully made and covered with its green-and-brown spread, and on the desk were my school books arranged in a neat pile. Someone had brought them home for me after the ball game, and there they were, on the desk, as though I had never been away. I went over to the window and stared out at the alleyway. I could see a cat lying in the shade of our wall, and beyond was the grass of our back lawn and the ailanthus tree with the sun on its leaves. I turned, sat down on the window seat, and stared at the *New York Times* war maps I had put on the wall over my bed. There were maps of the North African, Sicilian, and Italian campaigns, and now I would have to add a map of Europe, too. Over the maps was the large picture of Franklin Delano Roosevelt I had cut out of a *New York Times* Sunday magazine section, and next to it was the picture of Albert Einstein I had taken years ago from an issue of *Junior Scholastic*. I looked at my desk. My pens and pencils were neatly tucked into the holder alongside my lamp, and on top of a pile of papers was the recent issue of the WQXR *Bulletin*. I remembered I had wanted to listen to a Tchaikovsky symphony on Sunday night, the night of the ball game which I had been so certain we would win.

At the head of the bed was the door that led to my father's study. The door was closed, and I could hear my father working at his typewriter inside. There was no way to get to the living room except through the study, and I walked around behind my desk, opened the door, stepped inside, and closed it quietly behind me.

My father's study was the same size as my room, but it had no windows. The wall alongside the door was lined with floor-to-ceiling bookcases. Along the opposite wall were curtained French doors bounded by two large Ionic columns. What was left of that wall was also covered with bookcases, as was the wall adjoining it to the right. My father's desk stood near the outside wall of the house, in almost the exact position where I had asked to have my own desk placed. But it was a good deal larger than mine, with dark, polished wood, deep drawers, and a large, green, leather-bordered blotter that covered almost its entire top. It was strewn with papers now, and my father was working intently over his old Underwood typewriter. The study was the darkest room in the apartment because it had no windows, and my father always worked with the desk lamp on, the yellow light bathing the desk and the floor around it. He sat there now, wearing his small, black skullcap and pecking at the typewriter with his index fingers, a thin, frail man in his fifties, with gray hair, gaunt cheeks, and spectacles. I looked at him and suddenly realized that he hadn't coughed once since he had come to take me from the hospital. He glanced up at me for a moment, frowned, then went back to his work. He didn't like me to disturb him while he was at his desk, and I went quietly through the study, walking on the gray rug that covered the floor, then through the French doors into the living room.

Sunlight poured through the three wide windows that faced the street and spread gold across the gray rug, the French-style sofa, chairs and end tables, the polished, glass-topped coffee table, and along the white walls. I stood near the sofa for a moment, blinking my eyes which always hurt a little whenever I came from the darkness of my father's study into the brightness of our living room.

The windows were open, and I could hear children playing in the street. A warm breeze came into the room and lifted the lace curtains that fronted the windows.

I stood in that room for a long time, watching the sunlight and listening to the sounds on the street outside. I stood there, tasting the room and the sunlight and the sounds, and thinking of the long hospital ward with its wide aisle and its two rows of beds and little Mickey bouncing a ball and trying to find someone who would play catch with him. I wondered if little Mickey had ever seen sunlight come through the windows of a front room apartment.

I turned, finally, and went back through the apartment and through the door that led from my father's bedroom onto our wooden back porch. I sat on the lounge chair in the shade that covered the porch and looked out at the back lawn. Somehow everything had changed. I had spent five days in a hospital and the world around seemed sharpened now and pulsing with life. I lay back and put the palms of my hands under my head. I thought of the baseball game, and I asked myself, Was it only last Sunday that it happened, only five days ago? I felt I had crossed into another world, that little pieces of my old self had been left behind on the black asphalt floor of the school yard alongside the shattered lens of my glasses. I could hear the shouts of children on the street and the sounds of my father's typewriter. I remembered that tomorrow Danny would be over to see me. I lay very still on the lounge chair and thought a long time about Danny.

CHAPTER SIX
↦✠✠✠✠✠✠✠✠✠✠✠✠✠✠✠↤

THAT NIGHT as we sat at the kitchen table, with the Shabbat meal over and Manya gone until the morning, my father answered some of my questions about Danny Saunders.

It was a warm night, and the window between the stove and the sink was open. A breeze blew into the kitchen, stirring the ruffled curtains and carrying with it the odors of grass and flowers and orange blossoms. We sat at the table dressed in our Shabbat clothes, my father sipping his second glass of tea, both of us a little tired and sleepy from the heavy meal. There was color now in my father's face, and his cough had disappeared. I watched him sip his tea and listened to the soft rustling of the curtains as they moved in the breeze. Manya had done the dishes quickly after we had chanted the Grace After Meals, and now we sat alone, embraced by the warm June night, the memories of the past week, and the gentle silences of the Shabbat.

It was then that I asked my father about Danny. He was holding his glass of tea in his hands, the bottom of the glass resting upon his left palm, the body of the glass encircled by his right hand, and he put the glass on the white cloth that covered the table, looked at me, and smiled. He sat silent for a while, and I knew his answer would take a long time. Whenever he did not respond immediately to one of my questions, the answer was always a lengthy one. I could see he was arranging it in his mind, so that it would be carefully organized. When he finally spoke, his voice was soft, and the words came out slowly.

He told me he would have to go back a long time into the history of our people in order for me to understand his answer. He asked me if I had the patience to sit and listen

97

quietly, and I nodded. He sat back in his chair and began to speak.

I knew enough Jewish history, he said, not to make him have to start at the beginning. He would start, instead, with the history I had not yet learned in school, with the centuries of horror our people had experienced in Poland. Because it was really in Poland, or, more accurately, in the Slavic countries of eastern Europe, that Danny's soul had been born.

"Poland was different from the other countries of Europe, Reuven. Poland actually encouraged the Jews to come and live and be part of her people. This was in the thirteenth century, during a time when the Jews of western Europe, especially in Germany, were going through terrible persecutions. Jews had been living in Poland before this century, but they were not a very large community. Why did Poland want Jews when almost every other country was persecuting them? Because Poland was a very poor country, with a bankrupt aristocracy and a crushed peasantry. Her upper-class nobles would not engage in work and instead managed to survive by what they could squeeze out of the labor of the serfs. Poland wanted people who would build her economy, organize her affairs, and bring her to life. Jews had a reputation for possessing these abilities, and so the Polish nobles were eager to have Jews settle in their country. They came by the thousands from western Europe, especially from Germany. They ran the nobles' estates, collected the taxes, developed Polish industry, and stimulated her trade. Poland became a kind of Jewish Utopia.

"But the Jews did not only prosper economically. They also built many great academies of learning throughout the country. Every community had its Talmudic scholars, and by the end of the sixteenth century the Jewish academies in Poland had become centers of learning for all of European Jewry.

"And then, Reuven, a great tragedy occurred. It is a tragedy that happens often to anyone who acts as a buffer. The Jews were helping the nobility, but in doing so, in collecting taxes from the serfs and peasants, for example, they were building up against themselves the hatred of these oppressed classes. And the hatred finally exploded into violence. In the borderland east of Ukrainia in Russia, there was a community of Cossacks who were members of the Greek Orthodox Church. This community belonged to Poland, and the Polish nobles, who were Catholics, treated the Cossacks who lived there with cruelty and contempt. They not only taxed the lands and the cattle of the Cossacks but also their churches and religious customs. And who collected these taxes? The Jews. Who had possession of the keys to the Cossack churches? The Jews. Who did the Cossacks need to go to if they wanted to open their churches for a christening service or for a marriage or a funeral? The Jews. All of whom were acting in behalf of the Polish lords.

"Nothing happened for a long time, because the Cossacks, like the Polish peasants, were afraid of the Polish nobles. But in the year 1648, a man named Bogdan Chmielnicki became the leader of the Cossacks, and he led an uprising against Poland. The Jews became the victims of the Polish peasants, who hated them, and of the Cossacks, who also hated them. The revolution lasted ten years, and in that time something like seven hundred Jewish communities were destroyed and about one hundred thousand Jews were slain. When the horror was over, the great Jewish community of Poland had been almost completely destroyed."

My father paused for a long moment. The window curtains moved softly in the cool night breeze. When he spoke again, his voice was low, tense, subdued.

"Reuven, what could our people say to God during the Chmielnicki uprising? They could not thank Him for the slaughter going on before their eyes, and they would not deny His existence. So many of them began to believe the Messiah was coming. Remember, Reuven, that those Jews who believe in the Messiah believe also that just before the Messiah comes there will be an era of great disaster. At the moment when there seems to be no meaning in life, at that moment a person must try to find new meaning. And so thousands upon thousands of Jews in both eastern and western Europe began to look upon the Chmielnicki disaster as the prelude to the coming of the Messiah. They prayed and fasted and did penance —all in an effort to hasten his coming. And he came. His name was Shabbtai Zvi. He revealed himself about the same time as the massacres began. More than half the Jewish world became his followers. Years later, when it turned out that he was a fraud, you can imagine what the effect was. The Chmielnicki uprising was a physical disaster; the false Messiah was a spiritual disaster.

"We are like other people, Reuven. We do not survive disaster merely by appealing to invisible powers. We are as easily degraded as any other people. That is what happened to Polish Jewry. By the eighteenth century, it had become a degraded people. Jewish scholarship was dead. In its place came empty discussions about matters that had no practical connection with the desperate needs of the masses of Jews. Pilpul, these discussions are called—empty, nonsensical arguments over minute points of the Talmud that have no relation at all to the world. Jewish scholars became interested in showing other Jewish scholars how much they knew, how many texts they could manipulate. They were not in the least bit interested in teaching the masses of Jews, in communicating their knowledge and uplifting the people. And so there grew up a great wall between the scholars and the people. It was also a time of terrible superstition. Our people believed that there were demons and ghosts everywhere that tortured the Jew, wracked his body, and terrorized his soul. These fears affected all Jews. But they affected the unlearned masses worst of all. At least the scholar had his pilpul to keep him alive.

"Now, Reuven, if everywhere around you there are forces that wish to harm you, what is it that you can do to help yourself? Of course, you try to destroy those forces. But the masses of Jews did not believe they had the power to do this. Only very skillful people possessed such power, they felt. And so there came upon the scene Jews who claimed to be experts in the chasing away of demons and spirits. Such men were looked upon as saints, and they became very popular in Poland. They claimed that their power came from their ability to manipulate the various letters that spelled out the mystical names of God. That is why they were called Ba'ale Shem—Masters of the Name. To drive away evil spirits they wrote magical amulets, prescribed medicines, performed wild dances, wearing the tallit and tefillin over white robes; they used black candles, sounded the shofar, recited psalms, screamed, pleaded, threatened—anything to drive the evil spirits out of a person who, for example, might be ill, or away from a mother who was about to have a child. To such a level had our people sunk in Poland by the eighteenth century. And here, Reuven, is where my answer to your questions about Reb Saunders' son really begins."

My father paused for a moment and finished his tea. Then he looked at me and smiled. "Are you tired yet, Reuven?"

"No, abba."

"I am not sounding too much like a schoolteacher?"

"I don't mind it when you sound like a schoolteacher," I said.

"It is not a lecture," he said. "I will not ask you questions afterward."

"I want you to go on," I said.

He nodded and smiled again. "I will want some more tea," he said. "But a little later. Now let me tell you about a man who was born in that century, and I think you will begin to have your answer.

"There are many legends about his birth, but I am not interested in telling you legends. He was born about the year 1700 in Poland. His name was Israel. His parents were very poor and not learned, and they both died while he was still a child. The people of his village cared for him and sent him to school. But he did not like school, and whenever he could he would sneak away and escape to the woods where he would walk under the trees, look at the flowers, sit by a brook, listen to the songs of the birds and to the noise of the wind in the leaves. As often as his teachers brought him back, so often did he run away to these woods, and after a while they gave up and left him alone. When he was thirteen, he became an assistant to a schoolmaster, but instead of helping the master teach the little children, he often took them also to the woods where they would sing or stand in silence, listening to the birds in the trees. When he grew older, he became the beadle of the village synagogue. All day long he would sit around, listening to the learned discussions that went on inside the synagogue walls, and at night, when everyone else slept, he would take the holy books in his hands and study them carefully. But it was not the Talmud that he studied, it was the Kabbalah, the books of Jewish mysticism. The rabbis had forbidden the study of the Kabbalah, and so Israel had to study in secret. He married, finally, but almost nothing is known about his wife. She died soon afterward, and Israel, a full-grown man now, became a schoolteacher. He had a wonderful way with children, and he achieved a great reputation as a teacher. He was a kind and gentle person, honest and unaffected, and often people would come to him and ask him to settle their quarrels. He came to be regarded as a wise and holy man, and one day the father of Rabbi Abraham Gershon of the city of Brody came to him and asked him to settle a business dispute he had with another man. He was so impressed with Israel that he offered to give him his daughter Hannah in marriage. Israel agreed, but asked that the betrothal documents be kept a secret for the time being. And now, an interesting event occurred. The father of Hannah died, and Israel traveled to Brody, to the house of the great Rabbi Abraham Gershon, Hannah's brother, in order to claim his bride. He was dressed in the clothes of a peasant, torn boots and coarse garments, and you can imagine how shocked the rabbi was when he saw the betrothal agreement in Israel's hands. His sister should marry a peasant? What shame and dishonor that would bring upon the family name! He tried to persuade his sister to reject her father's choice, but somehow Hannah saw something in Israel which the good rabbi of Brody did not, and she refused. After their marriage, Rabbi Abraham Gershon tried to improve his brother-in-law's education. He began by teaching him Talmud, but Israel seemed very uninterested in Talmud. He made him his coachman, but Israel was a failure at that, too. Finally, the rabbi gave up and ordered his sister and brother-in-law to leave Brody so as not to dishonor his good name, and they left.

"And now, Reuven, you will begin to have the answer to your question. I am sorry I am taking so long."

"Please go on, abba."

"All right. Israel and his wife left Brody and settled in the Carpathian Mountains in a village near Brody. They were very poor, but very happy. Israel earned a living by selling the lime which they dug in the mountains. The Carpathian Mountains are beautiful, and Israel built a little house and spent many days there alone, praying, dreaming, and singing to the great hills. Very often he would remain alone throughout the entire week, and return to his wife Hannah only for

Shabbat. She must have suffered terribly because of their poverty, but she believed in him and was very devoted.

"Reuven, it was in these mountains that Israel gave birth to Hasidism. He was there many years, thinking, meditating, singing his strange songs, listening to the birds, learning from peasant women how to heal sickness with grasses and herbs, to write amulets, to drive out evil spirits. The people of the village loved him, and soon his reputation as a holy man began to spread throughout all of Poland. Legends began to grow about him. He was not yet forty, and already there were legends about him. You can imagine what kind of person he must have been.

"His brother-in-law, Rabbi Abraham Gershon, finally regretted his cruelty and asked Israel and Hannah to return to Brody. He acquired a tavern for them to operate, but it was Hannah who really managed it while Israel wandered about in the woods and meadows outside of Brody, meditating. Finally, he began to travel, and he became a Ba'al Shem. He was kind and saintly and godly, and he seemed to want to help people not for the money they paid him but for the love he had for them. And so they came to call him the Ba'al Shem Tov—the Kind or Good Master of the Name. He mingled with the people and talked to them about God and His Torah in plain, simple language that they could easily understand. He taught them that the purpose of man is to make his life holy—every aspect of his life: eating, drinking, praying, sleeping. God is everywhere, he told them, and if it seems at times that He is hidden from us, it is only because we have not yet learned to seek Him correctly. Evil is like a hard shell. Within this shell is the spark of God, is goodness. How do we penetrate the shell? By sincere and honest prayer, by being happy, and by loving all people. The Ba'al Shem Tov —his followers later shortened his name and called him the Besht—believed that no man is so sinful that he cannot be purified by love and understanding. He also believed—and here is where he brought down upon himself the rage of the learned rabbis—that the study of Talmud was not very important, that there need not be fixed times for prayers, that God could be worshiped through a sincere heart, through joy and singing and dancing. In other words, Reuven, he opposed any form of mechanical religion. There was nothing new in what he taught. You will find it all in the Bible, Talmud, and Kabbalah. But he gave it a special emphasis and taught it at a key time to people who were hungry for this kind of teaching. And these people listened and loved him. Many great rabbis came to mock him and went away converted to his way of thinking. When he died, his followers opened their own synagogues. Before the end of that century, about half of eastern European Jewry consisted of Hasidim, as his followers were called, pious ones. So great was the need of the masses for a new way to approach God.

"There was another man born in that century, Rabbi Elijah of Vilna, a great Talmudist, a genius, and a strong opponent of Hasidism. But even his opposition could not stop Hasidism from growing. It flourished and became a great movement in Jewish life. For a long time there was terrible bitterness between the Mitnagdim, the opponents of Hasidism, and the followers of the Besht. For example, if the son of a Hasid married the daughter of a Mitnaged, both fathers would say Kaddish after their children, considering them to be dead and buried. So great was the bitterness.

"The Hasidim had great leaders—tzaddikim, they were called, righteous ones. Each Hasidic community had its own tzaddik, and his people would go to him with all their problems, and he would give them advice. They followed these leaders blindly. The Hasidim believed that the tzaddik was a superhuman link between themselves and God. Every act of his and every word he spoke was holy. Even the food he touched became holy. For example, they would grab the food scraps he left on his plate and eat them, because the food had become holy through his touch, and they wanted some of this holiness inside themselves. For a while, the tzaddikim were kind and gentle souls, like the Besht himself. But in the next century the movement began to degenerate. Many of the positions of tzaddik became inherited posts, going automatically from father to son, even if the son was not a great leader. Many tzaddikim lived like Oriental monarchs. Some of them were out-and-out frauds, and they exploited their people terribly. Others were very sincere, and a few were even great scholars of the Talmud. In some Hasidic sects, the study of the Talmud became as important as it had been before the time of the Besht. Secular literature was forbidden, and the

Hasidim lived shut off from the rest of the world. Anything that was not Jewish and Hasidic was forbidden. Their lives became frozen. The clothes they wear today, for example, are the same Polish-style clothes they wore hundreds of years ago. Their customs and beliefs are also the same as they were hundreds of years ago. But not all of the Hasidic communities are identical, Reuven. The Hasidim of Russia, Germany, Poland, and Hungary are different one from the other. Not very different, but they are different. There are even Hasidic groups that believe their leaders should take upon themselves the sufferings of the Jewish people. You are surprised? But it is true. They believe that their sufferings would be unendurable if their leaders did not somehow absorb these sufferings into themselves. A strange belief, but a very important one, as far as they are concerned.

"Reuven, Reb Saunders is a great Talmudist and a great tzaddik. He has a reputation for brilliance and compassion. It is said that he believes the soul is as important as the mind, if not more so. He inherited his position from his father. When he dies, the position will go automatically to Danny."

My father stopped, looked at me with a smile, and said, "You are not asleep yet, Reuven?"

"No, abba."

"You are a very patient student. I think I am going to have another glass of tea. My throat is a little dry."

I took his glass, poured into it some strong-brewed tea from the teapot, filled it with water from the kettle, then brought it back to him. He put a cube of sugar between his teeth and sipped slowly from the glass, letting the tea soak through the sugar. Then he put the glass down.

"Tea is a blessing," he said, smiling. "Especially to a schoolteacher who must always give long answers to short questions."

I smiled back at him and waited patiently.

"All right," my father said. "I see you want me to continue. Now I am going to tell you another story, also a true story, about a Jewish boy who lived in Poland in the second half of the eighteenth century. As I tell you the story, think of Reb Saunders' son, and you will have your answer.

"This boy, Reuven, was brilliant, literally a genius. His name was Solomon, and later in life he changed his long Polish name to Maimon. When he was young, he found that the Talmud could not satisfy his hunger for knowledge. His mind would not let him rest. He wanted to know what was happening in the outside world. German was by then a great scientific and cultural language, and he decided to teach himself to read German. But even after he learned German he was not satisfied, because the reading of secular books was forbidden. Finally, at the age of twenty-five, he abandoned his wife and child and after many hardships came to Berlin where he joined a group of philosophers, read Aristotle, Maimonides, Spinoza, Leibniz, Hume, and Kant, and began to write philosophical books. It is astonishing how he was able to gobble up complicated philosophical treatises with such ease. He had a great mind, but it never left him in peace. He wandered from city to city, never finding roots anywhere, never satisfied, and finally died at forty-seven on the estate of a kind-hearted Christian who had befriended him.

"Reuven, Reb Saunders' son has a mind like Solomon Maimon's, perhaps even a greater mind. And Reb Saunders' son does not live in Poland. American is free. There are no walls here to hold back the Jews. Is it so strange, then, that he is breaking his father's rules and reading forbidden books? He cannot help himself. It is unbelievable what he has read these past few months. You are a brilliant student. I tell you that now very proudly. But he is a phenomenon. Once in a generation is a mind like that born.

"Now, Reuven, listen very carefully to what I am going to tell you. Reb Saunders' son is a terribly torn and lonely boy. There is literally no one in the world he can talk to. He needs a friend. The accident with the baseball has bound him to you, and he has already sensed in you someone he can talk to without fear. I am very proud of you for that. He would never have told you about his library visits if he believed for a moment you would not keep his words a secret trust. And I want you to let him be your friend and to let yourself be his friend. I am certain you and Reb Saunders' son can help each other in such a friendship. I know you, and I know him. And I know what I am saying. And now, Reuven, the lecture is over, I am going to finish my tea, and we will go to bed. What a lecture it has been! Do you want some tea?"

"No, abba."

We sat in silence, while my father sipped from his glass.

"You are very quiet," he said finally.

"It all started with a silly baseball game," I said. "I can't believe it."

"Reuven, as you grow older you will discover that the most important things that will happen to you will often come as a result of silly things, as you call them—'ordinary things' is a better expression. That is the way the world is."

I shook my head. "I just can't believe it," I said again. "This whole week has been like something from another world. The hospital, the people I met there, Mr. Savo, little Mickey, Billy—all because of a ball game."

My father sipped his tea and looked at me over the rim of the glass. He said nothing, but he was watching me intently.

"I don't understand it," I said. "Weeks and weeks go by, one Shabbat follows another, and I'm the same, nothing has changed, and suddenly one day something happens, and everything looks different."

"Different? What do you mean, different?"

I told him how I had felt that afternoon when I had come home from the hospital. He listened quietly, all the while sipping his tea. When I finished, I saw him smile. He put down the glass, sighed, and said, "Reuven, it is a tragedy your mother is not alive to—" He stopped, his voice breaking. He was quiet for a moment. Then he looked at the clock on the shelf over the refrigerator. "It is very late," he said. "We will talk some more tomorrow."

"Yes, abba."

"Reuven—"

"Yes?"

"Never mind. Go to sleep. I am going to sit here for a while and have another glass of tea."

I left him sitting at the kitchen table, staring down at the white cloth.

CHAPTER SEVEN
✦✦✦✦✦✦✦✦✦✦✦✦✦✦✦✦✦✦✦

THE NEXT DAY I met Danny's father.

My father and I woke early so as to be in our synagogue by eight-thirty. Manya came in a little before eight and served us a light breakfast. Then my father and I started out on the three-block walk to the synagogue. It was a beautiful day, and I felt happy to be out on the street again. It was wonderful to be outside that hospital, looking at the people and watching the traffic. When it didn't rain and wasn't too cold, my father and I always enjoyed our Shabbat walks to and from the synagogue.

There were many synagogues in Williamsburg. Each Hasidic sect had its own house of worship—shtibblach, they were called—most of them badly lighted, musty rooms, with benches or chairs crowded together and with windows that seemed always to be closed. There were also those synagogues in which Jews who were not Hasidim worshiped. The synagogue where my father and I prayed had once been a large grocery store. It stood on Lee Avenue, and though the bottom half of its window was curtained off, the sun shone in through the uncurtained portion of the glass, and I loved to sit there on a Shabbat morning, with the gold of the sun on the leaves of my prayer book, and pray.

The synagogue was attended mostly by men like my father —teachers from my yeshiva, and others who had come under the influence of the Jewish Enlightenment in Europe and whose distaste for Hasidism was intense and outspoken. Many of the students in the yeshiva I attended prayed there, too, and it was good to be able to be with them on a Shabbat morning.

When my father and I came into the synagogue that morning, the service had just begun. We took our usual seats a

few rows up from the window and joined in the prayers. I
saw Davey Cantor come in. He nodded to me, looking
gloomy behind his glasses, and took his seat. The prayers
went slowly; the man at the podium had a fine voice and
waited until each portion of the service had been completed
by everyone before he began to chant. I glanced at my father
during the Silent Devotion. He stood in his long prayer
shawl, its silver trim bathed in sunlight, its fringes dangling
almost to the floor. His eyes were closed—he always prayed
from memory, except during a Festival or a High Holiday
Service—and he was swaying slightly back and forth, his lips
murmuring the words. I did not wear a prayer shawl; they
were worn only by adults who were or had once been married.

During the Torah Service, which followed the Silent Devotion, I was one of the eight men called up to the podium to
recite the blessing over the Torah. Standing at the podium, I
listened carefully to the reader as he chanted the words from
the scroll. When he was done, I recited the second blessing
and the prayer that thanks God when a serious accident has
been avoided. As I left the podium and walked back to my
seat, I wondered what blessing, if any, I would have recited
had my eye been blinded. What blessing would Mr. Savo
make if he were a Jew? I asked myself. For the rest of the
service, I thought constantly of Mr. Savo and Billy.

Lunch was ready for us when we got home, and Manya
kept adding food to my plate and urging me to eat; food was
necessary for someone who had just come back from the hospital, she told me in her broken English. My father talked
about my work at school. I must be careful not to read until
Dr. Snydman gave me his permission, he said, but there was
nothing wrong if I attended classes and listened. Perhaps he
could help me study. Perhaps he could read to me. We would
try it and see. After the Grace, my father lay down on his
bed to rest for a while, and I sat on the porch and stared at
the sunlight on the flowers and the ailanthus. I sat like that
for about an hour, and then my father came out to tell me he
was going over to see one of his colleagues.

I lay back on the lounge chair and stared up at the sky. It
was a deep blue, with no clouds, and I felt I could almost
touch it. It's the color of Danny's eyes, I thought. It's as blue

as Danny's eyes. What color are Billy's eyes? I asked myself.
I think they're also blue. Both Danny's and Billy's eyes are
blue. But one set of eyes is blind. Maybe they're not blind
anymore, I thought. Maybe both sets of eyes are okay now. I
fell asleep, thinking about Danny's and Billy's eyes.

It was a light, dreamless sleep, a kind of half-sleep that re-
freshes but does not shut off the world completely. I felt the
warm wind and smelled newly cut grass, and a bird perched
on a branch of the ailanthus and sang for a long time before
it flew away. Somehow I knew where that bird was, though I
did not open my eyes. There were children playing on the
street, and once a dog barked and a car's brakes screeched.
Someone was playing a piano nearby, and the music drifted
slowly in and out of my mind like the ebb and flow of ocean
surf. I almost recognized the melody, but I could not be sure;
it slipped like a cool and silken wind from my grasp. I heard
a door open and close and there were footsteps against wood,
and then silence, and I knew someone had come onto the
porch, but I would not open my eyes. I did not want to lose
that twilight sleep, with its odors and sounds and whispered
flow of music. Someone was on the porch, looking at me. I
felt him looking at me. I felt him slowly push away the sleep,
and, finally, I opened my eyes, and there was Danny, standing
at the foot of the lounge chair, with his arms folded across
his chest, clicking his tongue and shaking his head.

"You sleep like a baby," he said. "I feel guilty waking
you."

I yawned, stretched, and sat up on the edge of the lounge
chair. "That was delicious," I added, yawning again. "What
time is it?"

"It's after five, sleepyhead. I've been waiting here ten minutes for you to wake up."

"I slept almost three hours," I said. "That was some sleep."

He clicked his tongue again and shook his head. "What
kind of infield is that?" He was imitating Mr. Galanter.
"How can we keep that infield solid if you're asleep there,
Malter?"

I laughed and got to my feet.

"Where do you want to go?" he asked.

"I don't care."

"I thought we'd go over to my father's shul. He wants to meet you."

"Where is it?" I asked him.

"It's five blocks from here."

"Is my father inside?"

"I didn't see him. Your maid let me in. Don't you want to go?"

"Sure," I said. "Let me wash up and put a tie and jacket on. I don't have a caftan, you know."

He grinned at me. "The uniform is a requirement for members of the fold only," he said.

"Okay, member of the fold. Come on inside with me."

I washed, dressed, told Manya that when my father came in she should let him know where I had gone, and we went out.

"What does your father want to see me about?" I asked Danny as we went down the stone stairway of the house.

"He wants to meet you. I told him we were friends."

We turned up the street, heading toward Lee Avenue.

"He always has to approve of my friends," Danny said. "Especially if they're outside the fold. Do you mind my telling him that we're friends?"

"No."

"Because I really think we are," Danny said.

I didn't say anything. We walked to the corner, then turned right on Lee Avenue. The street was busy with traffic and crowded with people. I wondered what any of my classmates would think if they saw me walking with Danny. It would become quite a topic of conversation in the neighborhood. Well, they would see me with him sooner or later.

Danny was looking at me, his sculptured face wearing a serious expression. "Don't you have any brothers or sisters?" he asked.

"No. My mother died soon after I was born."

"I'm sorry to hear that."

"How about you?"

"I have a brother and a sister. My sister's fourteen and my brother is eight. I'm going on sixteen."

"So am I," I said.

We discovered that we had been born in the same year, two days apart.

"You've been living five blocks away from me all these years, and I never knew who you were," I said.

"We stick pretty close together. My father doesn't like us to mix with outsiders."

"I hope you don't mind my saying this, but your father sounds like a tyrant."

Danny didn't disagree. "He's a very strong-willed person. When he makes up his mind about something, that's it, finished."

"Doesn't he object to your going around with an apikoros like me?"

"That's why he wants to meet you."

"I thought you said your father never talks to you."

"He doesn't. Except when we study Talmud. But he did this time. I got up enough courage to tell him about you, and he said to bring you over today. That's the longest sentence he's said to me in years. Except for the time I had to convince him to let us have a ball team."

"I'd hate to have my father not talk to me."

"It isn't pleasant," Danny said very quietly. "But he's a great man. You'll see when you meet him."

"Is your brother going to be a rabbi, too?"

Danny gave me a queer look. "Why do you ask that?"

"No special reason. Is he?"

"I don't know. Probably he will." His voice had a strange, almost wistful quality to it. I decided not to press the point. He went back to talking about his father.

"He's really a great man, my father. He saved his community. He brought them all over to America after the First World War."

"I never heard about that," I told him.

"That's right," he said, and told me about his father's early years in Russia. I listened in growing astonishment.

Danny's grandfather had been a well-known Hasidic rabbi in a small town in southern Russia, and his father had been the second of two sons. The firstborn son had been in line to inherit his father's rabbinic position, but during a period of study in Odessa he suddenly vanished. Some said he had been murdered by Cossacks; for a time there was even a rumor that he had been converted to Christianity and had gone to live in France. The second son was ordained at the age of seventeen, and by the time he was twenty had achieved an awesome reputation as a Talmudist. When his father died, he automatically inherited the position of rabbinic leadership. He was twenty-one years old at the time.

He remained the rabbi of his community throughout the years of Russia's participation in the First World War. One week before the Bolshevist Revolution, in the autumn of 1917, his young wife bore him a second child, a son. Two months later, his wife, his son, and his eighteen-month-old daughter were shot to death by a band of marauding Cossacks, one of the many bandit gangs that roamed through Russia during the period of chaos that followed the revolution. He himself was left for dead, with a pistol bullet in his chest and a saber wound in his pelvis. He lay unconscious for half a day near the bodies of his wife and children, and then the Russian peasant who tended the stove in the synagogue and swept its floor found him and carried him to his hut, where he extracted the bullet, bathed the wounds, and tied him to the bed so he would not fall out during the days and nights he shivered and screamed with the fever and delirium that followed.

The synagogue had been burned to the ground. Its Ark was a gutted mass of charred wood, its four Torah scrolls were seared black, its holy books were piles of gray ash blown about by the wind. Of the one hundred eighteen Jewish families in the community only forty-three survived.

When it was discovered that the rabbi was not dead but was being cared for by the Russian peasant, he was brought into the still-intact home of a Jewish family and nursed back to health. He spent the winter recovering from his wounds. During that winter the Bolshevists signed the treaty of Brest-Litovsk with Germany, and Russia withdrew from the war. The chaos inside the country intensified, and the village was raided four times by Cossacks. But each of those times the Jews were warned by friendly peasants and were concealed in the woods or in huts. In the spring, the rabbi announced to his people that they were done with Russia, Russia was Esav and Edom, the land of Satan and the Angel of Death. They would travel together to America and rebuild their community.

Eight days later, they left. They bribed and bargained their

way through Russia, Austria, France, Belgium, and England.
Five months later, they arrived in New York City. At Ellis
Island the rabbi was asked his name, and he gave it as Senders. On the official forms, Senders became Saunders. After
the customary period of quarantine, they were permitted to
leave the island, and Jewish welfare workers helped them settle in the Williamsburg section of Brooklyn. Three years later
the rabbi married once again, and in 1929, two days before
the stock market crash, Danny was born in the Brooklyn Memorial Hospital. Eighteen months later his sister was born,
and five and a half years after the birth of his sister, his
brother was born by Caesarean section, both in that same
hospital.

"They all followed him?" I asked. "Just like that?"

"Of course. They would have followed him anywhere."

"I don't understand that. I didn't know a rabbi had that
kind of power."

"He's more than a rabbi," Danny said. "He's a tzaddik."

"My father told me about Hasidism last night. He said it
was a fine idea until some of the tzaddikim began to take advantage of their followers. He wasn't very complimentary."

"It depends upon your point of view," Danny said quietly.

"I can't understand how Jews can follow another human
being so blindly."

"He's not just another human being."

"Is he like God?"

"Something like that. He's a kind of messenger of God, a
bridge between his followers and God."

"I don't understand it. It almost sounds like Catholicism."

"That's the way it is," Danny said, "whether you understand it or not."

"I'm not offending you or anything. I just want to be honest."

"I want you to be honest," Danny said.

We walked on in silence.

A block beyond the synagogue where my father and I
prayed, we made a right turn into a narrow street crowded
with brownstones and sycamores. It was a duplicate of the
street on which I lived, but a good deal older and less neatly
kept. Many of the houses were unkempt, and there were very
few hydrangea bushes or morning glories on the front lawns.

The sycamores formed a solid, tangled bower that kept out the sunlight. The stone banisters on the outside stairways were chipped, their surfaces blotched with dirt, and the edges of the stone steps were round and smooth from years of use. Cats scrambled through the garbage cans that stood in front of some of the houses, and the sidewalks were strewn with old newspapers, ice cream and candy wrappers, worn cardboard cartons, and torn paper bags. Women in long-sleeved dresses, with kerchiefs covering their heads, many with infants in their arms, others heavily pregnant, sat on the stone steps of the stairways, talking loudly in Yiddish. The street throbbed with the noise of playing children who seemed in constant motion, dodging around cars, racing up and down steps, chasing after cats, climbing trees, balancing themselves as they tried walking on top of the banisters, pursuing one another in furious games of tag—all with their fringes and earlocks dancing wildly in the air and trailing out behind them. We were walking quickly now under the dark ceiling of sycamores, and a tall, heavily built man in a black beard and black caftan came alongside me, bumped me roughly to avoid running into a woman, and passed me without a word. The liquid streams of racing children, the noisy chatter of long-sleeved women, the worn buildings and blotched banisters, the garbage cans and the scrambling cats all gave me the feeling of having slid silently across a strange threshold, and for a long moment I regretted having let Danny take me into his world.

We were approaching a group of about thirty black-caftaned men who were standing in front of the three-story brownstone at the end of the street. They formed a solid wall, and I did not want to push through them so I slowed my steps, but Danny took my arm with one hand and tapped his other hand upon the shoulder of a man on the outer rim of the crowd. The man turned, pivoting the upper portion of his body—a middle-aged man, his dark beard streaked with gray, his thick brows edging into a frown of annoyance—and I saw his eyes go wide. He bowed slightly and pushed back, and a whisper went through the crowd like a wind, and it parted, and Danny and I walked through, Danny holding me by the arm and nodding his head at the greetings in Yiddish that came in quiet murmurs from the people he passed. It

was as if a black-waved, frozen sea had been sliced by a
scythe, forming black, solid walls along a jelled path. I saw
black- and gray-bearded heads bow toward Danny and dark
brows arch sharply over eyes that stared questions at me and
at the way Danny was holding me by the arm. We were almost halfway through the crowd now, walking slowly together, Danny's fingers on the part of my arm just over the
elbow. I felt myself naked and fragile, an intruder, and my
eyes, searching for anything but the bearded faces to look at,
settled, finally, upon the sidewalk at my feet. Then, because I
wanted something other than the murmured greetings in Yiddish to listen to, I began to hear, distinctly, the tapping
sounds of Danny's metal-capped shoes against the cement
pavement. It seemed a sharp, unnaturally loud sound, and my
ears fixed on it, and I could hear it clearly as we went along.
I listened to it intently—the soft scrape of the shoe and the
sharp tap-tap of the metal caps—as we went up the stone
steps of the stairway that led into the brownstone in front of
which the crowd stood. The caps tapped against the stone of
the steps, then against the stone of the top landing in front of
the double door—and I remembered the old man I often saw
walking along Lee Avenue, moving carefully through the
busy street and tapping, tapping, his metal-capped cane,
which served him for the eyes he had lost in a First World
War trench during a German gas attack.

The hallway of the brownstone was crowded with black-
caftaned men, and there was suddenly a path there, too, and
more murmured greetings and questioning eyes, and then
Danny and I went through a door that stood open to our
right, and we were in the synagogue.

It was a large room and looked to be the exact size of the
apartment in which my father and I lived. What was my father's bedroom was here the section of the synagogue that
contained the Ark, the Eternal Light, an eight-branched
candelabrum, a small podium to the right of the Ark, and a
large podium about ten feet in front of the Ark. The two po-
diums and the Ark were covered with red velvet. What was
our kitchen, hallway, bathroom, my bedroom, my father's
study and our front room, was here the portion of the synagogue where the worshipers sat. Each seat consisted of a
chair set before a stand with a sloping top, the bottom edge

of which was braced with a jutting strip of wood to prevent what was on the stand from sliding to the floor. The seats extended back to about twenty feet from the rear wall of the synagogue, the wall opposite the Ark. A small portion of the synagogue near the upper door of the hallway had been curtained off with white cheesecloth. This was the women's section. It contained a few rows of wooden chairs. The remaining section of the synagogue, the section without chairs, was crowded with long tables and benches. Through the middle of the synagogue ran a narrow aisle that ended at the large podium. The walls were painted white. The wooden floor was a dark brown. The three rear windows were curtained in black velvet. The ceiling was white, and naked bulbs hung from it on dark wires, flooding the room with harsh light.

We stood for a moment just inside the door near one of the tables. Men passed constantly in and out of the room. Some remained in the hallway to chat, others took seats. Some of the seats were occupied by men studying Talmud, reading from the Book of Psalms, or talking among themselves in Yiddish. The benches at the tables stood empty, and on the white cloths that covered the tables were paper cups, wooden forks and spoons, and paper plates filled with pickled herring and onion, lettuce, tomatoes, gefülte fish, Shabbat loaves—the braided bread called chalah—tuna fish, salmon, and hard-boiled eggs. At the edge of the table near the window was a brown leather chair. On the table in front of the chair was a pitcher, a towel, a saucer, and a large plate covered with a Shabbat cloth—a white satin cloth, with the Hebrew word for the Shabbat embroidered upon it in gold. A long serrated silver knife lay alongside the plate.

A tall, heavyset boy came in the door, nodded at Danny, then noticed me, and stared. I recognized him immediately as Dov Shlomowitz, the player on Danny's team who had run into me at second base and knocked me down. He seemed about to say something to Danny, then changed his mind, turned stiffly, went up the narrow aisle, and found a seat. Sitting in the seat, he glanced at us once over his shoulder, then opened a book on his stand, and began to sway back and forth. I looked at Danny and managed what must have been a sick smile. "I feel like a cowboy surrounded by Indians," I told him in a whisper.

Danny grinned at me reassuringly and let go of my arm. "You're in the holy halls," he said. "It takes getting used to."

"That was like the parting of the Red Sea out there," I said. "How did you do it?"

"I'm my father's son, remember? I'm the inheritor of the dynasty. Number one on our catechism: Treat the son as you would the father, because one day the son will be the father."

"You sound like a Mitnaged," I told him, managing another weak smile.

"No, I don't," he said. "I sound like someone who reads too much. Come on. We sit up front. My father will be down soon."

"You live in this house?"

"We have the upper two floors. It's a fine arrangement. Come on. They're beginning to come in."

The crowd in the hallway and in front of the building had begun coming through the door. Danny and I went up the aisle. He led me to the front row of seats that stood at the right of the large podium and just behind the small podium. Danny sat down in the second seat and I sat in the third. I assumed that the first seat was for his father.

The crowd came in quickly, and the synagogue was soon filled with the sounds of shuffling shoes, scraping chairs, and loud voices talking Yiddish. I heard no English, only Yiddish. Sitting in the chair, I glanced over at Dov Shlomowitz, and found him staring at me, his heavy face wearing an expression of surprise and hostility, and I suddenly realized that Danny was probably going to have as much trouble with his friends over our friendship as I would have with mine. Maybe less, I thought. I'm not the son of a tzaddik. No one steps aside for me in a crowd. Dov Shlomowitz looked away but I saw others in the crowded synagogue staring at me too, and I looked down at the worn prayer book on my stand, feeling exposed and naked again, and very alone.

Two gray-bearded old men came over to Danny, and he got respectfully to his feet. They had had an argument over a passage of Talmud, they told him, each of them interpreting it in a different way, and they wondered who had been correct. They mentioned the passage, and Danny nodded, immediately identified the tractate and the page, then coldly and mechanically repeated the passage word for word, giving his interpretation of it, and quoting at the same time the interpretations of a number of medieval commentators like the Me'iri, the Rashba, and the Maharsha. The passage was a difficult one, he said, gesticulating with his hands as he spoke, the thumb of his right hand describing wide circles as he emphasized certain key points of interpretation, and both men had been correct; one had unknowingly adopted the interpretation of the Me'iri, the other of the Rashba. The men smiled and went away satisfied. Danny sat down.

"That's a tough passage," he said. "I can't make head or tail out of it. Your father would probably say the text was all wrong." He was talking quietly and grinning broadly. "I read some of your father's articles. Sneaked them off my father's desk. The one on that passage in *Kiddushin* about the business with the king is very good. It's full of real apikorsische stuff."

I nodded, and tried another smile. My father had read that article to me before he had sent it off to his publisher. He had begun reading his articles to me during the past year, and spent a lot of time explaining them.

The noise in the synagogue had become very loud, almost a din, and the room seemed to throb and swell with the scraping chairs and the talking men. Some children were running up and down the aisle, laughing and shouting, and a number of younger men lounged near the door, talking loudly and gesticulating with their hands. I had the feeling for a moment I was in the carnival I had seen recently in a movie, with its pushing, shoving, noisy throng, and its shouting, arm-waving vendors and pitchmen.

I sat quietly, staring down at the prayer book on my stand. I opened the book and turned to the Afternoon Service. Its pages were yellow and old, with ragged edges and worn corners. I sat there, staring at the first psalm of the service and thinking of the almost new prayer book I had held in my hands that morning. I felt Danny nudge me with his elbow, and I looked up.

"My father's coming," he said. His voice was quiet and, I thought, a little strained.

The noise inside the synagogue ceased so abruptly that I felt its absence as one would a sudden lack of air. It stopped in swift waves, beginning at the rear of the synagogue and

ending at the chairs near the podium. I heard no signal and
no call for silence; it simply stopped, cut off, as if a door had
slammed shut on a playroom filled with children. The silence
that followed had a strange quality to it: expectation, eagerness, love, awe.

A man was coming slowly up the narrow aisle, followed by
a child. He was a tall man, and he wore a black satin caftan
and a fur-trimmed black hat. As he passed each row of seats,
men rose, bowed slightly, and sat again. Some leaned over to
touch him. He nodded his head at the murmur of greetings
directed to him from the seats, and his long black beard
moved back and forth against his chest, and his earlocks
swayed. He walked slowly, his hands clasped behind his back,
and as he came closer to me I could see that the part of his
face not hidden by the beard looked cut from stone, the nose
sharp and pointed, the cheekbones ridged, the lips full, the
brow like marble etched with lines, the sockets deep, the eyebrows thick with black hair and separated by a single wedge
like a furrow plowed into a naked field, the eyes dark, with
pinpoints of white light playing in them as they do in black
stones in the sun. Danny's face mirrored his exactly—except
for the hair and the color of the eyes. The child who followed him, holding on to the caftan with his right hand, was
a delicate miniature of the man, with the same caftan, the
same fur-trimmed hat, the same face, the same color hair,
though beardless, and I realized he was Danny's brother. I
glanced at Danny and saw him staring down at his stand, his
face without expression. I saw the eyes of the congregants
follow the man as he came slowly up the aisle, his hands
clasped behind his back, his head nodding, and then I saw
them on Danny and me as he came up to us. Danny rose
quickly to his feet, and I followed, and we stood there, waiting, as the man's dark eyes moved across my face—I could
feel them moving across my face like a hand—and fixed
upon my left eye. I had a sudden vision of my father's gentle
eyes behind their steel-rimmed spectacles, but it vanished
swiftly, because Danny was introducing me to Reb Saunders.

"This is Reuven Malter," he said quietly in Yiddish.

Reb Saunders continued to stare at my left eye. I felt
naked under his gaze, and he must have sensed my discom-
fort, because quite suddenly he offered me his hand. I raised

my hand to take it, then realized, as my hand was going up, that he was not offering me his hand but his fingers, and I held them for a moment—they were dry and limp—then let my hand drop.

"You are the son of David Malter?" Reb Saunders asked me in Yiddish. His voice was deep and nasal, like Danny's, and the words came out almost like an accusation.

I nodded my head. I had a moment of panic, trying to decide whether to answer him in Yiddish or English. I wondered if he knew English. My Yiddish was very poor. I decided to answer in English.

"Your eye," Reb Saunders said in Yiddish. "It is healed?"

"It's fine," I said in English. My voice came out a little hoarse, and I swallowed. I glanced at the congregants. They were staring at us intently, in complete silence.

Reb Saunders looked at me for a moment, and I saw the dark eyes blink, the lids going up and down like shades. When he spoke again it was still in Yiddish.

"The doctor, the professor who operated, he said your eye is healed?"

"He wants to see me again in a few days. But he said the eye is fine."

I saw his head nod slightly and the beard go up and down against his chest. The lights from the naked bulb on the ceiling gleamed off his satin caftan.

"Tell me, you know mathematics? My son tells me you are very good in mathematics."

I nodded.

"So. We will see. And you know Hebrew. A son of David Malter surely knows Hebrew."

I nodded again.

"We will see," Reb Saunders said.

I glanced out of the sides of my eyes and saw Danny looking down at the floor, his face expressionless. The child stood a little behind Reb Saunders and stared up at us, his mouth open.

"Nu," Reb Saunders said, "later we will talk more. I want to know my son's friend. Especially the son of David Malter." Then he went past us and stood in front of the little podium, his back to the congregation, the little boy still holding on to his caftan.

Danny and I sat down. A whisper moved through the congregation, followed by the rustle of pages as prayer books were opened. An old, gray-bearded man went up to the large podium, put on a prayer shawl, and started the service.

The old man had a weak voice, and I could barely hear him over the prayers of the worshipers. Reb Saunders stood with his back to the congregation, swaying back and forth, occasionally clapping his hands together, and the child stood at his right, swaying too, in obvious imitation of his father. Throughout the entire service, Reb Saunders stood with his back to the congregation, sometimes raising his head toward the ceiling, or raising his hands to cover his eyes. He turned only when the Torah was taken from the Ark and read.

The service ended with the Kaddish, and then Reb Saunders walked slowly back up the aisle, followed by the child, who was still clinging to his father's caftan. As the child passed me, I noticed his dark eyes were very large and his face was deathly pale.

Danny nudged me with his elbow and motioned with his head toward the rear of the synagogue. He rose, and the two of us followed Reb Saunders up the aisle. I could see the eyes of the congregants on my face, and then feel them on my back. I saw Reb Saunders go to the leather chair at the table near the end window and sit down. The child sat on the bench to his left. Danny led me to the table and sat on the bench to his father's right. He motioned me to sit down next to him, and I did.

The congregants rose and came toward the rear of the synagogue. The silence was gone now, burst as abruptly as it had begun, and someone started chanting a tune, and others took it up, clapping their hands in rhythm to the melody. They were filing out the door—probably to wash their hands, I thought—and soon they were coming back in and finding seats at the tables, the benches scraping loudly as they were moved back and forth. The singing had stopped. Our table filled rapidly, mostly with older men.

Reb Saunders stood up, poured water over his hands from the pitcher, the water spilling into the saucer, then wiped his hands, removed the white satin cloth that covered the chalah, said the blessing over bread, cut a section off the end of the chalah, swallowed it, and sat down. Danny got to his feet, washed his hands, cut two slices from the chalah, handed me one, took one for himself, made the blessing, ate, and sat. He passed the pitcher to me, and I repeated the ritual, but I remained seated. Then Danny cut the remainder of the chalah into small pieces, gave a piece to his brother, and handed the plate to the old man sitting next to me. The pieces of chalah disappeared swiftly, grabbed up by the men at the table. Reb Saunders put some salad and fish on his plate and ate a small piece of the fish, holding it in his fingers. A man from one of the other tables came over and took the plate. Danny filled another plate for his father. Reb Saunders ate slowly, and in silence.

I was not very hungry, but I made some attempt at eating so as not to insult anyone. Frequently during the meal, I felt rather than saw Reb Saunders' eyes on my face. Danny was quiet. His little brother pecked at the food on his plate, eating little. The skin of his face and hands was almost as white as the tablecloth, drawn tightly over the bones, and the veins showed like blue branches in his face and on the tops of his hands. He sat quietly, and once he began to pick his nose, saw his father look at him, and stopped, his lower lip trembling a little. He bent over his plate and poked at a slice of tomato with a thin, stubby finger.

Danny and I said nothing to each other throughout that entire meal. Once I looked up and saw his father staring at me, his eyes black beneath the thick brows. I looked away, feeling as though my skin had been peeled away and my insides photographed.

Someone began to sing Atah Echad, one of the prayers from the Afternoon Service. The meal was over, and the men began to sway slowly, in unison with the melody. The singing filled the synagogue, and Reb Saunders sat back in his leather seat and sang too, and then Danny was singing. I knew the melody and I joined in, hesitantly at first, then strongly, swaying back and forth. At the end of the song, another melody was begun, a light, fast, wordless tune, sung to the syllables cheeree bim, cheeree bam, and the swaying was a little faster now, and hands were clapped in time to the rhythm. Then tune followed tune, and I felt myself begin to relax as I continued to join the singing. I found that most of the melodies were familiar to me, especially the slow, somber ones

that were meant to convey the sadness of the singers over the
conclusion of the Shabbat, and the tunes I did not know I
was able to follow easily, because the basic melody lines were
almost all the same. After a while I was singing loudly, swaying back and forth and clapping my hands, and once I saw
Reb Saunders looking at me, and his lips curved into a
shadow of a smile. I smiled at Danny and he smiled back at
me, and we sat there for about half an hour, singing, swaying, and clapping, and I felt light and happy and completely
at ease. So far as I could see, Reb Saunders' little son was the
only one in the synagogue not singing; he sat pecking at his
food and poking at the slice of tomato on his paper plate
with his thin, veined hand. The singing went on and on—and
then it stopped. I glanced around to see what had happened,
but everyone was sitting very still, looking over at our table.
Reb Saunders washed his hands again, and others spilled
what was left of the water in their paper cups over their
hands. The introductory psalm to the Grace was sung together, and then Reb Saunders began the Grace. He chanted
with his eyes closed, swaying slightly in his leather chair.
After the opening lines of the Grace, each man prayed
quietly, and I saw Danny lean forward, put his elbows on the
table, cover his eyes with his right hand, his lips whispering
the words. Then the Grace was done, and there was silence
—a long, solid silence in which no one moved and everyone
waited and eyes stared at Reb Saunders, who was sitting in
his chair with his eyes closed, swaying slightly back and
forth. I saw Danny take his elbows from the table and sit up
straight. He stared down at his paper plate, his face expressionless, and I almost had the feeling that he had gone rigid,
tense, as a soldier does before he jumps from shelter into
open combat.

Everyone waited, and no one moved, no one coughed, no
one even took a deep breath. The silence became unreal and
seemed suddenly filled with a noise of its own, the noise of a
too long silence. Even the child was staring now at his father,
his eyes like black stones against the naked whiteness of his
veined face.

And then Reb Saunders began to speak.

He swayed back and forth in the leather chair, his eyes
closed, his left hand in the crook of his right elbow, the fin-

gers of his right hand stroking his black beard, and I could see everyone at the tables lean forward, eyes staring, mouths slightly open, some of the older men cupping their hands behind their ears to catch his words. He began in a low voice, the words coming out slowly in a singsong kind of chant.

"The great and holy Rabban Gamaliel," he said, "taught us the following: 'Do His will as if it were thy will, that He may do thy will as if it were His will. Nullify thy will before His will that He may nullify the will of others before thy will.' What does this mean? It means that if we do as the Master of the Universe wishes, then He will do as we wish. A question immediately presents itself. What does it mean to say that the Master of the Universe will do what we wish? He is after all the Master of the Universe, the Creator of heaven and earth, the King of kings. And what are we? Do we not say every day, 'Are not all the mighty as naught before Thee, the men of renown as though they had not been, the wise as if without knowledge, and the men of understanding as if without discernment'? What are we that the Master of the Universe should do our will?"

Reb Saunders paused, and I saw two of the old men who were sitting at our table look at each other and nod. He swayed back and forth in his leather chair, his fingers stroking his beard, and continued to speak in a quiet, singsong voice.

"All men come into the world in the same way. We are born in pain, for it is written, 'In pain shall ye bring forth children.' We are born naked and without strength. Like dust are we born. Like dust can the child be blown about, like dust is his life, like dust is his strength. And like dust do many remain all their lives, until they are put away in dust, in a place of worms and maggots. Will the Master of the Universe obey the will of a man whose life is dust? What is the great and holy Rabban Gamaliel teaching us?" His voice was beginning to rise now. "What is he telling us? What does it mean to say the Master of the Universe will do our will? The will of men who remain dust? Impossible! The will of what men, then? We must say, the will of men who do *not* remain dust. But how can we raise ourselves above dust? Listen, listen to me, for this is a mighty thing the rabbis teach us."

He paused again, and I saw Danny glance at him, then stare down again at his paper plate.

"Rabbi Halafta son of Dosa teaches us, 'When ten people sit together and occupy themselves with the Torah, the Presence of God abides among them, as it is said, "God standeth in the congregation of the godly." And whence can it be shown that the same applies to five? Because it is said, "He had founded his band upon the earth." And whence can it be shown that the same applies to three? Because it is said, "He judgeth among the judges." And whence can it be shown that the same applies to two? Because it is said, "Then they that feared the Lord spake one with the other, and the Lord gave heed and heard." And whence can it be shown that the same applies even to one? Because it is said, "In every place where I cause my name to be remembered I will come into thee and I will bless thee."' Listen, listen to this great teaching. A congregation is ten. It is nothing new that the holy Presence resides among ten. A band is five. It is also nothing new that the holy Presence resides among five. Judges are three. If the holy Presence did not reside among judges there would be no justice in the world. So this, too, is not new. That the Presence can reside even among two is also not impossible to understand. But that the Presence can reside in one! In one! Even in one! That already is a mighty thing. Even in one! If one man studies Torah, the Presence is with him. If one man studies Torah, the Master of the Universe is already in the world. A mighty thing! And to bring the Master of the World *into* the world is also to raise oneself up from the dust. Torah raises us from the dust! Torah gives us strength! Torah clothes us! Torah brings the Presence!"

The singsong chant had died away. He was talking in a straight, loud voice that rang through the terrible silence in the synagogue.

"But to study Torah is not such a simple thing. Torah is a task for all day and all night. It is a task filled with danger. Does not Rabbi Meir teach us, 'He who is walking by the way and studying, and breaks off his study and says, "How fine is that tree, how fine is that field," him the Scripture regards as if he had forfeited his life'?"

I saw Danny glance quickly at his father, then lower his

eyes. His body sagged a little, a smile played on his lips, and I thought I even heard him sigh quietly.

"He had forfeited his life! His life! So great is the study of Torah. And now, listen, listen to this word. Whose task is it to study Torah? Of whom does the Master of the Universe demand 'Ye shall meditate over it day and night'? Of the world? No! What does the world know of Torah? The world is Esav! The world is Amalek! The world is Cossacks! The world is Hitler, may his name and memory be erased! Of whom, then? Of the people of Israel! *We* are commanded to study His Torah! *We* are commanded to sit in the light of the Presence! It is for this that we were created! Does not the great and holy Rabbi Yochanan son of Zakkai teach us, 'If thou hast learnt much Torah, ascribe not any merit to thyself, for thereunto wast thou created'? Not the world, but the people of Israel! The people of Israel must study His Torah!"

His voice stormed the silence. I found myself holding my breath, my heart thumping in my ears. I could not take my eyes off his face, which was alive now, or his eyes, which were open and filled with dark fire. He struck the table with his hand, and I felt myself go cold with fright. Danny was watching him now, too, and his little brother stared at him as though in a trance, his mouth open, his eyes glazed.

"The world kills us! The world flays our skin from our bodies and throws us to the flames! The world laughs at Torah! And if it does not kill us, it tempts us! It misleads us! It contaminates us! It asks us to join in its ugliness, its impurities, it abominations! The world is Amalek! It is not the world that is commanded to study Torah, but the people of Israel! Listen, listen to this mighty teaching." His voice was suddenly lower, quieter, intimate. "It is written, 'This world is like a vestibule before the world-to-come; prepare thyself in the vestibule, that thou mayest enter into the hall.' The meaning is clear: The vestibule is this world, and the hall is the world-to-come. Listen. In gematriya, the words 'this world' come out one hundred sixty-three, and the words 'the world-to-come' come out one hundred fifty-four. The difference between 'this world' and 'the world-to-come' comes out to nine. Nine is half of eighteen. Eighteen is chai, life. In this world there is only half of chai. We are only half alive in this world! Only half alive!"

A whisper went through the crowd at the tables, and I could see heads nod and lips smile. They had been waiting for this apparently, the gematriya, and they strained forward to listen. One of my teachers in school had told me about gematriya. Each letter of the Hebrew alphabet is also a number, so that every Hebrew word has a numerical value. The word for "this world" in Hebrew is "olam hazeh," and by adding the numerical value of each letter, the total numerical value of the word becomes one hundred and sixty-three. I had heard others do this before, and I enjoyed listening because sometimes they were quite clever and ingenious. I was beginning to feel relaxed again, and I listened carefully.

"Hear me now. Listen. How can we make our lives full? How can we fill our lives so that we are eighteen, chai, and not nine, not half chai? Rabbi Joshua son of Levi teaches us, 'Whoever does not labor in the Torah is said to be under the divine censure.' He is a nozuf, a person whom the Master of the Universe hates! A righteous man, a tzaddik, studies Torah, for it is written, 'For his delight is in the Torah of God, and over His Torah doth he meditate day and night.' In gematriya, 'nozuf' comes out one hundred forty-three, and 'tzaddik' comes out two hundred and four. What is the difference between 'nozuf' and 'tzaddik'? Sixty-one. To whom does a tzaddik dedicate his life? To the Master of the Universe! La-el, to God! The word, 'La-el' in gematriya is sixty-one! It is a life dedicated to God that makes the difference between the nozuf and the tzaddik!"

Another murmur of approval went through the crowd. Reb Saunders was very good at gematriya, I thought. I was really enjoying myself now.

"And now listen to me further. In gematriya, the letters of the word 'traklin,' hall, the hall that refers to the world-to-come, come out three hundred ninety-nine, and 'prozdor,' the vestibule, the vestibule that is this world, comes out five hundred thirteen. Take 'traklin' from 'prozdor,' and we have one hundred fourteen. Now listen to me. A righteous man, we said, is two hundred four. A righteous man lives by Torah. Torah is mayim, water; the great and holy rabbis always compare Torah to water. The word 'mayim' in gematriya is ninety. Take 'mayim' from 'tzaddik' and we also have one hundred fourteen. From this we learn that the righteous man who removes himself from Torah also removes himself from the world-to-come!"

The whisper of delight was loud this time, and men nodded their heads and smiled. Some of them were even poking each other with their elbows to indicate their pleasure. That one had really been clever. I started to go over it again in my mind.

"We see that without Torah there is only half a life. We see that without Torah we are dust. We see that without Torah we are abominations." He was saying this quietly, almost as if it were a litany. His eyes were still open, and he was looking directly at Danny now. "When we study Torah, *then* the Master of the Universe listens. *Then* He hears our words. *Then* He will fulfill our wishes. For the Master of the Universe promises strength to those who preoccupy themselves in Torah, as it is written, 'So ye may be strong,' and He promises length of days, as it is written. 'So that your days may be lengthened.' May Torah be a fountain of waters to all who drink from it, and may it bring to us the Messiah speedily and in our day. Amen!"

A chorus of loud and scattered amens answered.

I sat in my seat and saw Reb Saunders looking at Danny, then at me. I felt completely at ease, and I somewhat brazenly smiled and nodded, as if to indicate that I had enjoyed his words, or at least the gematriya part of his words. I didn't agree at all with his notions of the world as being contaminated. Albert Einstein is part of the world, I told myself. President Roosevelt is part of the world. The millions of soldiers fighting Hitler are part of the world.

I thought that the meal was ended now and we would start the Evening Service, and I almost began to get out of my seat when I realized that another silence had settled upon the men at the tables. I sat still and looked around. They seemed all to be staring at Danny. He was sitting quietly, smiling a little, his fingers playing with the edge of his paper plate.

Reb Saunders sat back in his leather chair and folded his arms across his chest. The little boy was poking at the tomato again and glancing at Danny from the tops of his dark eyes. He twirled a side curl around one of his fingers, and I saw his tongue dart out of his mouth, run over his lips, then dart back in. I wondered what was going on.

Reb Saunders sighed loudly and nodded at Danny, "Nu, Daniel, you have something to say?" His voice was quiet, almost gentle.

I saw Danny nod his head.

"Nu, what is it?"

"It is written in the name of Rabbi Yaakov, not Rabbi Meir," Danny said quietly, in Yiddish.

A whisper of approval came from the crowd. I glanced around quickly. Everyone sat staring at Danny.

Reb Saunders almost smiled. He nodded, and the long black beard went back and forth against his chest. Then I saw the thick black eyebrows arch upward and the lids go about halfway down across the eyes. He leaned forward slightly, his arms still folded across his chest.

"And nothing more?" he asked very quietly.

Danny shook his head—a little hesitantly, I thought.

"So," Reb Saunders said, sitting back in the leather chair, "there is nothing more."

I looked at the two of them, wondering what was happening. What was this about Rabbi Yaakov and Rabbi Meir?

"The words were said by Rabbi Yaakov, not by Rabbi Meir," Danny repeated. "Rabbi Yaakov, not Rabbi Meir, said, 'He who is walking by the way and studying, and breaks off his study and—"

"Good," Reb Saunders broke in quietly. "The words were said by Rav Yaakov. Good. You saw it. Very good. And where is it found?"

"In *Pirkei Avos*," Danny said. He was giving the Talmudic source for the quote. Many of the quotes Reb Saunders had used had been from *Pirkei Avos*—or *Avot*, as my father had taught me to pronounce it, with the Sephardic rather than the Ashkenazic rendering of the Hebrew letter "tof." I had recognized the quotes easily. *Pirkei Avot* is a collection of Rabbinic maxims, and a chapter of it is studied by many Jews every Shabbat between Passover and the Jewish New Year.

"Nu," Reb Saunders said, smiling, "how should you not know that? Of course. Good. Very good. Now, tell me—"

As I sat there listening to what then took place between Danny and his father, I slowly realized what I was witnessing. In many Jewish homes, especially homes where there are yeshiva students and where the father is learned, there is a tradition which takes place on Shabbat afternoon: The father quizzes the son on what he has learned in school during the past week. I was witnessing a kind of public quiz, but a strange, almost bizarre quiz, more a contest than a quiz, because Reb Saunders was not confining his questions only to what Danny had learned during the week but was ranging over most of the major tractates of the Talmud and Danny was obviously required to provide the answers. Reb Saunders asked where else there was a statement about one who interrupts his studies, and Danny coolly, quietly answered. He asked what a certain medieval commentator had remarked about that statement, and Danny answered. He chose a minute aspect of the answer and asked who had dealt with it in an altogether different way, and Danny answered. He asked whether Danny agreed with this interpretation, and Danny said he did not, he agreed with another medieval commentator, who had given another interpretation. His father asked how could the commentator have offered such an interpretation when in another passage in the Talmud he had said exactly the opposite, and Danny, very quietly, calmly, his fingers still playing with the rim of the paper plate, found a difference between the contradictory statements by quoting two other sources where one of the statements appeared in a somewhat different context, thereby nullifying the contradiction. One of the two sources Danny had quoted contained a biblical verse, and his father asked him who else had based a law upon this verse. Danny repeated a short passage from the tractate *Sanhedrin,* and then his father quoted another passage from *Yoma* which contradicted the passage in *Sanhedrin,* and Danny answered with a passage from *Gittin* which dissolved the contradiction. His father questioned the validity of his interpretation of the passage in *Gittin* by citing a commentary on the passage that disagreed with his interpretation, and Danny said it was difficult to understand this commentary—he did not say the commentary was wrong, he said it was difficult to understand it—because a parallel passage in *Nedarim* clearly confirmed his own interpretation.

This went on and on, until I lost track of the thread that held it all together and sat and listened in amazement to the feat of memory I was witnessing. Both Danny and his father spoke quietly, his father nodding his approval each time

Danny responded. Danny's brother sat staring at them with his mouth open, finally lost interest, and began to eat some of the food that was still on his plate. Once he started picking his nose, but stopped immediately. The men around the tables were watching as if in ecstasy, their faces glowing with pride. This was almost like the pilpul my father had told me about, except that it wasn't really pilpul, they weren't twisting the texts out of shape, they seemed more interested in b'kiut, in straightforward knowledge and simple explanations of the Talmudic passages and commentaries they were discussing. It went on like that for a long time. Then Reb Saunders sat back and was silent.

The contest, or quiz, had apparently ended, and Reb Saunders was smiling at his son. He said, very quietly, "Good. Very good. There is no contradiction. But tell me, you have nothing more to say about what I said earlier?"

Danny was suddenly sitting very straight.

"Nothing more?" Reb Saunders asked again. "You have nothing more to say?"

Danny shook his head, hesitantly.

"Absolutely nothing more to say?" Reb Saunders insisted, his voice flat, cold, distant. He was no longer smiling.

I saw Danny's body go rigid again, as it had done before his father began to speak. The ease and certainty he had worn during the Talmud quiz had disappeared.

"So," Reb Saunders said. "There is nothing more. Nu, what should I say?"

"I did not hear—"

"You did not hear, you did not hear. You heard the first mistake, and you stopped listening. Of course you did not hear. How could you hear when you were not listening?" He said it quietly and without anger.

Danny's face was rigid. The crowd sat silent. I looked at Danny. For a long moment he sat very still—and then I saw his lips part, move, curve slowly upward, and freeze into a grin. I felt the skin on the back of my neck begin to crawl, and I almost cried out. I stared at him, then looked quickly away.

Reb Saunders sat looking at his son. Then he turned his eyes upon me. I felt his eyes looking at me. There was a long, dark silence, during which Danny sat very still, staring

fixedly at his plate and grinning. Reb Saunders began to play
with the earlock along the right side of his face. He caressed
it with the fingers of his right hand, wound it around the index
finger, released it, then caressed it again, all the time looking
at me. Finally, he sighed loudly, shook his head, and put his
hands on the table.

"Nu," he said, "it is possible I am not right. After all, my
son is not a mathematician. He has a good head on him, but
it is not a head for mathematics. But we have a mathematician with us. The son of David Malter is with us. He is a
mathematician." He was looking straight at me, and I felt my
heart pound and the blood drain from my face. "Reuven,"
Reb Saunders was saying, looking straight at me, "you have
nothing to say?"

I found I couldn't open my mouth. Say about what? I
hadn't the faintest idea what he and Danny had been talking
about.

"You heard my little talk?" Reb Saunders asked me
quietly.

I felt my head nod.

"And you have nothing to say?"

I felt his eyes on me and found myself staring down at the
table. The eyes were like flames on my face.

"Reuven, you liked the gematriya?" Reb Saunders asked
softly.

I looked up and nodded. Danny hadn't moved at all. He
just sat there, grinning. His little brother was playing with the
tomato again. And the men at the tables were silent, staring
at *me* now.

"I am very happy," Reb Saunders said gently. "You liked
the gematriya. Which gematriya did you like?"

I heard myself say, lamely and hoarsely, "They were all
very good."

Reb Saunders' eyebrows went up. "All?" he said. "A very
nice thing. They were all very good. Reuven, were they *all*
very good?"

I felt Danny stir and saw him turn his head, the grin gone
now from his lips. He glanced at me quickly, then looked
down again at his paper plate.

I looked at Reb Saunders. "No," I heard myself say
hoarsely. "They were not all good."

There was a stir from the men at the tables. Reb Saunders sat back in his leather chair.

"Nu, Reuven," he said quietly, "tell me, which one was not good?"

"One of the gematriyot was wrong," I said. I thought the world would fall in on me after I said that. I was a fifteen-year-old boy, and there I was, telling Reb Saunders he had been wrong! But nothing happened. There was another stir from the crowd, but nothing happened. Instead, Reb Saunders broke into a warm, broad smile.

"And which one was it?" he asked me quietly.

"The gematriya for 'prozdor' is five hundred and three, not five hundred and thirteen," I answered.

"Good. Very good," Reb Saunders said, smiling and nodding his head, the black beard going back and forth against his chest, the earlocks swaying. "Very good, Reuven. The gematriya for 'prozdor' comes out five hundred three. Very good." He looked at me, smiling broadly, his teeth showing white through the beard, and I almost thought I saw his eyes mist over. There was a loud murmur from the crowd, and Danny's body sagged as the tension went out of him. He glanced at me, his face a mixture of surprise and relief, and I realized with astonishment that I, too, had just passed some kind of test.

"Nu," Reb Saunders said loudly to the men around the tables, "say Kaddish!"

An old man stood up and recited the Scholar's Kaddish. Then the congregants broke to go back to the front section of the synagogue for the Evening Service.

Danny and I said nothing to each other throughout the service, and though I prayed the words, I did not know what I was saying. I kept going over what had happened at the table. I couldn't believe it. I just couldn't get it through my head that Danny had to go through something like that every week, and that I myself had gone through it tonight.

The followers of Reb Saunders obviously had been pleased with my performance, because I could see they were no longer staring questions at me but were glancing at me admiringly. One of them, an old man with a white beard who was sitting in my row, even nodded at me and smiled, the corners of his eyes crinkling. I had clearly passed the test. What a ridiculous way to gain admiration and friendship!

The Evening Service was over very quickly, and afterward one of the younger men chanted the Havdalah, the brief service that marks the end of the Shabbat. Danny's brother held the braided candle, his hand trembling a little as the molten wax spilled onto his fingers. Then the congregants wished one another and Reb Saunders a good week and began to leave the synagogue. It was late, and I thought my father would probably be worried about me by now, but I stood there and waited until the last congregant was gone and the synagogue was empty—except for me, Danny, Reb Saunders, and the little boy. The synagogue seemed to me suddenly very small without its throng of black-hatted, black-bearded, black-caftaned men.

Reb Saunders was stroking his beard and looking at Danny and me. He leaned an elbow upon the large podium, and then the hand that was stroking the beard began to play with an earlock. I heard him sigh and saw him shake his head slowly, his dark eyes moist and brooding.

"Reuven, you have a good head on you," he said quietly in Yiddish. "I am happy my Daniel has chosen you for a friend. My son has many friends. But he does not talk about them the way he talks about you."

I listened and said nothing. His voice was gentle, almost a caress. He seemed so altogether different now from the way he had been at the table. I glanced at Danny. He was looking at his father, and the rigid lines were gone from his face.

Reb Saunders clasped his hands behind his back.

"I know of your father," he said to me quietly. "I am not surprised you have such a head. Your father is a great scholar. But what he writes, ah, what he writes!" He shook his head. "I worry myself about my son's friends, especially if such a friend is the son of David Malter. Ah, what your father writes! Criticism. Scientific criticism. Ah! So when he tells me you are now his friend, I worry myself. The son of David Malter should be my Daniel's friend? But your father is an observer of the Commandments, and you have his head, and so I am happy you are friends. It is good my Daniel has a friend. I have many responsibilities, I am not always able to talk to him." I saw Danny stare down at the floor, his face hardening. "It is good he has acquired a friend. Just so his friend does not teach him scientific criticism." Reb Saunders looked at me, his eyes dark and brooding. "You think a friend is an easy thing to be? If you are truly his friend, you will discover otherwise. We will see. Nu, it is late and your father is certainly worried that you are away so long. Have a good week, Reuven. And come pray with us again. There will be no more mistakes in gematriya."

He was smiling broadly and warmly now, his eyes wrinkling at the corners, the hard lines of his face almost gone. And then he offered me his hand, his entire hand this time, not only the fingers, and I took it, and he held my hand a long time. I almost had the feeling he wanted to embrace me. Then our hands separated, and he went slowly up the aisle, his hands clasped behind his back, tall, a little stooped and, I thought, a little majestic. His young son trailed behind him, holding on to the caftan.

Danny and I remained alone in the synagogue. It occurred to me suddenly that not a single word had passed between him and his father all evening, except for the Talmud contest.

"I'll walk you part of the way home," Danny offered, and we went out of the brownstone and down the stone stairway to the street. I could hear the caps of his shoes clearly against the stone of the stairway, and then against the cement pavement of the sidewalk.

It was night now, and cool, and a breeze blew against the sycamores and moved softly through the leaves. We walked in silence until Lee Avenue, then turned left. I was walking quickly, and Danny kept pace with my steps.

Walking along Lee Avenue, Danny said quietly, "I know what you're thinking. You think he's a tyrant."

I shook my head. "I don't know what to think. One minute he's a tyrant, the next minute he's kind and gentle. I don't know what to think."

"He's got a lot on his mind," Danny said. "He's a pretty complicated person."

"Do you always go through that routine at the table?"

"Oh, sure. I don't mind it. I even enjoy it a little."

"I've never seen anything like it in my life."

"It's a family tradition," Danny explained. "My father's father used to do it with him. It goes all the way back."

"It would scare me sick."

"It's not that bad. The bad part is waiting until he makes the mistake. After that it's all right. But the mistakes aren't really very hard to find. He makes ones that he knows I can find. It's a kind of game almost."

"Some game!"

"The second mistake tonight caught me off guard. But he made that one for you, really. That was very good, the way you caught it. He knew I wouldn't catch it. He just wanted to catch me, so he could tell me I wasn't listening. He was right. I wasn't listening. But I wouldn't have caught it even if I had listened. I'm no good in math. I've got a photographic memory for everything except math. You can't memorize math. You have to have a certain kind of head for it."

"I hate to tell you what I think about that game," I said, a little heatedly. "What happens if you miss the mistake?"

"I haven't missed in years."

"What happens when you *do* miss?"

He was silent a moment. "It's uncomfortable for a while," he said quietly. "But he makes a joke or something, and we go into a Talmud discussion."

"What a game!" I said. "In front of all those people!"

"They love it," Danny said. "They're very proud to see us like that. They love to hear the Talmud discussed like that. Did you see their faces?"

"I saw them," I said. "How could I not see them? Does your father always use gematriya when he talks?"

"Not always. Very rarely, as a matter of fact. The people love it and always hope for it. But he does it rarely. I think he did it tonight only because you were there."

"He's good at it, I'll say that much."

"He wasn't too good tonight. Some of it was a little forced. He was fantastic a few months ago. He did it with Talmudic laws then. He was really great."

"I thought it wasn't bad tonight."

"Well, it wasn't too good. He hasn't been feeling too well. He's worried about my brother."

"What's wrong with your brother?"

"I don't know. They don't talk about it. Something about his blood. He's been sick for a few years now."

"I'm sorry to hear that, Danny.

"He'll be all right. There's a pretty big doctor taking care of him now. He'll be all right." His voice had the same strange quality it had had when he had talked about his brother on our way over to the synagogue earlier in the day —hope, wistfulness, almost an eagerness for something to take place. I thought Danny must love his little brother very much, though I didn't remember his saying a word to him all the time they had been together. "Anyway," Danny said, "these contests, as you call them, are going to end as soon as I start studying with Rav Gershenson."

"Who?"

"Rav Gershenson. He's a great scholar. He's at Hirsch College. He teaches Talmud there. My father says that when I'm old enough to study with Rav Gershenson, I'll be old enough for him not to worry whether I can catch him at mistakes or not. Then we'll just have the Talmud discussions. I'll like that."

I was restraining my delight with considerable difficulty. The Samson Raphael Hirsch Seminary and College was the only yeshiva in the United States that offered a secular college education. It was located on Bedford Avenue, a few blocks from Eastern Parkway. My father had told me once that it had been built in the early twenties by a group of Orthodox Jews who wanted their sons to have both a Jewish and a secular education. Its college faculty was supposed to be excellent, and its rabbinic faculty consisted of some of the greatest Talmudists in the United States. A rabbinic ordination from its Talmud faculty was looked upon as the highest of Orthodox Jewish honors. It had been a foregone conclusion on my father's part and on mine that I would go on to there after high school for my bachelor's degree. When I told Danny that, his face burst into a smile.

"Well, that's wonderful!" he said. "I'm happy to hear that. That's really wonderful!"

"So we'll be going to the same college," I said. "Will you be going for a B.A.?"

"Sure. You have to. They don't let you study just Talmud in that college. I'll be majoring in psychology."

We had come to the corner of the synagogue in which my father and I prayed. Danny stopped.

"I have to go back," he said. "I've got schoolwork to do."

"I'll call you at your house tomorrow afternoon."

"I'll probably be in the library tomorrow afternoon, doing some reading in psychology. Why don't you come over there?"

"I won't be able to read anything."

"That's right," Danny smiled. "I forgot. You didn't duck."

"I'll come over anyway. I'll sit and think while you read."

"Wonderful. I'd like to watch you sit and think."

"Mitnagdim can think too, you know." I said.

Danny laughed. "I'll see you tomorrow."

"Right," I said, and watched him walk away, tall and lean in his black caftan and black hat.

I hurried home and came into the apartment just as my father was beginning to dial the phone. He put the phone down and looked at me.

"Do you know what time it is?" he asked.

"Is it very late?" I glanced at my watch. It was almost ten-thirty. "I'm sorry, abba. I couldn't just walk out."

"You were at Reb Saunders' synagogue all this time?"

"Yes."

"Next time you are out so late you will call, yes? I was ready to telephone Reb Saunders to find out what happened. Come into the kitchen and sit down. What are you looking so excited about? Sit down. I'll make some tea. Did you eat? What happened that you were away so long?"

I sat at the kitchen table and slowly told my father every-thing that had taken place in Reb Saunders' synagogue. He sipped his tea and listened quietly. I saw him grimace when I began to go over the gematriyot. My father did not particu-larly care for gematriya. He had once referred to it as non-sense numerology and had said that anything could be proved that way, all that had to be done was to shift letters around adroitly so as to make the values come out any way you wanted. So he sat there, sipping his tea and grimacing, as I reviewed Reb Saunders' gematriyot. When I started to tell him what had happened afterward, the grimace left his face, and he listened intently, nodding his head from time to time and sipping his tea. And when I got to the part where Reb

Saunders had asked me about the wrong gematriya, his face took on a look of astonishment, and he put the glass down on the table. Then I told him what Reb Saunders had said to me after Havdalah and what Danny and I had talked about on his way home, and he smiled proudly and nodded to indicate his happiness.

"Well," my father said, sipping his tea again, "you had some day, Reuven."

"It was an experience, abba. The way Danny had to answer his father's questions like that in front of everybody. I thought that was terrible."

My father shook his head. "It is not terrible, Reuven. Not for Danny, not for his father, and not for the people who listened. It is an old tradition, this kind of Talmudic discussion. I have seen it many times, between great rabbis. But it does not only take place between rabbis. When Kant became a professor, he had to follow an old tradition and argue in public on a philosophical subject. One day when you are a professor in a university and read a paper before your colleagues, you will also have to answer questions. It is part of Danny's training."

"But in public like that, abba!"

"Yes, Reuven. In public like that. How else would Reb Saunders' people know that Danny has a head for Talmud?"

"It just seemed so cruel to me."

My father nodded. "It is a little cruel, Reuven. But that is the way the world is. If a person has a contribution to make, he must make it in public. If learning is not made public, it is a waste. But the business about the mistakes I never heard before. That is something new. That is Reb Saunders' innovation. It is clear, but I am not sure I like it very much. No, I do not think I like it at all."

"Danny said the mistakes are always easy to find."

"Perhaps," my father said. "A man can do whatever he wishes to test his son's knowledge. But there are other ways than the way of Reb Saunders. At any rate, Reuven, it is good training for Danny. He will be involved in such things all his life."

"Reb Saunders is a very complicated man, abba. I can't make him out. One minute he's hard and angry, the next minute he's soft and gentle. I don't understand him."

"Reb Saunders is a great man, Reuven. Great men are always difficult to understand. He carries the burden of many people on his shoulders. I do not care for his Hasidism very much, but it is not a simple task to be a leader of people. Reb Saunders is not a fraud. He would be a great man even if he had not inherited his post from his father. It is a pity he occupies his mind only with Talmud. If he were not a tzaddik he could make a great contribution to the world. But he lives only in his own world. It is a great pity. Danny will be the same way when he takes his father's place. It is a shame that a mind such as Danny's will be shut off from the world."

My father sipped his tea again, and we sat quietly for a while.

"I am very proud of the way you handled yourself today," my father said, looking at me over the rim of the glass. "I am glad Reb Saunders will let you be Danny's friend. I was worried about Reb Saunders."

"I'm awfully sorry I came back so late, abba."

My father nodded. "I am not angry," he said. "But next time you will be so late, you will call, yes?"

"Yes, abba."

My father glanced at the clock on the shelf over the refrigerator. "Reuven, it is late, and tomorrow you are going to school. You should go to sleep now."

"Yes, abba."

"Remember, you must not read. I will read to you in the evenings and we will see if we can study that way. But you must not read by yourself."

"Yes, abba. Good night."

"Good night, Reuven."

I left him sitting at the kitchen table over his glass of tea and went to bed. I lay awake a long time before I was able to sleep.

CHAPTER EIGHT
╫╫╫╫╫╫╫╫╫╫╫╫╫╫╫╫╫╫╫╫

WHEN I GOT BACK to school the next morning, I found I had
become a hero, and during the fifteen-minute morning recess
my friends, and even some boys I did not know, all crowded
around me, wanting to know how I was and telling me what
a great game I had played. Near the end of the recess, I went
over to the pitcher's position and stood on the exact spot
where I had been hit by the ball. I looked—tried to look; the
yard was crowded with students—at home plate and imagined Danny standing there, grinning at me. I remembered his
grinning that way again yesterday, and I closed my eyes for a
moment, then went over and stood near the wire fence behind the plate. The bench on which the young rabbi had sat
was still there, and I stared at it for a moment. It seemed impossible to me that the ball game had taken place only a
week ago. So many things had happened, and everything
looked so different.

Sidney Goldberg came over to me and started talking
about the game, and then Davey Cantor joined us and added
his opinion about "those murderers." I nodded at what they
were saying without really listening. It seemed silly to me, the
way they kept talking about the game, they both sounded so
childish, and I got a little angry when Davey Cantor started
talking about "that snooty Danny Saunders," but I didn't say
anything.

I got out of school at two o'clock and took a trolley car
over to the public library where I was supposed to meet
Danny. The library was a huge, three-story, graystone building, with thick Ionic columns, and with the words BEAUTY IS
TRUTH, TRUTH BEAUTY, THAT IS ALL YE KNOW ON EARTH, AND
ALL YE NEED TO KNOW—JOHN KEATS engraved in the stone
over its four glass entrance doors. It stood on a wide boule-

vard and there were tall trees in front of it and a grassy lawn bordered by flowers. On the right-hand wall of the vestibule, just inside the doors, there was a mural of the history of great ideas, beginning with a drawing of Moses holding the Ten Commandments, going on to Jesus, Mohammed, Galileo, Luther, Copernicus, Kepler, Newton, and ending with Einstein gazing at the formula $E=MC^2$. On the other wall there was a mural showing Homer, Dante, Tolstoi, Balzac, and Shakespeare engaged in conversation. They were beautiful murals, done in bright colors, and the great men in them looked alive. Probably because I had become so sensitive about eyes the past week, I noticed for the first time that Homer's eyes seemed glazed, almost without pupils, as if the artist had been trying to show that he had been blind. I had never noticed that before, and it frightened me a little to see it now.

I went quickly through the first floor, with its marble floors, its marble pillars, its tall bookcases, its long reference tables, its huge windows through which the sun streamed, and its glass-topped desks at which the librarians sat. I found Danny on the third floor against the far wall, partly hidden by a bookcase, wearing a black suit, a tieless shirt, and a skullcap. He was sitting at a small table, bent over a book, his long earlocks dangling down the sides of his face and almost reaching to the top of the table.

There were not many people on this floor; its stacks were filled mostly with bound volumes of scholarly journals and pamphlets. It was a large floor, and the closely set stacks gave it a mazelike appearance. They went from floor to ceiling, and they seemed to me to contain everything of importance that had ever been written on any subject in the world. There were journals in English, French, German, Russian, Italian, and even one collection in Chinese. Some of the English journals had names I couldn't pronounce. This was the one floor of the three-floored library I did not know well. I had been up here once to find an article in the *Journal of Symbolic Logic* which had been recommended to me by my mathematics teacher, an article which I had only dimly understood, and once to meet my father. Now was the third time in all the years I had belonged to this library that I was on its third floor.

I stood near a bookcase a few feet away from the table at

which Danny was sitting, and I watched him read. His elbows were on the table, and he held his head in the palms of his hands, the fingers covering his ears completely, his eyes staring down at the book. Occasionally, the fingers of his right hand would play with his earlock, and once they stroked the tufts of sand-colored hair on his chin for a few seconds, then went back to the side of his face. His mouth was slightly open, and I could not see his eyes; they were hidden by the lids. He seemed impatient each time he came to the foot of a page, and he flipped the page with a quick gesture of his right hand, wetting the forefinger with his tongue and turning the page by pushing upward with the finger against the lower right-hand corner, the way one does a page of Talmud—except that with a Talmud the left forefinger usually pushes against the lower left-hand corner because it is read from right to left. He was reading with phenomenal speed. I could almost *see* him read. He would start at the head of a page, his head tilted slightly upward, and then his head would move downward in a straight line until he got to the foot of the page. Then it would tilt upward again and either move sideways to the right page or remain fixed in its upward position until the page was turned, and then start downward again. He did not seem to be reading from side to side but up and down, and, watching him, I had the distinct impression that he was reading the middle of the page only and was somehow able to ignore, or absorb without actually reading, what was written on the sides.

I decided not to disturb him, and I sat down at another table a few feet away and continued to watch him read. It was frustrating to be sitting there surrounded by all those journals and not be able to read a thing myself, and I decided after a while to review by heart some of the symbolic logic I had been studying. I closed my eyes and went over the propositional calculus, trying to visualize the truth tables for conjunction, disjunction, equivalence, and material implication. They were fairly simple, and I had no difficulty. I tried to do some problems, but after a while it became complicated, I couldn't remember all the deductive steps, and I stopped. I was about to begin going over the steps of indirect proof when I heard Danny say, "You're always sleeping!

What a sleepyhead you are!" and I opened my eyes. Danny was sitting up in his chair and looking at me.

"I was reviewing my logic," I told him. "I wasn't sleeping."

"Of course," he said, smiling. But his voice sounded sad.

"I was just going into the indirect proof. Do you want to hear it?"

"No. I can't stand that stuff. Why didn't you tell me you were here?"

"I didn't want to disturb you."

"You're nice. For a Misnaged." He gave the Hebrew letter "tof" its Ashkenazic pronunciation. "Come over here. I want you to see something."

I went over to his table and sat down next to him. "I'm not allowed to read, you know."

"I want you to hear this. I'll read it to you."

"What is it?"

"It's from Graetz's *History of the Jews.*" He sounded unhappy, and there was a somber look on his face. "It's about Hasidim. Listen. Graetz is talking about Dov Baer, who was the follower of the Besht. He just finished saying that Dov Baer invented the idea of the tzaddik." He looked down at the book on the table and began to read aloud. " 'Baer's idea, however, was not meant to remain idle and unfruitful, but to bring him honor and revenue. While the tzaddik cared for the conduct of the world, for the obtaining of heavenly grace, and especially for Israel's preservation and glorification, his adherents had to cultivate three kinds of virtues. It was their duty to draw nigh to him, to enjoy the sight of him, and from time to time to make pilgrimages to him. Further, they were to confess their sins to him. By these means alone could they hope for pardon from their iniquities.' That means sins," he told me.

"I know what it means," I said.

He went on. " 'Finally, they had to bring him presents, rich gifts, which he knew how to employ to the best advantage. It was also incumbent upon them to attend to his personal wants. It seems like a return to the days of the priests of Baal, so vulgar and disgusting do these perversities appear.' "

He looked up from the book. "That's pretty strong language, 'vulgar and disgusting.' " His eyes were dark and brooding. "It feels terrible to have a great scholar like Graetz call Hasidism vulgar and disgusting. I never thought of my father as a priest of Baal."

I didn't say anything.

"Listen to what else he says about Dov Baer." He turned a page. "He says here that Dov Baer used to crack vulgar jokes to make his people happy, and that he used to encourage his followers to drink alcohol, so they would pray fervently. He says that Rabbi Elijah of Vilna was a great opponent of the Hasidim, and that when he died—let me read it to you." He shuffled pages. "Here it is. Listen. 'After his death, the Hasidim took vengeance upon him by dancing upon his grave, and celebrating the day of his decease as a holiday, with shouting and drunkenness.' " He looked at me. "I never knew about any of these things. You were in our shul yesterday. Did anyone look drunk to you during the service?"

"No," I said.

"My father isn't like that at all." His voice was sad, and it trembled a little. "He really worries about his people. He worries about them so much he doesn't even have time to talk to me."

"Maybe Graetz is only talking about the Hasidim of his own day," I offered.

"Maybe," he said, not convinced. "It's awful to have someone give you an image like that of yourself. He says that Dov Baer had expert spies worthy of serving in the secret service. Those are his words, 'worthy of serving in the secret service.' He says they would go around discovering people's secrets and tell them to Dov Baer. People who came to see him about their personal problems would have to wait around until the Saturday after they came, and in the meantime these spies would investigate them and report back to him, so that when the person finally got to see him, Dov Baer would know everything, and the person would be impressed and think that Dov Baer had some sort of magical ability to look into his heart." He shuffled some more pages. "Listen to this. 'In the first interview Baer, in a seemingly casual manner, was able, in a skillfully arranged discourse, to bring in allusions to these strangers, whereby they would be convinced that he had looked into their hearts and knew their past.' " He shook his head sadly. "I never knew about anything like that. When my father talks about Dov Baer, he almost makes him out to be a saint."

"Did my father give you that book to read?"

"Your father said I should read Jewish history. He said the first important step in anyone's education is to know your own people. So I found this work by Graetz. It's a lot of volumes. I'm almost done with it. This is the last volume." He shook his head again, and the earlocks danced and brushed against the ridge of his jaw and the hollow of his cheeks. "What an image it gives me of myself."

"You ought to discuss it with my father first," I told him, "before you go believing any of that. He told me a lot about Hasidism on Friday night. He wasn't very complimentary, but he didn't say anything about drunkenness."

Danny nodded slowly. "I'll talk to him," he said. "But Graetz was a great scholar. I read up on him before I started reading his history. He was one of the greatest Jewish scholars of the last century."

"You ought to discuss it with my father," I repeated.

Danny nodded again, then slowly closed the book. His fingers played idly with the spine of the binding.

"You know," he brooded, "I read a psychology book last week in which the author said that the most mysterious thing in the universe to man is man himself. We're blind about the most important thing in our lives, our own selves. How could a man like Dov Baer have the gall to fool other people into thinking that he could look inside their hearts and tell them what they were really like inside?"

"You don't know that he did. You only know Graetz's version of it."

He ignored me. I had the feeling he was talking more to himself than to me.

"We're so complicated inside," he went on quietly. "There's something in us called the unconscious that we're completely unaware of. It practically dominates our lives, and we don't even know it." He paused, hesitating, his hand moving from the book and playing now with an earlock. I was reminded of the evening in the hospital when he had stared out the window at the people on the street below and had talked of God and ants and the reading he did in this library. "There's so much to read," he said. "I've only really been reading for a few months. Did you know about the subconscious?" he asked me, and when I somewhat hesitantly nodded, he said, "You see? You're not even interested in psychology, and you know about it. I have so much catching up to do." He was suddenly conscious of the way his fingers were playing with the earlock, and he let his hand drop to the table. "Did you know that very often the subconscious expresses itself in dreams? 'The dream is the product of a transaction between conscious and unconscious wishes,'" he quoted, "'and the results during sleep are naturally very different from those during waking hours.'"

"What's this about dreams?" I asked.

"It's true," he said. "Dreams are full of unexpressed fears and hopes, things that we never even think of consciously. We think of them unconsciously deep down inside ourselves, and they come out in dreams. They don't always come out straight, though. Sometimes they come out in symbols. You have to learn to interpret the symbols."

"Where did you find out about that?"

"In my reading. There's a lot of work been done on dreams. It's one of the ways they have of getting to a person's unconscious."

I must have had a strange expression on my face, because he asked me what was the matter.

"I dream all the time," I told him.

"Everyone does," he said. "We just don't remember a lot of them. We repress them. We sort of push them away and forget them, because sometimes they're too painful."

"I'm trying to remember mine," I said. "Some of them weren't very pleasant."

"A lot of times they're not pleasant. Our unconscious isn't a nice place—I call it a place; it isn't a place, really; the book I read says it's more like a process—it isn't a nice place at all. It's full of repressed fears and hatreds, things that we're afraid to bring out into the open."

"And these things rule our lives?"

"According to some psychologists they do."

"You mean these things go on and we don't know anything about them?"

"That's right. That's what I said before. What's inside us is the greatest mystery of all."

"That's a pretty sad thing to think about. To be doing things without really knowing why you're doing them."

Danny nodded. "You can find out about it, though. About your unconscious, I mean. That's what psychoanalysis is all about. I haven't read too much about it yet, but it's a long process. Freud started it. You've heard about Freud. He started psychoanalysis. I'm teaching myself German, so I can read him in the original. He discovered the unconscious, too."

I stared at him and felt a shock of coldness move inside me. "You're studying German?"

He seemed surprised at my reaction. "What's wrong with studying German? Freud wrote in German. What are you looking at me like that for?"

"Aren't his writings translated into English?"

"Not all of them. Besides, I want to read a lot of other things in German that haven't been translated yet. What's the matter with you? You've got the funniest look on your face."

I didn't say anything.

"Just because Hitler speaks German doesn't mean that the language is corrupt. It's the most important scientific language in the world. What are you looking at me like that for?"

"I'm sorry," I said. "It just seems strange to me, your studying German."

"What's so strange about it?"

"Nothing. How are you teaching it to yourself?"

"There's a grammar book in the reference library. I'm almost done memorizing it. It's an interesting language. Very technical and precise. It's amazing the way they put nouns together. Do you know what the word for 'mysterious' is in German?"

"I don't know any German."

"It's *'geheimnisvoll.'* It means 'full of secret.' That's what the subconscious is, *'geheimnisvoll.'* The word for 'sympathetic' is *'teilnahmsvoll'*—literally 'full of part-taking.' The word for charity is *'Nächstenliebe'*—literally, it means—"

"All right," I said. "I'm impressed."

"It's quite a language. Yiddish is a lot like it. Yiddish was originally Middle German. When the German Jews came into Poland, they brought it with them."

"You mean in the thirteenth century, when Poland encouraged the Jews to come in?"

"That's right. You know about that."

"I didn't know about Yiddish being German."

"My father doesn't, either. At least, I don't think he does. He thinks Yiddish is almost holy. But it's really from Middle German."

I was going to ask him what the Middle meant in Middle German, but I decided not to push the conversation any further. I was upset enough as it was about his learning German. And it had nothing to do with Hitler, either. I kept remembering what my father had told me about Solomon Maimon. It all sounded so weird. I almost had the feeling I was talking to Maimon's ghost.

We talked some more about Graetz's version of Hasidism, and then somehow we got onto the subject of Danny's brother. He had been examined by a big doctor that morning, and the doctor had said he would be all right, but that he would have to be careful, no strenuous studying or exercising. He had gone with his father, and Danny said his father was now very upset. But at least his brother would be all right. It had something to do with his blood chemistry, Danny said, and the doctor had prescribed three different pills for him to take. He hadn't been very optimistic about the condition clearing up, either. He said he would have to take the pills as long as it persisted. "It might persist his whole life," Danny said sadly. Again, I got the impression that he loved his brother very much, and I wondered why he hadn't said a word to him during all the time I had seen them together yesterday in the synagogue.

Finally, we decided it was getting late, and we started down the wide marble staircase. When we were about halfway down the staircase to the second floor, Danny stopped and looked carefully around. He did the same when we were going down to the main floor. He replaced the Graetz book, and we went outside.

It was cloudy and seemed ready to rain, so we decided to take a trolley car back rather than walk. Danny got off at his block, and I rode the rest of the way alone, my head full of what we had talked about, especially his teaching himself German.

I told my father about it over the supper table.

"What does Danny want to read in German?" he asked me.

"He wants to read Freud."

My father's eyes went wide behind their spectacles.

"He was very excited about it," I said. "He was talking about the unconscious and dreams. He was also reading Graetz on Hasidism."

"The unconscious and dreams," my father muttered. "And Freud. At the age of fifteen." He shook his head gloomily. "But it will not be possible to stop him."

"Abba, was Graetz right in what he said about Hasidism?"

"Graetz was biased, and his sources were not accurate. If I remember correctly, he calls the Hasidim vulgar drunkards, and he calls the tzaddikim priests of Baal. There is enough to dislike about Hasidism without exaggerating its faults."

I met Danny again in the library later that week, but he wasn't too enthusiastic when I told him what my father had said about Graetz. He told me he had read another book on Hasidism, and while the author hadn't accused the tzaddikim of encouraging drinking, he had accused them of almost everything else. I asked him how he was coming along with his German, and he said he had finished memorizing the grammar text and was reading a book he had borrowed from the German section of the library. He said he hoped to start reading Freud in a few weeks. I didn't tell him what my father had said about that. He looked upset and tense, and he kept playing with an earlock all the time we talked.

My father told me that night that there had been a serious question in his mind about how ethical it was for him to give Danny books to read behind his father's back.

"How would I feel if someone gave you books to read which I believed might be harmful to you?"

I asked him why he had done it.

"Because Danny would have continued to read anyway on his own. At least this way he has some direction from an adult. It was a fortunate accident that he stumbled upon me. But it is not a comfortable feeling, Reuven. I dislike doing this to Reb Saunders. He is certain to find out one day. It will be an uncomfortable situation when he does. But he will not be able to stop Danny from reading. What will he do when his son goes to college?"

I pointed out to my father that Danny was anyway reading on his own now, without direction from an adult. My father certainly hadn't told him to read Freud.

My father nodded his agreement. "But he will come to me to discuss what he reads," he said. "At least there will be a balance. I will give him other books to read, and he will see that Freud is not God in psychology. Freud yet. At fifteen." And he shook his head gloomily.

Danny and I arranged to spend Shabbat afternoon together with his father, studying *Pirkei Avot*. When I turned off Lee Avenue that Shabbat and started up the sunless street on which Danny lived, the feeling of having crossed into a twilight world was only a little less strong than it had been the week before. It was just after three o'clock, and there were no bearded, caftaned men or kerchief-wearing women on the street, but the children were outside, playing, shouting, running. Except for the children, the sidewalk in front of the three-story brownstone at the end of the block was deserted. I remembered how the black-caftaned men had parted for Danny and me the week before, and I remembered, too, the tapping of Danny's capped shoes on the pavement as we had gone through the crowd and up the wide stone staircase. The door in the hallway that led into the synagogue was open, but the synagogue was empty—except for the echoes it contained. I stood just inside the synagogue. The tables were covered with white cloths, but the food had not yet been put out. I stared at the table where I had sat, and I could still hear the gematriyot tumbling out of Reb Saunders' mouth and then his question to Danny, "Nothing more? You have nothing more to say?" I saw the idiot grin spread itself slowly across Danny's lips. I turned quickly and went back out into the hall.

I stood at the foot of the inside stairway and called up, "Hello! Anybody home?" After a moment, Danny appeared at the head of the stairs, wearing his black caftan, black pants, and a black skullcap, and told me to come on up.

He introduced me to his mother and sister. His sister was almost as tall as I, with dark, vivacious eyes and a face al-

most exactly like Danny's, except that the sculptured lines
were a good deal softer. She wore a long-sleeved dress, and
her dark hair was combed back severely and dangled in a
thick braid behind her. She smiled at me and said, "I know
all about you, Reuven Malter. Danny never stops talking
about you." His mother was short, with blue eyes and a
roundish body. Her head was covered with a kerchief, and
there were faint tufts of sand-colored hair on her upper lip.
They were both sitting in the living room and had apparently
been reading or studying what looked to me to be a Yiddish
book when we had interrupted them. I told them politely that
it was nice to meet them and was rewarded with another
smile from Danny's sister.

We left them and started up the stairway to the third floor.
Danny explained that the third floor contained his room, his
father's study, and a conference room. The second and third
floors were completely separated, just as they were in any
three-story brownstone. They had thought once of moving
the family to the third floor, Danny said, so as to avoid the
noise made by the people who were constantly climbing the
stairs to see his father. But his mother wasn't well, and a
three-floor climb would be too much for her.

I asked him how his brother was feeling.

"All right, I guess," he told me. "He's asleep now."

Danny took me through the third-floor rooms. They were
identical with the ones in which my father and I lived. Danny's bedroom was located exactly where my father's bedroom
was, the kitchen had been left intact—to serve the visiting
dignitaries tea, Danny said with a grin—the bathroom was
next to the kitchen, the study was where my father's study
was—except that one of its walls had been knocked out so
that it also included what in our apartment was my room—
and the living room contained a long glass-topped conference table and leather chairs. Danny took me into the
conference room first—we went through the outside hallway
door—then into his room, which had a narrow bed, a bookcase full of old Hebrew and Yiddish books, and a desk clut-
tered with papers. A Talmud lay open on top of the papers.
The walls were white and bare. All the walls were white and
bare. I saw no photographs or paintings anywhere, neither on

the floor where his family lived, nor here on the floor where he lived and his father worked.

We stood outside his father's study, and Danny knocked softly on the door. "He doesn't like me to barge in on him when he's in there," he whispered with a grin. His father said to come in, and we went in.

Reb Saunders sat behind a massive, black wood, glass-topped desk, wearing a black caftan and a tall, round, black skullcap. He was sitting in a straight-backed red leather chair with intricately carved wooden arms. A single light bulb glowed white behind its ceiling fixture. The study, with its additional room, seemed enormous. A thick red carpet covered its floor, and its walls were lined with glass-enclosed wooden bookcases jammed tight with books. There were books everywhere—on the two wooden chairs near the desk, on the desk itself, on the wooden file cabinet that stood near the door, on cardboard boxes piled in a corner, on the small wooden step-ladder, on the black leather easy chair that stood in another corner, even on the window seat. Many of the books were bound in black, red, and brown leather. One book had been bound in white, and it stood out prominently on a shelf among the black-bound books around it. Danny told me later that it contained the sayings of the Ba'al Shem Tov and had been presented to his father as a gift on his fiftieth birthday by the members of his congregation. All the books seemed to be in Hebrew or Yiddish, and many of them were very old and in their original bindings. There was a musty odor in the room, the odor of old books with yellow leaves and ancient bindings.

Reb Saunders told us to clear the books off the two chairs near the desk. The desk stood in almost the exact spot where my father had his desk. Danny sat at his father's right, I at his left.

Reb Saunders wanted to know about my eye. I told him it wasn't bothering me at all and that I was supposed to see the doctor this Monday morning. He understood I was not permitted to read. I nodded. "So you will listen," he told me, playing with an earlock. "You are a good mathematician. Now we will see what you know about more important things." He said it with a smile on his lips, and I did not feel it as a challenge. I knew I could not match him and Danny in the breadth of their knowledge, but I wondered if I might not be able to keep up with them in terms of depth. Rabbinic literature can be studied in two different ways, in two directions, one might say. It can be studied quantitatively or qualitatively—or, as my father once put it, horizontally or vertically. The former involves covering as much material as possible, without attempting to wrest from it all its implications and intricacies; the latter involves confining oneself to one single area until it is exhaustively covered, and then going on to new material. My father, in his classes and when he studied with me at home, always used the latter method. The ideal, of course, was to be able to do both, but none of the students in my school had that kind of time available to him because of the school's heavy emphasis on English studies.

Reb Saunders had a text of *Pirkei Avot* open in front of him. He began to read from it, stopping at the end of each passage. Danny and I took turns explaining each alternating passage. I realized soon enough that the *Pirkei Avot* text was merely being used as a sort of jumping-off point for them, because they were soon ranging through most of the major tractates of the Talmud again. And it wasn't a quiz or a quiet contest this time, either. It was a pitched battle. With no congregants around, and with me an accepted member of the family, Danny and his father fought through their points with loud voices and wild gestures of their hands almost to where I thought they might come to blows. Danny caught his father in a misquote, ran to get a Talmud from a shelf, and triumphantly showed his father where he had been wrong. His father checked the margin of the page for the textual corrections of Rabbi Elijah—the same Rabbi Elijah who had persecuted Hasidim!—and showed Danny that he had been quoting from the corrected text. Then they went on to another tractate, fought over another passage, and this time Reb Saunders agreed, his face glowing, that his son was correct. I sat quietly for a long time, watching them battle. There was an ease about them, an intimacy, which had been totally lacking from the show they had put on before the congregants last week. There was no tension here at all but a battle between equals, with Reb Saunders losing only a little less frequently than his son. And I soon realized something else: Reb Saunders was far happier when he lost to Danny than

when he won. His face glowed with fierce pride and his head
nodded wildly—the nod beginning from the waist and including the entire upper portion of his body, with the beard moving back and forth against his chest—each time he was
forced to acquiesce to Danny's rendition of a passage or to
Danny's incisive counter-questioning. The battle went on for
a long time, and I slowly became aware of the fact that both
Danny and his father, during a point they might be making
or listening to, would cast inquisitive glances at me, as if to
ask what I was doing just sitting there while all this excitement was going on: Why in the world wasn't I joining in the
battle? I listened to them for a few minutes longer, and then
I realized that though they knew so much more material
than I did, once a passage was quoted and briefly explained, I
was on almost equal footing with them. I had this time been
able to retain hold of the chain of the argument—probably
because there was no tension now—and so when Reb Saunders cited and explained a passage that seemed to contradict
a point that had just been made by Danny, I suddenly found
myself on the field of combat, offering an interpretation of
the passage in support of Danny. Neither of them seemed at
all surprised to hear my voice—I had the feeling they were
surprised they hadn't heard it sooner—and from that point
on the three of us seesawed back and forth through the infi-
nite intricacies of the Talmud. I discovered that my father's
method of teaching me Talmud and his patient insistence that
I learn Talmudic grammar—I had painfully memorized an
Aramaic grammar book—was now standing me in good
stead. I saw allusions in passages that Danny and his father
overlooked, and I resolved a contradiction with an appeal to
grammar. "Grammar!" Reb Saunders threw up his hands.
"Grammar we need yet!" But I insisted, explained, cajoled,
raised my voice, gestured with my hands, quoted whatever
proof texts I could remember from the grammar book, and
finally he accepted my explanations. I found I was enjoying it
all immensely, and once I even caught myself reading aloud
from a Talmud—it was the grammatical discussion of the
gender of "derech," road, in the tractate *Kiddushin*—before
Reb Saunders realized what I was doing and told me to stop,
I wasn't allowed to use my eye yet, Danny would read the
passage. Danny didn't need to read the passage—he quoted it

by heart with mechanical swiftness. It became clear quickly
enough that though I was unequal to Danny in breadth, I was
easily equal to him in depth, and this seemed to please Reb
Saunders enormously. Danny and I were soon involved in a
heated discussion concerning two contradictory commentaries
on the same passage, and Reb Saunders sat back quietly and
listened. Our argument ended in a draw; we agreed that the
passage was obscure and that as it stood it could be explained
either way.

There was a pause.

Reb Saunders suggested quietly that Danny might go down
and bring us some tea.

Danny left.

The silence that now replaced our loud voices was almost
uncomfortable. Reb Saunders sat quietly, stroking his beard
with his right hand. I heard Danny's capped shoes in the
apartment hallway outside the study. Then the door opened
and closed. Reb Saunders stirred and looked at me.

"You have a good head," he said softly. The Yiddish
phrase he used was, literally translated, "an iron head." He
nodded, seemed to listen for a moment to the silence in the
study, then folded his arms across his chest. He sighed
loudly, his eyes suddenly sad. "Now we will see about your
soul," he said softly. "Reuven, my son will return soon. We
have little time to talk. I want you to listen to me. I know
that my Daniel spends hours almost every day in the public
library. No, do not say anything. Just listen. I know you are
surprised that I know. It is not important how I found it out.
The neighborhood is not so big that he could hide this from
me forever. When my son does not come home in the afternoons week after week, I want to know where he is. Nu, now
I know. I also know that he is sometimes with you in the
library and sometimes with your father. I want you to tell me
what he reads. I could ask my son, but it is difficult for me to
speak to him. I know you do not understand that. But it is
true. I cannot ask my son. One day perhaps I will tell you the
reason. I know the mind he has, and I know I can no longer
tell him what yes to read and what not to read. I am asking
you to tell me what he reads."

I sat frozen and felt a long moment of blind panic. What
my father had anticipated was now actually happening. But

he hadn't anticipated it happening to *me*. He had thought Reb Saunders would confront *him*, not me. My father and I had acted behind Reb Saunders' back; now Reb Saunders was asking me to act behind Danny's back. I didn't know what to say.

Reb Saunders looked at me and sighed again. "Reuven," he said very quietly, "I want you to hear me out. No one lives forever. My father led his people before me, and my grandfather before him, and my great-grandfather before him. For six generations now we have led our people. I will not live forever. Daniel will one day take my place—" His voice broke, and he stopped. He put a finger to one of his eyes. Then he went on, his voice a little hoarse now. "My son is my most precious possession. I have nothing in the world compared to my son. I must know what he is reading. And I cannot ask him." He stopped and looked down at an open Talmud on his desk. "How did he come to meet your father in the library?" he asked, looking down at the Talmud.

I sat very still and said nothing. I realized I was sitting on top of a possible explosion between Danny and his father. How long would Reb Saunders remain silent about his son's visits to the library? And I didn't like the way my father seemed to appear in all of this—as if he were conspiring behind Reb Saunders' back to contaminate his son. I took a deep breath and began to talk slowly, choosing my words with care. I told Reb Saunders everything, how Danny had met my father, why my father was suggesting books for him to read, what he was reading, how my father was helping him —omitting that Danny was studying German, that he planned to read Freud, and that he had read some books on Hasidism.

When I finished, Reb Saunders just sat there and stared at me. I could see he was controlling himself with great effort. He covered his eyes and nose with his right hand and leaned forward, his elbow on the open Talmud, the upper portion of his body swaying slowly back and forth. I saw his lips move beneath the hand, and I heard the words "Psychology. Master of the Universe, psychology. And Darwin." They came out as a soft, whispered moan. He took the hand away from his face and let it drop to the Talmud. "What can I do?" he asked himself softly. "I can no longer speak to my own son.

The Master of the Universe gave me a brilliant son, a phenomenon. And I cannot speak to him." He looked at me and
seemed suddenly aware again of my presence. "The pain of
raising children," he said quietly. "So many troubles. So
many troubles. Reuven, you and your father will be a good
influence on my son, yes?"

I nodded slowly, afraid now to speak.

"You will not make a goy out of my son?"

I shook my head, feeling numb at what I was hearing. His
voice was an ache, a plea. I saw him stare up at the ceiling.

"Master of the Universe," he almost chanted. "You gave
me a brilliant son, and I have thanked you for him a million
times. But you had to make him *so* brilliant?"

I listened to his voice and felt myself go cold. There was
so much pain in it, so much bewildered pain.

The apartment door opened and closed. Reb Saunders sat
up in his chair, his face quickly regaining its composure.
Clearly, almost like an echo in a cave, I heard the tap-tap-tap
of Danny's metal-capped shoes against the linoleum hallway
floor. Then he was in the study, carrying a tray with three
glasses of tea, sugar, spoons, and some of his mother's cookies. I pushed some books aside on the desk, and he put the
tray down.

From the moment he entered the room and saw my face, I
knew he was aware that something had happened during his
absence. We sipped our tea in silence, and I saw him glance
at me from over the rim of his glass. He knew, all right. He
knew something had happened between his father and me.
What was I supposed to tell him? That his father now knew
he was reading forbidden books and was not going to try to
stop him? Reb Saunders hadn't said anything about not telling Danny what had gone on between us. I looked at him for
a clue, but he was sipping his tea calmly. I hoped Danny
wouldn't ask me today. I wanted to talk to my father first.

Reb Saunders put his glass down and folded his arms
across his chest. He was acting as though nothing at all had
happened.

"Tell me more about grammar in the Talmud, Reuven," he
said to me, with a gentle hint of mockery in his voice. "All
my life I have studied Talmud and paid no attention to
grammar. Now you tell me a person must know grammar to

know Talmud. You see what happens when you have a father who is a Misnaged? Grammar yet. Mathematics—nu, all
right. Mathematics I can understand. But grammar!"

The three of us sat there and talked until it was time for
the Afternoon Service. Danny found his father's deliberate
mistake easily, and I was able to follow the ensuing Talmudic
discussion without too much difficulty, though I did not join
in.

After the Evening Service, Danny said he would walk me
part of the way home, and as we turned into Lee Avenue he
asked me what had happened between me and his father that
afternoon.

I told him everything. He listened in silence, not seeming
at all surprised that his father somehow had learned of his
secret visits to the library.

"I knew he would find out about it sooner or later," he
said softly, looking very sad.

"I hope you don't mind my telling him, Danny. I had to."

He shrugged. His eyes were moist and gloomy. "I almost
wish he had asked *me* instead," he said quietly. "But we don't
talk anymore, except when we study Talmud."

"I don't understand that."

"It's what I told you in the hospital. My father believes in
silence. When I was ten or eleven years old, I complained to
him about something, and he told me to close my mouth and
look into my soul. He told me to stop running to him every
time I had a problem. I should look into my own soul for the
answer, he said. We just don't talk, Reuven."

"I don't understand that at all."

"I'm not so sure I understand it myself," he said gloomily.
"But that's the way he is. I don't know how he found out I
was reading behind his back, but I'm glad he knows about
it. At least I won't have to walk around in that library scared
to death. I just feel bad having had to fool my father like
that. But what else could I have done?"

I agreed with him that he couldn't have done anything else,
but I told him I wished he could somehow get around to talking about it with his father.

"I can't," he said, shaking his head. "I just can't. You don't
know what torture it was talking to him about organizing a

ball team. We just don't talk, Reuven. Maybe it sounds a little crazy to you. But it's true."

"I think you ought to at least try."

"I *can't!*" he said, a little angry now. "Don't you listen to what I'm saying? I just can't!"

"I don't understand it," I told him.

"Well, I can't explain it to you any better than I have," he said angrily.

When we stopped in front of the synagogue where my father and I prayed, he muttered his "Good night," turned, and walked slowly away.

My father seemed astonished when I told him what Danny had said to me.

"Silence? What do you mean, Danny is being brought up in silence?" His eyes were wide.

"They never talk, abba. Except when they study Talmud. That's what Danny told me."

He stared at me for a long time. Then he seemed to remember something, and his eyes narrowed suddenly.

"Once in Russia I heard something," he murmured softly, speaking to himself. "But I did not believe it."

"Heard what, abba?"

He looked at me, his eyes somber, and shook his head. "I am happy Reb Saunders knows now about his son's reading," he said quietly, evading my question. "I was concerned about all this subterfuge."

"But why can't he talk to Danny about it?"

"Reuven, he has already talked to Danny about it. He has talked to Danny through you."

I stared at him.

He sighed softly.

"It is never pleasant to be a buffer, Reuven," he told me quietly. And he would say nothing more about the strange silence between Reb Saunders and his son.

CHAPTER NINE
❧❧❧❧❧❧❧❧❧❧❧❧❧❧❧❧❧❧❧

I WENT STRAIGHT HOME from school the next day and spent the afternoon and evening listening to my father read to me from my textbooks. At nine o'clock on Monday morning, my father took me to Dr. Snydman's office on Eastern Parkway. We were both nervous and silent on the way over. I had taken my school books with me, because we planned to go straight from Dr. Snydman's office to the school. Dr. Snydman looked at my eye and told me I was fine, it had healed perfectly, I could read now, play ball, swim, do whatever I wanted, just so long as I didn't try to stop a fast ball anymore with my head. My father's eyes were misty when we left the office, and I cried a little during the trolley ride to school. We stood outside the school, my father kissed my forehead and said thank God that it had all ended well, and now he had to go to his class, he had already missed one class today because of the doctor's appointment and the students were probably making the substitute teacher's life miserable. I grinned, then nodded when he told me to go to my class. He went off. As I climbed the stairs to the second floor, I realized I had forgotten to ask Dr. Snydman about Billy. I decided I would call Billy later in the week after my exams, and go over to see him.

That was a busy week. The final exams began that Monday afternoon. It was wonderful to be able to read and write again, and I didn't mind it at all that my first reading and writing in fifteen days was being done over final examinations. It was a kind of wild, soaring experience to be able to hold a pen again and look into a book or at a piece of paper with writing on it. I took my exams and enjoyed them immensely.

I didn't see Danny that entire week. He called me on

Wednesday night, sounding sad, and we talked for a while. I asked him what he would be doing that summer, and he told me he always stayed home in the summer, studying Talmud. He added that he would probably also be reading Freud this summer. I said I would come over to his house that Shabbat and we could talk some more then, I was busy now studying for finals, and I hung up. His voice had been quiet, subdued, and I wondered if he had been reading any more books on Hasidism.

I took the last exam on Friday morning, and then the year was over; I was free until September. I wasn't worried about my grades. I knew I had done well.

When I came home from school early Friday afternoon, Manya asked me if I was hungry, and I said yes, I could eat a horse, a kosher horse, of course, and she quickly put a lunch on the table. My father came in a few minutes later and joined me. There had been a terrible storm in Europe that entire week, he told me, and it had hurt the invasion, but it was over now, thank God. I hadn't heard anything about it, I had been so busy with my exams.

My father left right after lunch, and I went over to the telephone to call Billy. I found his father's name in the phone book and dialed the number.

"Hello," a man's voice said.

"Mr. Merrit?"

"That's right."

"This is Reuven Malter, sir."

"Who?"

"Reuv—Bobby Malter. I had the bed next to Billy in the hospital."

"Oh, yes. Yes. Bobby Malter."

"Do you remember me, sir?"

"Of course. Of course I remember you."

"How is Billy, sir?"

There was a pause.

"Sir?"

"Yes?"

"Is Billy all right?"

"I'm afraid not. The surgery was not successful."

I felt myself break out into a cold sweat. The hand holding

the phone began to tremble and I had to push the phone against my face to keep it steady.

"Hello?"

"Yes, sir."

"How is *your* eye, Bobby?"

"It's fine, sir. It's all healed."

"I'm happy to hear that. No, Billy's surgery was not successful."

"I'm awfully sorry to hear that, sir."

There was another pause. I thought I could hear Mr. Merrit breathing into the phone.

"Sir?"

"Yes?"

"May I come over to visit Billy?"

"Billy is in Albany with friends of mine. My company has transferred me to Albany. We're being moved out today."

I didn't say anything.

"Goodbye, Bobby. I'm glad your eye is all right. Be careful with your eyes."

"Yes, sir. Goodbye."

I hung up the phone and stood still for a minute, trying to calm myself. It didn't do any good. I went into my room and sat by the window for a while. I opened a book, stared at it blankly, then closed it. I kept hearing Mr. Savo saying, "Crazy world. Cockeyed." I began to wander aimlessly through the rooms of the apartment. My hands were freezing. I went out onto the porch, sat in the lounge chair, and stared across the yard at the ailanthus. Its leaves were bathed in sunlight, and its musky odor reached me faintly in the breeze that blew against the back of the house. Something moved faintly across the edge of the field of vision of my left eye, but I ignored it and kept staring at the sunlight on the ailanthus leaves. It moved again, and I heard a faint buzzing sound. I turned my head and looked at the wooden rail of the porch. A spider had spun a web across the corner of the upper rail, and there was a housefly trapped in it now, its wings spread-eagled, glued to the strands of the web, its legs flaying the air frantically. I saw its black body arching wildly, and then it managed to get its wings free, and there was the buzzing sound again as the wings struggled to free the body to which they were attached. Then the wings were trapped again by the filmy, almost invisible strands of the web, and the black legs kicked at the air. I saw the spider, a small, gray, furry-looking spider, with long, wispy legs and black eyes, move across the web toward the fly. I rose from the chair and went over to the web. The fly's tiny black legs flayed the air fiercely, then its wings were free again, buzzing noisily, but its body remained glued fast. I bent and blew hard against the web. It swayed, but remained intact. I blew again, harder now, and the strands seemed suddenly to melt. The fly fell on its back to the wooden floor of the porch, righted itself, then flew off, buzzing loudly. The spider tumbled from the broken web, hung by a single strand a few inches above the floor, then swiftly climbed the strand, scrambled across the top front rail of the porch, and disappeared. I went back to the lounge chair, sat down, and continued to stare at the sunlight on the ailanthus.

CHAPTER TEN
✛✛✛✛✛✛✛✛✛✛✛✛✛✛✛✛

DANNY AND I were together almost every day during the first month of that summer. It was a hot, humid month, with a fierce summer sun that left a heat shimmer over the streets and softened the asphalt. Manya was forever muttering about the streaks of black tar that clung to my shoes and sneakers and rubbed off on the floor of the apartment.

Danny spent his mornings studying Talmud, either alone or with his father, while I spent Monday, Wednesday, and Friday mornings playing ball with my yeshiva friends, none of whom seemed to be bothered by my friendship with Danny—they accepted it and just didn't talk about it—and Sunday, Tuesday, and Thursday mornings studying Talmud with my father, either on our back porch when it was a nice day or in his study when it was not. My father and I were studying *Sanhedrin*—slowly, patiently, intensively, not leaving a passage until my father was satisfied that, at least for the present, we understood it fully. Often, we were only able to do about ten lines at a time. Danny, on the other hand, had his daily Talmud goal increased to three blatt by his father. It didn't seem to affect him very much; he was still able to spend all his afternoons on the third floor of the library, reading. I joined him there every afternoon, and frequently my father came with me. He was writing another article, on a passage in *Avodah Zarah*, which, he said, he was only now beginning to understand, and he needed one of the journal collections. So the three of us sat there in the afternoons, reading or talking quietly, until it was time for supper. Once I invited Danny to come home and eat with us, but he refused the invitation with a lame excuse, looking a little embarrassed. On our way home, my father told me that Danny probably didn't eat anywhere except in his own home, or in the home of one of his father's followers, because of kash-ruth, and that it would be wise for me not to embarrass him again with another invitation.

On Shabbat afternoons I would walk to Danny's house. Danny would take me up to his father's study, and we would all do battle again over the Talmud. Then would come the glass of tea, the Afternoon Service, the ritual of the contest —Danny didn't once miss finding his father's deliberate er-rors—the Evening Service, and the Havdalah. Reb Saunders didn't talk to me again about Danny's reading, but I knew he was bothered by it terribly. I could tell from the occasional silence that filled the study while Danny would be downstairs getting the tea. And Danny didn't talk about it, either. He just went on reading.

Only the evenings were unscheduled. We sort of played them by ear, as Mr. Galanter might have said, deciding dur-ing the afternoon whether we would spend the evening walk-ing, or in my house or his, or alone. Often, I went to the movies either with my father or with some of my school friends. Danny never went to the movies. They were forbid-den by his father, he said.

My father and I followed the war news very carefully, and there were now many more *New York Times* maps on the wall of my room. From the fourth to the tenth of July there was a violent battle in the La-Haye-du-Puits area. A panzer counterattack west of the Vire was smashed on the eleventh of July, but the American drive toward St.-Lô was stopped by a German parachute corps. Caen was finally captured, and then on the eighteenth of July St.-Lô fell. A war correspond-ent triumphantly announced that the lodgment area from which the Allied Armies would soon launch their major of-fensive into the heart of occupied France was now adequate and secure.

My father and I listened to the news broadcasts, read the *Times,* and studied the maps. It seemed to us that, despite the many announcements of victories, the war was going very slowly. My father looked grim as he studied the war maps that showed the Allied advance between D day and the third week of July. Then the weather in France changed, and the war seemed to have come to a complete halt, swallowed by endless rain.

In the beginning of the third week of July, my father's research for the article he was writing made it necessary for him to travel to the library of the Jewish Theological Seminary in Manhattan. There were manuscripts there which he needed for the purpose of checking variant readings of the Talmudic passage on which he was working. So every day that week right after lunch he took the subway to Manhattan, and I went alone to the library to be with Danny. That was the week Danny began to read Freud in German.

It was difficult for him at first, and he admitted it openly. Not only was the language still a problem but also the terminology and ideas he encountered were strange and bewildering to him. This wasn't Graetz on Jewish history, he told me, or Minkin on Hasidism, or Hemingway, Fitzgerald, Dreiser, and Dickens. It wasn't even the Ogden and Flügel psychology books he had been reading. This was primary source material, research papers based on direct experimental data, involved theoretical constructions utilizing a complex vocabulary and containing a wealth of original ideas—and he was breaking his head on it.

I listened to him talk and felt a little awed by it all. Five or so weeks ago, he had talked of the unconscious and of dreams almost as a child talks about his first tricycle. Now he was talking about direct experimental data and involved theoretical constructions.

He spent the first part of that third week in July leafing through a collection of Freud's writings—to get a taste of the material, he said—while I sat opposite him, trying to make my way through the first volume of *Principia Mathematica* and finally giving it up as too difficult and settling for a re-reading of the article my math teacher had recommended in the *Journal of Symbolic Logic*—it was called "Conditions Affecting the Application of Symbolic Logic," and I understood it a lot better this time—and for a book on logic by Susanne K. Langer. The first sections of the book were a little too easy for me, but the final chapter on logistics, in which she showed how *Principia Mathematica* provides a basis from which the concepts, operations, and relations of arithmetic and other branches of mathematics may be derived, I found to be very exciting.

By Thursday, Danny's side of the table was piled high with

books, and he was looking thoroughly unhappy. He was sitting there, twisting an earlock and biting his lower lip, his face a mask of frustration. It was impossible, he said finally. The whole thing was ridiculous and impossible; he wasn't getting anywhere. It wasn't so much the German itself anymore as the technical terminology. He wasn't making any headway at all. Not only that, but he had begun to use English translations of the German works he had been reading, and they did nothing but confuse him even more. He showed me where in one translation the German word *"Unlust"* had been translated as "pain," in quotations marks, and the word *"Schmerz"* had been translated as "pain," without quotation marks. How was he supposed to know what the translator had had in mind when he had used "pain" with and "pain" without quotation marks? And look at the word *"Besetzung,"* he said angrily. What did it mean to translate it as "investment" or "charge"? And what good did it do to translate it as "cathexis"? What did "cathexis" mean? *"Angst"* was "anxiety," *"Furcht"* was "fear," *"Schreck"* was "fright." How was he supposed to know what the difference between "fear" and "fright" was? He wasn't getting anywhere, he would probably have to drop the whole thing; who did he think he was anyway trying to read Freud at the age of fifteen? He went home angry and disgusted, his face a picture of bewildered frustration.

When I got to Danny's house that Shabbat afternoon, I found him in an ugly mood. He was waiting for me outside. He greeted me with a curt nod of his head and muttered something about not really being in the mood for Talmud now but we had to go up anyway. He was very quiet during the first few minutes of the Talmud battle, and though I tried to make up for his silence by increasing the volume of my own enthusiasm, I could see that Reb Saunders was becoming more and more annoyed by his son's lack of participation. Danny was tense and edgy, his face still masked by frustration, his mind obviously not on what we were discussing. He's probably eating himself up alive over Freud, I thought, hoping his father wouldn't lose his temper. But Reb Saunders remained patient and left his son alone.

In the middle of a heated debate over an impossible passage in *Kiddushin* I heard Danny take a sudden loud breath,

as if he had been punched in the stomach. Reb Saunders and I
broke off our discussion and looked at him. He was staring
down at the Talmud, and smiling. His face had come to life,
and there was a light in his eyes. He jumped up from his
chair, circled the room, then sat down again, and Reb Saunders and I just sat there, staring at him. Something is the
matter? Reb Saunders wanted to know. There is a joke in the
Talmud we did not see? What was so funny? Danny shook
his head, still smiling, bent over the Talmud, and began to
give his version of the passage. His voice trembled a little.
There was a pause when he finished, and I thought for a moment that Reb Saunders would again ask his son what had
been so funny. Instead, I heard him sigh a little, then offer a
brief passage from *Baba Bathra* that contradicted Danny's explanation. We returned to the battle, and Danny more than
made up for his previous silence.

He was quiet as he walked me part of the way home that
night, and when we got to the synagogue where my father
and I prayed he muttered something about seeing me in the
library the next day, then turned and went quickly back.

When I got to the library the next afternoon, I found him
seated at his table. There were three books open in front of
him. He smiled broadly and waved me to a chair. He had
worked out a method of doing Freud, he said, and seemed to
be going all right, so far. He pointed to the three books. One
was a volume of Freud's early papers, he told me. Some of
them Freud had written together with Josef Breuer, a Vi-
ennese physician; others he had written alone. Another was
the Cassell's German-English Dictionary. The third was a
dictionary of psychological terms edited by someone called
Warren. The Freud volume was open to a paper entitled *"Ein
Fall Von Hypnotischer Heilung."* *"Fall"* meant "case," he
said. The rest of the title I could figure out for myself from
my Yiddish, he told me.

"I forgot what it was like to study Talmud," he said excitedly. "Talmud is so easy for me now, I didn't remember what
I used to go through when I first started it as a kid. Can you
study Talmud without the commentaries? Imagine Talmud
without Rashi. How far would you get?"

I agreed with him that I wouldn't get very far at all.

He had been going at it all wrong, he said, his eyes bright

with excitement. He had wanted to *read* Freud. That had been his mistake. Freud had to be *studied*, not read. He had to be studied like a page of Talmud. And he had to be studied with a commentary.

But Danny didn't know of any commentaries on Freud, so he had settled for the next best thing. He had needed something that would explain Freud's technical terminology, that would clarify the various shades of meaning the German words had—and he had found this dictionary of psychological terms. He was reading Freud now sentence by sentence. He didn't go on to the next sentence until the prior sentence was perfectly clear in his mind. If he came across a German word he did not know, he looked up its English meaning in the Cassell's. If the Cassell's gave him a translation he didn't understand, one that wouldn't fit the meaning of the sentence, he looked the English word up in the psychology dictionary. That psychological dictionary was his commentary. It had, for example, already explained to him the technical difference between "fear" and "fright." It had also explained the term "cathexis." It was working. He had already studied two and a half pages that afternoon.

Was Freud worth all that effort? I wanted to know.

Freud was a genius, Danny told me. Of course he was worth all that effort. Was symbolic logic worth all my effort?

I had nothing to say to that, except admit that he was probably right.

So I continued reading the Langer book, while Danny bent over the table studying Freud. He shuffled pages impatiently whenever he had to look something up in one of his dictionaries. The sounds of the shuffling pages were loud in the silence of the library.

On Thursday, I told him that my father and I would be leaving next Tuesday morning for the cottage near Peekskill where we always stayed in August, and I gave him two books I thought he might like to read. One was *The Making of the Modern Jew* by Milton Steinberg, the other was *The Nineteen Letters of Ben Uzziel* by Samson Raphael Hirsch. He thanked me and said he would read them. When my father and I left for Peekskill on Tuesday morning, Danny had completed the first paper and was started on the second, entitled *"Die Abwehr-Neuropsychosen."* We had agreed not to

write to each other—probably out of an unspoken feeling
that two boys our age writing one another when we were
only going to be separated for a month was a little childish
—and I didn't see him again until after Labor Day.

My father and I returned home the day after Labor Day,
and I called Danny immediately. His mother answered and
told me she was delighted I had had a good vacation but she
was sorry, Danny wasn't home, he had gone with his father
to visit a family friend in Lakewood. Danny called me later
that evening, happy to hear I was back. He had missed me,
he said. How was the trip to Lakewood? I wanted to know.
Miserable, he said. Had I ever sat in a bus with my father for
hours and not exchanged a single word of conversation, except for a short discussion about a passage of Talmud? No, I
told him quietly, I had never had that kind of experience. I
always talked to my father. I was lucky, he said. I didn't
know how really lucky I was, he added, a little bitterly.

We chatted for a while, and agreed to meet in the library
the following afternoon. I found him at his table, looking a
little pale, but happy. His tufts of beard had grown a bit
thicker, he blinked his eyes a little too often, as if weary
from all his reading, but otherwise he was the same, everything was the same, and it was as though we had not seen
each other for, at most, a single night of dream-filled sleep.
Yes, he had read the two books I had given him. They had
been very good, and he had learned a lot from them about
the problems of contemporary Judaism. His father had
thrown some poisonous looks at him when he had taken
them into the house, but the looks had disappeared when
Danny had somehow gotten up the courage to tell him that
the books had come from Reuven Malter. He would give
them back to me tomorrow. He had also read a great deal
of Freud, he said. He had finished almost all of the first volume, and he wanted to talk to me about a paper of Freud's
called *"Die Sexualität in der Ätiologie der Neurosen."* It had
been something of a shock to him to read that, he said, and
he had no one else to talk to about it except me, he didn't
want to discuss it with my father. I said fine, we could talk
about it on Shabbat when I came over to his house.

But somehow we never got around to talking about it that

Shabbat, and on Sunday morning we were both back in school again. The year—the real year of a person going to school—began, and for a long while I had no time at all to think about, let alone discuss, the writings of Sigmund Freud.

CHAPTER ELEVEN
✚✚✚✚✚✚✚✚✚✚✚✚✚✚✚✚✚✚✚✚✚

FOR THE FIRST TWO MONTHS of that school year, Danny and I were able to get together regularly only on Shabbat afternoons. Only once did we manage to see each other during the week. I had been elected president of my class, and I found myself suddenly involved in student politics. The evenings that I might have spent with Danny I spent instead at student council or committee meetings. We talked frequently by phone, though, and neither of us felt our friendship was suffering any. But we never got around to discussing what he was reading in Freud.

During November, I managed to go over to his house one evening in the middle of the week. I brought him a half a dozen books on Jewish subjects that my father had suggested he read, and he thanked me for them gratefully. He looked a little weary, but otherwise he was fine—except for his eyes, which tired easily, he said. He had been to a doctor, but he didn't need glasses, so everything was really all right. I asked him how he was coming along with Freud, and he said, looking uncomfortable, that he was rarely in the library these days, there was too much schoolwork, but he did manage to read a little of Freud now and then, and it had become very upsetting.

"One of these days I want to have a long talk with you about it," he told me, blinking his eyes.

But we had no real opportunity for any long talk. The Shabbat day grew shorter and shorter, my schoolwork seemed endless, and student politics took up every moment of my spare time.

And then, in the middle of December, just when it seemed that the war would be over very soon, the Germans launched a major offensive in the Ardennes region, and the Battle of the Bulge began. There were reports of frightful American casualties—some newspaper said that two thousand American soldiers were being killed and wounded every day.

It was a cold, bitter winter in New York, bleak with the news of the fighting in the Ardennes, and at night, as I sat working at my desk, I could hear the radio in the kitchen where my father would be sitting with his war maps, following the news.

The Battle of the Bulge ended about the middle of January, with the newspapers reporting seventy-seven thousand Allied casualties and one hundred twenty thousand German casualties.

Throughout the entire month of that battle—from the middle of December to the middle of January—I did not see Danny once. We spoke on the phone a few times; he told me his brother was sick again and might have to spend some time in a hospital. But the next time I called him his brother was all right—the doctor had changed his pills, Danny said, and that seemed to work. He sounded tired and sad, and once or twice I could barely hear his voice over the phone. The Battle of the Bulge? Yes, he said vaguely, a terrible business. When was I coming over to see him? As soon as I could breathe a little, I said. He said not to wait too long, he needed to talk to me. Was it very important? I wanted to know. No, it could wait, it wasn't *very* important, he said, sounding sad.

So it waited. It waited through my midyear exams and through the first two weeks of February, when I managed to get to Danny's house twice and we fought our customary Talmud battles together with his father but didn't get a chance to be alone long enough for us to talk. And then the news of the war in Europe suddenly reached a peak of feverish excitement. The Russians captured Königsberg and Breslau and came within thirty miles of Berlin, and at the end of the first week in March American troops reached the Rhine River at Remagen and discovered, to their astonishment, that the Ludendorff Bridge had, for some reason, not been destroyed by the Germans. My father almost wept with joy when we heard the news. There had been talk of bloody battles and high casualties in crossing the Rhine. Instead, American troops poured across the bridge, the Remagen beachhead was

quickly enlarged and held against German counterattacks—
and everyone began to talk of the war ending in two months.

My father and I were overjoyed, and even Danny, whom I
saw again in the middle of March and who generally took
little interest in the details of the war, began to sound excited.

"It is the end of Hitler, may his name and memory be
erased," Reb Saunders said to me that Shabbat afternoon.
"Master of the Universe, it has taken so long, but now the
end is here."

And he trembled as he said it and was almost in tears.

Danny caught the flu in the last week of March and was in
bed for more than a week. During that time, the Saar and
Silesia were taken, the Ruhr was encircled by American
troops, and another bridgehead was formed across the Rhine
by soldiers of General Patton's army. Almost every day now
there were rumors that the war had ended. But each rumor
proved to be false and did nothing but add to the already in-
tolerable anxiety and suspense my father and I were feeling
as we read the papers and listened to the radio.

Danny returned to school at the end of the first week in
April, apparently too soon, for he was back in bed two days
later with bronchitis. I called his mother to ask if I could visit
him, but she said, no, he was too sick, and besides what he
had was contagious, even his brother and sister weren't permitted into his room. I asked if I could speak to him, but she
told me he was running a high fever and could not could not
leave his bed to come to the phone. She sounded worried. He
was coughing a great deal, she told me, and was exhausted
from the sulfa he was taking. Yes, she would give him my
wishes for his speedy recovery.

On the Thursday afternoon of the second week in April, I
was sitting at a meeting of the student council. The meeting
had started pleasantly enough with the usual reading of the
minutes and committee reports, when Davey Cantor burst
into the room, looking as though he was crying, and shouted
breathlessly that someone had just told him President Roosevelt was dead.

He was standing by the open door of the classroom, and
there was a sudden movement of heads as everyone turned
and gaped at him in total astonishment. I had been in the

middle of a sentence, and I turned, too, remaining on my feet next to my desk, and I heard myself saying angrily that he had a hell of a nerve barging in here like that, he wasn't being one bit funny.

"It's true!" he shouted, crying. "Mr. Weinberg just told me! He heard it on the radio in the faculty room!"

I stared at him and felt myself slide slowly back onto my desk. Mr. Weinberg taught English. He was a short, bald man, with no sense of humor, and his motto was "Believe nothing of what you hear and only half of what you see." If Mr. Weinberg had told Davey Cantor that President Roosevelt was dead . . .

I found myself in a sudden cold sweat. Someone in the room giggled, someone else moaned, "Oh, no!" and our faculty advisor stood up and suggested that the meeting be adjourned.

We left the building and came out onto the street. All the way down the three flights of stairs I wouldn't believe it. I couldn't believe it. It was like God dying. Davey Cantor had said something about a cerebral hemorrhage. I didn't believe it. Until I got to the street.

It was a little after five o'clock, and there was still sunlight. The late afternoon traffic was heavy. Trucks, cars and a trolley choked the street, waiting for the corner light to change. I crossed quickly, ran for the trolley, and made it just as the light changed. I found a seat next to a middle-aged lady who sat staring straight ahead, weeping silently. I looked around. No one in the trolley was talking. It was crowded, and it became more crowded as it went along, but there was only the silence inside. I saw one man put his hands over his eyes and just sit there like that for a while. I stared out the window. People stood around in small groups on the sidewalks. They didn't seem to be talking. They just stood there, together, like an animal herd bunching up for protection. An old gray-haired woman, walking with a child, held a handkerchief to her mouth. I saw the child look up at her and say something, but I couldn't hear it. I found myself crying too, and felt a gnawing emptiness, as though I had been scraped clean inside and there was nothing in me now but a terrible darkness. I was feeling as though it had been my father who had died.

The whole ride home was like that: silence in the trolley

car, weeping men and women, groups of people standing about dazedly in the streets, little children looking bewildered and wondering what had happened.

Manya and my father were home. I heard the radio in the kitchen as I opened the door, quickly put my books in my room, and joined them. Manya was cooking supper, and sobbing. My father was sitting at the table, his face ashen, his cheeks hollow, his eyes red, looking as he had when he had visited me in the hospital. I sat at the table and listened to the news announcer. He was talking in a hushed voice and giving details of President Roosevelt's death. Harry S Truman was now President of the United States. I sat there and listened and couldn't believe it. How could President Roosevelt die? I had never even thought of him as being mortal. And to die now, especially now, when the war was almost over, when there was to be a meeting soon of the new United Nations. How could a man like that die?

We ate our supper listening to the radio—something we had never done before; my father never liked to have the radio on during a meal. But it was on during that meal and every other meal we ate that entire weekend—except for the Shabbat—and it stayed on every moment either my father or Manya or I was home.

I tried calling Danny on Friday afternoon, but he was still too sick to come to the phone. My father and I spent Shabbat morning in the synagogue, where the pain of death showed itself clearly on every face, and where my friends and I just stood around aimlessly after the service, not knowing what to say. My father began to cough again, the deep, dry, racking cough that shook his frail body and frightened me terribly. On Shabbat afternoon, he talked of President Roosevelt, of the hope he had brought to the country during the Depression.

"You do not remember the Depression, Reuven," he told me. "Those were terrible days, black days. It is impossible to believe he is gone. It is like when—" His voice broke, and he was suddenly sobbing. I stared at him, feeling helpless and terrified. He went into his bedroom and stayed there the rest of the afternoon, and I lay on my bed, staring up at the ceiling, my hands clasped behind my head, trying to grasp what had happened. I couldn't. I saw only emptiness and fear and a kind of sudden, total end to things that I had never experienced before. I lay on my bed and thought about it a long time. It was senseless, as—I held my breath, feeling myself shiver with fear—as Billy's blindness was senseless. That was it. It was as senseless, as empty of meaning, as Billy's blindness. I lay there and thought of Roosevelt being dead and Billy being blind, and finally I turned over and lay with my face on the pillow and felt myself crying. I cried a long time. Then I slept fitfully. When I woke, the room was dark, and I heard the radio going again in the kitchen. I lay on the bed a while, then joined my father. We sat together in the kitchen. It was after midnight when we went to sleep.

The next day, President Roosevelt was buried. Our school was closed for the funeral, and my father and I sat in the kitchen all that day and listened to the radio.

Danny called me a few hours after the funeral. He sounded tired, and he coughed a good deal. But his temperature was down to normal, he said, and had been normal for twenty-four hours now. Yes, Roosevelt's death was a terrible thing, he said. His parents were all right. His brother was sick, though. He was running a high fever, and coughing. Could I come over during the week? he asked me. I didn't think so. Could I come over on Saturday, then? Yes, I could. I would see him on Shabbat, I said. He sounded relieved when we hung up, and I wondered what was happening.

But on Wednesday I came home from school with a fever, and by Thursday afternoon I was running 103.6. The doctor called it the flu and warned my father to keep me in bed or there might be complications. I asked my father to call Danny and tell him. I was in bed for ten days, and when I finally got back to school I found I had missed so much work that for two weeks I dropped all my student council activities and spent every moment I had catching up. I used Shabbat afternoons for reading, and by the first week of May I had caught up enough to be able to begin attending student council meetings again. Then Reb Saunders became ill, and at the same time my father also took to his bed with the flu, a severe case that bordered on pneumonia for a while and frightened me terribly. Both Reb Saunders and my father were quite ill on the day in May when word finally came that the war in Europe was over.

I was with my father when we heard the news over the
radio in his bedroom.

"Thank God!" my father said, his eyes wet with joy.
"What a price to have paid for Hitler and his madmen!" And
he lay back on the pillow and closed his eyes.

And then, together with the official report of the signing of
the unconditional surrender on May 7, there came the news, at
first somewhat guarded, then, a few days later, clear and outspoken, of the German concentration camps. My father, recuperating slowly and looking worn and weary, sat in his bed
propped on pillows, and read the newspaper stories of the
horrors that had occurred in those camps. His face was grim
and ashen. He seemed unable to believe what he was reading.

It was while my father read to me an account of what had
happened at Teresienstadt, where the Germans had impris-
oned and murdered European Jews of culture and learning,
that I saw him break down and weep like a child.

I didn't know what to say. I saw him lie back on his pillows and cover his face with his hands. Then he asked me to
leave him alone, and I walked out and left him there, crying,
and went to my room.

I just couldn't grasp it. The numbers of Jews slaughtered
had gone from one million to three million to four million,
and almost every article we read said that the last count was
still incomplete, the final number would probably reach six
million. I couldn't begin to imagine six million of my people
murdered. I lay in my bed and asked myself what sense it
made. It didn't make any sense at all. My mind couldn't hold
on to it, to the death of six million people.

Danny called me a few days later, and I went over to his
house the next Shabbat afternoon. We did not study Talmud.
Instead, his father talked of the Jewish world in Europe, of
the people he had known who were now probably dead, of
the brutality of the world, of his years in Russia with the
Cossack bands looting and plundering.

"The world kills us," he said quietly. "Ah, how the world
kills us."

We were sitting in his study, and he was in his straight-
backed chair. His face was lined with suffering. His body
swayed slowly back and forth, and he talked in a quiet singsong, calling up the memories of his youth in Russia and tell-

ing us of the Jewish communities of Poland, Lithuania, Russia, Germany, and Hungary—all gone now into heaps of bones and ashes. Danny and I sat silent and listened to him talk. Danny was pale and seemed tense and distraught. He tugged constantly at an earlock, his eyes blinking nervously.

"How the world drinks our blood," Reb Saunders said. "How the world makes us suffer. It is the will of God. We must accept the will of God." He was silent for a long moment. Then he raised his eyes and said softly. "Master of the Universe, how do you permit such a thing to happen?"

The question hung in the air like a sigh of pain.

Danny could not walk me back that night, he had too much schoolwork to do, so I went home alone and found my father in his bedroom, listening to the radio. He was in pajamas, and he wore his small black skullcap. The announcer was talking about the United Nations. I sat in a chair and listened, and when the news program was over my father turned off the radio and looked at me.

"How is Reb Saunders?" he asked quietly.

I told him what Reb Saunders had talked about that afternoon.

My father nodded slowly. He was pale and gaunt, and his skin had a yellowish tint to it and was parchmentlike on his face and hands.

"Reb Saunders wanted to know how God could let something like his happen," I told him quietly.

My father looked at me, his eyes somber.

"And did God answer him?" he asked. His voice had a strange quality of bitterness to it.

I didn't say anything.

"Did God answer him, Reuven?" my father asked again, that same bitterness in his voice.

"Reb Saunders said it was God's will. We have to accept God's will, he said."

My father blinked his eyes. "Reb Saunders said it was God's will," he echoed softly.

I nodded.

"You are satisfied with that answer, Reuven?"

"No."

He blinked his eyes again, and when he spoke his voice was soft, the bitterness gone. "I am not satisfied with it, either, Reuven. We cannot wait for God. If there is an answer, we must make it ourselves."

I was quiet.

"Six million of our people have been slaughtered," he went on quietly. "It is inconceivable. It will have meaning only if we give it meaning. We cannot wait for God." He lay back on the pillows. "There is only one Jewry left now in the world," he said softly, staring up at the ceiling. "It is here, in America. We have a terrible responsibility. We must replace the treasures we have lost." His voice was hoarse, and he coughed. Then he was quiet for a long time. I saw him close his eyes, and I heard him say, "Now we will need teachers and rabbis to lead our people." He opened his eyes and looked at me. "The Jewish world is changed," he said, almost in a whisper. "A madman has destroyed our treasures. If we do not rebuild Jewry in America, we will die as a people." Then he closed his eyes again and was silent.

My father recovered slowly, and it was only at the end of May that he was able to return to his teaching.

Two days after I took my final examination, he suffered a heart attack. He was rushed by ambulance to the Brooklyn Memorial Hospital and put into a semiprivate room one floor below the eye ward. Manya took care of me during the first nightmarish days of blind panic when my mind collapsed and would not function. Then Reb Saunders called me one night and invited me to live in his house while my father recovered. How could I live alone with only a housekeeper to care for me? he wanted to know. Why should I stay alone in the apartment at night? Who knew, God forbid, what could happen? It was terrible for a boy my age to be left alone. They could put another bed in Danny's room, and I could sleep there. When I told my father, he said it would be wise for me to accept the offer. And he told me to tell Reb Saunders how grateful he was to him for his kindness.

On the first day of July I packed a bag and took a cab to Reb Saunders' house. I moved into Danny's room.

CHAPTER TWELVE
✢✢✢✢✢✢✢✢✢✢✢✢✢✢✢✢✢✢✢✢✢✢✢✢

FROM THE DAY I entered Reb Saunders' house to the day I left to go with my father to our cottage near Peekskill where he was to convalesce, I was a warmly accepted member of Danny's family. Danny's mother, who had some kind of heart condition and needed to rest frequently, was forever adding food to my plate. Danny's sister, I noticed for the first time, was a very pretty girl, with dark eyes and long dark hair combed back into a single braid, and vivacious hands that seemed always in motion when she spoke. She was forever teasing Danny and me and referring to us as David and Jonathan. Danny's brother, Levi, was forever poking at his food when he sat at the kitchen table, or walking ghostlike around the house, picking his nose. And Danny's father was forever silent, withdrawn, his dark eyes turned inward, brooding, as if witnessing a sea of suffering he alone could see. He walked bent forward, as though there were some kind of enormous burden on his shoulders. Dark circles had formed around his eyes, and sometimes at the kitchen table I would see him begin to cry suddenly, and he would get up and walk out of the room, then return a few minutes later and resume eating. No one in the family talked about these sudden moments of weeping. And I didn't either, though they frightened and bewildered me.

Danny and I did everything together that month. We would rise a little before seven, go down to the synagogue to pray the Morning Service with the congregation, have breakfast with the family, then go out onto his porch if the day was nice, or stay in his room if it wasn't, and spend the morning studying Talmud. After lunch, we would go together to the library, where we would spend the early hours of the afternoon. Danny was reading Freud, and I was doing sym-

183

bolic logic. It was in the library that we did all the talking we had been unable to do during the year. Then, at about four o'clock, we would take the trolley together to the Brooklyn Memorial Hospital and visit my father. We would have supper together with Danny's family, then spend the evening either chatting with his sister and mother in the living room or reading quietly—Danny used the evenings to read the books on Jewish subjects I kept giving him—or, if his father was free, we would go up to the study and do battle over the Talmud. But Reb Saunders was rarely free. There seemed to be an endless number of people coming into the house and walking up the three flights of stairs to see him, and by the time we were ready for supper he was always visibly fatigued, and he would sit lost in thought, his eyes dark and brooding. And once, during a supper meal, I saw tears come slowly from his eyes and disappear into the tangle of the dark beard. He did not leave the table this time. He sat there, weeping in silence, and no one said anything. And then he dried his eyes with a handkerchief, took a deep, trembling breath, and went back to his food.

During the entire month I spent in Reb Saunders' house, the only time I ever saw him talk to Danny was when we argued over the Talmud. There was never any simple, intimate, human kind of conversation between him and his son. I almost had the impression that they were physically incapable of communicating with each other about ordinary things. It troubled me, but I said nothing about it.

Danny and I talked often about his reading of Freud. We sat at our table in the third floor of the library, surrounded by the mazelike stacks, and he told me what he had read during the past year and what he was reading now. Freud had clearly upset him in a fundamental kind of way—had thrown him off balance, as he once put it. But he couldn't stop reading him, he said, because it had become increasingly obvious to him that Freud had possessed an almost uncanny insight into the nature of man. And that was what Danny found upsetting. Freud's picture of man's nature was anything but complimentary, it was anything but religious. It tore man from God, as Danny put it, and married him off to Satan.

Danny knew enough about Freud now—his method of study had been so thoroughly successful—that he was able to use Freud's technical terminology with the same kind of natural ease that characterized our use of the technical terminology of the Talmud. For the first two weeks of July, Danny spent part of our reading time in the library patiently explaining to me some of Freud's basic concepts. We sat at our table, Danny in his dark suit—he wore a dark suit no matter how hot it was—his tieless shirt, his fringes, his skullcap, his long earlocks, and his beard, which was thick and full now, almost an adult beard, and me in my sport shirt, summer trousers, and skullcap, and we talked about Sigmund Freud. What I heard was new, so new that I couldn't grasp it at first. But Danny was patient, as patient as my father, and slowly I began to understand the system of psychological thought Freud had constructed. And I, too, became upset. Freud contradicted everything I had ever learned. What I found particularly upsetting was the fact that Danny didn't seem to have rejected what Freud taught. I began to wonder how it was possible for the ideas of the Talmud and the thinking of Freud to live side by side within one person. It seemed to me that one or the other would have to give way. When I told this to Danny, he shrugged, said nothing, and went back to his reading.

Had my father been well at that time, I would have talked to him about it, but he was in the hospital, recuperating slowly, and I didn't want to upset him with an account of Danny's reading. He was upset enough as it was with his own reading. Whenever Danny and I came to visit him, we found newspapers strewn all over his bed. He was reading everything he could find that told of the destruction of European Jewry. He talked of nothing else but European Jewry and the responsibility American Jews now carried. Occasionally he spoke of the importance of Palestine as a Jewish homeland, but mostly he was concerned about American Jewry and the need for teachers and rabbis. Once he asked Danny and me what we were reading these days, and Danny answered honestly that he was going through Freud. My father sat in his hospital bed, propped up on pillows, looked at him, and blinked. He had grown very thin—I hadn't thought he could ever get any thinner than he had been before his heart attack, but it seemed to me he had lost at least ten pounds—and he

seemed to become easily upset by little things. I was frightened for a moment, because I didn't want him to get involved
in an argument with Danny about Freud. But he only shook
his head and sighed. He was very tired, he said; he would
talk to Danny about Freud another time. Danny shouldn't
think that Freud was the final word in psychoanalysis; many
great thinkers disagreed with him. He let it go at that, and
went back to talking about the destruction of European
Jewry. Did we know, he asked us, that on December 17,
1942, Mr. Eden got up in the House of Commons and gave
the complete details of the Nazi plan, already in full operation, to massacre the entire Jewish population of Europe?
Did we know that Mr. Eden, though he had threatened the
Nazis with retribution, hadn't said a word about practical
measures to save as many Jews as possible from what he
knew would be their inevitable fate? There had been public
meetings in England, protests, petitions, letters—the whole
machinery of democratic expression had been set in motion
to impress upon the British Government the need for action
—and not a thing was done. Everyone was sympathetic, but
no one was sympathetic enough. The British let some few
Jews in, and then closed their doors. America hadn't cared
enough, either. No one had cared enough. The world closed
its doors, and six million Jews were slaughtered. What a
world! What an insane world! "What do we have left to us
now, if not American Jewry?" he said. "Some Jews say we
should wait for God to send the Messiah. We cannot wait for
God! We must make our own Messiah! We must rebuild
American Jewry! And Palestine must become a Jewish homeland! We have suffered enough! How long must we wait for
the Messiah?"

It was bad for my father to get excited that way, but there
was nothing I could do to stop him. He could talk of nothing
else but the destruction of European Jewry.

One morning at breakfast Reb Saunders came out of a
brooding silence, sighed, and for no apparent reason began
telling us, in a soft, singsong chant, the story of an old, pious
Hasid who had set out on a journey to Palestine—Eretz Yisroel, Reb Saunders called it, giving the land its traditional
name and accenting the "E" and the "ro"—so as to be able
to spend the last years of his life in the Holy Land. Finally,

he reached the Wailing Wall in Jerusalem, and three days later he died while praying at the Wall for the Messiah to come and redeem his people. Reb Saunders swayed slowly back and forth as he told the story, and when he was done I said quietly, not mentioning my father's name, that a lot of people were now saying that it was time for Palestine to become a Jewish homeland and not only a place where pious Jews went to die. The reaction on the part of the entire family was instantaneous; it was as though someone had thrown a match onto a pile of straw. I could almost feel the heat that replaced the family warmth around the table. Danny went rigid and stared down at the plate in front of him. His brother let out a little whimper, and his sister and mother seemed frozen to their chairs. Reb Saunders stared at me, his eyes suddenly wild with rage, his beard trembling. And he pointed a finger at me that looked like a weapon.

"Who are these people? Who are these people?" he shouted in Yiddish, and the words went through me like knives. "Apikorsim! Goyim! Ben Gurion and his goyim will build Eretz Yisroel? They will build for us a Jewish land? They will bring Torah into this land? Goyishkeit they will bring into the land, not Torah! God will build the land, not Ben Gurion and his goyim! When the Messiah comes, we will have Eretz Yisroel, a Holy Land, not a land contaminated by Jewish goyim!"

I sat there stunned and terrified, engulfed by his rage. His reaction had caught me so completely by surprise that I had quite literally stopped breathing, and now I found myself gasping for breath. I felt as if I were being consumed by flames. The silence that followed his outburst had a fungus quality to it, as though it were breeding malignancies, and I had the uncanny feeling that I had somehow been stripped naked and violated. I didn't know what to do or say. I just sat there and gaped at him.

"The land of Abraham, Isaac, and Jacob should be built by Jewish goyim, by contaminated men?" Reb Saunders shouted again. "Never! Not while I live! Who says these things? Who says *we* should now build Eretz Yisroel? And where is the Messiah? Tell me, we should forget completely about the Messiah? For this six million of our people were slaughtered? That we should forget completely about the Messiah, that we should forget completely about the Master of the Universe?

Why do you think I brought my people from Russia to
America and not to Eretz Yisroel? Because it is better to live
in a land of true goyim than to live in a land of Jewish
goyim! Who says *we* should build Eretz Yisroel, ah? I'll tell
you who says it! Apikorsim say it! Jewish goyim say it! True
Jews do not say such a thing!"

There was a long silence. Reb Saunders sat in his chair,
breathing hard and trembling with rage.

"Please, you should not get so angry," Danny's sister
pleaded softly. "It is bad for you."

"I'm sorry," I said lamely, not knowing what else to say.

"Reuven was not talking for himself," Danny's sister said
quietly to her father. "He was only—"

But Reb Saunders cut her off with an angry wave of his
hand. He went rigidly through the Grace, then left the
kitchen, wearing his rage visibly.

Danny's sister stared down at the table, her eyes dark and
sad.

Later, when Danny and I were alone in his room, Danny
told me to think ten thousand times the next time I wanted
to mention anything like that again to his father. His father
was fine, he said, until he was confronted by any idea that he
felt came from the contaminated world.

"How was I supposed to know that Zionism is a contaminated idea?" I said. "My God, I feel as if I've just been
through the seven gates of Hell."

"Herzl didn't wear a caftan and side curls," Danny said.
"Neither does Ben Gurion."

"You can't be serious."

"I'm not talking about myself. I'm talking about my father.
Just don't talk about a Jewish state anymore. My father takes
God and Torah very seriously, Reuven. He would die for
them both quite gladly. A secular Jewish state in my father's
eyes is a sacrilege, a violation of the Torah. You touched a
raw nerve. Please don't do it again."

"I'm glad I didn't mention it was my father who said it. He
might have thrown me out of the house."

"He *would* have thrown you out of the house," Danny said
grimly.

"Is he—is he feeling all right?"

"How do you mean?"

"The way he cries all the time like that. Is he—is something wrong?"

Danny's hand went slowly to an earlock, and I watched him tug at it nervously. "Six million Jews have died," he said. "He's—I think he's thinking of them. He's suffering for them."

I looked at him. "I thought he might be sick. I thought your sister said—"

"He's not sick," Danny broke in. He lowered his hand. "I —I really don't want to talk about it."

"All right," I said quietly. "But I don't think I want to study any Talmud this morning. I'm going to take a long walk."

He didn't say anything. But his face was sad and brooding as I went out of his room.

When I saw Reb Saunders again at lunch, he seemed to have forgotten the incident completely. But I found myself thinking carefully now before I said anything to him. And I was constantly on my guard with him from that time on.

During an afternoon in the last week of July, Danny began talking about his brother. We were sitting in the library, reading, when he suddenly looked up, rested his head in the palm of his right hand, the elbow on the table, and said his eyes were bothering him again and that he wouldn't be at all surprised if he ended up wearing glasses soon, his brother was having glasses made and he was only nine. I told him his brother didn't seem to be doing much reading, what did he need glasses for.

"It has nothing to do with reading," Danny said. "His eyes are just plain bad, that's all."

"Your eyes look bloodshot," I told him.

"They are bloodshot," he said.

"Your eyes look as if you've been reading Freud."

"Ha-ha," Danny said.

"What does Freud say about an ordinary thing like bloodshot eyes?"

"He says to rest them."

"A genius," I said.

"You know, my brother's a good kid," Danny said. "His sickness is quite a handicap, but everything considered he's a good kid."

"He's quiet, I'll say that for him. Does he study at all?"

"Oh, sure. He's bright, too. But he has to be careful. My father can't pressure him."

"Lucky boy."

"I don't know. I wouldn't want to be sick all my life. I'd much rather be pressured. He's a nice kid, though."

"Your sister's pretty nice, too," I said.

Danny didn't seem to have heard me—or if he had, he chose to ignore my words completely. He went on talking about his brother. "It must really be hell to walk around sick all the time and have to depend upon pills. He's really a sweet kid. And bright, too." He seemed to be rambling, and I wasn't quite sure I knew what he was trying to say. His next words jarred me. "He'd probably make a fine tzaddik," he said.

I looked at him. "How's that again?"

"I said my brother would probably make a fine tzaddik," Danny said quietly. "It occurred to me recently that if I didn't take my father's place I wouldn't be breaking the dynasty after all. My brother could take over. I had talked myself into believing that if I didn't take his place I would break the dynasty. I think I had to justify to myself having to become a tzaddik."

I was frightened and said tightly, "Your home hasn't blown up recently, so I take it you haven't told your father."

"No, I haven't. And I'm not going to, either. Not yet."

"When will you tell him? Because I'm going to be out of town that day."

"No," he said quietly. "I'm going to need you around that day."

"I was only kidding," I told him, feeling sick with dread.

"It also occurred to me recently that all my concern about my brother's health was a fake. I don't have much of a relationship with him at all. He's such a kid. I pity him a little, that's all. I was really concerned about his health because all along I've wanted him to be able to take my father's place. That was something, all right, when I realized that. How am I doing? Are you bored yet?"

"I'm bored stiff," I said. "I can't wait until the day you tell your father."

"You'll wait," Danny said tightly, blinking his eyes. "You'll wait, and you'll be around, too, because I'm going to need you."

"Let's talk about your sister for a change," I said.

"I heard you the first time. Let's not talk about my sister, if you don't mind. Let's talk about my father. You want to know how I feel about my father? I admire him. I don't know what he's trying to do to me with this weird silence that he's established between us, but I admire him. I think he's a great man. I respect him and trust him completely, which is why I think I can live with his silence. I don't know why I trust him, but I do. And I pity him, too. Intellectually, he's trapped. He was born trapped. I don't ever want to be trapped the way he's trapped. I want to be able to breathe, to think what I want to think, to say the things I want to say. I'm trapped now, too. Do you know what it's like to be trapped?"

I shook my head slowly.

"How could you possibly know?" Danny said. "It's the most hellish, choking, constricting feeling in the world. I scream with every bone in my body to get out of it. My mind cries to get out of it. But I can't. Not now. One day I will, though. I'll want you around on that day, friend. I'll *need* you around on that day."

I didn't say anything. We sat in silence a long time. Then Danny slowly closed the Freud book he had been reading.

"My sister's been promised," he told me quietly.

"What?"

"My father promised my sister to the son of one of his followers when she was two years old. It's an old Hasidic custom to promise children away. She'll be married when she reaches eighteen. I think we ought to go over and visit your father now."

That was the only time Danny and I ever talked about his sister.

A week later, I went up with my father to our cottage near Peekskill. While we were there, America destroyed Hiroshima and Nagasaki with atomic bombs, and the war with Japan came to an end.

I didn't tell my father about that last conversation I had with Danny, and I had many nightmares that year in which

Reb Saunders screamed at me that I had poisoned his son's mind.

That September Danny and I entered Hirsch College. I had grown to five feet nine inches, an inch shorter than Danny, and I was shaving. Danny hadn't changed much physically during his last year in high school. The only thing different about him was that he was now wearing glasses.

BOOK THREE

A word is worth one coin; silence is worth two.
—The Talmud

CHAPTER THIRTEEN
✳✳✳✳✳✳✳✳✳✳✳✳✳✳✳✳✳✳✳✳✳✳✳✳✳✳

BY THE END of our first week in college, Danny was feeling thoroughly miserable. He had discovered that psychology in the Samson Raphael Hirsch Seminary and College meant experimental psychology only, and that the chairman of the department, Professor Nathan Appleman, had an intense distaste for psychoanalysis in general and for Freud in particular.

Danny was quite vocal about his feelings toward Professor Appleman and experimental psychology. We would meet in the mornings in front of my synagogue and walk from there to the trolley, and for two months he did nothing during those morning trolley rides except talk about the psychology textbook he was reading—he didn't say "studying," he said "reading"—and the rats and mazes in the psychology laboratory. "The next thing you know they'll stick me with a behaviorist," he lamented. "What do rats and mazes have to do with the *mind?*"

I wasn't sure I knew what a behaviorist was, and I didn't want to make him more miserable by asking him. I felt a little sorry for him, mostly because I had found college to be exciting and was thoroughly enjoying my books and my teachers, while he seemed to be going deeper and deeper into misery.

The building that housed the college stood on Bedford Avenue. It was a six-story whitestone building, and it occupied half a block of a busy store-filled street. The noise of the traffic on the street came clearly through the windows and into our classrooms. Behind the college was a massive brownstone armory, and a block away, across the street, was a Catholic church with a huge cross on its lawn upon which was the crucified figure of Jesus. In the evenings, a green

spotlight shone upon the cross, and we could see it clearly
from the stone stairs in front of the college.

The street floor of the building consisted of administrative
offices, an auditorium, and a large synagogue, a section of
which contained chairs and long tables. The entire second
floor was a library, a beautiful library, with mazelike stacks
that reminded me of the third floor of the library in which
Danny and I had spent so much time together. It had bright
fluorescent lights—that didn't flicker or change color, I noticed immediately the first time I walked in—and a trained,
professional library staff. It also contained a large reading
room, with long tables, chairs, a superb collection of reference books, and an oil painting of Samson Raphael Hirsch
which was prominently displayed on a white wall—Hirsch
had been a well-known Orthodox rabbi in Germany during
the last century and had fought intelligently through his writings and preachings against the Jewish Reform movement of
his day. The third and fourth floors had white-painted, modern classrooms and large, well-equipped chemistry, physics
and biology laboratories. There were also classrooms on the
fifth floor, as well as a psychology laboratory, which contained rats, mazes, screens, and a variety of instruments for
the measuring of auditory and visual responses. The sixth
floor consisted of dormitory rooms for the out-of-town students.

It was a rigidly Orthodox school, with services three times
a day and with European-trained rabbis, many of them in
long, dark coats, all of them bearded. For the first part of the
day, from nine in the morning to three in the afternoon, we
studied only Talmud. From three-fifteen to six-fifteen or sev-
en-fifteen, depending on the schedule of classes we had chosen
for ourselves, we went through a normal college curriculum.
On Fridays from nine to one, we attended the college; on
Sundays, during that same time span, we studied Talmud.

I found that I liked this class arrangement very much; it
divided my work neatly and made it easy for me to concentrate separately upon Talmud and college subjects. The length
of the school day, though, was something else; I was frequently awake until one in the morning, doing homework.
Once my father came into my room at ten minutes to one,
found me memorizing the section on river flukes from my

biology textbook, asked me if I was trying to do four years of college all at once, and told me to go to bed right away. I went to bed—half an hour later, when I had finished the memorizing.

Danny's gloom and frustration grew worse day by day, despite the fact that the students in his Talmud class looked upon him with open-mouthed awe. He had been placed in Rav Gershenson's class, the highest in the school, and I had been placed one class below. He was the talk of the Talmud Department by the end of two weeks and the accepted referee of all Talmudic arguments among the students. He was also learning a great deal from Rav Gershenson, who, as Danny put it, loved to spend at least three days on every two lines he taught. He had quickly become the leader of the few Hasidic students in the school, the ones who walked around wearing dark suits, tieless shirts, beards, fringes, and earlocks. About half of my high school class had entered the college, and I became friendly enough with many of the other non-Hasidic students. I didn't mix much with the Hasidim, but the extent to which they revered Danny was obvious to everyone. They clung to him as though he were the reincarnation of the Besht, as though he were their student tzaddik, so to speak. But none of this made him too happy; none of it was able to offset his frustration over Professor Appleman, who, by the time the first semester ended, had him so thoroughly upset that he began to talk about majoring in some other subject. He just couldn't see himself spending four years running rats through mazes and checking human responses to blinking lights and buzzing sounds, he told me. He had received a B for his semester's work in psychology because he had messed up some math equations on the final examination. He was disgusted. What did experimental psychology have to do with the human mind? he wanted to know.

We were in the week between semesters at the time. Danny was sitting on my bed and I was at my desk, wishing I could help him, he looked so thoroughly sad. But I didn't know a thing about experimental psychology, so there was little I could offer by way of help, except to urge him to stick out the year, something might come of it, he might even get to like the subject.

"Did you ever get to like my father and his planned mistakes?" he asked testily.

I shook my head slowly. Reb Saunders had stopped inserting deliberate errors into his Shabbat evening talks the week we had entered college, but the memory of it still rankled. I told Danny that I had disliked the mistake business and had never really gotten used to it, despite my having witnessed it many times.

"So what makes you think sitting long enough through something you hate will get you to like it?"

I had nothing to say to that, except to urge him again to stick out the year with Professor Appleman. "Why don't you talk to him about it?" I asked.

"About what? About Freud? The one time I mentioned a Freudian theory in class, all I got out of Appleman was that dogmatic psychoanalysis was related to psychology as magic was related to science. 'Dogmatic Freudians,'" Danny was imitating Professor Appleman—or so I assumed; I didn't know Professor Appleman, but Danny's voice had taken on a somewhat professorial quality—"'Dogmatic Freudians are generally to be regarded as akin to the medieval physicists who preceded the era of Galileo. They are interested solely in confirming highly dubious theoretical hypotheses by the logic of analogy and induction, and make no attempt at refutation or intersubjective testing.' That was my introduction to experimental psych. I've been running rats through mazes ever since."

"Was he right?" I asked.

"Was who right?"

"Professor Appleman."

"Was he right about what?"

"About Freudians being dogmatic?"

"What followers of a genius *aren't* dogmatic, for heaven's sake? The Freudians have plenty to be dogmatic about. Freud was a genius."

"What do they do, make a tzaddik out of him?"

"Very funny," Danny said bitterly. "I'm getting a lot of sympathy from *you* tonight."

"I think you ought to have a heart-to-heart talk with Appleman."

"And tell him what? That Freud was a genius? That I hate

experimental psychology? You know what he once said in class?" He assumed the professorial air again. " 'Gentlemen, psychology may be regarded as a science only to the degree to which its hypotheses are subjected to laboratory testing and to subsequent mathematization.' Mathematization yet! What should I tell him, that I hate mathematics? I'm taking the wrong course. *You* should be taking that course, not me!"

"He's right, you know," I said quietly.

"Who?"

"Appleman. If the Freudians aren't willing to try testing their theories under laboratory conditions, then they *are* being dogmatic."

Danny looked at me, his face rigid. "What makes you so wise about Freudians all of a sudden?" he asked angrily.

"I don't know a thing about the Freudians," I told him quietly. "But I know a lot about inductive logic. One of these days remind me to give you a lecture on inductive logic. If the Freudians—"

"Damn it!" Danny exploded. "I never even mentioned the followers of Freud in class! I was talking about Freud himself! Freud was a scientist. Psychoanalysis is a scientific tool for exploring the mind. What do rats have to do with the human mind?"

"Why don't you ask Appleman?" I said quietly.

"I think I will," Danny said. "I think I'll do just that. Why not? What have I got to lose? It can't make me any more miserable than I am now."

"That's right," I said.

There was a brief silence, during which Danny sat on my bed and stared gloomily down at the floor.

"How are your eyes these days?" I asked quietly.

He sat back on the bed, leaning against the wall. "They still bother me. These glasses don't help much."

"Have you seen a doctor?"

He shrugged. "He said the glasses should do it. I just have to get used to them. I don't know. Anyway, I'll talk to Appleman next week. The worst that could happen is I drop the course." He shook his head grimly. "What a miserable business. Two years of reading Freud, and I have to end up doing experimental psychology."

"You never know," I said. "Experimental psychology might come in handy some day."

"Oh, sure. All I need to do is get to love mathematics and rats. Are you coming over this Saturday?"

"I'm studying with my father Shabbat afternoon," I told him.

"Every Saturday afternoon?"

"Yes."

"My father asked me last week if you were still my friend. He hasn't seen you in two months."

"I'm studying Talmud with my father," I said.

"You review?"

"No. He's teaching me scientific method."

Danny looked at me in surprise, then grinned. "You're planning to try scientific method on Rav Schwartz?"

"No," I said. Rav Schwartz was my Talmud teacher. He was an old man with a long, gray beard who wore a black coat and was constantly smoking cigarettes. He was a great Talmudist, but he had been trained in a European yeshiva, and I didn't think he would take kindly to the scientific method of studying Talmud. I had once suggested a textual emendation in class, and he had given me a queer look. I didn't think he even understood what I had said.

"Well, good luck with your scientific method," Danny told me, getting to his feet. "Just don't try it on Rav Gershenson. He knows all about it and hates it. When will my father get to see you?"

"I don't know," I said.

"I've got to go home. What's your father doing in there?" The sound of my father's typewriter had been clearly heard throughout the time we had been talking.

"He's finishing another article."

"Tell him my father sends his regards."

"Thanks. Are you and your father talking to each other these days?"

Danny hesitated a moment before answering. "Not really. Only now and then. It's not really talking."

I didn't say anything.

"I think I had really better go home," Danny said. "It's late. I'll meet you in front of your shul Sunday morning."

"Okay."

I walked him to the door, then stood there listening to the tapping of his metal-capped shoes on the hallway floor. He went out the double door and was gone.

I came back to my room and found my father standing in the doorway that led to his study. He had a bad cold and was wearing a woolen sweater and a scarf around his throat. This was his third cold in five months. It was also the first time in weeks that he had been home at night. He had become involved in Zionist activities and was always attending meetings where he spoke about the importance of Palestine as a Jewish homeland and raised money for the Jewish National Fund. He was also teaching an adult studies course in the history of political Zionism at our synagogue on Monday nights and another adult course in the history of American Jewry at his yeshiva on Wednesday nights. He rarely got home before eleven. I would always hear his tired steps in the hallway as he came in the door. He would have a glass of tea, come into my room and chat with me for a few minutes, telling me where he had been and what he had done that night, then he would remind me I didn't have to do four years of college all at once, I should go to bed soon, and he would go into his study to prepare for the classes he would be teaching the next day. He had begun taking his teaching with almost ominous seriousness these past months. He had always prepared for his classes, but there was a kind of heaviness to the way he went about preparing now, writing everything down, rehearsing his notes aloud—as if he were trying to make certain that nothing of significance would remain unsaid, as if he felt the future hung on every idea he taught. I never knew when he went to sleep; no matter what time I got to bed he was still in his study. He had never regained the weight he had lost during the weeks he had spent in the hospital after his heart attack, and he was always tired, his face pale and gaunt, his eyes watery.

He stood now in the doorway to his study, wearing the woolen sweater, the scarf, and the round, black skullcap. His feet were in bedroom slippers and his trousers were creased from all the sitting over the typewriter. He was visibly tired, and his voice cracked a few times as he asked me what

Danny had been so excited about. He had heard him through the door, he said.

I told him about Danny's misery over Professor Appleman and experimental psychology.

He listened intently, then came into my room and sat down on my bed with a sigh. "So," he said, "Danny is discovering that Freud is not God."

"I told him at least to talk it over with Professor Appleman."

"And?"

"He'll talk to him next week."

"Experimental psychology," my father mused. "I know nothing about it."

"He said there was a lot of math in it."

"Ah. And Danny does not like mathematics."

"He hates it, he says. He's feeling pretty low. He feels he wasted two years reading Freud."

My father smiled and shook his head but remained silent.

"Professor Appleman sounds a lot like Professor Flesser," I said. Professor Abraham Flesser was my logic teacher, an avowed empiricist and an enemy of what he called "Obscurantist Continental philosophies," which, he explained, included everything that had happened in German philosophy from Fichte to Heidegger, with the exception of Vaihinger and one or two others.

My father wanted to know what it was the two professors had in common, and I told him what Professor Appleman had said about psychology being a science only to the extent to which its hypotheses can be mathematized. "Professor Flesser made the same remark once about biology," I said.

"You talk about biology in a symbolic logic class?" my father asked.

"We were discussing inductive logic."

"Ah. Of course. The point about mathematizing hypotheses was made by Kant. It is one of the programs of the Vienna Circle logical positivists."

"Who?"

"Not now, Reuven. It is too late, and I am tired. You should go to sleep soon. Take advantage of the nights when you have no schoolwork."

"You'll be working late tonight, abba?"

"Yes."

"You're not taking care of yourself, you know. Your voice sounds awful."

He sighed again. "It is a bad cold," he said.

"Does Dr. Grossman know you're working so hard?"

"Dr. Grossman worries a little bit too much about me," he said, smiling.

"Are you going for another checkup soon?"

"Soon," he said. "I am feeling fine, Reuven. You worry like Dr. Grossman. Worry better about your schoolwork. I am fine."

"How many fathers do I have?" I asked.

He didn't say anything, but he blinked his eyes a few times.

"I wish you'd take it a little easy," I said.

"This is not a time to take things easy, Reuven. You read what is happening in Palestine."

I nodded slowly.

"This is a time to take things easy?" my father asked, his hoarse voice rising. "The Haganah and Irgun boys who die are taking it easy?"

He was talking about what was now going on in Palestine. Two Englishmen, an army major and a judge, had been kidnaped recently by the Irgun, the Jewish terrorist group in Palestine, and were being held as hostages. A captured member of the Irgun, Dov Gruner, had been sentenced to hanging by the British, and the Irgun had announced instant retaliation against these hostages should the sentence be carried out. This was the latest of a growing list of terrorist activities against the British Army in Palestine. While the Irgun engaged in terror—blowing up trains, attacking police stations, cutting communications lines—the Haganah continued smuggling Jews through the British naval blockade in defiance of the British Colonial Office, which had sealed Palestine off to further Jewish immigration. Rarely did a week go by now without a new act of terror against the British. My father would read the newspaper accounts of these activities, and I could see the anguish in his eyes. He hated violence and bloodshed and had an intense distaste for the terrorist policy of the Irgun, but he hated the British non-immigration policy even more. Irgun blood was being shed for the sake of a future Jewish state, and he found it difficult to give voice to his feelings of opposition to the acts of terror that were regularly making front-page headlines now. Invariably, the headlines spurred him on to new bursts of Zionist activity and to loud, excited justification of the way he was driving himself in his fund-raising and speechmaking efforts in behalf of a Jewish state.

I could see he was beginning to get excited now, too, so to change the subject quickly, I told him Reb Saunders had sent his regards. "He wonders why he doesn't see me," I said.

But my father didn't seem to have heard me. He sat on the bed, lost in thought. We were quiet for a long time. Then he stirred and said softly, "Reuven, do you know what the rabbis tell us God said to Moses when he was about to die?"

I stared at him. "No," I heard myself say.

"He said to Moses, 'You have toiled and labored, now you are worthy of rest.'"

I stared at him and didn't say anything.

"You are no longer a child, Reuven," my father went on. "It is almost possible to see the way your mind is growing. And your heart, too. Inductive logic, Freud, experimental psychology, mathematizing hypotheses, scientific study of the Talmud. Three years ago, you were still a child. You have become a small giant since the day Danny's ball struck your eye. You do not see it. But I see it. And it is a beautiful thing to see. So listen to what I am going to tell you." He paused for a moment, as if considering his next words carefully, then continued. "Human beings do not live forever, Reuven. We live less than the time it takes to blink an eye, if we measure our lives against eternity. So it may be asked what value is there to a human life. There is so much pain in the world. What does it mean to have to suffer so much if our lives are nothing more than the blink of an eye?" He paused again, his eyes misty now, then went on. "I learned a long time ago, Reuven, that a blink of an eye in itself is nothing. But the eye that blinks, *that* is something. A span of life is nothing. But the man who lives that span, *he* is something. He can fill that tiny span with meaning, so its quality is immeasurable though its quantity may be insignificant. Do you understand what I am saying? A man must fill his life with meaning, meaning is not automatically given to life. It is hard work to fill one's

life with meaning. *That* I do not think you understand yet. A
life filled with meaning is worthy of rest. I want to be worthy
of rest when I am no longer here. Do you understand what I
am saying?"

I nodded, feeling myself cold with dread. That was the first
time my father had ever talked to me of his death, and his
words seemed to have filled the room with a gray mist that
blurred my vision and stung as I breathed.

My father looked at me, then sighed quietly. "I was a little
too blunt," he said. "I am sorry. I did not mean to hurt you."

I couldn't say anything.

"I will live for many more years, with God's help," my father said, trying a smile. "Between my son and my doctor, I
will probably live to be a very old man."

The gray mist seemed to part. I took a deep breath. I
could feel cold sweat running down my back.

"Are you angry at me, Reuven?"

I shook my head.

"I did not want to sound morbid. I only wanted to tell you
that I am doing things I consider very important now. If I
could not do these things, my life would have no value.
Merely to live, merely to exist—what sense is there to it? A
fly also lives."

I didn't say anything. The mist was gone now. I found the
palms of my hands were cold with sweat.

"I am sorry," my father said quietly. "I can see I upset
you."

"You frightened me," I heard myself say.

"I am sorry."

"Will you please go for that checkup?"

"Yes," my father said.

"You really frightened me, talking that way. Are you sure
you're all right?"

"I have a bad cold," my father said. "But I am fine otherwise."

"You'll go for that checkup?"

"I will call Dr. Grossman tomorrow and make an appointment for next week. All right?"

"Yes."

"Fine. My young logician is satisfied. Good. Let us talk of
happier things. I did not tell you that I saw Jack Rose yester-

day. He gave me a thousand-dollar check for the Jewish National Fund."

"Another thousand dollars?" Jack Rose and my father had been boyhood friends in Russia and had come to America on the same boat. He was now a wealthy furrier and a thoroughly nonobservant Jew. Yet, six months ago, he had given my father a thousand-dollar contribution to our synagogue.

"It is strange what is happening," my father said. "And it is exciting. Jack is on the Building Committee of his synagogue. Yes, he joined a synagogue. Not for himself, he told me. For his grandchildren. He is helping them put up a new building so his grandchildren can go to a modern synagogue and have a good Jewish education. It is beginning to happen everywhere in America. A religious renaissance, some call it."

"I can't see Jack Rose in a synagogue," I said. On the few occasions when he had been over to our apartment, I had found his open disregard for Jewish tradition distasteful. He was a short man, with round, pink features, always immaculately dressed, always smoking long, expensive cigars. Once I asked my father why they had remained friends, their views about almost everything of importance were so different. He replied by expressing dismay at my question. Honest differences of opinion should never be permitted to destroy a friendship, he told me. "Haven't you learned that yet, Reuven?" Now I was tempted to tell my father that Jack Rose was probably using his money to salve a bad conscience. But I didn't. Instead, I said, a little scornfully, "I don't envy his rabbi."

My father shook his head soberly. "Why not? You should envy him, Reuven. American Jews have begun to return to the synagogue."

"God help us if synagogues fill up with Jack Roses."

"They will fill up with Jack Roses, and it will be the task of rabbis to educate them. It will be your task if you become a rabbi."

I looked at him.

"*If* you become a rabbi," my father said, smiling at me warmly.

"*When* I become a rabbi, you mean."

My father nodded, still smiling. "You would have been a fine university professor," he said. "I would have liked you to become a university professor. But I think you have already decided. Am I right?"

"Yes," I said.

"Even with a synagogue full of Jack Roses?"

"Even with a synagogue full of Jack Roses," I said. "God help me."

"America needs rabbis," my father said.

"Well, it's better than being a boxer," I told him.

My father looked puzzled.

"A bad joke," I said.

"Will you have some tea with me?"

I said I would.

"Come. Let us have some tea and continue to talk about happy things."

So we drank tea and talked some more. My father told me about the Zionist activities he was engaged in, the speeches he was making, the funds he was raising. He said that in a year or two the crisis in Palestine would come to a head. There would be terrible bloodshed, he predicted, unless the British would give over the problem to the United Nations. Many American Jews were not yet aware of what was going on, he said. The English papers did not tell the entire story. A Jew had to read the Yiddish press now if he wished to know everything that was happening in Palestine. American Jews had to be awakened to the problem of a Jewish state. His Zionist group was planning a mass rally in Madison Square Garden, he told me. The publicity would be going out this week, and there would be a large ad soon in the *New York Times,* announcing the rally. It was scheduled for late February.

"I wonder how Reb Saunders will feel when he finds out that Danny is the friend of the son of a Zionist," I mused. I had told my father about Reb Saunders' explosion.

My father sighed. "Reb Saunders sits and waits for the Messiah," he said. "I am tired of waiting. Now is the time to bring the Messiah, not to wait for him."

We finished our tea. My father returned to his study, and I went to bed. I had some terrible dreams that night, but I could remember none of them when I woke in the morning.

It was Friday, and I had nothing planned. Danny always

spent his mornings studying Talmud, so I decided that rather than waste the day I would go over to the college library and see if I could find something on experimental psychology. It was a little before ten o'clock when I woke, and my father had already left to teach, so Manya served me breakfast alone, calling me a lazy sleepyhead and a few other things in Russian which I didn't understand, and then I took the trolley over to the college.

The library had a large section devoted to psychology. I found some books on experimental psychology and leafed through them slowly, then checked the indexes and bibliographies. What I discovered made it very clear why Danny was feeling so miserable.

I had chosen the books at random, but even a quick glance at them made it apparent that they were all structured along similar lines. They dealt only with experimental data and were filled with graphs, charts, tables, photographs of devices for the measuring of auditory, visual, and tactile responses, and with mathematical translations of laboratory findings. Most of the books didn't even cite Freud in their bibliographies. In one book, Freud was referred to only once, and the passage was far from complimentary.

I checked the indexes under "unconscious." Some of the books didn't even have it listed. One book had this to say:

> It is impossible here to discuss the "new psychology of the unconscious," but exaggerated as are many of the statements made as to the revolution in psychology caused by psychoanalysis there is little doubt that it has influenced psychology permanently. And it is well that the teacher should study something of it, partly because of its suggestiveness in many parts of his work, and partly to be on guard against the exaggerated statements of extremists, and the uncritical advocacy of freedom from all discipline, based upon them.

That "uncritical advocacy of freedom from all discipline" sounded a lot like Professor Appleman. Then I found something that really sounded like Professor Appleman:

> Magic depends on tradition and belief. It does not welcome observation, nor does it profit by experiment. On the other hand, science is based on experience; it is open to correction by observation and experiment.

The book in which I found that passage was full of tables and graphs showing the results of experiments on frogs, salamanders, rats, apes, and human beings. It didn't mention Freud or the unconscious anywhere.

I felt sorry for Danny. He had spent two years studying about the mind from the point of view of Freudian analysis. Now he was studying about the mind from the point of view of physiology. I understood what he had meant when he said that experimental psychology had nothing to do with the human mind. In terms of psychoanalytic theory, it had very little to do with the human mind. But psychoanalysis aside, I thought the books were very valuable. How else could a science of psychology be built except by laboratory findings? And what else could you do in a laboratory except experiment with the physiology of animals and men? How could you experiment with their *minds?* How could anyone subject Freud's concept of the unconscious to a laboratory test?

Poor Danny, I thought. Professor Appleman, with his experimental psychology, is torturing your mind. And your father, with his bizarre silence—which I still couldn't understand, no matter how often I thought about it—is torturing your soul.

I went home, feeling sad and a little helpless. Danny would have to work out his own problem. I couldn't help him much with psychology.

The second semester of college began the following Monday, and during lunch Danny told me he planned to speak to Professor Appleman that afternoon. He looked tense and nervous. I suggested that he be polite but honest, and that he listen to what Appleman might have to say. I was a little nervous myself, but I told him I had done some reading in experimental psychology on Friday and that I thought it had a lot to contribute. How could you have a science without experimentation? I wanted to know. And how could anyone experiment on the unconscious, which, by definition, seemed to defy laboratory techniques of testing?

I saw Danny become tight-lipped with anger. "Thanks a lot," he said bitterly. "That's just what I need now. A kick in the pants from my best friend."

"I'm telling you how I feel," I said.

"And I'm telling you how *I* feel!" he almost shouted. "Thanks a million!"

He stormed angrily out of the lunchroom, leaving me to finish the meal alone.

We usually met outside the building after our final class and went home together, but that evening he didn't show up. I waited about half an hour, then went home alone. The next morning, as I walked up Lee Avenue, I saw him waiting for me in front of the synagogue where my father and I prayed.

"Where were you last night?" he asked.

"I waited half an hour," I said. "What time did you get out?"

"A quarter after seven."

"You were with him an *hour?*"

"We had a long talk. Listen, I'm sorry I blew up like that yesterday at lunch."

I told him I had a pretty thick skin and, besides, what was a friend for if not to be blown up at every now and then.

We were walking toward the trolley station. It was a bitter cold morning. Danny's earlocks lifted and fell in the stiff wind that blew through the streets.

"What happened?" I asked.

"It's a long story," Danny said, looking at me sideways and grinning. "We had a long talk about Freud, Freudians, psychology, psychoanalysis, and God."

"And?"

"He's a very fine person. He said he's been waiting all term for me to talk to him."

I didn't say anything. But now *I* was grinning.

"Anyway, he knows Freud forwards and backwards. He told me that he wasn't objecting to Freud's conclusions as much as to his methodology. He said Freud's approach was based on his own limited experiences. He generalized on the basis of a few instances, a few private patients."

"That's the problem of induction in a nutshell," I said. "How do you justify jumping from a few instances to a generalization?"

"I don't know anything about the problem of induction," Danny said. "That's your department. Appleman said something else, though, that made a lot of sense to me. He admitted that Freud was a genius and a cautious scientist, but he said that Freud evolved a theory of behavior based only on the study of *abnormal* cases. He said that experimental psychology was interested in applying the methodology of the natural sciences to discover how *all* human beings behaved. It doesn't generalize about personality behavior only on the basis of a certain segment of people. That makes a lot of sense."

"Well, well," I said, grinning broadly.

"He also said his quarrel was mainly with the Freudians, not so much with Freud himself. He said they were happy to earn their fat fees as analysts and refused to let anyone challenge their hypotheses."

"There's our trolley," I said. "Come on!"

The trolley was waiting for a light, and we made it just in time. Some of the people inside stared curiously at Danny as we went up the aisle looking for seats. I had grown accustomed to people staring at Danny, at his beard and side curls. But Danny had become increasingly self-conscious about his appearance ever since the time he had read Graetz on Hasidism. He looked straight ahead, trying to ignore the stares. We found seats in the rear of the trolley and sat down.

"So he said analysts don't let anyone challenge their hypotheses," I said. "What happened then?"

"Well, we talked a lot about experimental psychology. He told me that it was almost impossible to study human subjects because it was too difficult to control the experiments. He said we use rats because we can vary the conditions. He repeated a lot of things he'd already said in class, but he made a lot more sense this time. At least, I think he made a lot more sense. Maybe after what he said about Freud being a genius I was just more willing to listen to him. He said he admired my knowledge of Freud but that in science no one was God, not even Einstein. He said even in religion people differed about what God was, so why shouldn't scientists take issue with other scientists? I couldn't argue with that. He said experimental psychology would be a healthy balance to my knowledge of Freud. Maybe. I still don't think it has anything to do with the human mind. It's more physiology than anything else, I think. Anyway, Appleman told me that if I had any problem with math he was willing to help me as much as he could. But his time is limited, he said, so he suggested I get a friend to help me on a regular basis."

I didn't say anything.

He looked at me and grinned.

"Okay," I said. "I don't charge very much."

"It won't make me love running rats through mazes," Danny said. "But at least he's sympathetic. He's really a fine person."

I smiled at him but didn't say anything. Then I noticed the psychology textbook he was carrying. It was one of the books I had seen on Friday that didn't mention Freud once. I asked him what he thought of it, and he said it was a grind. "If I ever get to love experimental psychology after this book I'll assume the Messiah has come," he said.

"Well, just call on your friendly tzaddik for help," I told him.

He looked at me queerly.

"I meant me," I said.

He looked away and didn't say anything. We rode the rest of the way to school in silence.

So I began coaching Danny in math. He caught on very quickly, mostly by memorizing steps and procedures. He wasn't really interested in the *why* of a mathematical problem but in the *how*. I enjoyed coaching him and learned a lot of experimental psychology. I found it fascinating, a lot more substantial and scientific than Freud had been, and a lot more fruitful in terms of expanding testable knowledge on how human beings thought and learned.

Throughout the early weeks of February, Danny and I met in the lunchroom, sat at a table by ourselves, and discussed the difficulties he was having with his mathematical translations of psychological experiments. I showed him how to set up his graphs, how to utilize the tables in his textbook, and how to reduce experimental findings to mathematical formulas. I also kept arguing for the value of experimentation. Danny remained convinced of his original argument that experimental psychology had nothing to do with the human mind, though he began to see its value as an aid to learning theory and intelligence testing. His frustration over it went up and down like a barometer, the climate being the extent to which he was able to comprehend and resolve whatever mathematical problem preoccupied him at any given moment.

I saw very little of my father during those early weeks of February. Except for breakfast, supper, and Shabbat, he was never home. Sometime between eleven and twelve every night, he would return from wherever he had been, have a glass of tea, spend a few minutes with me in my room, then go into his study. I never knew what time he went to bed, though his tired, stooped body and his haggard face made it clear that he was sleeping very little. He had gone for his checkup, and Dr. Grossman had been satisfied with his health, though he had suggested that he get more rest. My father took a vitamin pill every morning now with his orange juice, but they didn't seem to be doing much good. He completely ignored Dr. Grossman's suggestion that he rest more, and every time I brought up the subject he either waved it away or talked about the violence now going on in Palestine. It was impossible to talk to him about his health. There was nothing more important to him now than the two ideas around which his life revolved: the education of American Jewry and a Jewish state in Palestine. So he continued teaching his adult classes and planning for the Madison Square Garden rally due to take place in the last week of February.

Not only had my home life been affected by Palestine but my school life as well. Every shade of Zionist thought was represented in Hirsch College, from the Revisionists, who supported the Irgun, to the Neturai Karta, the Guardians of the City, the city being Jerusalem. This latter group was composed of severely Orthodox Jews, who, like Reb Saunders, despised all efforts aimed at the establishment of a Jewish state prior to the advent of the Messiah. A recent influx of Hungarian Jews into our neighborhood had swelled their ranks, and they formed a small but highly vocal element of the school's student population. Even the rabbinic faculty was split, most of the rabbis voicing their hope for a Jewish state, some of them opposing it, while all of the college faculty seemed to be for it. There were endless discussions during the afternoon college hours about the problem of dual loyalty— what sort of allegiance could an American Jew have toward a

foreign Jewish state?—and invariably these arguments revolved around this hypothetical question: On what side
would an American Jew fight should America ever declare
war against a Jewish state? I always answered that the question was silly, America would never send Jews to fight against
a Jewish state; during the Second World War she had sent
Japanese Americans to fight the Germans, not the Japanese.
But my answer never seemed to satisfy anyone. What if
America *did* want to send Jews to fight against a Jewish
state? the theorists countered. What then? The discussions
were quite heated at times, but they went on only among
those students and teachers who favored a Jewish state. Many
of the Hasidim ignored the question completely. Despising as
they did all efforts in behalf of a Jewish state, they despised
as well all discussions that had to do with even its possible
existence. They called such discussions bitul Torah, time
taken away from the study of Torah, and looked upon all the
disputants with icy disgust.

Toward the middle of February, the various factions began
to firm up their ranks as the entire spectrum of Zionist youth
movements moved into the school in a drive for membership,
the second such drive since I had entered the college. From
that time on—the recruitment drive lasted a few days—every
student's position was clearly defined by the Zionist philosophy of the group he had joined. Most of the pro-Zionist students, myself included, joined a religious Zionist youth group;
a few joined the youth arm of the Revisionists. The anti-
Zionist students remained aloof, bitter, disdainful of our
Zionism.

In the lunchroom one day, one of the Hasidim accused a
member of the Revisionist youth group of being worse than
Hitler. Hitler had only succeeded in destroying the Jewish
body, he shouted in Yiddish, but the Revisionists were trying
to destroy the Jewish soul. There was almost a fistfight, and
the two students were kept apart with difficulty by members
of their respective sides. The incident left a bitter taste in everyone's mouth and succeeded only in increasing the tension
between the pro-Zionist and anti-Zionist students.

As I expected, Danny did not join any of the Zionist
groups. Privately, he told me he wanted to join my group.
But he couldn't. Did I remember his father's explosion over

Zionism? he wanted to know. I told him I had had nightmares about that explosion. How would I like an explosion
like that with every meal? Danny asked me. I didn't think the
question required an answer and told him so. Danny nodded
grimly. Besides, he added, the anti-Zionists among the Hasidic students looked upon him as their leader. How would it
be if he joined a Zionist group? It would do nothing but add
to the already existing bitterness. He was trapped by his
beard and earlocks, he said, and there was nothing he could
do. But one day . . . He did not finish the sentence. He remained aloof, however, never participating in the quarrels between the pro-Zionist and anti-Zionist groups. And during the
near fistfight in the lunchroom, his face went rigid as stone,
and I saw him look with hatred at the Hasidic student who
had started the quarrel. But he said nothing, and after the
disputants had been half carried, half dragged, from the
lunchroom he returned immediately to the math problem we
had been discussing.

In the third week of February, the newspapers reported
that British Foreign Minister Bevin had announced his intention to bring the Palestine issue to the United Nations in September. My father was delighted, despite the fact that the
news cost him some extra nights of work rewriting the speech
he was to give at the rally.

He read the speech to me the Shabbat afternoon before the
rally. In it he described the two-thousand-year-old Jewish
dream of a return to Zion, the Jewish blood that had been
shed through the centuries, the indifference of the world to
the problem of a Jewish homeland, the desperate need to
arouse the world to the realization of how vital it was that
such a homeland be established immediately on the soil of
Palestine. Where else could the remnant of Jewry that had
escaped Hitler's ovens go? The slaughter of six million Jews
would have meaning only on the day a Jewish state was established. Only then would their sacrifice begin to make some
sense; only then would the songs of faith they had sung on
their way to the gas chambers take on meaning; only then
would Jewry again become a light to the world, as Ahad
Ha'am had foreseen.

I was deeply moved by the speech, and I was very proud
of my father. It was wonderful to know that he would soon

be standing in front of thousands of people, reading the same words he read to me that Shabbat.

The day before the scheduled date of the Madison Square Garden rally there was a violent snowstorm, and my father walked like a ghost through our apartment, staring white-faced out the window at the swirling snow. It fell the entire day, then stopped. The city struggled to free itself of its white burden, but the streets remained choked all the next day, and my father left in the evening for the rally, wearing a look of doom, his face ashen. I couldn't go with him because I had a logic exam the next day and had to remain home to study. I forced myself to concentrate on the logic problems, but somehow they seemed inconsequential to me. I kept seeing my father standing at the rostrum in front of a vast, empty hall, speaking to seats made vacant by the snow. I dreaded the moment I would hear his key in the lock of our apartment door.

I did as much studying as I could, hating Professor Flesser for springing the exam on us the way he had done; then I wandered aimlessly through the apartment, thinking how stupid it was to have all my father's work ruined by something like a snowstorm.

Shortly before one in the morning, I heard him open the door. I was in the kitchen, drinking milk, and I ran out into the hallway. His face was flushed with excitement. The rally had been a wild success. The Garden had been packed, and two thousand people had stood on the street outside, listening to the speeches over loudspeakers. He was elated. We sat at the kitchen table, and he told me all about it. The police had blocked off the street; the crowd's response to the speeches urging an end to the British mandate and the establishment of a Jewish state had been overwhelming. My father's talk had been wildly cheered. A senator who had spoken earlier had come up to him after the rally and had enthusiastically shaken his hand, promising him his complete support. There was no question that the rally had been a success. It had been a stunning success—despite the snow-choked streets.

It was after three in the morning when we finally went to bed.

The rally made the front pages of all the New York papers the next day. The English papers carried excerpts of the senator's speech and briefly mentioned my father. But all the Yiddish papers quoted him extensively. I was the center of considerable attention on the part of the Zionist students and the target of icy hatred from the ranks of the anti-Zionists. I paid no attention to the fact that Danny did not meet me in the lunchroom. Between my fatigue over lack of sleep and my excitement over the rally, I did quite poorly in the logic exam. But I didn't care. Logic didn't seem at all important now. I kept seeing my father's excited face and heard his voice telling me over and over again about the rally.

That evening I waited for Danny more than half an hour just inside the double door of the school before I decided to go home alone. The next morning he wasn't in front of the synagogue. I waited as long as I could, then took the trolley to school. I was sitting at a table preparing for the Talmud session, when I saw him pass me and nod his head in the direction of the door. He looked white-faced and grim, and he was blinking his eyes nervously. He went out, and a moment later I followed. I saw him go into the bathroom, and I went in after him. The bathroom was empty. Danny was urinating into one of the urinals. I stood next to him and assumed the urinating position. Was he all right? I wanted to know. He wasn't all right, he told me bitterly. His father had read the account of the rally in the Yiddish press. There had been an explosion yesterday at breakfast, last night at supper, and this morning again at breakfast. Danny was not to see me, talk to me, listen to me, be found within four feet of me. My father and I had been excommunicated from the Saunders family. If Reb Saunders even once heard of Danny being anywhere in my presence, he would remove him immediately from the college and send him to an out-of-town yeshiva for his rabbinic ordination. There would be no college education, no bachelor's degree, nothing, just a rabbinic ordination. If we tried meeting in secret, Reb Saunders would find out about it. My father's speech had done it. Reb Saunders didn't mind his son reading forbidden books, but *never* would he let his son be the friend of the son of a man who was advocating the establishment of a secular Jewish state run by Jewish goyim. It was even dangerous for Danny to meet me in the bathroom, but he had to tell me. As if to emphasize how dangerous it was, a Hasidic student came into the bathroom just then, took one look at me, and chose the urinal farthest away from me. A moment later, Danny walked out. When I came into the hallway, he was gone.

I had expected it, but now that it had happened I couldn't believe it. Reb Saunders had drawn the line not at secular literature, not at Freud—assuming he knew somehow that Danny had been reading Freud—but at Zionism. I found it impossible to believe. My father and I had been excommunicated—not only from the Saunders family, apparently, but also from the anti-Zionist element of the Hasidic student body. They avoided all contact with me, and even stepped out of my way so I would not brush against them in the halls. Occasionally I overheard them talking about the Malter goyim. During lunch I sat at a table with some of my non-Hasidic classmates and stared at the section of the room the Hasidic students always took for themselves. They sat together in the lunchroom, and my eyes moved slowly over them, over their dark clothes, fringes, beards, and earlocks— and it seemed to me that every word they were saying was directed against me and my father. Danny sat among them, silent, his face tight. His eyes caught mine, held, then looked slowly away. I felt cold with the look of helpless pleading I saw in them. It seemed so incredible to me, so outrageously absurd. Not Freud but Zionism had finally shattered our friendship. I went through the rest of the day alternating between violent rage at Reb Saunders' blindness and anguished frustration at Danny's helplessness.

When I told my father about it that night, he listened in silence. He was quiet for a long time afterward; then he sighed and shook his head, his eyes misty. He had known it would happen, he said sadly. How could it not happen?

"I don't understand it, abba." I was almost in tears. "In a million years I'll never understand it. He let Danny read all the books I gave him, he let us be friends all these years even though he knew I was your son. Now he breaks us up over this. I just don't understand it."

"Reuven, what went on between you and Danny all these years was private. Who really knew? It was probably not difficult for Reb Saunders to answer questions from his followers, assuming there were any questions, which I doubt, simply by saying that I was at least an observer of the Commandments. But he has no answer anymore to my Zionism. What can he tell his people now? Nothing. He had to do what he did. How could he let you continue to be friends? I am sorry I was the cause of it. I brought you together, and now I am the cause of your separation. I am deeply sorry."

"He's such a—a fanatic!" I almost shouted.

"Reuven," my father said quietly, "the fanaticism of men like Reb Saunders kept us alive for two thousand years of exile. If the Jews of Palestine have an ounce of that same fanaticism and use it wisely, we will soon have a Jewish state."

I couldn't say anything else. I was afraid my anger would bring me to say the wrong words.

I went to bed early that night but lay awake a long time, trying to remember all the things Danny and I had done together since the Sunday afternoon his ball had struck me in the eye.

CHAPTER FOURTEEN
+++++++++++++++++++++++++++

FOR THE REST of that semester, Danny and I ate in the same lunchroom, attended the same classes, studied in the same school synagogue, and often rode in the same trolley car—and never said a single word to each other. Our eyes met frequently, but our lips exchanged nothing. I lost all direct contact with him. It was an agony to sit in the same class with him, to pass him in the hallway, to see him in a trolley, to come in and out of the school building with him—and not say a word. I grew to hate Reb Saunders with a venomous passion that frightened me at times, and I consoled myself with wild fantasies of what I would do to him if he ever fell into my hands.

It was an ugly time and it began to affect my schoolwork to a point where some of my college teachers called me into their offices and wanted to know what was happening, they expected better from me than they were receiving. I made vague allusions to personal problems and went away from them cold with despair. I talked about it with my father as often as I could, but there seemed to be little he could do to help me. He would listen somberly, sigh, and repeat that he had no intention of quarreling with Reb Saunders, he respected his position in spite of its fanaticism.

I wondered often during those months whether Danny was also going through these same dreadful experiences. I saw him frequently. He seemed to be losing weight, and I noticed he was wearing different eyeglasses. But he was very carefully avoiding me, and I knew enough to stay away from him. I didn't want word to get back to his father that we had been seen together.

I hated the silence between us and thought it unimaginable that Danny and his father never really talked. Silence was ugly, it was black, it leered, it was cancerous, it was death. I hated it, and I hated Reb Saunders for forcing it upon me and his son.

I never knew myself capable of the kind of hatred I felt toward Reb Saunders all through that semester. It became, finally, a blind, raging fury, and I would find myself trembling with it at odd moments of the day—waiting to get into a trolley car, walking into a bathroom, sitting in the lunchroom, or reading in the library. And my father only added to it, for whenever I began to talk to him of my feelings toward Reb Saunders he invariably countered by defending him and by asserting that the faith of Jews like Reb Saunders had kept us alive through two thousand years of violent persecution. He disagreed with Reb Saunders, yes, but he would countenance no slander against his name or his position. Ideas should be fought with ideas, my father said, not with blind passion. If Reb Saunders was fighting him with passion, that did not mean that my father had to fight Reb Saunders with passion.

And Reb Saunders was fighting with passion. He had organized some of the Hasidic rebbes in the neighborhood into a group called The League for a Religious Eretz Yisroel. The work of this organization had begun mildly enough in early March with the handing out of leaflets. Its aims were clear: no Jewish homeland without the Torah at its center; therefore, no Jewish homeland until the coming of the Messiah. A Jewish homeland created by Jewish goyim was to be considered contaminated and an open desecration of the name of God. By the end of March, however, the leaflets had become inflammatory in tone, threatening excommunication to all in the neighborhood who displayed allegiance to Zionism, even at one point threatening to boycott neighborhood stores owned by Jews who contributed to, participated in, or were sympathetic with Zionist activities. A mass anti-Zionist rally was announced for a date a few days before Passover. It was poorly attended, but it made some of the English papers, and the reports of what had been said were ugly.

The student body of the college was tense with suppressed violence. An angry fistfight broke out in a classroom one afternoon, and it was only because the Dean threatened immediate expulsion to any future participants in such quarrels that more fistfights were avoided. But the tension was felt everywhere; it spilled over into our studies, and arguments over Milton, Talleyrand or deductive procedures in logic were often clear substitutes for the outlawed fistfights over Zionism.

I took the finals in the middle of June and came away from them sick with despair. I had botched my midterms badly, and I didn't do too much better on my finals. My father didn't say a word when he saw my report card at the end of June. Both of us were by that time looking forward very eagerly to the quiet month of August when we would be together in the cottage near Peekskill. It had been a terrible time, these past four months, and we wanted to get away from the city.

But the cottage proved to be not far enough away. We took to it the horrifying news that the Irgun had hanged two innocent British sergeants in retaliation for the three Irgunists who were hanged on the twenty-ninth of July. My father was outraged by the Irgun act, but said nothing more about it after his first burst of anger. Two weeks after we left for the cottage we were back in the city. Urgent Zionist meetings had been called to plan for the coming United Nations session that was to discuss the Palestine problem. My father was on the Executive Committee of his Zionist group and had to attend the meetings.

For the rest of August, I saw my father only on Shabbat. He was gone in the mornings when I woke and he returned at night when I was asleep. He was filled with fiery excitement, but it was clear that he was wearing himself out. I couldn't talk to him at all about his health. He refused to listen. Our Shabbat afternoon Talmud sessions had stopped; my father spent all of Shabbat resting so as to be prepared for each coming week of furious activity. I haunted the apartment, wandered the streets, barked at Manya, and thought of Danny. I remembered him telling me how much he admired and trusted his father, and I couldn't understand it. How could he admire and trust someone who wouldn't talk to him, even if that someone was his father? I hated his father. Once I even went up to the third floor of the public library, hoping I might find Danny there. Instead, I found an old man sitting in the chair Danny had once occupied, staring nearsightedly at the pages of a scholarly journal. I went away from there and walked the streets blindly until it was time to go home to a lonely supper.

In the second week of September, I returned to school for the preregistration student assembly and found myself sitting in the auditorium a few seats away from Danny. He looked thin and pale, and constantly blinked his eyes. During the registrar's brief words of instruction concerning registration procedure, I saw Danny turn his head, stare at me for a moment, then turn slowly away. His face had remained expressionless; he hadn't even nodded a greeting. I sat very still, listening to the registrar, and felt myself get angry. To hell with you, Danny Saunders, I thought. You could at least show you know I'm alive. To hell with you and your fanatic father. I became so completely absorbed in my anger that I stopped listening to the instructions. I had to ask one of my classmates to repeat them to me after the assembly. To hell with you, Danny Saunders, I kept saying to myself all that day. I can live without your beard and earlocks with no trouble at all. You're not the center of the world, friend. To hell with you and your damn silence.

By the time the fall semester officially began two days later, I had promised myself to forget Danny as quickly as possible. I wasn't going to let him ruin another semester's work. One more report card like the one I had shown my father at the end of June and I wouldn't even be graduated *cum laude*. To hell with you, Danny Saunders, I kept saying to myself. You could a least have nodded your head.

But it proved to be a good deal more difficult to forget him than I had anticipated, mostly because I had been moved up into Rav Gershenson's Talmud class where Danny's presence was always felt.

Rav Gershenson was a tall, heavy-shouldered man in his late sixties, with a long, pointed gray beard and thin, tapered fingers that seemed always to be dancing in the air. He used his hands constantly as he talked, and when he did not talk his fingers drummed on his desk or on the open Talmud in front of him. He was a gentle, kindly person, with brown eyes, an oval face, and a soft voice, which at times was almost inaudible. He was an exciting teacher, though, and he taught Talmud the way my father did, in depth, concentrating for days on a few lines and moving on only when he was satisfied that we understood everything thoroughly. He laid heavy emphasis on the early and late medieval Talmudic commentators, and we were always expected to come to class knowing the Talmud text and these commentators in advance. Then he would call on one of us to read and explain the text—and the questions would begin. "What does the Ramban say about Rabbi Akiva's question?" he might ask of a particular passage, speaking in Yiddish. The rabbis spoke only Yiddish in the Talmud classes, but the students could speak Yiddish or English. I spoke English. "Everyone agrees with the Ramban's explanation?" Rav Gershenson might go on to ask. "The Me'iri does not. Very good. What does the Me'iri say? And the Rashba? How does the Rashba explain Abaye's answer?" And on and on. There was almost always a point at which the student who was reading the text would become bogged down by the cumulative intricacies of the questions and would stare down at his Talmud, drowning in the shame produced by his inability to answer. There would be a long, dreaded silence, during which Rav Gershenson's fingers would begin to drum upon his desk or his Talmud. "Nu?" he would ask quietly. "You do not know? How is it you do not know? Did you review beforehand? Yes? And you still do not know?" There would be another long silence, and then Rav Gershenson would look around the room and say quietly, "Who does know?" and, of course, Danny's hand would immediately go up, and he would offer the answer. Rav Gershenson would listen, nod, and his fingers would cease their drumming and take to the air as they accompanied his detailed review of Danny's answer. There were times, however, when Rav Gershenson did not nod at Danny's answer but questioned him on it instead, and there would then ensue a lengthy dialogue between the two of them, with the class sitting by and listening in silence. Most often these dialogues took only a few minutes, but by the end of September there had already been two occasions when they had lasted more than three quarters of an hour. I was constantly being reminded by these dialogues of the way Danny argued Talmud with his father. It made it not only difficult to forget him but quite impossible. And now it was also I and not only Reb Saunders who was able to listen to Danny's voice only through a Talmudic disputation.

The hours of the Talmud classes in the school were arranged in such a way that we were able to spend from nine in the morning to noon preparing the material to be studied with Rav Gershenson. We would then eat lunch. And from one to three we would have the actual Talmud session itself, the shiur, with Rav Gershenson. No one in the class knew who would be called on to read and explain, so all of us worked feverishly to prepare. But it never really helped, because no matter how hard we worked there would always be that dreaded moment of silence when the questions could no longer be answered and Rav Gershenson's fingers would begin their drumming.

There were fourteen students in the class, and each one of us, with the exception of Danny, sooner or later tasted that silence personally. I was called on in the first week of October and tasted the silence briefly before I managed to struggle through with an answer to an almost impossible question. The answer was accepted and amplified by Rav Gershenson, thereby forestalling Danny's poised hand. I saw him look at me briefly afterward, while Rav Gershenson dealt with my answer. Then he looked away, and a warm smile played on his lips. My anger at him melted away at the sight of that smile, and the agony of not being able to communicate with him returned. But it was a subdued agony now, a sore I was somehow able to control and keep within limits. It was no longer affecting my schoolwork.

By the middle of October everyone in the class, except me, had been called on at least twice. I prepared feverishly, expecting to hear my name called any day. But it wasn't. By the end of October, I began to feel uneasy. By the middle of November I still hadn't been called on again. I took part in the class discussions, asked questions, argued, raised my hand almost as frequently as Danny raised his in response to Rav Gershenson's "Who does know?"—but I was not called on to read. I couldn't understand it, and it began to upset me. I wondered if this was his way of participating in Reb Saunders' ban against me and my father.

There were other things, too, that were upsetting me at the time. My father had begun to look almost skeletal as a result

of his activities, and I dreaded the nights he came wearily
home, drank his glass of tea, spent some minutes with me in
my room, looking hollow-eyed and not really listening to
what I told him, and then went into his study. Instead of
studying Talmud with him on the Shabbat, I studied alone
while he slept. The Palestine issue was being debated now by
the United Nations, and the Partition Plan would soon be
voted upon. Every day there were headlines announcing new
acts of terror and bloodshed; every week, it seemed, there
was another massive rally in Madison Square Garden. I was
able to attend two of those rallies. The second time I went I
made sure to arrive early enough to get a seat inside. The
speeches were electrifying, and I joined in the applause and
the cheering until my hands were sore and my voice was
hoarse. My father spoke at that rally, his voice booming out
clearly through the public address system. He seemed so huge
behind the microphones, his voice giving his body the stature
of a giant. When he was done, I sat and listened to the wild
applause of the crowd, and my eyes filled with tears of pride.

In the midst of all this, Reb Saunders' League for a Religious Eretz Yisroel continued putting out its anti-Zionist
leaflets. Everywhere I went I found those leaflets—on the
streets, in the trolley cars, in my classroom desks, on my
lunch table, even in the school bathrooms.

It became clear as November went by that the United Nations vote on the Partition Plan would take place sometime at
the end of the month. My father was at a meeting on Saturday evening, November 29, when the vote was finally held,
and I listened to it over the kitchen radio. I cried like a baby
when the result was announced, and later, when my father
came home, we embraced and wept and kissed, and our tears
mingled on our cheeks. He was almost incoherent with joy.
The death of the six million Jews had finally been given
meaning, he kept saying over and over again. It had happened. After two thousand years, it had finally happened. We
were a people again, with our own land. We were a blessed
generation. We had been given the opportunity to see the
creation of the Jewish state. "Thank God!" he said. "Thank
God! Thank God!" We alternately wept and talked until after
three in the morning when we finally went to bed.

I woke groggy from lack of sleep but still feeling the sense of exhilaration, and was eager to get to school to share the joy with my friends. My exhilaration was dampened somewhat during breakfast when my father and I heard over the radio that a few hours after the United Nations vote a bus on its way from Tel Aviv to Jerusalem had been attacked by Arabs and seven Jews had been killed. And my exhilaration was snuffed out and transformed into an almost uncontrollable rage when I got to school and found it strewn with the leaflets of Reb Saunders' anti-Zionist league.

The leaflets denounced the United Nations vote, ordered Jews to ignore it, called the state a desecration of the name of God, and announced that the league planned to fight its recognition by the government of the United States.

Only the Dean's threat of immediate expulsion prevented me from engaging in a fistfight that day. I was tempted more than once to scream at the groups of anti-Zionist students huddling together in the halls and classrooms that they ought to go join the Arabs and the British if they were so opposed to the Jewish state. But I managed somehow to control myself and remain silent.

In subsequent weeks, I was grateful for that silence. For as Arab forces began to attack the Jewish communities of Palestine, as an Arab mob surged through Princess Mary Avenue in Jerusalem, wrecking and gutting shops and leaving the old Jewish commercial center looted and burned, and as the toll of Jewish dead increased daily, Reb Saunders' league grew strangely silent. The faces of the anti-Zionist Hasidic students in the school became tense and pained, and all anti-Zionist talk ceased. I watched them every day at lunch as they read to each other the accounts of the bloodshed reported in the Jewish press and then talked about it among themselves. I could hear sighs, see heads shaking and eyes filling with sadness. "Again Jewish blood is being spilled," they whispered to one another. "Hitler wasn't enough. Now more Jewish blood, more slaughter. What does the world want from us? Six million isn't enough? More Jews have to die?" Their pain over this new outbreak of violence against the Jews of Palestine outweighed their hatred of Zionism. They did not become Zionists; they merely became silent. I was glad during those weeks that I had restrained my anger.

I received straight A's in my college courses at the end of

that semester. I also received an A in Talmud, despite the fact that Rav Gershenson had only called on me once during the entire four-month period I had spent in his class. I planned to talk to him about it during the inter-semester break, but my father suffered a second heart attack on the first day of that break.

He collapsed at a Jewish National Fund meeting and was rushed to the Brooklyn Memorial Hospital by ambulance. He hovered tenuously between life and death for three days. I lived in a nightmare of hallucinatory dread, and if it hadn't been for Manya constantly reminding me with gentle kindness that I had to eat or I would get sick, I might well have starved.

My father was beginning to recover when the second semester began, but he was a shell of a man. Dr. Grossman told me that he would be in the hospital at least six weeks, and that it would take from four to six more months of complete rest before he would be able to return to his work.

My classmates had all heard the news by the time the semester began, but their words of consolation didn't help very much. The look on Danny's face, though, when I saw him for the first time, helped a little. He passed me in the hallway, his face a suffering mask of pain and compassion. I thought for a moment he would speak to me, but he didn't. Instead, he brushed against me and managed to touch my hand for a second. His touch and his eyes spoke the words that his lips couldn't. I told myself it was bitter and ironic that my father needed to have a heart attack in order for some contact to be established once again between myself and Danny.

I lived alone. Manya came in the mornings and left after supper, and during the long winter nights of January and February I was all alone in the house. I had been alone before, but the knowledge that my father would return from his meetings and spend a few minutes with me had made the loneliness endurable. Now he wasn't attending meetings and wasn't coming into my room, and for the first few days the total silence inside the apartment was impossible for me to take, and I would go out of the house and take long walks in the bitter, cold winter nights. But my schoolwork began to suffer, and I finally took hold of myself. I spent as much of the early parts of every evening as I could visiting my father in the hospital. He was weak and could barely talk and kept asking me if I was taking care of myself. Dr. Grossman had warned me not to tire him, so I left as soon as I could, went home, ate, then spent the night studying.

By the time my father had been in the hospital three weeks, the evenings had become almost an automatic routine. The dread of his possible death was gone. It was now a matter of waiting out the silence until he came home. And I waited out the silence by studying.

I began especially to study Talmud. In the past, I had done all my Talmud studying on Shabbat and during the morning preparation periods. Now I began to study Talmud in the evenings as well. I tried to finish my college work as quickly as I could, then I would turn to the passage of Talmud we were studying with Rav Gershenson. I would study it carefully, memorize it, find the various commentaries—those which were not printed in the Talmud itself could always be found in my father's library—and memorize them. I tried to anticipate Rav Gershenson's tangled questions. And then I began to do something I had never done before with the Talmud I studied in school. After I was done memorizing the text and the commentaries, I began to go over the text again critically. I checked the Talmudic cross-references for parallel texts and memorized whatever differences I found. I took the huge volumes of the Palestinian Talmud from my father's library— the text we studied in school was the Babylonian Talmud— and checked its parallel discussions just to see how it differed from the discussions in the Babylonian Talmud. I worked carefully and methodically, using everything my father had taught me and a lot of things I now was able to teach myself. I was able to do all of this in real depth because of Rav Gershenson's slow-paced method of teaching. And by doing all of this, I was able to anticipate most of Rav Gershenson's questions. I also became more and more certain of when he would call on me again.

He had never called on me since that day in October. And it was now the middle of February. As a result of my night sessions with Talmud, I had pulled ahead of the class by at least five or six days and was tangled in one of the most com-

plicated discussions I had ever encountered. The complication
was caused not only by the Talmud text itself, which seemed
filled with gaps, but by the commentaries that struggled to explain it. The text consisted of nine lines. One of the commentaries on the text ran to two and a half pages, another ran to
four pages. Neither was very clear. A third commentary,
however, explained the text in six lines. The explanation was
terse, clipped, and simple. The only thing wrong with it was
that it seemed not to be based on the text it was explaining.
A later commentary tried to reconcile the three commentaries
by the method of pilpul, the result being a happy one for
someone who enjoyed pilpul but quite strained as far as I was
concerned. It looked to be a hopeless situation.

As we came closer and closer to this text, I became more
and more convinced that Rav Gershenson was going to call
on me to read and explain it. I didn't quite know *why* I was
convinced of that; I just knew that I was.

I began painfully to unravel the puzzle. I did it in two
ways. First, in the traditional way, by memorizing the text
and the commentaries, and then inventing all sorts of questions that Rav Gershenson might ask me. I would ride the
trolley, walk the streets, or lie in bed—and ask myself questions. Second, in the way my father had taught me, by attempting to find or reconstruct the correct text, the text the
commentator who had offered the simple explanation must
have had before him. The first way was relatively simple; it
was a matter of brute memorization. The second way was
tortuous. I searched endlessly through all the cross-references
and all the parallel passages in the Palestinian Talmud. When
I was done, I had four different versions of the text on my
hands. I now had to reconstruct the text upon which the simple commentary had been based. I did it by working backward, using the commentary as a base, then asking myself
what passage among the four versions the commentator could
have had before him as he wrote the commentary. It was
painstaking work, but I finally thought I had it down right. It
had taken hours and hours of precious time, but I was satisfied I had the correct text, the only text that really made
sense. I had done it this way only to satisfy myself. When
Rav Gershenson called on me, I would, of course, only use
the first method of explanation. When my father returned

from the hospital, I would show him what I had done with the second method. I felt very proud of my accomplishment.

Three days later, we came to that passage in our Talmud class, and for the second time that year Rav Gershenson called out my name and asked me to read and explain.

The class was deathly silent. Some of my friends had told me earlier that they dreaded being called on for that passage; they hadn't been able to make any sense at all out of it and the commentaries were impossible. I was a little frightened, too, but very eager to show off what I had learned. When I heard my name called, I felt myself tingle with a mixture of fear and excitement, as if a tiny electric shock had gone through my body. Most of the students had been waiting apprehensively to hear who would be asked to read. They had sat staring down at their texts, afraid to meet Rav Gershenson's eyes. Now they were all looking at me, even Danny was looking at me, and from one of the students at my right came a barely audible sigh of relief. I bent over my Talmud, put the index finger of my right hand below the first word of the passage, and began to read.

Every Talmudic passage is composed of what, for the sake of convenience, might best be called thought units. Each thought unit is a separate stage of the total discussion that makes up the passage. It might consist of a terse statement of law, or a question on the statement, an answer to the question, a brief or lengthy commentary on a Biblical verse, and so on. The Talmud contains no punctuation marks, and it is not always a simple matter to determine where a thought unit begins and ends; occasionally, a passage will have a tight, organic flow to it which makes breaking it up into thought units difficult and somewhat arbitrary. In most instances, however, the thought units are clearly discernible, and the decision on how to break up a passage into such units is a matter of common sense and a feel for the rhythm of the argument. The need to break up a passage into its thought units is simple enough. One has to decide when to stop reading and start explaining, as well as when to appeal to the commentaries for further explanation.

I had broken up the passage into its thought units as I had studied it, so I knew precisely at what points I would stop reading and begin my explanations. I read aloud a thought unit that consisted of a citation from the Mishnah—the Mishnah is the written text of rabbinic oral law; in form and content it is for the most part terse and clipped, a vast collection of laws upon which are based almost all the rabbinic discussions which, together with the Mishnah, compose the Talmud. When I came to the end of the Mishnaic thought unit, I stopped, and reviewed it briefly, together with the commentaries of Rashi and the Tosafists. I tried to be as clear as I could, and acted as if I myself were teaching the class rather than merely acting as a springboard for Rav Gershenson's comments. I finished the explanation of the Mishnaic text and read the next thought unit, which consisted of another Mishnah found in a different tractate from the one we were now studying. This second Mishnah flatly contradicted the first. I explained the Mishnah carefully, showed why there was a contradiction, then read from the commentaries of Rashi and the Tosafists, both of which are printed on the same page as the Talmud text. I expected to be stopped at any moment by Rav Gershenson, but nothing happened. I continued reading and explaining, my eyes fixed on the text as I read and looking at Rav Gershenson as I explained. He let me continue without interruption. By the time I was four lines into the passage, the discussion had become so involved that I had already begun to appeal to one of the medieval commentaries that were not printed on the same page as the text but were rather placed separately at the end of the tractate. I kept a finger of my right hand on the appropriate place in the text, flipped the Talmud to where the commentary had been printed, and read from it. I then indicated that other commentaries had offered different explanations, and I cited them by heart because they were not found in the Talmud edition the class used. Having said that, I returned to the passage and continued to read. When I raised my eyes to explain the thought unit I had just read, I saw that Rav Gershenson had sat down—the first time since I had come into the class that he was sitting during a shiur. He was holding his head in the palms of his hands, the elbows on the open Talmud in front of him, and listening intently. As I continued with my explanation of the thought unit I had just read, I glanced at my wristwatch and discovered to my amazement that I had been talking for almost an hour and a half without interruption. I had to utilize all the commentaries this time and was able to finish explaining the thought unit a moment before the three o'clock bell sounded. Rav Gershenson said nothing. He just sat there and dismissed the class with a wave of his hand.

The next day he called on me again, and I continued to read and explain. I spent two hours on seven words, and again sometime during the session he sat down, with his head in the palms of his hands. He said not a single word. The bell caught me in the middle of a lengthy explanation of the four-page commentary, and when he called on me again the third day I read the seven words quickly, briefly went through my explanations of the day before, then continued where I had stopped.

Between the third and fourth day, my mood jumped back and forth erratically from wild exhilaration to gloomy apprehension. I knew I was doing well, otherwise Rav Gershenson would have stopped me, but I kept wishing he would say something and not just stand or sit in complete silence.

Some of the Hasidic students in the class were giving me mixed looks of awe and jealousy, as if they couldn't restrain their feelings of admiration over how well I was doing but at the same time were asking themselves how someone like me, a Zionist and the son of a man who wrote apikorsische articles, could possibly know Talmud so well. Danny, though, seemed absolutely delighted over what was happening. He never looked at me while I read and explained, but I could see him nodding his head and smiling as I went through my explanations. And Rav Gershenson remained silent and impassive, listening intently, his face expressionless, except for an occasional upward curving along the corners of his lips whenever I clarified a particularly difficult point. By the end of the third day, it began to be something of a frustrating experience. I wished he would at least say or do something, nod his head, smile, even catch me at a mistake—anything but that awful silence.

I was prepared for Rav Gershenson to call on me again the fourth day, and he did. There was by now only one more thought unit left in the passage, and I had decided in advance that when I was done explaining I would quickly review the entire passage and all the commentaries, outlining the difficulties they had found in the text and showing the different ways they had explained these difficulties. Then I would go into the attempt of the late medieval commentary to reconcile the diverse explanations of the commentaries. All of that took me just under an hour, and when I was satisfied that I had done the best I could, I stopped talking. Rav Gershenson was sitting behind his desk, looking at me intently. It felt strange to me for a moment not to be hearing my own voice anymore. But I had nothing more to say.

There was a brief silence, during which I saw one of the Hasidic students grin and lean over to whisper something into another Hasidic student's ear. Then Rav Gershenson got to his feet and folded his arms across his chest. He was smiling a little now, and the upper part of his body was swaying slowly back and forth.

He asked me to repeat a point I had made two days earlier, and I did. He asked me to make myself a little clearer on a passage in one of the commentaries, and I repeated the passage by heart and explained it again as best I could. He asked me to go over the difficulties I had found in the various commentaries, and I repeated them carefully. Then he asked me to show how the late medieval commentary had attempted to reconcile these difficulties, and I went over that, too.

Again, there was a brief silence. I glanced at my watch and saw it was two-thirty. I wondered if he would start on the next passage with only half an hour left to the shiur. He usually preferred to start a new passage—or inyan, as it is called—at the beginning of a shiur, so as to give the class time to get into it. I was feeling very satisfied with the way I had explained the passage and answered his questions. I promised myself that I would tell my father about it when I visited him in the hospital that evening.

Then I heard Rav Gershenson ask me whether I was satisfied with the late medieval commentary's attempt at reconciliation.

It was a question I hadn't expected. I had regarded the effort at reconciliation as the rock bottom of the entire discussion on the passage and had never thought that Rav Gershenson would question it. For a long moment, I felt myself wallowing in that dreaded silence that always followed a question of his that a student couldn't answer, and I waited for the drumming of his fingers to begin. But his arms remained folded across his chest, and he stood there, swaying slowly back and forth, and looking at me intently.

"Nu," he said again, "there are no questions about what he says?"

I waited for Danny's hand to go up, but it didn't. I glanced at him and saw his mouth had fallen slightly open. The question had caught him by surprise, too.

Rav Gershenson stroked his pointed beard with his right hand, then asked me for the third time if I was satisfied with what the commentary said.

I heard myself tell him that I wasn't.

"Ah," he said, smiling faintly. "Good. And why not?"

"Because it's pilpul," I heard myself say.

There was a stir from the class. I saw Danny stiffen in his seat, throw me a quick, almost fearful glance, then look away.

I was suddenly a little frightened at the disparaging way I had uttered the word pilpul. The tone of disapproval in my voice hung in the air of the classroom like a threat.

Rav Gershenson slowly stroked his pointed gray beard. "So," he said softly, "it is pilpul. I see you do not like pilpul. . . . Nu, the great Vilna Gaon also did not like pilpul." He was talking about Rabbi Elijah of Vilna, the eighteenth-century opponent of Hasidism. "Tell me, Reuven"—that was the first time he had ever called me by my first name—"why is it pilpul? What is wrong with his explanation?"

I answered that it was strained, that it attributed nuances to the various conflicting commentaries that were not there, and that, therefore, it really was not a reconciliation at all.

He nodded his head slowly. "Nu," he said, not speaking only to me but to the entire class now, "it is a very difficult inyan. And the commentaries"—he used the term "Rishonim," which indicates the early medieval Talmudic commentators—"do not help us." Then he looked at me. "Tell me, Reuven," he said quietly, "how do *you* explain the inyan?"

I sat there and stared at him in stunned silence. If the commentators hadn't been able to explain it, how could I? But he didn't let the silence continue this time. Instead, he repeated his question, his voice soft, gentle. "You cannot explain it, Reuven?"

"No," I heard myself say.

"So," Rav Gershenson said. "You cannot explain it. You are sure you cannot explain it?"

For a moment I was almost tempted to tell him the text was wrong and to give him the text I had reconstructed. But I didn't. I was afraid. I remembered Danny telling me that Rav Gershenson knew all about the critical method of studying Talmud, and hated it. So I kept silent.

Rav Gershenson turned to the class. "Can anyone explain the inyan?" he asked quietly.

He was answered by silence.

He sighed loudly. "Nu," he said, "no one can explain it. . . . The truth is, I cannot explain it myself. It is a difficult inyan. A very difficult inyan." He was silent for a moment, then he shook his head and smiled. "A teacher can also sometimes not know," he said softly.

That was the first time in my life I had ever heard a rabbi admit that he didn't understand a passage of Talmud.

We sat there in an uncomfortable silence. Rav Gershenson stared down at the open Talmud on his desk. Then he closed it slowly and dismissed the class.

As I was gathering up my books, I heard him call my name. Danny heard him, too, and looked at him. "I want to talk with you a minute," Rav Gershenson said. I went up to his desk.

Standing near him, I could see how wrinkled his face and brow were. The skin on his hands looked dry, parchmentlike, and his lips formed a thin line beneath the heavy tangle of gray beard. His eyes were brown and gentle, and deep wrinkles spread from their outside corners like tiny furrows.

He waited until all the students were out of the classroom. Then he asked me quietly, "You studied the inyan by yourself, Reuven?"

"Yes," I said.

"Your father did not help you?"

"My father is in the hospital."

He looked shocked.

"He's better now. He had a heart attack."

"I did not know," he said softly. "I am sorry to hear that."

He paused for a moment, looking at me intently. "So," he said. "You studied the inyan alone."

I nodded.

"Tell me, Reuven," he said gently, "do you study Talmud with your father?"

"Yes," I said.

"Your father is a great scholar," he said quietly, almost wistfully. "A very great scholar." His brown eyes seemed misty. "Reuven tell me, how would your father have answered my question?"

I stared at him and didn't know what to say.

He smiled faintly, apologetically. "You do not know how your father would have explained the inyan?"

The class was gone, we were alone, and somehow I felt an intimacy between us that made it not too difficult for me to say what I then said. I didn't say it without feeling a little frightened, though. "I think I know what he would have said."

"Nu," Rav Gershenson prodded me gently. "What?"

"I think he would have said the text is wrong."

I saw him blink his eyes a few times, his face expressionless. "Explain what you mean," he said quietly.

I explained how I had reconstructed the text, then quoted the reconstructed text from memory, showing him how it fitted perfectly to the explanation offered by the simplest of all the commentaries. I ended by saying I felt certain that was the text of the Talmud manuscript the commentator had had before him when he had written his commentary.

Rav Gershenson was silent for a long moment, his face impassive. Then he said slowly, "You did this by yourself, Reuven?"

"Yes."

"Your father is a good teacher," he told me quietly. "You are blessed to have such a father."

His voice was soft, reverent.

"Reuven?"

"Yes?"

"I must ask you never to use such a method of explanation in my class." He was speaking gently, almost apologetically. "I am myself not opposed to such a method. But I must ask you never to use it in my class. Do you understand me?"

"Yes."

"I will call on you often now," he said, smiling warmly. "Now that you understand, I will call on you very often. I have been waiting all year to see how good a teacher your father is. He is a great teacher and a great scholar. It is a joy to listen to you. But you must not use this method in my class. You understand?"

"Yes," I said again.

And he dismissed me with a quiet smile and a gentle nod of his head.

That evening after my last class, I went to the school library and looked for Rav Gershenson's name in the Hebrew and English catalogues. His name wasn't listed anywhere. It was then that I understood why my father was not teaching in this school.

CHAPTER FIFTEEN
****

MY FATHER RETURNED from the hospital in the middle of March. He was weak and gaunt, confined to his bed and almost completely incapable of any kind of physical activity. Manya cared for him as though he were a child, and Dr. Grossman visited him twice a week, on Mondays and Thursdays, until the end of April, when the visits were reduced to once a week. He was satisfied with my father's progress, he kept telling me. There was nothing to worry about anymore, except to make sure that he had complete rest. During the first four weeks my father was home a night nurse came in every evening, stayed awake through the night in my father's room, then left in the morning. Talking tired him quickly; even listening seemed to tire him. We weren't able to spend too much time together the first six weeks he was home. But it was wonderful to have him there, to know he was back in his room again and out of the hospital, and to know that the dark silence was finally gone from the apartment.

I had told him about my experience with Rav Gershenson while he had still been in the hospital. He had listened quietly, nodded, and had said that he was very proud of me. He hadn't said anything at all about Rav Gershenson. I was being called on regularly now in the Talmud class, and there were no silences when I read and explained a passage.

I saw Danny all the time in school, but the silence between us continued. I had finally come to accept it. We had begun to communicate with our eyes, with nods of our heads, with gestures of our hands. But we did not speak to each other. I had no idea how he was getting along in psychology, or how his family was. But I heard no bad news, so I assumed things were more or less all right.

The grim faces of the teachers and the students in school

reflected the newspaper headlines that told of Arab riots and attacks against the Jews of Palestine, Jewish defense measures, many of which were being hampered by the British, and continued Irgun activities. The Arabs were attacking Jewish settlements in the Upper Galilee, the Negev and around Jerusalem, and were incessantly harassing supply convoys. Arabs were killing Jews, Jews were killing Arabs, and the British, caught uncomfortably in the middle, seemed unable and at times even unwilling to stop the rising tide of slaughter.

The Zionist youth groups in the school became increasingly active, and on one occasion some of the members of my group were asked to cut our afternoon classes and go down to a warehouse in Brooklyn to help load uniforms, helmets, and canteens onto huge ten-ton trucks that were waiting outside. We were told that the supplies would soon be on a ship heading for Palestine and would be used by the Haganah. We worked long and hard, and somehow loading those trucks made me feel intimately bound up with the news bulletins that I kept hearing on the radio and seeing in the papers.

In April, Tiberias, Haifa, and Safed were occupied by the Haganah, and the Irgun, with the help of the Haganah, captured Jaffa.

My father was a good deal stronger now and had begun walking around a bit inside the house. We were able to talk at length, and we talked of little else but Palestine. He told me that before his heart attack he had been asked to go as a delegate to the Zionist General Council that was to meet in Palestine during the coming summer. "Now I will be glad if I can go to the cottage this summer," he said, and there was a wry smile on his lips.

"Why didn't you tell me?" I asked him.

"I did not want to upset you. But I could not keep it to myself any longer. So I am telling you now."

"Why didn't you tell me when they asked you?"

"They asked me the night I had the attack," he said.

We never talked about it again. But if I was around, I always knew when he thought about it. His eyes would become dreamy, and he would sigh and shake his head. He had worked so hard for a Jewish state, and that very work now kept him from seeing it. I wondered often during the coming months what meaning he could possibly give to that. I didn't know, and I didn't ask him.

We wept quite openly that Friday in the second week of May when Israel was born. And on my way to the synagogue the next morning, I saw the newspaper headlines announcing the birth of the Jewish state. They also announced that the Arab armies had begun their threatened invasion.

The next few weeks were black and ugly. The Etzion area in the Hebron Mountains fell, the Jordanian Army attacked Jerusalem, the Iraqi Army invaded the Jordan Valley, the Egyptian Army invaded the Negev, and the battle for Latrun, the decisive point along the road to Jerusalem, turned into a bloodbath. My father became grim and silent, and I began to worry again about his health.

In early June, a rumor swept through the school that a recent graduate had been killed in the fighting around Jerusalem. The rumor ran wild for a few days, and was finally confirmed. I hadn't know him at all, he had been graduated before I had entered, but apparently most of the present members of the senior class remembered him well. He had been a brilliant mathematics student, and very popular. He had gone to the Hebrew University in Jerusalem to get his doctorate, had joined the Haganah and been killed trying to get a convoy through to Jerusalem. We were stunned. We had never thought the war would come so close.

On a day in the second week of June, the same week the United Nations truce went into effect and the fighting in Israel ceased, the entire school attended an assembly in memory of the student. Everyone was there, every rabbi, student, and college teacher. One of his Talmud teachers described his devoutness and dedication to Judaism, his mathematics professor talked about his brilliance as a student, and one of the members of the senior class told of the way he had always spoken of going to Israel. Then we all stood as a prayer was chanted and the Kaddish was said.

Reb Saunders' anti-Zionist league died that day as far as the students in Hirsch College were concerned. It remained alive outside the school, but I never again saw an anti-Zionist leaflet inside the school building.

The final examinations were not too much of a problem to me that semester, and I made all A's. July came and brought

sweltering heat, and the happy announcement from Dr.
Grossman that my father was now well enough to be able to
go to the cottage in August and resume teaching in September. But he was to rest in the cottage, not work. Yes, he
could write—since when was writing work? My father
laughed at that, the first time he had laughed in months.

In September, my father resumed his teaching, and I entered my third year of college. Since symbolic logic was part
of philosophy, I had chosen philosophy as my major subject,
and I was finding it very exciting. The weeks passed quickly.
My father was doing nothing but teaching for the first few
months; then, with the approval of Dr. Grossman, he went
back to some of his Zionist activities and to teaching an adult
class one night a week.

The war in Israel continued sporadically, especially in the
Negev. But the initiative had passed to the Israelis, and the
tension was gone from it by now.

Reb Saunders' anti-Zionist league seemed to have gone out
of existence. I heard nothing about it, even in my own neighborhood. And one day in the late spring of that year, while I
was eating lunch, Danny came over to my table, smiled hesitantly, sat down, and asked me to give him a hand with his
experimental psychology; he was having difficulty setting up a
graph for a formula involving variables.

CHAPTER SIXTEEN
+++++++++++++++++++++++++

I FELT A LITTLE SHIVER hearing his voice.

"Welcome back to the land of the living," I said, staring up at him and feeling my heart turn over. It had been over two years now that we hadn't talked to each other.

He smiled faintly and rubbed his beard, which was quite thick. He was wearing his usual dark suit, tieless shirt, fringes, and skull cap. His earlocks hung down along the sides of his sculptured face, and his eyes were bright and very blue.

"The ban has been lifted," he said simply.

"It feels good to be kosher again," I told him, not without some bitterness in my voice.

He blinked his eyes and tried another smile. "I'm sorry," he said quietly.

"I'm sorry, too. I needed you around for a while. Especially when my father was sick."

He nodded, and his eyes were sad.

"How do you do it?" I asked.

He blinked again. "Do what?"

"How do you take the silence?"

He didn't say anything. But his face tightened.

"I hated it," I told him. "How do you take it?"

He pulled nervously at an earlock, his eyes dark and brooding.

"I think I would lose my mind," I said.

"No you wouldn't," he said softly. "You'd learn to live with it."

"Why does he do it?"

The hand pulling at the earlock dropped down to the table. He shook his head slowly. "I don't know. We still don't talk."

"Except when you study Talmud or he explodes."

He nodded soberly.

"I hate to tell you what I think of your father."

"He's a great man," Danny said evenly. "He must have a reason."

"I think it's crazy and sadistic," I said bitterly. "And I don't like your father at all."

"You're entitled to your opinion," Danny said softly. "And I'm entitled to mine."

We were silent for a moment.

"You've lost weight," I told him.

He nodded but remained silent. He sat there slumped over, looking small and uncomfortable, like a bird in pain.

"How are your eyes?" I asked.

He shrugged. "They bother me sometimes. The doctor says it's nervous tension."

There was another silence.

"It's good to have you back," I said. And I grinned.

He smiled hesitantly, his blue eyes bright and shining.

"You and your crazy way of hitting a baseball," I said. "You and your father with his crazy silences and explosions."

He smiled again, deeply now, and straightened up in the chair. "Will you help me with this graph?" he asked.

I told him it was about time he helped himself with graphs, and then showed him what to do.

When I told my father about it that night, he nodded soberly. He had expected it, he said. The Jewish state was not an issue anymore but a fact. How long would Reb Saunders have continued his ban over a dead issue?

"How is Danny feeling?" he wanted to know.

I told him Danny didn't look well and had lost a lot of weight.

He was thoughtful for a moment. Then he said, "Reuven, the silence between Danny and Reb Saunders. It is continuing?"

"Yes."

His face was sad. "A father can bring up a child any way he wishes," he said softly. "What a price to pay for a soul."

When I asked him what he meant, he wouldn't say anything more about it. But his eyes were dark.

So Danny and I resumed our old habits of meeting in front

of my synagogue, of riding to school together, eating lunch together, and going home together. Rav Gershenson's class became a particular joy, because the ease between Danny and myself now permitted us to engage in a constant flow of competitive discussion that virtually monopolized the hours of the shiur. We dominated the class to such an extent that one day, after a particularly heated Talmudic battle between Danny and me that had gone on uninterrupted for almost a quarter of an hour, Rav Gershenson stopped us and pointed out that this wasn't a private lesson he was giving; there were twelve other students in the class—didn't anyone else have something to say? But he said it with a warm smile, and Danny and I were delighted by his oblique compliment.

A few days after we had resumed talking, Danny told me that he had resigned himself to experimental psychology and was even beginning to enjoy it. When he talked about psychology now, he invariably used the technical language of the experimentalist: variables, constants, manipulation, observation, recording of data, testing hypotheses, and the advantages of attempting to refute hypotheses as against confirming them. Mathematics no longer seemed to be much of a problem to him. Only rarely now did he need my help.

We were sitting in the lunchroom one day when he told me of a conversation he had had with Professor Appleman. "He said if I ever wanted to make any kind of valuable contribution to psychology I would have to use scientific method. The Freudian approach doesn't really provide a method of accepting or rejecting hypotheses, and that's no way to acquire knowledge."

"Well, well." I grinned. "Goodbye Freud."

He shook his head. "No. It's not goodbye Freud. Freud was a genius. But he was too circumspect in his findings. I want to know a lot more than just the things Freud dealt with. Freud never really did anything with perception, for example. Or with learning. How people see, hear, touch, smell, taste, and learn is a fascinating subject. Freud never went into any of that. But he was a genius, all right, in what he did go into."

"You're going to become an experimentalist?"

"I don't think so. I want to work with people, not with rats and mazes. I talked to Appleman about it. He suggested I go into clinical psychology."

"What's that?"

"Well, it's the same as the difference between theoretical and applied physics, say. The experimental psychologist is more or less the theoretician; the clinical psychologist applies what the experimentalist learns. He gets to work with people. He examines them, tests them, diagnoses them, even treats them."

"What do you mean, treats them?"

"He does therapy."

"You're going to become an analyst?"

"Maybe. But psychoanalysis is only one form of therapy. There are many other kinds."

"What kinds?"

"Oh, many kinds," he said vaguely. "A lot of it is still very experimental."

"You're planning to experiment on people?"

"I don't know. Maybe. I really don't know too much about it yet."

"Are you going on for a doctorate?"

"Sure. You can't move in this field without a doctorate."

"Where are you planning to go?"

"I don't know yet. Appleman suggested Columbia. That's where he got his doctorate."

"Does your father know yet?"

Danny gave me a tight, strained look. "No," he said quietly.

"When will you tell him?"

"The day I receive my smicha." "Smicha" is the Hebrew term for rabbinic ordination.

"That's next year," I said.

Danny nodded grimly. Then he looked at his watch. "We'd better move or we'll be late for the shiur," he said.

We raced up the stairs to Rav Gershenson's class and made it just a moment before he called on someone to read and explain.

During another one of our lunchroom conversations, Danny asked me what good symbolic logic was going to be for me when I entered the rabbinate. I told him I didn't

know, but I was doing a lot of reading in philosophy and theology, and some good might come of that.

"I always thought that logic and theology were like David
and Saul," Danny said.

"They are. But I might help them get better acquainted."

He shook his head. "I can't get over your becoming a
rabbi."

"I can't get over your becoming a psychologist."

And we looked at each other in quiet wonder.

In June, Danny's sister was married. I was invited to the
wedding and was the only one there who wasn't a Hasid. It
was a traditionally Hasidic wedding, with the men and
women sitting separately and with a lot of dancing and singing. I was shocked when I saw Reb Saunders. His black
beard had begun to go gray, and he seemed to have aged a
great deal since I had seen him last. I went over to congratu-
late him, and he shook my hand warmly, his eyes dark and
piercing. He was surrounded by people, and we didn't have a
chance to talk. I didn't care. I wasn't particularly eager to
talk to him. Levi had grown up a little, but he still looked
white-skinned, and his eyes seemed large behind his shell-
rimmed glasses. Danny's sister had become a beautiful girl.
The boy she married was a Hasid, with a black beard, long
earlocks, and dark eyes. He looked rather severe, and I
quickly decided that I didn't like him. When I congratulated
him after the wedding and shook his hand, his fingers were
limp and moist.

When the school year ended and July came around, I went
over to Danny's house one morning. Except for the wedding,
I hadn't seen Reb Saunders at all since Danny and I had
begun talking again, because my father was teaching me Talmud on Shabbat afternoons. So I decided it would be the polite thing to do to go over one morning after the school year.
Danny took me up to his father's study. The third-floor hallway was crowded with dark-caftaned men, waiting around in
silence to see his father. They nodded and murmured respect-
ful greetings to Danny, and one of them, an incredibly old
man with a white beard and a bent body, reached out and
touched his arm as we passed. I found the gesture distasteful.
I was beginning to find everything connected with Reb Saun-

ders and Hasidism distasteful. We waited until the person who was with his father came out, then we went in.

Reb Saunders sat in his straight-backed red leather chair surrounded by books and the musty odor of old bindings. His face seemed lined with pain, but his voice was soft when he greeted me. He was, he said quietly, very happy to see me. He hesitated, looked at me, then at Danny. His eyes were dark and brooding. Where was I keeping myself, he asked, and why wasn't I coming over anymore on Shabbos afternoons? I told him my father and I were studying Talmud together on Shabbat. His eyes brooded, and he sighed. He nodded vaguely. He wished he could spend more time talking to me now, he said, but there were so many people who needed to see him. Couldn't I come over some Shabbos afternoon? I told him I would try, and Danny and I went out.

That was all he said. Not a word about Zionism. Not a word about the silence he had imposed upon Danny and me. Nothing. I found I disliked him more when I left than when I had entered. I did not see him again that July.

CHAPTER SEVENTEEN
✦✦✦✦✦✦✦✦✦✦✦✦✦✦✦✦✦✦✦✦✦✦✦✦✦✦✦

OUR LAST YEAR of college began that September. Over lunch one day I told Danny a mild anti-Hasidic story I had heard, and he laughed loudly. Then, without thinking, I mentioned a remark one of the students had made a few days back: "The tzaddik sits in absolute silence, saying nothing, and all his followers listen attentively," and the laughter left his lips as suddenly as if he had been slapped, and his face froze.

I realized immediately what I had said, and felt myself go cold. I muttered a helpless apology.

For a long moment, he said nothing. His eyes seemed glazed, turned inward. Then his face slowly relaxed. He smiled faintly. "There's more truth to that than you realize," he murmured. "You can listen to silence, Reuven. I've begun to realize that you can listen to silence and learn from it. It has a quality and a dimension all its own. It talks to me sometimes. I feel myself alive in it. It talks. And I can hear it."

The words came out in a soft singsong. He sounded exactly like his father.

"You don't understand that, do you?" he asked.

"No."

He nodded. "I didn't think you would."

"What do you mean, it talks to you?"

"You have to want to listen to it, and then you can hear it. It has a strange, beautiful texture. It doesn't always talk. Sometimes—sometimes it cries, and you can hear the pain of the world in it. It hurts to listen to it then. But you have to."

I felt myself go cold again, hearing him talk that way. "I don't understand that at all."

He smiled faintly.

"Are you and your father talking these days?"

He shook his head.

I didn't understand any of it, but he seemed so somber and strange that I didn't want to talk about it anymore. I changed the subject. "You ought to get yourself a girl," I told him. I was dating regularly now on Saturday nights. "It's a wonderful tonic for a suffering soul."

He looked at me, his eyes sad. "My wife has been chosen for me," he said quietly.

I gaped at him.

"It's an old Hasidic custom, remember?"

"It never occurred to me," I said, shocked.

He nodded soberly. "That's another reason it won't be so easy to break out of the trap. It doesn't only involve my own family."

I didn't know what to say. There was a long, uncomfortable silence. And we walked together in that silence to Rav Gershenson's shiur.

Danny's brother's bar mitzvah celebration, which I attended on a Monday morning during the third week in October, was a simple and unpretentious affair. The Morning Service began at seven-thirty—early enough to enable Danny and me to attend and not come late to school—and Levi was called to recite the blessing over the Torah. After the service there was a kiddush, consisting of schnapps and some cakes and cookies. Everyone drank l'chaim, to life, then left. Reb Saunders asked me quietly why I wasn't coming over to see him anymore, and I explained that my father and I were studying Talmud together on Shabbat afternoons. He nodded vaguely and walked slowly away, his tall frame somewhat stooped.

Levi Saunders was now tall and thin. He seemed a ghostly imitation of Danny, except that his hair was black and his eyes were dark. The skin on his hands and face was milky white, almost translucent, showing the branching veins. There was something helplessly fragile about him; he looked as if a wind would blow him down. Yet at the same time his dark eyes burned with a kind of inner fire that told of the tenacity with which he clung to life and of his growing awareness of the truth that for the rest of his days his every breath would depend upon the pills he put into his mouth at regular intervals. The eyes told you that he had every intention of holding on to his life, no matter what the pain.

As if to emphasize the tenuousness of Levi Saunders' existence, he became violently ill the day following his bar mitzvah and was taken by ambulance to the Brooklyn Memorial Hospital. Danny called me during supper as soon as the ambulance pulled away from in front of his house, and I could tell from his voice that he was in a panic. There wasn't much I could say to him over the phone, and when I asked him if he wanted me to come over, he said no, his mother was almost hysterical, he would have to stay with her, he had only wanted to let me know. And he hung up.

My father apparently had heard my troubled voice, because he was standing now outside the kitchen, asking me what was wrong.

I told him.

We resumed our supper. I wasn't very hungry now, but I ate anyway to keep Manya happy. My father noticed how disturbed I was, but he said nothing. After the meal, he followed me into my room, sat on my bed while I sat at my desk, and asked me what was wrong, why was I so upset by Levi Saunders' illness, he had been ill before.

It was at that point that I told my father of Danny's plans to go on for a doctorate in psychology and abandon the position of tzaddik he was to inherit one day from Reb Saunders. I also added, feeling that I ought to be completely honest about it now, that Danny was in a panic over his brother's illness because without his brother it might not be possible for him to break away from his father; he did not really want to destroy the dynasty.

My father's face became more and more grim as he listened. When I was done, he sat for a long time in silence, his eyes grave.

"When did Danny tell you this?" he asked finally.

"The summer I lived in their house."

"That long ago? He knew already that long ago?"

"Yes."

"And all this time you did not tell me?"

"It was a secret between us, abba."

He looked at me grimly. "Does Danny know what pain this will cause his father?"

"He dreads the day he'll have to tell him. He dreads it for both of them."

"I knew it would happen," my father said. "How could it not happen?" Then he looked at me sharply. "Reuven, let me understand this. Exactly what is Danny planning to tell Reb Saunders?"

"That he's going on for a doctorate in psychology and doesn't intend to take his place."

"Is Danny thinking to abandon his Judaism?"

I stared at him. "I never thought to ask him," I said faintly.

"His beard, his earlocks, his clothes, his fringes—all this he will retain in graduate school?"

"I don't know, abba. We never talked about it."

"Reuven, how will Danny become a psychologist while looking like a Hasid?"

I didn't know what to say.

"It is important that Danny know exactly what he will tell his father. He must anticipate what questions will be on Reb Saunders' mind. Talk to Danny. Let him think through exactly what he will tell his father."

"All this time I never thought to ask him."

"Danny is now like a person waiting to be let out of jail. He has only one desire. To leave the jail. Despite what may be waiting for him outside. Danny cannot think one minute beyond the moment he will have to tell his father he does not wish to take his place. Do you understand me?"

"Yes."

"You will talk to him?"

"Of course."

My father nodded grimly, his face troubled. "I have not talked to Danny in so long," he said quietly. He was silent for a moment. Then he smiled faintly. "It is not so easy to be a friend, is it, Reuven?"

"No," I said.

"Tell me, Danny and Reb Saunders still do not talk?"

I shook my head. Then I told him what Danny had said about silence. "What does it mean to hear silence, abba?"

That seemed to upset him more than the news about Danny's not becoming a tzaddik. He sat up straight on the bed, his body quivering. "Hasidim!" I heard him mutter, almost contemptuously. "Why must they feel the burden of the world is only on their shoulders?"

I looked at him, puzzled. I had never heard that tone of contempt in his voice before.

"It is a way of bringing up children," he said.

"What is?"

"Silence."

"I don't understand—"

"I cannot explain it. I do not understand it completely myself. But what I know of it, I dislike. It was practiced in Europe by some few Hasidic families." Then his voice went hard. "There are better ways to teach a child compassion."

"I don't—"

He cut me short. "Reuven, I cannot explain what I do not understand. Danny is being raised by Reb Saunders in a certain way. I do not want to talk about it anymore. It upsets me. You will speak to Danny, yes?"

I nodded.

"Now I have work I must do." And he went from the room, leaving me as bewildered as I had been before.

I had planned to talk to Danny the next day, but when I saw him he was in such a state of panic over his brother that I didn't dare mention what my father had said. The doctors had diagnosed his brother's illness as some kind of imbalance in the blood chemistry caused by something he had eaten, Danny told me over lunch, looking pale and grim, and blinking his eyes repeatedly. They were trying out some new pills, and his brother would remain in the hospital until they were certain the pills worked. And he would have to be very careful from now on with his diet. Danny was tense and miserable all that day and throughout the week.

Levi Saunders was discharged from the Brooklyn Memorial Hospital the following Wednesday afternoon. I saw Danny in school the next day. We sat in the lunchroom and ate for a while in silence. His brother was fine, he said finally, and everything seemed to have settled down. His mother was in bed with high blood pressure, though. But the doctor said it was caused by her excitement over Levi's illness and all she needed now was to rest. She would be better soon.

He told me quietly that he was planning to write to three

universities that day—Harvard, Berkeley, and Columbia—and apply for a fellowship in psychology. I asked him how long he thought he would be able to keep his applications a secret.

"I don't know," he said, his voice a little tight.

"Why don't you tell your father now and get it over with?"

He looked at me, his face grim. "I don't want explosions with every meal," he said tightly. "All I get are either explosions or silence. I've had enough of his explosions."

Then I told him what my father had said. As I spoke, I could see him become more and more uncomfortable.

"I didn't want you to tell your father," he muttered angrily.

"My father kept your library visits a secret from me," I reminded him. "Don't worry about my father."

"I don't want you to tell anyone else."

"I won't. What about what my father said? Are you going to remain an Orthodox Jew?"

"Whatever gave you the notion that I had any intention of not remaining an Orthodox Jew?"

"What if your father asks about the beard, the caftan, the—"

"He won't ask me."

"What if he does?"

He pulled nervously at an earlock. "Can you see me practicing psychology and looking like a Hasid?" he asked tightly.

I hadn't really expected any other answer. Then something occurred to me. "Won't your father see the mail you get from the graduate schools you've applied to?"

He stared at me. "I never thought of that," he said slowly. "I'll have to intercept the mail." He hesitated, his face rigid. "I can't. It comes after I leave for school." And his eyes filled with fear.

"I think you ought to have a talk with my father," I said.

Danny came over to our apartment that night, and I took him into my father's study. My father came quickly around from behind his desk and shook Danny's hand.

"I have not seen you in such a long time," he said, smiling warmly. "It is good to see you again, Danny. Please sit down."

My father did not sit behind his desk. He sat next to us on

the kitchen chair he had asked me earlier to bring into the study.

"Do not be angry at Reuven for telling me," he said quietly to Danny. "I have had practice with keeping secrets."

Danny smiled nervously.

"You will tell your father on the day of your ordination?"

Danny nodded.

"There is a girl involved?"

Danny nodded again, giving me a momentary glance.

"You will refuse to marry this girl?"

"Yes."

"And your father will have to explain to her parents and to his followers."

Danny was silent, his face tight.

My father sighed softly. "It will be a very uncomfortable situation. For you and for your father. You are determined not to take your father's place?"

"Yes," Danny said.

"Then you must know exactly what you will tell him. Think carefully of what you will say. Think what your father's questions will be. Think what he will be most concerned about after he hears of your decision. Do you understand me, Danny?"

Danny nodded slowly.

There was a long silence.

Then my father leaned forward in his chair. "Danny," he said softly, "you can hear silence?"

Danny looked at him, startled. His blue eyes were wide, frightened. He glanced at me. Then he looked again at my father. And, slowly, he nodded his head.

"You are not angry at your father?"

Danny shook his head.

"Do you understand what he is doing?"

Danny hesitated. Then he shook his head again. His eyes were wide and moist.

My father sighed again. "It will be explained to you," he said softly. "Your father will explain it to you. Because he will want you to carry it on with your own children one day."

Danny blinked his eyes nervously.

"No one can help you with this, Danny. It is between you

and your father. But think carefully of what you will say to him and of what his questions will be."

My father came with us to the door of our apartment. I could hear Danny's capped shoes tapping against the outside hallway floor. Then he was gone.

"What is this again about hearing silence, abba?" I asked.

But my father would say nothing. He went into his study and closed the door.

Danny received letters of acceptance from each of the three universities to which he had applied. The letters came in the mail to his home and lay untouched on the vestibule table until he returned from school. He told me about it in early January, a day after the third letter had come. I asked him who usually picked up the mail.

"My father," he said, looking tense and bewildered. "Levi's in school when it comes, and my mother doesn't like climbing stairs."

"Were there return addresses on the envelopes?"

"Of course."

"Then how can't he know?" I asked him.

"I don't understand it," he said, his voice edged with panic. "What is he waiting for? Why doesn't he say something?"

I felt sick with his fear and said nothing.

Danny told me a few days later that his sister was pregnant. She and her husband had been over to the house and had informed his parents. His father had smiled for the first time since Levi's bar mitzvah, Danny said, and his mother had wept with joy. I asked him if his father gave any indication at all of knowing what his plans were.

"No," he said.

"No indication at all?"

"No, I get nothing from him but silence."

"Is he silent with Levi, too?"

"No."

"Was he silent with your sister?"

"No."

"I don't like your father," I told him. "I don't like him at all."

Danny said nothing. But his eyes blinked his fear.

A few days later, he told me, "My father asked me why you're not coming over anymore on Shabbat."

"He talked to you?"

"He didn't talk. That isn't talking."

"I study Talmud on Shabbat."

"I know."

"I'm not too eager to see him."

He nodded unhappily.

"Have you decided which university you're going to?"

"Columbia."

"Why don't you tell him and get it over with?"

"I'm afraid."

"What difference does it make? If he's going to throw you out of the house, he'll do it no matter when you tell him."

"I'll have my degree in June. I'll be ordained."

"You can live with us. No, you can't. You won't eat at our house."

"I could live with my sister."

"Yes."

"I'm afraid. I'm afraid of the explosion. I'm afraid of anytime I'll have to tell him. God, I'm afraid."

My father would say nothing when I talked to him about it. "It is for Reb Saunders to explain," he told me quietly. "I cannot explain what I do not completely understand. I cannot do it with my students, and I cannot do it with my son."

A few days later, Danny told me that his father had asked again why I wasn't coming over to their house anymore.

"I'll try to get over," I said.

But I didn't try very hard. I didn't want to see Reb Saunders. I hated him as much now as I had when he had forced his silence between me and Danny.

The weeks passed and winter melted slowly into spring. Danny was working on an experimental psychology project that had to do with the relationship between reinforcement and rapidity of learning, and I was doing a long paper on the logic of ought statements. Danny pushed himself relentlessly in his work. He grew thin and gaunt, and the angles and bones of his face and hands jutted like sharp peaks from beneath his skin. He stopped talking about the silence between him and his father. He seemed to be shouting down the silence with his work. Only his constantly blinking eyes gave any indication of his mounting terror.

The day before the start of the Passover school vacation period, he told me that his father had asked him once again why I wasn't coming over to their house anymore. Could I possibly come over on Passover? he had wanted to know. He especially wanted to see me the first or second day of Passover.

"I'll try," I said halfheartedly, without the slightest intention of trying at all.

But when I talked to my father that night, he said, with a strange sharpness in his voice, "You did not tell me Reb Saunders has been asking to see you."

"He's been asking all along."

"Reuven, when someone asks to speak to you, you must let him speak to you. You still have not learned that? You did not learn that from what happened between you and Danny?"

"He wants to study Talmud, abba."

"You are sure?"

"That's all we've ever done when I go over there."

"You only study Talmud? You have forgotten so quickly?"

I stared at him. "He wants to talk to me about Danny," I said, and felt myself turn cold.

"You will go over the first day of the holiday. On Sunday."

"Why didn't he tell me?"

"Reuven, he did tell you. You have not been listening."

"All these weeks—"

"Listen next time. Listen when someone speaks to you."

"Maybe I should go over tonight."

"No. They will be busy preparing for the holiday."

"I'll go over on Shabbat."

"Reb Saunders asked you to come on Passover."

"I told him we study Talmud on Shabbat."

"You will go on Passover. He has a reason if he asked you to come especially on Passover. And listen next time when someone speaks to you, Reuven."

He was angry, as angry as he had been in the hospital years ago when I had refused to talk to Danny.

I called Danny and told him I would be over on Sunday.

He sensed something in my voice. "What's wrong?"

"Nothing's wrong. I'll see you on Sunday."

"Nothing's wrong?" His voice was tight, apprehensive.

"No."

"Come over around four," he said. "My father needs to rest in the early afternoons."

"Four."

"Nothing's wrong?"

"I'll see you on Sunday," I told him.

CHAPTER EIGHTEEN
❋❋❋❋❋❋❋❋❋❋❋❋❋❋❋❋❋❋❋❋❋❋

ON THE AFTERNOON of the first day of Passover, I walked beneath the early spring sycamores on my street, then turned into Lee Avenue. The sun was warm and bright, and I went along slowly, past the houses and the shops and the synagogue where my father and I prayed. I met one of my classmates and we stopped to talk for a few minutes; then I went on alone, turning finally into Danny's street. The sycamores formed a tangled bower through which the sun shone brightly, speckling the ground. There were tiny buds on these sycamores now and on some I could see the green shoots of infant leaves. In a month, those leaves would shut out the sky, but now the sun came through and brushed streaks of gold across the sidewalks, the street, the talking women, and the playing children. I walked along slowly, remembering the first time I had gone up this street years ago. Those years were coming to an end now. In three months, in a time when the leaves would be fat and full, our lives would separate like the branches overhead that made their own way into the sunlight.

I went slowly up the wide stone staircase of Danny's house and through the wooden double door of the entrance. The hallway was dim and cold. The synagogue door stood open. I peered inside. Its emptiness whispered echoes at me: mistakes, gematriya, Talmud quizzes, and Reb Saunders staring at my left eye. You do not know yet what it is to be a friend. Scientific criticism, ah! Your father is an observer of the Commandments. It is not easy to be a true friend. Soft, silent echoes. It seemed tiny to me now, the synagogue, so much less neat than when I had seen it for the first time. The stands were scarred, the walls needed paint, the naked light bulbs seemed ugly, their bare, black wires like the dead branches of a stunted tree. What echoes will Reb Saunders' study have? I thought. And I felt myself go tight with apprehension.

I stood at the foot of the inner stairway and called Danny's name. My voice moved heavily through the silent house. I waited a moment, then called his name again. I heard the tapping of metal-capped shoes upon the third-floor stairway, then in the hallway over my head; and then Danny was standing at the head of the stairs, tall, gaunt, an almost spectral figure with his beard and earlocks and black satin caftan.

I climbed the stairs slowly, and he greeted me. He looked tired. His mother was resting, he said, and his brother was out somewhere. He and his father were studying Talmud. His voice was dull, flat, only faintly edged with fear. But his eyes mirrored clearly what his voice concealed.

We went up to the third floor. Danny seemed to hesitate before the door to his father's study, almost as if he was wishing not to have to go back in there again. Then he opened the door, and we stepped inside.

It had been almost a year since I had last been inside Reb Saunders' study, but nothing about it had changed. There was the same massive, black wood, glass-topped desk, the same red carpet, the same glass-enclosed wooden bookcases jammed tight with books, the same musty old-book odor in the air, the same single light bulb glowing white behind its ceiling fixture. Nothing had really changed—nothing, except Reb Saunders himself.

He sat in his straight-backed, red leather chair and looked at me from behind the desk. His beard had gone almost completely gray, and he sat stooped forward, bent, as though he were carrying something on his shoulders. His brow was criss-crossed with wrinkles, his dark eyes brooded and burned with some kind of invisible suffering, and the fingers of his right hand played aimlessly with a long, gray earlock.

He greeted me quietly, but did not offer me his hand. I had the feeling that a handshake was a physical effort he wanted to avoid.

Danny and I sat in the chairs by his desk, Danny to his right, I to his left. Danny's face was expressionless, closed. He tugged nervously at an earlock.

Reb Saunders moved forward slightly in the chair and put his hands on the desk. Slowly, he closed the Talmud from which he and Danny had been studying. Then he sighed, a deep, trembling sigh that filled the silence of the room like a wind.

"Nu, Reuven," he said quietly, "finally, finally you come to see me." He spoke in Yiddish, his voice quavering a little as the words came out.

"I apologize," I said hesitantly, in English.

He nodded his head, and his right hand went up and stroked his gray beard. "You have become a man," he said quietly. "The first day you sat here, you were only a boy. Now you are a man."

Danny seemed suddenly to become conscious of the way he was twisting his earlock. He put his hand on his lap, clasped both hands tightly together and sat very still, staring at his father.

Reb Saunders looked at me and smiled feebly, nodding his head. "My son, my Daniel, has also become a man. It is a great joy for a father to see his son suddenly a man."

Danny stirred faintly in his chair, then was still.

"What will you do after your graduation?" Reb Saunders asked quietly.

"I have another year to study for smicha."

"And then what?"

"I'm going into the rabbinate."

He looked at me and blinked his eyes. I thought I saw him stiffen for a moment, as though in sudden pain. "You are going to become a rabbi," he murmured, speaking more to himself than to me. He was silent for a moment. "Yes. I remember. . . . Yes. . . ." He sighed again and shook his head slowly, the gray beard moving back and forth. "My Daniel will receive his smicha in June," he said quietly. Then he added, "In June. . . . Yes. . . . His smicha. . . . Yes. . . ." The words trailed off, aimless, disconnected, and hung in the air for a long moment of tight silence.

Then, slowly, he moved his right hand across the closed Talmud, and his fingers caressed the Hebrew title of the tractate that was stamped into the spine of the binding. Then he clasped both hands together and rested them on top of the Talmud. His body followed the movements of his hands, and his gray earlocks moved along the sides of his aged face.

"Nu," he said, speaking softly, so softly I could barely hear him, "in June my Daniel and his good friend begin to go different ways. They are men, not children, and men go different ways. You will go one way, Reuven. And my son, my Daniel, he will—he will go another way."

I saw Danny's mouth fall open. His body gave a single convulsive shudder. Different ways, I thought. *Different* ways. Then he—

"I know," Reb Saunders murmured, as if he were reading my mind. "I have known it for a long time."

Danny let out a soft, half-choked, trembling moan. Reb Saunders did not look at him. He had not once looked at him. He was talking to Danny through me.

"Reuven, I want you to listen carefully to what I will tell you now." He had said: Reuven. His eyes had said: Danny. "You will not understand it. You may never understand it. And you may never stop hating me for what I have done. I know how you feel. I do not see it in your eyes? But I want you to listen.

"A man is born into this world with only a tiny spark of goodness in him. The spark is God, it is the soul; the rest is ugliness and evil, a shell. The spark must be guarded like a treasure, it must be nurtured, it must be fanned into flame. It must learn to seek out other sparks, it must dominate the shell. Anything can be a shell, Reuven. Anything. Indifference, laziness, brutality, and genius. Yes, even a great mind can be a shell and choke the spark.

"Reuven, the Master of the Universe blessed me with a brilliant son. And he cursed me with all the problems of raising him. Ah, what it is to have a brilliant son! Not a smart son, Reuven, but a brilliant son, a Daniel, a boy with a mind like a jewel. Ah, what a curse it is, what an anguish it is to have a Daniel, whose mind is like a pearl, like a sun. Reuven, when my Daniel was four years old, I saw him reading a story from a book. And I was frightened. He did not read the story, he swallowed it, as one swallows food or water. There was no soul in my four-year-old Daniel, there was only his mind. He was a mind in a body without a soul. It was a story in a Yiddish book about a poor Jew and his struggles to get to Eretz Yisroel before he died. Ah, how that man suffered! And my Daniel *enjoyed* the story, he *enjoyed* the last terrible page, because when he finished it he realized for the first time what a memory he had. He looked at me proudly and told me back the story from memory, and I cried inside my heart. I went away and cried to the Master of the Universe, 'What have you done to me? A mind like this I need for a son? A *heart* I need for a son, a *soul* I need for a son, *compassion* I want from my son, righteousness, mercy, strength to suffer and carry pain, *that* I want from my son, not a mind without a soul!' "

Reb Saunders paused and took a deep, trembling breath. I tried to swallow; my mouth was sand-dry. Danny sat with his right hand over his eyes, his glasses pushed up on his forehead. He was crying silently, his shoulders quivering. Reb Saunders did not look at him.

"My brother was like my Daniel," he went on quietly. "What a mind he had. What a mind. But he was also not like my Daniel. My Daniel, thank God, is healthy. But for many, many years my brother was ill. His mind burned with hunger for knowledge. But for many years his body was wasted with disease. And so my father did not raise him as he raised me. When he was well enough to go off to a yeshiva to study, it was too late.

"I was only a child when he left to study in Odessa, but I still remember what he was able to do with his mind. But it was a cold mind, Reuven, almost cruel, untouched by his soul. It was proud, haughty, impatient with less brilliant minds, grasping in its search for knowledge the way a conqueror grasps for power. It could not understand pain, it was indifferent to and impatient with suffering. It was even impatient with the illness of its own body. I never saw my brother again after he left for the yeshiva. He came under the influence of a Maskil in Odessa and went away to France where he became a great mathematician and taught in a university. He died in a gas chamber in Auschwitz. I learned of it four years ago. He was a Jew when he died, not an observer of the Commandments, but not a convert, thank God. I would like to believe that before he died he learned how much suffering there is in this world. I hope so. It will have redeemed his soul.

"Reuven, listen to what I am going to tell you now and remember it. You are a man, but it will be years before you understand my words. Perhaps you will never understand them. But hear me out, and have patience.

"When I was very young, my father, may he rest in peace, began to wake me in the middle of the night, just so I would cry. I was a child, but he would wake me and tell me stories of the destruction of Jerusalem and the sufferings of the people of Israel, and I would cry. For years he did this. Once he took me to visit a hospital—ah, what an experience that was! —and often he took me to visit the poor, the beggars, to listen to them talk. My father himself never talked to me, except when we studied together. He taught me with silence. He taught me to look into myself, to find my own strength, to walk around inside myself in company with my soul. When his people would ask him why he was so silent with his son, he would say to them that he did not like to talk, words are cruel, words play tricks, they disort what is in the heart, they conceal the heart, the heart speaks through silence. One learns of the pain of others by suffering one's own pain, he would say, by turning inside oneself, by finding one's own soul. And it is important to know of pain, he said. It destroys our self-pride, our arrogance, our indifference toward others. It makes us aware of how frail and tiny we are and of how much we must depend upon the Master of the Universe. Only slowly, very slowly, did I begin to understand what he was saying. For years his silence bewildered and frightened me, though I always trusted him, I never hated him. And when I was old enough to understand, he told me that of all people a tzaddik expecially must know of pain. A tzaddik must know how to suffer for his people, he said. He must take their pain from them and carry it on his own shoulders. He must carry it always. He must grow old before his years. He must cry, in his heart he must always cry. Even when he dances and sings, he must cry for the sufferings of his people.

"You do not understand this, Reuven. I see from your eyes that you do not understand this. But my Daniel understands it now. He understands it well.

"Reuven, I did not want my Daniel to become like my brother, may he rest in peace. Better I should have had no son at all than to have a brilliant son who had no soul. I looked at my Daniel when he was four years old, and I said to myself, How will I teach this mind what it is to have a soul? How will I teach this mind to understand pain? How will I teach it to *want* to take on another person's suffering?

How will I do this and not lose my son, my precious son whom I love as I love the Master of the Universe Himself? How will I do this and not cause my son, God forbid, to abandon the Master of the Universe and His Commandments? How could I teach my son the way I was taught by my father and not drive him away from Torah? Because this is America, Reuven. This is not Europe. It is an open world here. Here there are libraries and books and schools. Here there are great universities that do not concern themselves with how many Jewish students they have. I did not want to drive my son away from God, but I did not want him to grow up a mind without a soul. I knew already when he was a boy that I could not prevent his mind from going to the world for knowledge. I knew in my heart that it might prevent him from taking my place. But I had to prevent it from driving him away completely from the Master of the Universe. And I had to make certain his soul would be the soul of a tzaddik no matter what he did with his life."

He closed his eyes and seemed to shrink into himself. His hands trembled. He was silent for a long time. Tears rolled slowly down alongside the bridge of his nose and disappeared into his beard. A shuddering sigh filled the room. Then he opened his eyes and stared down at the closed Talmud on the desk. "Ah, what a price to pay. . . . The years when he was a child and I loved him and talked with him and held him under my tallis when I prayed. . . . 'Why do you cry, Father?' he asked me once under the tallis. 'Because people are suffering,' I told him. He could not understand. Ah, what it is to be a mind without a soul, what ugliness it is. . . . Those were the years he learned to trust me and love me. . . . And when he was older, the years I drew myself away from him. . . . 'Why have you stopped answering my questions, Father?' he asked me once. 'You are old enough to look into your own soul for the answers,' I told him. He laughed once and said, 'That man is such an ignoramus, Father.' I was angry. 'Look into his soul,' I said. 'Stand inside his soul and see the world through his eyes. You will know the pain he feels because of his ignorance, and you will not laugh.' He was bewildered and hurt. The nightmares he began to have. . . . But he learned to find answers for himself. He suffered and learned to listen to the suffering of others. In the silence between us, he began to hear the world crying."

He stopped. A sigh came from his lips, a long, trembling sigh like a moan. Then he looked at me, his eyes moist with his own suffering. "Reuven, you and your father were a blessing to me. The Master of the Universe sent you to my son. He sent you when my son was ready to rebel. He sent you to listen to my son's words. He sent you to be my closed eyes and my sealed ears. I looked at your soul, Reuven, not your mind. In your father's writings I looked at his soul, not his mind. If you had not found the gematriya mistake, Reuven, it would have made a difference? No. The gematriya mistake only told me you had a good mind. But your soul I knew already. I knew it when my Daniel came home and told me he wanted to be your friend. Ah, you should have seen his eyes that day. You should have heard his voice. What an effort it was for him to talk to me. But he talked. I knew your soul, Reuven, before I knew your mind or your face. A thousand times I have thanked the Master of the Universe that He sent you and your father to my son.

"You think I was cruel? Yes, I see from your eyes that you think I was cruel to my Daniel. Perhaps. But he has learned. Let my Daniel become a psychologist. I know he wishes to become a psychologist. I do not see his books? I did not see the letters from the universities? I do not see his eyes? I do not hear his soul crying? Of course I know. For a long time I have known. Let my Daniel become a psychologist. I have no more fear now. All his life he will be a tzaddik. He will be a tzaddik for the world. And the world needs a tzaddik."

Reb Saunders stopped and looked slowly over at his son. Danny still sat with his hand over his eyes, his shoulders trembling. Reb Saunders looked at his son a long time. I had the feeling he was preparing himself for some gigantic effort, one that would completely drain what little strength he had left.

Then he spoke his son's name.

There was silence.

Reb Saunders spoke his son's name again. Danny took his hand away from his eyes and looked at his father.

"Daniel," Reb Saunders said, speaking almost in a whisper,

"when you go away to study, you will shave off your beard and earlocks?"

Danny stared at his father. His eyes were wet. He nodded his head slowly.

Reb Saunders looked at him. "You will remain an observer of the Commandments?" he asked softly.

Danny nodded again.

Reb Saunders sat back slowly in his chair. And from his lips came a soft, tremulous sigh. He was silent for a moment, his eyes wide, dark, brooding, gazing upon his son. He nodded his head once, as if in final acknowledgment of his tortured victory.

Then he looked back at me, and his voice was gentle as he spoke. "Reuven, I—I ask you to forgive me . . . my anger . . . at your father's Zionism. I read his speech . . . I—I found my own meaning for my . . . brother's death . . for the death of the six million. I found it in God's will . . . which I did not presume to understand. I did not—I did not find it in a Jewish state that does not follow God and His Torah. My brother . . . the others . . . they could not—they could not have died for such a state. Forgive me . . . your father . . . it was too much . . . too much—"

His voice broke. He held himself tightly. His beard moved faintly with the trembling of his lips.

"Daniel," he said brokenly. "Forgive me . . . for everything . . . I have done. A—a wiser father . . . may have done differently. I am not . . . wise."

He rose slowly, painfully, to his feet. "Today is the—the Festival of Freedom." There was a soft hint of bitterness in his voice. "Today my Daniel is free. . . . I must go. . . . I am very tired. . . . I must lie down."

He walked heavily out of the room, his shoulders stooped, his face old and torn with pain.

The door closed with a soft click.

Then I sat and listened to Danny cry. He held his face in his hands, and his sobs tore apart the silence of the room and racked his body. I went over to him and put my hand on his shoulder and felt him trembling and crying. And then I was crying too, crying with Danny, silently, for his pain and for the years of his suffering, knowing that I loved him, and not knowing whether I hated or loved the long, anguished years of his life. He cried for a long time, and I left him in the chair and went to the window and listened to his sobs. The sun was low over the brownstones on the other side of the yard, and an ailanthus stood silhouetted against its golden rim, its budding branches forming a lace curtain through which a wind moved softly. I watched the sun set. The evening spread itself slowly across the sky.

Later, we walked through the streets. We walked for hours, saying nothing, and occasionally I saw him rub his eyes and heard him sigh. We walked past our synagogue, past the shops and houses, past the library where we had sat and read, walking in silence and saying more with that silence than with a lifetime of words. Late, late that night I left Danny at his home and returned alone to the apartment.

My father was in the kitchen and there was a strange brooding sadness on his face. I sat down and he looked at me, his eyes somber behind their steel-rimmed spectacles. And I told him everything.

When I was done, he was quiet for a very long time. Then he said softly, "A father has a right to raise his son in his own way, Reuven."

"In *that* way, abba?"

"Yes. Though I do not care for it at all."

"What kind of way is that to raise a son?"

"It is, perhaps, the only way to raise a tzaddik."

"I'm glad I wasn't raised that way."

"Reuven," my father said softly, "I did not have to raise you that way. I am not a tzaddik."

During the Morning Service on the first Shabbat in June, Reb Saunders announced to the congregation his son's intention to study psychology. The announcement was greeted with shocked dismay. Danny was in the synagogue at the time, and all eyes turned to stare at him in astonishment. Whereupon Reb Saunders further stated that this was his son's wish, that he, as a father, respected his son's soul and mind—in that order, according to what Danny later told me —that his son had every intention of remaining an observer of the Commandments, and that, therefore, he felt compelled to give his son his blessing. The turmoil among Reb Saunders' followers that was caused by this announcement was considerable. But no one dared to challenge Reb Saunders' tacit transference of power to his younger son. After all, the tzaddikate was inherited, and the charisma went automatically from father to son—all sons.

Two days later, Reb Saunders withdrew his promise to the family of the girl Danny was supposed to marry. There had been some fuss over that, Danny told me afterward. But it had quieted down after a while.

The reaction at Hirsch College, once the news of Reb Saunders' announcement was out, lasted all of about two or three days. The non-Hasidic students talked about it for a day or so, and then forgot it. The Hasidic students sulked, scowled, glowered, and then forgot it, too. Everyone was busy with final examinations.

That June Danny and I were among the seventy-eight students who were graduated from Hirsch College, to the accompaniment of numerous speeches, applause, honorary degrees, and family congratulations. Both of us had earned our degrees *summa cum laude*.

Danny came over to our apartment one evening in September. He was moving into a room he had rented near Columbia, he said, and he wanted to say goodbye. His beard and earlocks were gone, and his face looked pale. But there was a light in his eyes that was almost blinding.

My father smiled at him warmly. "Columbia is not so far," he said. "We will see you on Shabbat."

Danny nodded, his eyes glowing, luminous.

I asked him how his father had reacted when he had seen him without the beard and earlocks.

He smiled sadly. "He's not happy about it. He said he almost doesn't recognize me."

"He talked to you?"

"Yes," Danny said quietly. "We talk now."

There was a long, gentle silence. A cool breeze moved soundlessly through the open windows of the living room.

Then my father leaned forward in his chair. "Danny," he said softly, "when you have a son of your own, you will raise him in silence?"

Danny said nothing for a long time. Then his right hand

rose slowly to the side of his face and with his thumb and forefinger he gently caressed an imaginary earlock.

"Yes," he said. "If I can't find another way."

My father nodded, his eyes calm.

Later, I went down with Danny to the street.

"You'll come over sometimes on a Saturday and we'll study Talmud with my father?" he asked.

"Of course," I said.

We shook hands and I watched him walk quickly away, tall, lean, bent forward with eagerness and hungry for the future, his metal capped shoes tapping against the sidewalk. Then he turned into Lee Avenue and was gone.

ABOUT THE AUTHOR

Born and raised in New York City, Dr. Chaim Potok
was graduated from Yeshiva University in 1950 with
a B.A. *summa cum laude* in English literature. He then
received a rabbinic ordination in 1954 from the Jewish
Theological Seminary of America. Dr. Potok was a
member of the faculty of the University of Judaism
in Los Angeles and spent a year in Israel completing
his doctoral dissertation on philosophy; he received
his doctorate from the University of Pennsylvania in
1965. He has written numerous articles, reviews, and
stories, and in May 1966 he became editor of the Jewish Publication Society of America. *The Promise,* a
sequel to *The Chosen,* was published in 1969. His
most recent work is the novel *My Name Is Asher Lev.*